"I don't read much science fiction, but I got ahold of a manuscript copy of *StarDoc* and just loved it. Don't miss this one." —Catherine Coulter

"Continuously surprising and deviously written and splendidly full of new characters." —Anne McCaffrey

"Space opera somewhat reminiscent of C. J. Cherryh's early work." —*Chronicle*

"An entertaining, almost old-fashioned adventure. . . . The adventure and quirky mix of aliens and cultures makes a fun combination." —*Locus*

"An excellent protagonist. . . . [Viehl has] set the stage for an interesting series of interspecies medical adventures." —Space.com

"Space opera and medical melodrama mix with a dash of romance in this engaging novel . . . a rousing good yarn, with plenty of plot twists, inventive scene-setting, and quirky characters to keep readers thoroughly entertained . . . *StarDoc* is a fun adventure story, with an appealing heroine, a lot of action, a sly sense of humor, and wonders aplenty." —SF Site

"A fascinating reading experience . . . a wonderful heroine." —*Midwest Book Review*

Beyond Varallan

"[Cherijo is] an engaging lead character. . . . Viehl skillfully weaves in the clues to build a murder mystery with several surprising ramifications." —Space.com

continued . . .

Endurance

"An exciting science fiction tale . . . fast-paced and exciting. . . . SF fans will fully enjoy S. L. Viehl's entertaining entry in one of the better ongoing series today."
—*Midwest Book Review*

"[*Endurance*] gets into more eclectic and darker territory than most space opera, but it's a pretty engrossing trip. Recommended." —Hypatia's Hoard

"A rousing medical space opera. . . . Viehl employs misdirection and humor, while not defusing the intense plot development that builds toward an explosive conclusion." —*Romantic Times*

Shockball

"Genetically enhanced fun. . . . Cherijo herself has been justly praised as a breath of fresh air—smart [and] saucy. . . . The reader seems to be invited along as an amicable companion, and such is the force of Cherijo's personality that it sounds like fun."
—Science Fiction Weekly

"Fast-paced . . . an entertaining installment in the continuing adventures of the *StarDoc*." —*Locus*

"An exhilarating science fiction space adventure. The zestful story line stays at warp speed. . . . Cherijo is as fresh as ever. . . . Fans of futuristic outer space novels will want to take off with this tale and the three previous *StarDoc* books as all four stories take the audience where they rarely have been before."
—*Midwest Book Review*

Eternity Row

"Space opera at its very best. . . . Viehl has created a character and a futuristic setting that is second to none in its readability, quality, and social mores."
—*Midwest Book Review*

"S. L. Viehl serves readers her usual highly entertaining mix of humor and space opera. This episode is enlivened by the antics of her daughter, Marel, and by an exploration of aging and immortality. As usual I look forward to the next in an exciting series." —BookLoons

Rebel Ice

"Well-drawn cultures and fascinating aliens."
—*Publishers Weekly*

"It's fast, fun, character-driven and left me wanting more . . . one of my all-time favorite sci-fi series."
—Fresh Fiction

"Both gritty and realistic." —*Romantic Times*

"A thrilling addition to the series." —*Booklist*

"A wonderful piece of space opera." —SFRevu

"Seems very realistic—almost as if the author visited that world and decided to write about it. *Rebel Ice* is a terrific outer space science fiction novel."
—*Library Bookwatch*

Plague of Memory

"Another exciting adventure in this well-regarded series." —Monsters and Critics

DREAM CALLED TIME

A *StarDoc* Novel

S. L. Viehl

A ROC BOOK

ROC

Published by New American Library, a division of
Penguin Group (USA) Inc., 375 Hudson Street,
New York, New York 10014, USA

Penguin Group (Canada), 90 Eglinton Avenue East, Suite 700, Toronto,
Ontario M4P 2Y3, Canada (a division of Pearson Penguin Canada Inc.)
Penguin Books Ltd., 80 Strand, London WC2R 0RL, England
Penguin Ireland, 25 St. Stephen's Green, Dublin 2,
Ireland (a division of Penguin Books Ltd.)
Penguin Group (Australia), 250 Camberwell Road, Camberwell, Victoria 3124,
Australia (a division of Pearson Australia Group Pty. Ltd.)
Penguin Books India Pvt. Ltd., 11 Community Centre, Panchsheel Park,
New Delhi - 110 017, India
Penguin Group (NZ), 67 Apollo Drive, Rosedale, North Shore 0632,
New Zealand (a division of Pearson New Zealand Ltd.)
Penguin Books (South Africa) (Pty.) Ltd., 24 Sturdee Avenue,
Rosebank, Johannesburg 2196, South Africa

Penguin Books Ltd., Registered Offices:
80 Strand, London WC2R 0RL, England

First published by Roc, an imprint of New American Library,
a division of Penguin Group (USA) Inc.

First Printing, August 2010
10   9   8   7   6   5   4   3   2   1

Copyright © S. L. Viehl, 2010
All rights reserved

ROC REGISTERED TRADEMARK—MARCA REGISTRADA
Printed in the United States of America

This book is for
all the loyal *StarDoc* readers out there.
It took ten years for us to make this journey
through constant hardships
and endless heartaches,
but while I chose this path,
you never once let me
walk it alone.
Thank you.

Yesterday

When I woke up, it was in the oddest of circumstances. I was crammed into a very small space, with my legs tucked in and my shoulders pressing against what felt like a tiny console. I opened my eyes and found two small, slimy faces close to mine. "Who are you?"

"Rilken." One of the diminutive aliens reached out and prodded me with a sticky finger. "You Terran?"

"Uh-huh." I tried to sit up, found I couldn't, and swiveled onto my stomach instead. I was inside what had to be the smallest vessel I'd ever seen. A lavatory on the *Sunlace* was ten times bigger. "Why am I here?"

"We purchase you from Bartermen." One of the little guys went to an equally tiny helm and initiated some engines. "Prepare for launch."

"Wait a minute." I managed to hunch over and sit up, and immediately felt like Gulliver. I filled up half the passenger compartment, which had been designed for beings less than half a meter in height. "Where are we going?"

"We are leaving Oenrall," the other pip-squeak

said. "We are mercenaries. You will be returned to the Hsktskt for blood bounty."

Midget mercenaries. Well, why not? "You're friends with the lizards?"

He shrugged his tiny shoulders. "The Hsktskt offer more credits for you."

The tiny vessel lifted off and entered the upper atmosphere. Before the mercenaries could initiate their flightshield, something struck us.

"What is it?" The one guarding me ran up to the helm.

"A Jorenian ship, firing on us." Fear ran through the Rilken's voice. "They have disabled our stardrive."

Considering the size of the ship, Xonea must have used a peashooter. I crawled up behind both of them, and felt for the syrinpress I'd been carrying in my tunic pocket. It was gone, so I'd have to use more creative measures.

"Nighty-night, boys." I knocked their skulls together once, then watched them slide to the floor. I looked around me. "That's it? I don't get shot, stabbed, poisoned, whipped, burned, or anything else?"

The Rilkens didn't make a response.

Clunking them was certainly easier than using their communications array. I had to use one of my fingernails to operate the control panel. At last I raised the *CloudWalk* to let them know I was in control and all right.

"It is good to see you, council representative," the Jado ClanLeader said, and smiled. "There are two others here who wish to relay their happiness, as well."

He stepped aside, and the welcome sight of my husband and daughter appeared on the vid screen.

"Cherijo." My husband looked very relieved. "You escaped the Bartermen by yourself?"

"Mtulla helped. By the way, if you ever want to get kidnapped, pick Rilkens. Very easy species to overpower. Marel could do it." I thought of the peace talks. "Have I ruined everything for Captain Teulon?"

"No, it appears the negotiations are a success. The Torins retrieved Alunthri from the Jxin, and it has convinced the Taercal that your cure is a divine intervention, and that their god refuses to allow them to suffer, as was prophesied."

"About time." I moved one of the sleeping Rilkens out of my way and sat back against the interior hull wall. "Well, I think that wraps it up here. I'd really like that vacation now, please."

"Come and get us."

Reever told me how to fly the Rilken vessel to rendezvous with the Jado ship, then touched the screen with his hand. "I'll be waiting for you, *Waenara*."

I matched my fingertips to his. "Not for long, *Osepeke*."

Those last words we exchanged would come back to haunt me. I just didn't know it yet.

Because the shot from the Jado had wrecked the stardrive, I could only coax limping speed out of the propulsion system. I set the helm on autopilot, tied up the Rilkens so they wouldn't cause any more trouble when they woke, and tried to make myself comfortable by stretching out my legs on the deck. I'd always felt like a shrimp compared with most other beings, so it was kind of a novelty to experience for once what it was like to be a giant.

I didn't expect ClanLeader Jado to send a launch to meet me, so when one appeared on the exterior viewer, I reached for the dinky console to send a signal. "Reever told me how to use the ship's position to navigate to the *CloudWalk*, Captain. I won't get lost."

No one responded, and when I peered at the console, I saw several warning lights blinking. Someone was jamming my transceiver, which wasn't a good thing. Neither was the launch, the design of which wasn't Jorenian, but League.

I tried another signal, this time opening the relay so it could be picked up by the other vessel. "League transport, identify yourself, and your reasons for approaching my vessel."

A harsh voice responded with only four words. "Prepare to be boarded."

"Prepare my ass." I swung around and crouched over the console, taking it off auto control and changing course to evade the League transport.

I dodged them for a while, but their engines were working perfectly, as was their pulse array. They fired twice and took out what was left of the Rilkens' propulsion system, then used a third to destroy my transceiver.

I couldn't see the *CloudWalk* on the viewer, but I knew they were out there and monitoring my progress, as was the ship belonging to my adopted family, HouseClan Torin. They'd definitely pick up the pulse fire on their scanners. Any attack on a member of a Jorenian HouseClan resulted in a declaration of ClanKill, which meant my adopted kin would devote themselves to hunting down my assailants and subjecting them to an instant and painful death by manual evisceration.

"You guys are going to be so sorry you did this," I muttered as I looked around the cabin for weapons.

The Rilkens had a couple of pistols and rifles, but they were too small for me to handle comfortably. I settled for a dagger I took off one of my unconscious abductors, although I had to wrap the hilt with some plastape until it was large enough for me to grip. I staggered as the deck rocked; the viewer showed the transport's docking clamps engulfing the little ship.

I put my back against a wall and watched the upper access hatch. Energy crackled through the air, and then something knocked me away from the wall and threw me to the deck.

I crawled, my teeth still chattering from the power surge they'd sent through the hull, but there was no place big enough for me to hide. A pair of League boots appeared in front of my nose, and I raised my head to look into the business end of a pulse rifle.

"Colonel Shropana sends his compliments," the soldier said just before he reversed the weapon and slammed the stock into my face.

PART ONE

Today

One

Into whatever houses I enter, I will go for the benefit of the sick.

—Hippocrates

Hippocrates never had to deal with a patient like mine, or he'd have said to hell with his oath and run for the hills.

As I was currently on the *Sunlace*, a Jorenian interstellar star vessel, I didn't have hills or that luxury. What I did have was a body on the exam table in front of me: Terran, adult female, petite, thin, pale-skinned, and dark-haired. Uninjured but unconscious, waiting to be awakened, to be healed, to be saved.

Standing there in the cold, sterile brightness of the medical assessment room, dependent on the kindness of a bunch of strangers, I could relate.

Visually speaking, the patient did not appear to be a sterling example of her gender or her species. I'd never call her pretty, shapely, vibrant, or attractive. She didn't have the benefit of physical symmetry; her long-fingered, narrow hands appeared overly large for her bony wrists; her long torso seemed at odds with her short legs. Her translucent skin didn't have a mark on it, which made it look like a too-tight envirosuit, and displayed in outline a bit too much of her skeletal structure. Although I knew her to be in her midthirties, at first glance I'd have guessed her to be a moderately undernourished adolescent.

I picked up her chart. "Not much to look at, is she?" The herd of tall, blue-skinned Jorenian interns and nurses gathered around the table didn't respond. "Until we open the really boring package, and get a look at all the prizes inside."

"Healer, what say we summon your bondmate?" That came from a gorgeous female nurse whose name I didn't know. She wove her fingers through the air as she spoke in the eloquent hand gestures her species used as part of their language. "He would wish to be present."

I watched her white-within-white eyes, which were not at all as blind as they appeared. "Do you think I need my husband to hold my hand while I assess this patient, Nurse?"

She was two feet taller than me and a hundred pounds heavier, and could probably snap my neck with one jerk of her beautiful blue wrist, but she shuffled her feet and ducked her head like a scolded kid. "No, Healer."

"Good answer." I turned my attention back to the patient. "The Terran female here presents with a genetically enhanced immune system which renders her impervious to infection and disease," I said, not bothering to read from the chart. "Any injury she sustains, including the life-threatening variety, heals in a matter of hours. Her brain capacity is estimated to be several hundred times that of an average Terran, and includes exceptional intelligence, eidetic memory, and select superior motor skills." I glanced at the dismayed faces across from me. "Any of you know how she was created?"

This time one of the male interns spoke up. "Her parent replicated his own cells and genetically enhanced them to change her gender as well as her physiology."

"That's correct. You get to skip the pop quiz I'm giving later." I placed the chart back in the holder at the end of the exam table. "The end result was Dr. Cherijo Grey Veil, cloned and refined and engineered from birth to be the perfect physician. Would anyone like to take a stab at diagnosing her current condition?" I showed them some of my teeth. "I'm dying to know what it is."

"She is violating an order of bed rest," a low voice said from behind me.

I glanced back at the Senior Healer. Three-armed, one-legged, pink-hided with a bald head and a nest of white, thin, prehensile, meter-long gildrells around his mouth, the Omorr surgeon was my best friend and one of my oldest colleagues.

Judging by the flush currently darkening his features, he was also as pissed off as I was.

"Don't forget appropriating medical staff and using diagnostic equipment without proper authorization," I reminded him. "Nice to see you, Senior Healer. They told me you were on Joren." Although how he got there, I had no clue.

"I was. I jaunted out on a scout to meet the ship. Leave us," Squilyp said to the others as he hopped around to stand on the opposite side of the table.

Suppressing various expressions, gestures, and

sounds of relief, the interns and nurses almost trampled one another trying to get out of the entry panel.

The Omorr smelled a little like bile, and looked tired, or older—or maybe both. A lot of things had changed, and I didn't know why, but I was about to find out.

Or else.

"How many transitions did it take for you to get here," I asked, "and how many times did you puke?"

"Seven jumps," he said. "I vomited twice. What are you doing?"

"I'm putting together a workup on Dr. Grey Veil here." Or, at least, the dimensional image of her. I was the original, the prototype, the living, breathing version of the simulated woman who currently lay on my exam table, naked and flat on her back. My back. Whatever. "I thought it might be helpful in finding out what the hell is going on, since no one is telling me anything."

He started to say something, and then changed his mind. "You were advised to stay in your berth."

"I'll be happy to do that. Just as soon as I know how I got on this ship, where it is, who swapped out the crew, and what happened to my injuries."

"You don't remember?"

I folded my arms. "What do you think?"

"What have you been told?"

"Basically? Nothing. Every time I ask, they railroad me with some nonsense about psychological trauma. They removed nearly all the entries from my chart, and I've been locked out of the medical database." I brushed aside a thick section of her/our hair, creating a part along one side of her/our head. "Is this where I got conked? How bad was it?"

"I cannot say." He glanced at the simulation to avoid looking at me. "We were not present when you were injured, and the damage healed before you were recovered."

Obviously, or now I'd be leaking blood or brain matter all over the deck. "Then show me what you extrapolated from my scans after you took me back from the League."

"I do not have all the details on the incident—"

"God*damn* it, Squilyp." The last shred of my patience finally parted ways with my temper. "Tell me what the hell happened to me."

Shouting at him stiffened his gildrells into icicles—a sure sign he was offended—but he only addressed the control console. "Display program variation C-1."

Like an invisible killer with an unseen ax, the imager erased a good chunk of my twin's skull, vaporizing the bone and exposing the brain tissue. It was such a brutal injury that for a moment I forgot to breathe.

How could I have survived this? I felt ready to puke myself now. Thanks to my enhanced immune system, I could physically survive almost anything, but mentally . . . emotionally . . . "That's what that League pirate did to me?"

"Based on the initial head series I performed, and the few details we were able to garner from one eyewitness, this approximates the wound you sustained after your transport crash-landed on the surface of Akkabarr."

I glanced up. "What are you talking about? I wasn't anywhere near Akkabarr. I was on that dinky Rilken ship. One of Shropana's jackasses boarded it before he smacked me in the head with the end of a pulse rifle." I regarded the simulation again. "There's no way he did this much damage, unless he kept bashing my skull in after I fell unconscious."

"That is the last thing you remember?" he asked. "Being assaulted on the Rilken ship?"

"That's the last thing that happened to me." I didn't like the careful way he was talking to me. "Right?"

"Ah, no." His gildrells coiled into knots of agitation. "You were abducted and taken to Akkabarr by a League operative, but the atmospheric conditions caused your transport to crash on the surface. There you were attacked by a group of natives, and shot." He touched the control panel, creating a second, independent image of the brain and projecting the ruined organ above the body, where it slowly revolved. "Due to the weapon being fired at almost point-blank range, it caused considerable damage to the brain center, as well as significant vascular trauma and a substantial amount of tissue destruction."

I resisted the urge to touch my head. "You're telling me that after this League ship I was on crashed, the natives dragged me out of the wreckage, shot me in the head, and blew out half of my brains." He nodded, and I took in a shaky breath. "Any particular reason *why*?"

"As it was explained to me," he said, "they wished to kill and partially dismember you in order to collect a bounty from their masters."

"*Partially* dismember?" I almost shrieked.

"They skin the faces of unauthorized intruders," he explained, "which they trade for various rewards from their masters."

"Remind me never to jaunt to Akkabarr again." Not that I'd wanted to go in the first place. I took another good look at the holoimage. "What happened after that?"

"I cannot be certain," he said, not looking at me again, "but scans indicate that the tissue and bone spontaneously regenerated, probably within a matter of days. It was during that time that, I believe, you entered the primary phase of an extended dissociative fugue state."

"Getting shot in the head gave me an identity disorder." I snickered. "Sure. Who did I think I was? A P'Kotman with clogged mouth pores?"

"No." He seemed to be searching for words again. "Cherijo, do you recall anything else? Anything at all? Do you remember where you were or what you saw after the League soldier attacked you?"

"I woke up here, in Medical." His expression and my lack of wounds told me that couldn't be correct. "Squilyp, just how long was I unconscious?"

He had to try three times before he could speak. "I regret to say that you were abducted and taken to Akkabarr nearly five years ago."

All the strength went out of my legs, and I groped for a stool. Not five days, or five weeks. Not even five months. Five *years*. Absently I heard myself ask, "Did you try to bring me out of the coma before now?"

"Cherijo." He hopped around the exam table and bent his knee until he could look into my eyes. "There were some residual effects, but to our knowledge, you never became comatose."

"What?" I was still trying to process what he'd said. "Okay. So, where did the five years go? Did I freeze on that ice ball or something?"

"This will be difficult for you to accept." He wrapped the sensitive and extremely dexterous web of tissues at the end of his arms around my hands. "The attack destroyed your mind. You were lost to us."

"I'm right here, and my mind is working perfectly," I reminded him. "What did you do when you found me? You didn't put me in stasis, did you? Not for five years."

"There was no need. When we recovered you from Akkabarr, you were conscious and cognizant and functional." He hesitated. "You had acquired another personality. An Akkabarran persona."

I started to laugh, and just as quickly stopped. "You're saying that I've been a different *person* for the last five years of my life?" He nodded. "You know, if this is some kind of sick, tasteless practical joke to get back at me for being captured by the Rilkens, I will never forgive you or anyone else involved."

"Your memory center—along with possibly one-third of your brain tissue—was destroyed after the crash. Nothing of your personality remained." He put his membranes on my shoulders. "You were not unconscious, Cherijo. You were gone. After we recovered you from the Iisleg, I tried everything to bring you back. When nothing worked, I had to assume that the head injury had killed you."

"Unless you toss me into the nearest star or molecular disintegration unit, I can't be killed, and you know it." I rose and stepped away so that he wasn't touching me anymore. "Try again."

"I wish I had the answers you seek." Squilyp reached over and switched off the imager, and the body of my twin vanished. "We must speak of what has happened since you . . . when your body was occupied by—"

Oh, no, we didn't.

I turned and walked out into Medical Bay, letting the door shut off Squilyp's babbling. All the nurses working that shift had stopped whatever they were doing and now stood staring at me.

They'd been doing this nonsense practically since I'd woken up. "Hello. Anyone know where my clothes are?" Silence. "How about my husband? Duncan Reever? He waiting around somewhere?"

Everyone looked at each other and then at the deck. No one said a word to me.

"Thanks a lot." The thought of something alien occupying any part of me made my skin crawl, and I marched over to a garment storage unit and yanked out a set of scrubs.

No one tried to stop me from using the cleansing unit. Lucky them.

Showering and dressing in the scrubs calmed me down and made me feel a little more like myself, but as soon as I stepped out, I found the Omorr waiting for me.

"You cannot leave," he said, hopping in front of me to block my path to the main door panels. "I have not discharged you."

"You never admitted me," I countered. "I want to see Reever. Get out of my way."

"I understand how you must feel," he said, until I looked him in the eye. "No, of course, I cannot imagine what this must be like for you."

"Take a nap for sixty months," I suggested as I tried to go around him. When he cut me off a second time, I grabbed the front of his blue and white surgeon's tunic. "You don't want to do this with me, Doctor. I want to see Duncan. And Marel. Right now."

"You will, soon." He covered my fist with his web of a hand. "I promise. All I ask is that you allow me to assure you are well, and that there is no danger of a relapse."

"How?"

"I must examine you," he said, and, before I could tell him what I thought of that, added, "We do not yet know if your condition is stable."

"As long as no one tries to blow my head off again, I should be just peachy." I wasn't sure I'd ever go to sleep again voluntarily, but that wasn't my immediate problem. "Where's Reever? Why isn't he here with me? Where is my daughter?"

"Reever is on the ship," he assured me. "Marel is waiting for you both on Joren."

The last time I'd left them, they had been together on the *CloudWalk*. Everything was so screwed up I hardly knew what to think. Had something happened between me and Reever? Had that thing that took over my body—

A surge of panic shot through me. "Squilyp, why did Duncan walk away from me last night?"

"This has been a terrible shock for everyone. We had accepted that you were lost to us. Now that you are with us again, so suddenly, without any warning or explanation . . ." He made a helpless gesture. "It is a terrible shock."

"You keep saying terrible." As if my waking up had been a bad thing. "Being shot in the head is terrible. So is waking up and finding out you've lost five years of your life. The war between the League and the Hsktskt, that's really terrible—"

"The war is over," he said gently. "Teulon Jado

negotiated peace between the League and the Hsktskt."

"The Jado . . ." Pain lanced through my head, so sharp and sudden that it knocked the wind out of me. "Something happened to them. What?"

"Just after you took control of the Rilken ship, the League fleet attacked the *CloudWalk*, and massacred HouseClan Jado," Squilyp said, stunning me. "You were the only witness. They knew if they allowed you to escape, you would trigger a war between the Jorenians and the League."

"Why didn't they just kill me?" Then I answered my own question before he could. "Shropana. He wanted revenge for the attack on Joren, when I sold him and his fleet out to the Hsktskt. Is that why he attacked the *CloudWalk*?"

"Some believe it influenced his decision."

I remembered Akkabarr was a slaver world. "It's also why he kept me alive. He was going to sell me into slavery."

"Not all of the Jado were killed. Their ClanLeader, Teulon, also survived the massacre. Like you, he was abducted and taken to Akkabarr to be sold. He escaped to the surface and organized a rebellion. In time, he forced both the League and the Hsktskt to declare peace." Squilyp hesitated before adding, "Jarn helped him."

"Jarn." The name made my head spin. "That's what the nurses keep calling me." What my husband had muttered in that awful voice before he'd left me here.

"From the day the League transport you were on crashed on Akkabarr until last night," Squilyp said, "that is the person you have been."

*   *   *

The Omorr took his time examining me, performing a full-body series of scans before drawing blood samples and testing my physical and mental responses. As he worked, he filled me in on some of the events I'd missed during my extended nap—none of which involved me personally, I noted.

"I can see you being chief medical adviser to the Jorenian Ruling Council," I mentioned as he used a penlight to check my pupils, "but the father of twin boys?"

"My mate claims it was a deliberate attempt on my part to further subjugate her," Squilyp murmured as he used a scope to look at my retinas. "No matter how often I explain that in our species twinning is caused by a female hormonal surge at the point of conception, she still holds me responsible."

I thought of my daughter. I never liked being separated from my kid, but it would be another day before I saw her again. "Why did we leave Marel on Joren?"

"Many reasons," he assured me. "All of which had to do with protecting her."

I did some math. "She'd be almost nine years old now. Jesus." I'd already missed too much of her life. As soon as we returned to Joren, I was never letting the kid out of my sight again.

He straightened. "Have you felt any weakness, sensory disruption, or pain since regaining consciousness?"

My heart felt like a lump of arutanium, but the only cure for that evidently didn't want to see me. "That light is giving me a headache."

Not counting the abyssal gap in my memory, I

passed all of the Omorr's scans and tests. After he checked the results, he handed them to me.

"You are slightly underweight, but that is normal for you," Squilyp said as he transferred the last of the data from his scanner to my chart. "I would like to keep you under monitor for the next forty-eight hours, but I doubt your readings will change. Nor would the medical staff thank me for it."

I barely heard him. Throughout the exam I had stayed quiet, simply watching the door panel and waiting for it to open, and Reever to hurry in to check on me. He hadn't, and now I suspected he never would.

Why? What was wrong? What had I done?

"The ship looks different," I said as I finished dressing. "Did they relocate our quarters?"

"I believe so." He gave me a troubled look. "It might be wise to arrange separate accommodations for the moment."

"So Reever will have some time to get over the terrible shock of me waking up." Before he could lie to me again, I shook my head. "Never mind. He can tell me what the deal is between us when I find him."

"First allow me to signal the captain."

As it turned out, he didn't have to; Xonea Torin was waiting for us in Medical. As soon as I stepped out of the assessment room, he strode over to me, seven and a half feet of large, blue, grim-faced, warhardened Jorenian commander.

"Healer?"

"Captain." I glanced up at the new purple streak in his black hair. "You're starting to look like Pnor," I said, referring to the former captain of the *Sunlace*. "Next thing you know, you'll be tossing me into a detainment cell."

"Cherijo." He seized me, lifted me off my feet, and embraced me. "I knew the Mother would return you to us. I knew."

The ferocity of his affection unnerved me, and I gave his shoulder an awkward pat. "It's okay, big guy. Sorry it took so long."

He set me down but held on to my hands. All twelve of his fingers trembled as he looked over my head at the Senior Healer. "She has fully recovered? She will not leave us again?"

"I cannot be certain, Captain, but all of the tests I've run indicate that she is both stable and healthy." Squilyp turned to me. "Cherijo, I need to have a word with the captain. Will you wait here for me?"

I nodded and, as soon as they disappeared into the Senior Healer's office, I headed for the door panels.

"Healer Jarn," someone called after me. "You agreed to wait."

"I didn't say how long, and my name isn't Jarn." Once I was out in the corridor, I went straight for the lift. A few of the Jorenian crewmen I passed tried to stop me to chat, but I made a quick, apologetic gesture of urgency and kept going.

Once inside the lift, I told the panel to take me to the observation deck.

"No such location exists on this vessel," the computer responded politely.

I couldn't believe the Torins had removed the observation deck. It was Reever's favorite spot on the *Sunlace*. "Can you tell me where Linguist Duncan Reever is on the ship?"

"Affirmative," it replied. "Please verify by inputting security authorization code."

I didn't have a code, or a clue as to why I would need one. "Medical-emergency system override. Authorization Healer Cherijo Torin."

"No such name exists in this system."

Of course not. The minor headache caused by Squilyp's examination began to build. "Try authorization Healer Jarn."

"Authorization confirmed by voiceprint. Thank you, Healer Jarn. Linguist Reever is currently located on level eight, environome four."

So my husband had gone to play in a dimensional simulator instead of coming to Medical to see me. This was just getting better by the minute. "Then take me to level eight."

"Yes, Healer." The lift whirled smoothly into motion as it zipped around the spiraling outer curves of the hull.

"And while we're at it," I said to the panel, "display all of my security access and authorization codes."

I memorized the list of codes assigned to Jarn by the time I exited the lift, and used the one with the highest clearance to access the dimensional simulator. The program Reever had initiated wasn't a very complicated one. It generated a field on the surface of Joren, one solidly paved with silvery yiborra grass. Off in the distance I could see a white smudge that might have been the Torin pavilion, but it was only a projection, like the sky and the streamers of rainbow-colored cloud. Reever hadn't even bothered to program the simulation with the planet's heavier gravity field or the flowers that scented the air.

I spotted him in the center of the field, standing with his back to me. He'd cut short his golden hair, which now brushed the collar of his plain black tunic. His hands were loose at his sides as he stared at the horizon.

"Computer," I said, trying to keep the irony out of my tone. "End simulation."

The field and sky and the rest of Joren vanished, leaving me and Reever standing in an empty room, the walls, deck, and ceiling covered with a glowing yellow grid.

He turned, so slowly I knew he was making an effort, and walked toward me. He stopped a meter away. "Cherijo."

"Duncan." I inspected his expression, or lack thereof. He looked exactly as he had when I'd first met him on K-2: a man with no human emotions. "Are your legs broken?"

He glanced down. "No."

"Were you accidentally locked in here?" I gestured to the door panel, and he shook his head. "So you didn't come back to Medical to see if I was okay because . . . for some reason you desperately needed to commune with a fake alien pasture?"

He didn't answer me or even look at my face. He just stood there like a statue, staring at some point past my left shoulder.

"I guess there was no hurry," I continued, ignoring the cracks I could feel forming in my heart. "According to Squilyp, you've had my body around for the last five years—"

"Two years."

I raised my brows. "Excuse me?"

"It took two and a half years for me to find you on Akkabarr," he said. "Another six months to take you back from the rebels."

"But you didn't find *me*, Reever," I reminded him. "You found my remains, occupied and possessed by some alien body snatcher." Why was I being so snotty to him? With an effort I forced back some of my outrage. "It must have been pretty tough for you and Marel while I was gone." Now the shock would go, and he would tell me exactly how horrible it had been for them, and how much he missed me, and how glad he was that I had come back.

"You do not understand," he said flatly. "She was a woman, and a healer, and a person. Her name was Jarn."

I heard the anger in his voice; I simply didn't understand why he would be mad at me. Maybe it was, as Squilyp had said, a terrible shock. Me sniping at him wouldn't help matters.

"I know you thought I was dead, and that I was never coming back," I said carefully. "But I *am* back, sweetheart, and I assure you, I'm here to stay."

Reever said nothing.

"I'm also stable, healthy, and not suffering from any negative aftereffects." His lack of reaction was beginning to piss me off, though. "Tell me something. Did you even *miss* me while I was gone?"

He didn't like that. "I assumed that the loss was permanent. Squilyp tried to recover your memories and personality. He could not reverse the effects of the brain damage."

"Is that right." I planted my hands on my hips. "How many times did you ask him to *try*?"

"I have no wish to quarrel with you, Cherijo." Reever strode past me, as if he couldn't bear to spend another minute alone with me.

Me, the wife he hadn't seen for five years.

"Hold on." I grabbed him. "You walked out on me last night. You never came back. Aren't you even curious to see if the body snatcher—excuse me—if *Jarn* might find a way to kick me out again?"

Gently he removed my hand from his arm. "Jarn is not coming back."

"Is that right?" I shifted around so I blocked his path. "How do you know?"

"She killed herself so that you could return." Out he went.

Two

After Reever took off, I reinitiated the Jorenian yi-borra-field program and sat there for a while watching the simulated grass grow. Pain from my headache became laced with disorienting confusion. Nothing made sense, so I didn't bother to think. No doubt Xonea or Squilyp would soon come after me, and tell me all about it.

"Healer Torin."

I looked over my shoulder at the furry face of the strange healer who had attended me last night. Thick black fur covered the bipedal form of the lupine male, although much of it looked as if it had been recently shorn and was just now growing back. His mane, which grew from the top of his skull to the top of his shoulders, also had a shaggy, uneven look to it. The darkness of his body hair made his light green irises appear to glow a little.

The distinct muzzle and fanged teeth didn't worry me—I'd encountered a lot of frightening-looking beings in my time away from the homeworld, and most of them were more civilized than Terrans—but something about him made the hair on my neck rise.

Someone had told me his name and species. . . . "Healer Valtas. What do you want?"

"It would please me greatly if you would call me Shon." He made the traditional Jorenian gesture of greeting, briefly extending ten black, blunted claws before retracting them into his articulated paws. "The Omorr wishes you to return to Medical."

"I'm sure he does, Healer Valtas." I turned away, hoping he'd take the hint.

The oKiaf didn't; he came and sat down beside me. "Healer Squilyp indicated you have no memory of the last five years, so I assume you do not remember me."

I made a sound. Not a nice one.

"I was an intelligence officer alterformed by the League to serve as a spy," he said, resting his elbows on his knees. "When they attempted to force me to heal tortured prisoners in order to extend their suffering, I deserted, changed my identity, and became a healer. I accompanied the survey team to my home-world, where I tried to kill myself. In the process I was infected by a protocrystal life-form which is taking over the planet."

I guessed I was supposed to care. Crying shame that I didn't. "Do you tell everyone your life story five seconds after you meet them?"

"You thwarted my attempted suicide, and then removed the crystalline infection from my body before it could kill me," he said. "I would not be alive if not for you."

"It wasn't me, but you're welcome." I pulled up a blade of grass, which once separated from the simulator grid's energy matrix immediately lost coherence and disintegrated. My temper was about to do the same. "Now would you mind leaving me alone? Or do you need help with a second suicide attempt?"

"I remember what it was like, when I woke up after the alterforming process had been completed," he continued. "I did not know my own skin."

"I know mine. I just don't know who's been wearing it for the last five years." I destroyed some more phony grass. "Anything else happen between you and whatever possessed my body?"

He gazed at the fake horizon. "Jarn's efforts to save me are ultimately what led to the return of your persona."

That got my attention. "So you're the one who brought me back from oblivion?"

"I believe it to be so."

Maybe the body-snatching slave girl hadn't committed suicide after all . . . and was I going to tell Reever that?

Hell, no. "I guess that makes us even." I rose and straightened my tunic, and he did the same. "I'm hungry," I lied. "Want to share a meal interval with me?"

Judging by his expression, he didn't know quite what to make of that. Or me. Which made two of us.

At last he said, "If that is your wish."

"You'll have to show me where the galley is," I told him as we walked out of the environome. "They've changed everything around so much I don't know where it is."

"Of course." He led me to a lift, and then whisked us off to another deck.

The oKiaf didn't indulge in any small talk, but I welcomed the silence. Every time someone opened their mouth, I heard something else that I didn't want to know. It would be great to spend a couple of hours not knowing.

The galley was mostly empty, but the few crew members who were dining there only offered up a smile or a nod before returning their attention to their meals. I never knew Jorenians to be so standoffish, so either *that* had changed, too, or Xonea had said something to the crew.

At the prep unit, I pulled up the menu programmed for Terrans and read through the list. Most of the dishes were Reever's preferences, although there were several synpro dishes I didn't recognize. Since I usually couldn't stomach the alien fare my husband enjoyed, I selected one of the odd ones. The unit produced what appeared to be a small, slithery heap of gelatinous, uncooked flesh sprinkled with spike-edged purple and red leaves.

P.S., the odor was worse than the presentation.

"Where did Duncan pick up this recipe?" I muttered, examining the plate. "Waste world?"

"That is ptar belly with ice leaves," the oKiaf told me. "It is a delicacy on Akkabarr."

Oh. *Her* food. Raw flesh and ugly herbs. God only knew what she had been putting in my stomach for the last five years. I dumped the plate and its contents into the disposal unit. "Shon, is there anything on your menu a Terran can eat without a lot of puking afterward?"

He dialed up some sort of soup and flat bread. Since the scent of it didn't turn my stomach, I carried it to a table and sat down. He brought an identical meal for himself, and two servers of a hot, golden brew.

"Kapelat," he told me as he offered me one of the drinks. "It will settle your stomach."

I tried a sip. It wasn't tooth-numbingly sweet like so many Jorenian teas, but had a mellow tang that went down easily. "It's good. Thanks."

The soup, while unlike anything made by Terrans, was vegetable-based, and had a strange but agreeable flavor. The chewy flat bread had a strong, darker taste to it, but paired well with the soup. My tight throat didn't want to cooperate, but the kapelat was an effective soother, and I managed to finish half the meal.

My companion didn't make it obvious that he was watching me eat, but he stopped as soon as I did. That reminded me that some species considered it rude to continue dining when others had finished.

"Go ahead, keep eating," I said. "It's not the food. It's me."

"There are some matters I would discuss with you, Healer Torin," the oKiaf said.

"Cherijo."

He inclined his head. "As you have no memory of our—of my interactions with your former self, I feel I should tell you of them, and what I discovered from them."

"Are you going to use the word 'terrible'?" I demanded. He shook his head. "All right, then. Tell me."

"During the brief time that I knew Jarn, I developed intimate feelings for her. I fell in love with her." He sounded gruff, as if it was hard for him to admit. "And because of those emotions, I attempted to seduce her."

Was this the reason Reever was treating me like a contagious disease? Guilt over what the slave girl had done with my body? "Did she go for it?"

"Did she . . . ah, no."

"That's too bad." No, it wasn't, but I didn't have to stomp on the guy's heart. I was curious, though. "Why would you fall for a Terran? We're not exactly at the top of everyone's crossbreed-mating wish list." When he started unfastening the front of his tunic, I flashed up a hand. "Whoa, wait a second. I don't need you to show me anything."

"It is only this." He pulled aside his tunic to reveal two parallel vertical rows of golden fur.

"They're, uh, very attractive markings," I guessed.

"They indicate that I am a touch-healer."

"What do you know? So is Squilyp." A tingling of alarm made me draw back a little. "I don't really need to be touched or healed, though. Just FYI."

"I am like you, sister." He refastened his tunic. "I am never ill. I have survived every injury done to me. Even when I attempted to take my own life, I could not end it. I am immortal."

I blinked. "You were bioengineered? The way I was?"

"So it would seem, although I have no memory of it," he admitted. "You—Jarn—called me 'brother.' She seemed to recognize me."

Not one damn thing about him seemed familiar to me. "My surrogate mother once told me that there were others. At the time I didn't really believe her. Maybe you're one of them." I saw Xonea walk into the galley, and head toward our table. "Here comes another family member."

"Cherijo." Xonea sounded relieved. "You should be resting in Medical."

"I think I've slept long enough, ClanBrother." I forced my mouth to approximate a pleasant smile.

"I'd also like to pass on any debriefing you have in mind."

"As you say, ClanSister." With remarkable, un-Xonea-like calm he turned to address Shon. "She is well?"

The oKiaf nodded.

I hated being treated as if I were invisible, so I got to my feet. "Thank you for sharing the meal with me, Healer Valtas. Xonea, see you around." I headed for the lift.

Xonea caught up with me before I could make a clean getaway. "Cherijo, wait." He turned me around and took hold of my cold hands. "You are distressed."

It was ironic; the only person happy I was back was my ex-brother-in-law, whom I had once married and divorced. What did that say about me?

"I've had better days." Squilyp's suggestion prompted me to ask, "I'm going to need my own place. Got any vacant quarters near Medical that I can use for a while?"

"I have already arranged it." Some of the pleasure ebbed from his expression, and his grip on me tightened. "You have spoken to Duncan?"

"I tried. He's not interested in chatting with me right now." I glanced at the lift. "Where are my new rooms?"

He folded one of my arms over his. "I will escort you."

From there we went to the living quarters that Xonea had assigned to me. They were furnished for use by a Jorenian, which made them comfortable if a bit too large and colorful for me, but they would do. The data terminal was all I was interested in, but when I tried to access it, my codes were refused.

"Why am I locked out of the database?" I asked.

"The Omorr thought it best." Xonea brought me a server of jaspkerry tea. "You need not try to absorb the events of the past five years in one day." He saw my expression. "Perhaps Squilyp is being somewhat overprotective, but he is the Senior Healer. He has only your best interests in mind."

"That's why he let some alien run around with my body for the last five years?" Before he could reply, I added, "I've reviewed my medical records, Xonea. They removed the dates, but not the facts. The Omorr gave up on me. Just like everyone else did."

"I did not." He set aside the tea and crouched in front of me. Other species often found it hard to discern emotions from the Jorenians' all-white eyes, but I could see a kind of joyful pain, as if what he felt was too acute to put into words. "I prayed each day to the Mother, and implored her to return you to us. I never lost hope. I knew eventually she would hear me."

"Yeah, well, she took her sweet time, didn't she?" Now I had to know what it had cost me. "What is everyone keeping from me? What the hell did this Akkabarran do while I was gone?"

"There have been many repercussions since the rebellion—"

"I'm not interested in hearing about another stupid war," I told him. "What did she do to my husband?"

Lines of strain appeared around his mouth. "Duncan has not told you of this?"

"Duncan doesn't want to talk about it with me." And finally I understood why. "I see. He got involved with her. And Marel? Did she think . . . ?" I couldn't put it into words. "Did the Akkabarran play mother as well as wife?"

Xonea rose and walked over to the viewport to look out at the stars. He always did that when he didn't want to answer me.

This was what it felt like, to have your heart shattered. Interesting. Rather like a massive myocardial infarction, minus the copious sweating and respiratory distress.

After a long interval my ClanBrother finally spoke. "You should not blame them, Cherijo. Duncan truly believed that you had embraced the stars. So did the little one. They grieved for you in their own way, but . . . the path changes, and so, too, must the traveler."

As affirmations went, that was a resounding one. And it killed something inside me, some frail and puny faith that had kept me going since I'd woken up to this new world.

I had worked hard, compromised, sacrificed, and exhausted myself to care for so many. I'd died a couple of times in the process. I'd overlooked Reever's inhuman personality, the lack of emotions, the hundred or so stupid things he'd done since we'd met, and finally put my trust in him and the love he had always claimed to feel for me.

And this was my reward.

"Give me the codes, Xonea."

He came over to the terminal and inputted an override sequence. "I will remain with you."

"Not necessary." I accessed the ship's logs first.

"You will have questions."

"I'll find the answers myself." I turned away and began scanning the first report, and didn't stop until

I heard the door panel open and close. Then I got up, secured the panel, and leaned against the wall. Somehow I ended up in a huddle on the deck, hunched over, the heels of my hands grinding into my dry, burning eyes.

Jarn hadn't just helped herself to my body, and erased five years of my life. She'd stolen my family from me.

And my husband had let her.

I didn't waste my time weeping, or tearing out my hair, or otherwise collapsing into a helpless puddle of misery. It would serve no purpose, and if there was one thing I had been created to be, it was useful.

I spent the next forty-eight hours on the terminal in my quarters, reading first the ship's logs and then sifting through the database for records of the other events I had missed. I stopped only for food, cleansing, and lavatory visits. I also blocked all the signals that were sent to my quarters from Command, Medical Bay, and several crew terminals.

Once I'd read through all the data available on the main database, I encountered several new and interesting safeguards protecting the more sensitive data available only to the ship's commander and senior officers. Although neither my codes nor Xonea's override would bypass them, I tried one I thought Squilyp might use—the birth date of his twin boys—and gained full access to the restricted areas.

There I found all the information they were trying to keep from me: records of my whereabouts and activities, surveillance of my personal quarters both on the ship and on Joren, field reports on my movements and sojourns, and enough audio and video to keep me staring at a monitor for several months. Three enormous files contained all the known details from my visits to oKia, Trellus, and Vtaga.

My, my, my. I had no memory of any of it; the slave girl had been in possession at the time. She'd illegally trespassed on oKia, gotten herself marooned on Trellus, and nearly started a civil war on Vtaga. But to her credit, she'd discovered a new form of crystal, stopped an alien butcher, and cured a plague.

She'd also brought Reever back to life on Vtaga after SrrokVar—now, there was a name I'd never wanted to hear again—had killed him.

I had hoped to get in a third day of study before they came for me, but the Omorr wasn't known for his patience. He used a medical override to bypass the locking mechanism on my door panel and hopped in with the oKiaf and a Jorenian nurse in tow.

"Power down that terminal," he told me. "You are coming with me to Medical."

"I'm not deaf." I switched off the monitor. "You don't have to shout."

"I am not . . ." He exhaled and inhaled before speaking in a softer voice. "Forgive me. I am deeply concerned about you."

"Why?" I faced him. "I'm fine."

"You are anything but fine," he snapped. "You have shunned all interactions with the crew. You have not answered a single signal sent to these quarters. You are irrational, antisocial, and displaying obsessive-compulsive behavior."

I folded my arms. "Squilyp, we both know that's just me, even on a good day."

"I disagree. I believe you are suffering from post-traumatic stress disorder." He took a medical case from the nurse and opened it. "What would you classify a patient who for days refused to leave a computer terminal or sleep?"

"A busy insomniac who doesn't want to talk to anyone." I smiled. He turned a beautiful shade of dark rose pink whenever he was agitated. "I promise, I am not on the verge of an emotional collapse. How do you know I haven't been sleeping?"

"Deeply traumatic events such as you have endured often trigger such breaks." He removed a syrinpress and dialed up a dosage of something on it.

"No, that's not it." I glanced around my quarters, the quarters my ClanBrother had so thoughtfully arranged for me. "I didn't think to check for recording drones. You must have gotten quite a show whenever I cleansed. When did Xonea decide to sanction gross violations of personal privacy?"

"We thought it prudent to keep you under close monitor," the Omorr said, "in the event you required assistance."

"No one wants to see me naked anymore." I released a theatrical sigh and turned to Shon. "If the Senior Healer tries to sedate me, I will be leaving, and you'll have to take him back to Medical and surgically remove that syrinpress from his esophagus. Are you up for that, or should I explain the extraction procedure to you first?"

"Enough of this, Cherijo." Squilyp was shouting again.

Shon stepped between us. "Senior Healer, please." He regarded me. "Cherijo, the captain has received orders to return at once to Joren. To do so, he must make two interdimensional jumps. Now."

I'd never handled dimensional transitions very

well. "That's the real reason you wanted me back in Medical?" I asked Squilyp.

"Yes," Shon answered quickly for him.

"Why didn't you say so in the first place?" I slipped on my footgear.

Squilyp bided his time, following me to the lift and entering it along with the oKiaf and the nurse. All three of them tried to visually assess me while trying not to be obvious about it. Considering how small the lift was, that took some doing.

"I've been taking regular breaks to eat and cleanse," I said mildly. "I'm not experiencing any weakness, sensory disruption, or pain. No headaches, vision problems, new memory loss, or any other abnormal or unusual symptoms, either. So quit worrying."

"I do not worry," Squilyp snapped. "Are you giving yourself stimulants in order to remain awake?"

"No. I haven't felt tired." It was partly true. Something was driving me now, something big and dark and seething, and I didn't care to shine an internal light on it. "If it makes you feel better, I'll probably lose consciousness as soon as the ship transitions. Then you can poke and prod me as much as you like until I wake up."

If I woke up. No one questioned the possibility that the slave girl might come back instead, but they were all thinking it. So was I.

My calm demeanor was as much an act as my rational attitude, but they didn't know that, and I didn't want to go through transition alone. If I was strapped into a berth in Medical and something did go wrong, Squilyp was my best chance of surviving it.

I felt something soft and very warm touch my hand, and looked down to see Shon's paw curling around my fingers. His fur was much finer and silkier than it looked, and his body heat topped mine by a good ten degrees. I also became aware of how good he smelled: like trees and earth and growing things. I felt like wrapping him around me, but the icy cold was deep inside me, where all that lovely warmth couldn't reach.

I took my hand from his. If I was going to handle this, I couldn't depend on the kindness of strangers. Especially one who had been in love with *her*, not me.

I hung on to that frigid calm until they put me in a berth in an isolation room and a nurse began to attach monitor leads to my head and chest. Then my muscles went on strike, first stiffening and then knotting as I began to tremble.

"Leave us," the Omorr said as he scanned me.

I saw the oKiaf and the nurses go. "I'm all right."

"No, you are not." He checked his scanner and sighed. "Try to relax."

By that point the berth was shaking along with me. "Se-se-seizure?"

"Your heart rate and respiration have doubled, you are perspiring heavily and presenting involuntary rapid fine tremors, your glucose level is dropping, and your glands are attempting to compensate by releasing a substantial amount of adrenaline into your bloodstream," he said. "You are having an anxiety attack."

How wimpy of me. "S-s-sorry."

"Your recent activities have resulted in a serious B complex deficiency, which is contributing to your condition. I am giving you a vitamin booster to augment. Please do not shove the instrument down my throat," he added as he infused me and then finished wiring me to the equipment.

I clenched my teeth to keep them from chattering until the anxiety crested and then slowly dissolved. "Sedatives would have worked just as well."

He sighed. "Over the last years you have become immune to them."

But not to anxiety, evidently. The receding adrenaline left me feeling abruptly exhausted. "Would you do something for me, Senior Healer?"

"As long as it does not require you to leave this berth."

"If I don't wake up this time," I said carefully, "put my body in stasis until you can figure out how to bring me back."

"Cherijo—"

"Please." In spite of my best efforts to control my emotions, I felt a single tear roll down my cheek. "Don't let some alien take over my body again, Squilyp. Please. I'm begging you."

Squilyp did something very un-Squilyp then: He sat on the edge of the berth, pulled me up, and wrapped all three arms around me. "I promise."

He didn't let me go, so shortly thereafter when reality was sucked into a dizzying swirl of colors, I was still in his arms. As my tired brain upended itself, a wistful sadness filled me, and I wished I'd asked Squilyp to send for Reever. Despite what had happened, I regretted that the last words we'd exchanged had been angry and bitter.

As bitter as the words I'd said . . . that I had signaled . . .

Memories began pouring into my mind, a series of vivid sensory flashes that blotted out the disorienting effects of the ship's transition. I was back on the Rilken ship, jaunting toward the *CloudWalk*, only this time something was different. I saw myself on the deck, blood all over my face. The League soldier who had hit me lay across me, unconscious. I had to push him off and roll him to one side so I could reach the main console and initiate a relay. I watched myself doing those things, and felt as if I were doing them at the same time.

League command vessel, this is Dr. Cherijo Torin. I have to speak to Colonel Shropana immediately.

I didn't receive a response, so I switched relay channels and repeated the request, but that made no difference. The console began picking up transmissions between League ships, however, and I saw myself listening to them, and then attempting to signal first the Jorenians, and then the League command vessel.

No one would respond to my relays. My transceiver had been partially damaged; all I could do was listen.

The Rilkens' viewer displayed the *CloudWalk* as it fired on an approaching transport—a drone transport, according to the signals I'd overheard—programmed to provoke the Jorenians into an attack. I watched myself change tactics and try to send a signal to the Jorenians.

There are no living beings on that launch, I shouted. *They are trying to provoke you into an attack. Cease fire.*

All I heard in return was a satisfied male voice issuing an order to respond and destroy the *CloudWalk*.

ClanLeader Teulon, listen to me, I pleaded. *You have to stop this right now. It's nothing but a ruse. My husband and my daughter are on your ship. Shropana knows that. He's doing this to get to them. To get back at me. Listen to me, please.*

League ships began swarming around the Jado vessel. The viewer glowed brighter and brighter as explosions of pulse fire burst all around me.

No, please, Teulon. You have to cease fire. There are too many of them. Cease fire, for God's sake—

I saw but didn't see the League soldier rise up behind me. I kept sending my frantic transmissions until the viewer filled with white light, and the *CloudWalk*'s stardrive imploded.

The light blinded me just as the soldier clubbed me in the head.

I regained consciousness on what I assumed was the cargo compartment on the League transport. My head ached, and the restraints they'd put me in were cutting off the circulation to my hands and feet, but I was alive. They'd posted a heavily armed humanoid male as my guard; he was a canine species with narrow black eyes, a prominent muzzle, and brown-pelted skin. He wore combat-fitted body armor and looked as if he'd enjoy shooting me.

I knew Reever and Marel were not dead, but the part of me reliving this experience didn't. I couldn't breach the distance between our minds, and reassure myself. I could only feel the rage building again.

The Jorenians will come for you. Do you know what they do to anyone who harms their kin?

Keep your orifice shut. He had a magnificent set of sharp denticles. *Or I will gag you.*

I didn't know what he had been ordered to do, but I could guess. The hostility in his black eyes made his threats into promises. If I pushed hard enough, he might lose control and do more, perhaps even execute me early. Which was fine with me. I didn't want to live anymore, not without my family.

Your commander just wiped out an entire House-Clan, I told him. *Since there are no Jado left now, the Jorenian Ruling Council will designate the dead as ClanJoren. Do you know what that means, murderer?*

He came up to me and backhanded me. *I have not killed anyone. Be silent.*

It doesn't matter. Every HouseClan on the planet will be coming for your commander. Your fleet. I spit out some blood onto the front of his chest plate. *And you.*

Let them come. They may join their kin in death. He didn't sound quite as ferocious now.

They won't be coming alone, I promised. *While you and the Hsktskt have been playing war games, the Jorenians have been forming their own coalition with other neutral species. The treaties have included pacts of mutual protection against the League and the Faction. This massacre will not go unanswered. They'll call on their new allies as well as their old friends, most of whom have just been waiting for any decent excuse to move against the League. They'll disable your fleet. Then the Jorenians will board the ships and declare the crews ClanKill.* I leaned forward, straining against the restraints. *They'll hold them down, one by one, and use their claws to eviscerate them alive.*

He took an involuntary step back. *How could you know any of this? You are a fugitive from Terra. You are not even classified as a sentient creature.*

Is that what they told you? I asked sweetly. *Whatever the League thinks of me, the Jorenians adopted me. And after I saved their planet from an invasion, they made me a member of their Ruling Council.*

You were told not to interact with the prisoner, a familiar voice said.

I looked past the guard and saw the ugly, gloating face of one of my oldest enemies. *Shropana.*

Now you understand why you should have killed me when you had the chance, Cherijo.

Cherijo.

Cherijo.

"Cherijo."

I opened my eyes, and saw my face reflected in something dark and shiny. When I blinked, the mirror image didn't do the same. Only when cracks began spreading over it did I realize that I was seeing my face, encased in black crystal, and it was being slowly crushed.

I screamed.

Three

"It was only a bad dream," I told Squilyp as he removed the monitor leads from my temples. "Or a hallucination, caused by the effects of the jump. Maybe I saw your face and thought it was something else."

"According to the equipment, you never lost consciousness." He brushed some hair out of my eyes. "And I do not think my countenance, distorted or not, could have frightened you enough to cry out like that."

I hadn't described to him what I'd seen. It was bad enough that I had to remember it. "Whatever it was, it's over. Forget about it." As soon as the last line was off me, I swung my legs over the side of the berth. "Are we there yet?"

"The ship will be landing on Joren within the hour. You are not leaving Medical until it does." The Omorr handed me a stack of ceremonial garments. "If you feel well enough to get up, you can get dressed."

"I'm not wearing this. I look ridiculous in Jorenian robes." As I realized why he'd given them to me, I dropped them on the berth. "Oh, no. You didn't tell them I woke up."

"The captain signaled the planet before we transitioned. The entire HouseClan has assembled to celebrate your return. You are supposed to be surprised by this." He didn't smirk or even sound amused. "There are others waiting on planet who also wish to meet with you."

Uh-oh. "What others?"

"A diplomatic party from Vtaga. That is all Xonea told me," he added, before I could ask. "I will send a nurse to obtain some garments from your, ah, from Reever's quarters." He gave me a sympathetic look before he hopped out.

I thought about using the isolation room terminal to signal Command and tell Xonea what I thought of his surprise party, but I was too busy trying to understand why an entourage of Hsktskt had been allowed on planet.

The last time the Faction had sent its representatives to Joren, it had been strictly for the purposes of invading it, stripping it of its resources, and enslaving the populace. I'd traded Shropana and an entire fleet of League ships to stop that from happening. Thanks to Reever's own devious machinations, I'd also been enslaved myself, although eventually I'd freed myself and the League prisoners, and destroyed the Hsktskt slave depot on Catopsa in the process.

But that was no longer the status quo, as I knew from accessing Xonea's secured files. Jarn had helped end the war between the League and the Faction, and then she'd cured a devastating plague on the Hsktskt homeworld. She'd even convinced the lizards to revoke the blood bounty they'd put on my head after I'd destroyed their flesh-peddling prison outpost.

"If I'm supposed to feel grateful for what she

did," I muttered, "everyone is going to be very disappointed."

The nurse showed up with fresh garments, none of which I recognized. "Do you need assistance, Healer?"

"No, thanks." I shook out the tunic and trousers, both of which were in a shade of ivory that I never wore. The material smelled of unfamiliar organics: transfer from a musky plant or herb. Maybe it was some sort of perfume the slave girl had worn to make herself smell nice.

Had she done it for Reever? What else had she done for him? Was that how she had stolen him from me? With some weird alien sex?

A complicated, strapped contraption fell to the floor, and I picked it up. It didn't belong to me. "What's this?"

"It was left folded atop your undergarments," the nurse said. "I assumed it belonged to you."

"Why would I need all these straps?" It must have been Jarn's, but what kind of woman-hating culture had she come from, to have to bind herself up in something like this?

At second glance it didn't appear to be a body rig; it was more like a harness to be strapped across the shoulders and chest. Odd pockets and flaps had been sewn in the straps, and when I opened one, I discovered it was a sheath for a small, smooth-hilted blade.

I took out the dagger and examined it. "This looks like a weapon." I checked the other pockets, which held a variety of other knives—twenty in all. "Jesus Christ. What is this thing?"

The nurse smiled uneasily. "I would say it is a blade harness, Healer."

"I'm a physician," I pointed out. "We don't use weapons. We clean up the mess they make."

"The harness belonged to Jarn," Reever said as he came into the room. He turned to the nurse. "Would you excuse us, please?"

"As you wish, Linguist. Healer." The nurse practically ran out of the room.

"Hello, Duncan." I took out one of the slave girl's longer daggers and held it up to the light. "Omorr-forged, perfectly balanced." I didn't have to test the edge, which bore marks indicating it had been honed down to a lethal sharpness that would cut like a lascalpel. "This looks like one of yours."

"I gave it to Jarn when peace was declared." He seemed more interested in me now than he had in the environome. "She attended the injured and dying on battlefields. She was trained to carry weapons to defend herself."

"Considering what a lethal threat injured, dying rebels can be, that's completely understandable." I sheathed the dagger and dropped the contraption like the trash it was. "What do you want? Your knives back?" I kicked the harness across the deck to him. "There you go."

He bent over to retrieve the harness and slung it over his shoulder. "I did not come here to provoke you."

"Too late." I showed him some teeth. "And I'm sorry to disappoint you, but Jarn's still dead, and I'm not." I turned my back on him. "You know your way out."

He didn't go. "We should talk."

"Oh, *now* we should talk," I said to the berth. "*Not* when I woke up out of a five-year walking coma. *Not* when I found out how long I'd been gone. *Not* when I went looking for my husband and he treated me like a Tingalean leper in active contagion-molt. Certainly *not* at any time over the past thirty-six hours that I spent alone in my new quarters waiting for him to drop by and reassure me that despite his behavior he was happy I'd come back. I can see how those would have been totally inappropriate moments to have a conversation."

"I needed time to accept Jarn's loss." He moved a little closer. "But now I see that it was wrong of me to make you wait and suffer in solitude as I have. I apologize for my actions."

Jarn's loss. Not mine. Had he ever grieved like that for me? Why did he care now if I suffered or not?

Silently I counted to ten, thinking the entire time that it was a damn good thing he was holding that knife harness and not me.

"I am glad you have returned," he continued. "I regret that we were not able to effect the reinstatement of your personality sooner than this. You must have a great many questions about the gaps in your memory."

"Not really. While you were busy sobbing into your pillow and sulking, I broke into Xonea's secured files and read up on everything that's happened since we parted ways at Oenrall. Well, almost everything," I amended as I remembered the scent from the garments I'd never worn. "There are still some minor details that I'm sketchy on. For example, did you have sex with the Akkabarran?"

"I do not think—"

"Don't think, darling," I said, very softly, so that he

would understand just how angry I was. "Just answer the question."

"Yes," he said. "Jarn and I made love. She was as much my wife as you were."

Were. I was still dead to him. Having that confirmed extinguished the last, tiny flicker of hope in my heart. All that remained for me to do was to make arrangements for an appropriate burial.

Here lies Cherijo's true love, the grave marker would read. *Stolen by an alien, slowly strangled, and left alone to rot in solitude. Also known as the definition of living hell.*

A cold little voice in my head reminded me that I'd done this before, with Kao Torin. I survived that; I'd get over this. Maybe I'd visit Omorr and see if any of their single males were interested in an offworld mate. They wrote up legal contracts before they got into permanent relationships, and if they tried to leave a spouse for an alien entity, said spouse could have all their assets seized.

"Cherijo?" He sounded uneasy now.

"They're having a party for me on Joren," I said, stripping off the gown. "The usual overblown endless all-day, all-night revelry thing, I imagine. My *nine*-year-old daughter is there, and Squilyp says there are some Hsktskt waiting to see me, too. I'm sure I'm going to be very busy for the next several weeks." I pulled the tunic over my head and tugged it into place. "So when we land, you should really go."

"Go where?"

"Anywhere. Another province, planet, quadrant, galaxy, dimension, take your pick." I turned on him. "It doesn't matter, as long as it's away from me."

His eyes changed colors with his moods, and at that moment they were a bleak, dark gray. "You would have me leave you now?"

"You left me two years ago, Reever, when you and your little alien girlfriend decided to fall in love and use my body as a hotel." I pulled on my trousers. "This will simply make it official."

The new lines around his mouth tightened. "You forget that we have a daughter, Cherijo."

"Oh, no, *I* haven't forgotten anything," I said. "Once I file for legal separation, our counselors can get together and work out an amicable split-parenting agreement." I fastened the waistband before pulling down my tunic and adjusting the hem. "I believe the standard Terran arrangement for shared custody is three to four days per week and every other holiday on a rotational basis."

His hands knotted into fists. "Acting on your anger with me will not resolve anything."

"Acting on your infidelity will." I gathered up my hair, twisting and folding it, and secured the coil to the back of my head with a clip. "Adultery is still lawful justification for dissolution of marriage on quite a few planets, including the one we'll be orbiting in a half hour." I pretended to think. "In fact, I'm pretty sure that the Jorenian bondmate who cheats on his Chosen is expected to commit ritual suicide in front of the entire HouseClan to restore honor to his ex. So is his illicit lover, but, oh, right." I eyed him. "You don't have to worry about that part."

A muscle flicked in his jaw. "I was not unfaithful to you in the legal sense of the term."

"You know, you find out the most fascinating tidbits when you illegally access confidential command files," I advised him. "For example, did you know that Jarn resigned my position from the Jorenian Ruling Council? She cited her mental condition as making her unfit to serve. The council accepted her resignation, and referred to her as Jarn in all of the documentation, some of which was video, and all of which I am sure they etched on crystal. That qualifies her as a unique being, recognized as independent and completely separate from me." I turned on him. "So yes, sweetheart. Legally speaking, you *were* unfaithful to me."

"I have told you the truth, and I have apologized for my behavior," he said through his teeth. "What more do you want?"

Five years. "From you?" I uttered a chuckle. "Nothing, thanks."

He grabbed me by the shoulders and shook me. "Stop this foolishness. You are not leaving me, nor I you. We have a child. We have a life together."

I wanted to punch him in the face. I wanted to scream. I wanted to drop on my knees and hug his legs and beg him to tell me that this was all some sort of horrible mistake. That there had never been a Jarn. That this was some sort of bizarre medical test or psychological assessment being done to determine only if I was the real Cherijo.

None of that happened. It never would. My anger dissipated abruptly, and the despair it left behind swelled. If I didn't finish this, it was going to crush me from the inside out.

"Do you love me, Duncan? Or are you still in love with her? No." As he tried to turn his head away, I caught his jaw. "Look me in the eyes and tell me."

"Over time, I came to care for her. I cannot tell you

when it happened, or why, only that it did. I never felt such a thing for another. It seemed as if she were truly the other half of my . . ." He stopped and cleared his throat. "It is of no consequence now. She is gone. You came first in my life. You are here again, and in time I believe that we can be together as we once were."

"Sorry." Because Reever understood so little about human emotion, he had convinced himself that we still had a shot at this. Somewhere under the flattening weight of my own heartbreak, I felt for him. "Not going to happen."

"Why not?"

"When you lose someone you love, they take part of you with them. You're never the same again. You never get it back." I went to the door panel, stopped, and glanced back at him. "I understand how you feel much better than you think."

"You speak of losing Kao Torin." He nodded, still oblivious to what I was saying. "Yes. That is how it has been for me."

"I'm not talking about Kao." For a moment I let him see my sorrow. "I know how you feel about losing Jarn because I've lost you."

I didn't glance back as I left Medical and headed for launch bay.

Joren looked exactly as I remembered it: big, wide-open, beautiful, and dazzling with color. All the colors of the rainbow streamed across the sky in the form of prismatic cloud streaks; the immense fields of silver yiborra grass stretched out in every direction around HouseClan Torin's Main Transport facility. The air smelled of flowers, which bloomed everywhere in countless varieties and shades.

While Main Transport was a busy place, with ships landing and launching all around us, even the sight of Jorenians in their flight gear made me feel a little better. These were my people, the only species to take me in and accept what I was and still care for me like one of their own. Joren and its HouseClans were the home and kin of my soul.

I didn't realize there was going to be an official welcoming committee until Xonea and a detachment of guards in dress uniform surrounded me.

"Cherijo." My ClanBrother frowned at the ordinary garments I was wearing. "Where are your robes?"

"I left them on the ship." Along with Reever, who hadn't tried to disembark with the rest of us. Maybe he was planning to go out the back way. I glanced over at the passenger reception and departure building, and the hundreds of dark blue faces looking out from the view panels. "Can't I skip this and go see what the lizards want?"

"Not after so long an absence," he said in a firm voice, and put one big hand against my back. "Nor will you avoid the celebrations planned to honor your return."

"No, of course we can't miss all the eating and laughing and touching," I said, feeling glum.

"One might claim to be weary and in need of rest after so long a journey," Xonea suggested.

"I didn't go anywhere." I gave him a suspicious look. "Why are you being so helpful? You always liked parties. You certainly dragged me to enough of them."

"I have not felt in the celebratory mood for some time," was all he would say.

Something had changed about Xonea, although I

couldn't quite decide what it was. He'd been all sun-shine and happiness around me, but even that was different than it had been. Before I'd gotten booted out of my own body, Xonea had been like a brother to me. Now he was acting more like my parent: seeing to my rooms, holding my arm, ushering me around as if I couldn't be trusted alone.

"Did Jarn do something to upset or offend you?" I asked him. He didn't reply, so I stopped. "You might as well tell me."

"She did nothing to me."

"*Nothing* being like trying to take your command away from you?" I offered him a guileless look. "Oops. Someone must have let that slip."

"Indeed." He glowered down at me. "Now is not the time to discuss my interactions with the Akkabar-ran."

It was interesting, how he avoided using her name. "You didn't like her? I'm shocked. Everyone else did."

"If I could have declared her my ClanKill with-out harming your form," he assured me through his lovely, clenched white teeth, "she would never have stepped foot on my ship."

Whoa, that wasn't dislike; that was pure hatred. Another reason to love my adopted sibling. I slipped my hand into his and gave it a squeeze. "You're right, we'll talk about it later. Your pardon, Captain."

He laced his fingers through mine. "No pardon is required, Lady."

As we walked toward the building, I saw a small, ivory-skinned figure rush out toward us. She was blond and smiling and so grown-up I forgot to breathe.

"Jesus." I dragged in some air and clutched Xonea's

hand so tight his knuckles popped. "Is that little girl my baby?"

He smiled. "That is our Marel."

My daughter avoided the two Jorenians trotting after her and ran all the way to us, flinging herself into my arms. "Mama. You came back."

I picked her up and held her tight, burying my face in her golden curls. "Sweetheart." She still smelled the same. "God, you're so big. Did you miss me?"

My daughter lifted her face and looked into my eyes, her little face scrunching into a frown. "Mama? Did Daddy teach you to speak our kind of Terran while you were gone?"

"No, but I remembered it," I said carefully. "I remembered everything I forgot, baby. Including who I was."

She squirmed until I put her down on her feet, and looked at Xonea. Her face was so solemn, I felt tears sting my eyes. "Did it hurt her?" Marel asked Xonea.

The captain knelt before her. "Your ClanMother is not injured, Marel."

"No, I mean my other mama. My mama Jarn." She made a little choking sound. "Did it hurt her when she embraced the stars?"

Xonea exchanged a look with me before he said, "No, little one. She went with joy."

Marel swallowed and knuckled her eyes before she looked at me again, this time not so happy. "You are my birth mama. ClanMother Cherijo."

"Yes, I am." I wasn't going to lie to her, although if Jarn had been there, I would have gutted her with my bare hands. "Do you remember me?"

"A little." Marel sounded uncertain. "Will my real mama be coming back?"

I'm your real mother, I wanted to shriek, but I knew that wouldn't do anything but hurt my daughter. "Jarn didn't want to leave you, baby, but she had to go. She left so that you and I could be together again, the way we were before she came."

"I don't know you," Marel said slowly. "You look like my mama, but you don't feel like her. You sound different. You sound sad."

"If you were gone for a long time, and everyone forgot about you, and then you came back, would you feel sad?" She nodded. "That's why I sound that way."

"You could help me remember." Cautiously she took my hand, as if I were a stranger she wasn't sure she trusted entirely. "Then I think I would like you."

I wanted to hug her and never let her go, but I settled for a bright smile. "That sounds like a very good idea." And I'd also make sure she forgot all about the husband- and child-stealing slave girl who had done this to her.

Marel's face lit up, but not for me. "Daddy," she said, and ran past us into her father's arms.

Reever picked her up and held her close, but watched me over her head. He opened his mouth as if to call to me, and then closed it. As he kept looking at me, his eyes darkened.

He expects you to go running over to him. That's probably what she did every time he snapped his fingers.

I turned my back on him and said to Xonea, "Are the Hsktskt here at the pavilion?" I needed to focus on something more dangerous than my current emotional state. The lizards were the only thing that scared me more.

"No, they remain guests of the Adan in the capital,"

he said. "You need not meet with them until after the celebration has concluded."

"You people party for weeks," I reminded him as I started for the passenger terminal. "And as I remember, the Faction isn't that patient."

"Much has changed since TssVar became Hanar," Xonea said. "But that is a discussion for another hour. Come, my ClanParents await."

It hurt to walk away from my daughter and meet the Torin welcoming mob, but I had no intention of putting up a pretense or encouraging my soon-to-be ex-husband. I could be civil to him for Marel's sake, but that was all. It was typical of Reever not to realize how upsetting this situation was for me; he had only a rudimentary understanding of human emotion, and whatever he felt now was for Jarn, not me.

If he wants to hang around me while he pretends I'm her, I thought as I plastered a smile on my face for the Torins, *I'll declare him ClanKill myself.*

My adopted family didn't wait for me to enter the terminal, but came out in a flood of towering bodies and grinning dark faces. Dozens of hands danced around me as I was greeted and welcomed and passed through an almost-continuous gauntlet of affectionate voices speaking my name and blessings and prayers to the Mother. At the center of the crowd was Xonea's father and the Torin ClanLeader, Xonal, who touched his brow to mine before enveloping me in his arms.

"I have missed you, ClanDaughter," he said, pulling me off my feet and whirling me around as he might a child. Since I was child-sized compared with the Jorenians, this was understandable. "You are well?"

"Thanks to Squilyp, Xonea, and our kin, yes, Clan-

Leader. I am." I held on to his hands as I looked around at all the happy faces. "I thank you for this welcome," I said in the ceremonial form of their language. "That the Mother chose to lead me to this House again is the only path I could ever wish to follow."

Squilyp had coached me a little on the wording, and I didn't even attempt the hand gestures, which were more complicated than anything I could have managed. But they understood me all the same, and a resounding cheer went up, spread out through the air until it echoed around the dock.

I was glad, too. The atmosphere on the ship had grown so tense as to be almost unbearable. Now I didn't have to pretend people weren't staring at me. Here they wanted to look and see me. Here I was with family; I was loved; I was venerated. Here I was valued and treasured, an essential part of something big and wonderful and important. I was a daughter of the House, a child of its Clan, and they had missed me.

Finally, I was home.

The trip from Main Transport over to HouseClan Torin's pavilion took only a short time, during which I spoke at length with Xonal Torin in his private glidecar about the current political situation.

"We were not filled with joy at the prospect of allowing the Hsktskt delegation on planet," he admitted, "but their Hanar offered many assurances, and Teulon Jado gave his full endorsement to the request. Apparently the two have grown to trust each other since the peace negotiations concluded."

Despite their abandoning planetary raiding and slave trading, I wasn't entirely convinced that the Hsktskt had been transformed into a benign, peace-loving civilization. "Have we signed any treaties with the Faction?"

Xonal shook his head. "The Hsktskt have extended several offers, but to date the council has avoided agreeing to any formal settlements with the Hanar. Few have forgotten that the last time they sent their troops to Varallan, it was for the purpose of invasion and enslavement of our people."

"They wouldn't have come here at all unless Tss-Var thought he had no other choice," I said, thinking out loud. "We were never friends, ClanFather, only enemies with a healthy amount of mutual respect. Surely that hasn't changed."

"It has, somewhat, since Jarn went to Vtaga," he told me. "By doing so, she averted a rekindling of hostilities between the Faction and the League, and she was able to stop the spread of the mind-plague that was destroying their population. TssVar owes you— and, by extension, our people—a debt he can never repay."

"He owes me nothing." I wasn't going to take credit for what Jarn had done on Vtaga. I caught the look on Xonal's face. "Of course, I don't ever have to *tell* him that."

He grinned. "It is good to have you back, my Clan-Daughter."

A Jorenian celebration could never be called a paltry gathering. Every member of the House came, and each one brought something to the party. They weren't stingy. I saw enough food laid out on the banquet tables to feed five or six HouseClans.

Then there were the flowers, which my adopted people loved to use as decorations. Strung in swatches of color to imitate the multicolor skies, they festooned the ceilings and draped over entries and sprang in huge bunches from every imaginable type of container. The varieties and colors made me dizzy; it was a bit like being smacked in the face by ten thousand rainbows all at once.

"Cherijo." A tall, solemn-faced warrior came and made a formal gesture of greeting before grabbing me in a gentle hug. "Welcome home."

"Salo." I remembered seeing him chasing after Marel when she came running out of the passenger terminal. "Thanks for taking care of my kid."

He drew back and smiled. "She has brought much happiness to my bondmate and ClanDaughter."

"I imagine she brought some other things, too." I glanced at the young Jorenian female standing behind him. She was nearly as tall as Salo, but I didn't recognize her. "Who's this?"

"Healer Cherijo." The girl smiled. "Do you not know me?"

I knew the voice. "Fasala?" It was Salo's daughter, only much taller than I remembered. "Suns, you're all grown-up now. Just yesterday you were . . ." But yesterday for me was five years ago for everyone else. Awkwardly I finished with, "You look wonderful, honey."

"I thank you." She had Darea's regal smile, but mischief danced in her white eyes. "ClanMother says if I grow any taller, she will have to wear a neck brace when she speaks to me."

"She is not yet majority age," another familiar female voice grumbled, "and still I must alter the hems of her garments every season." Darea Torin put an arm around Fasala's waist before she regarded me. "Welcome back to Joren, Cherijo."

"Darea, it's lovely to see you." She had been one of my best friends on the *Sunlace*, but now it was as if we were strangers all over again. "I appreciate you and Salo looking after Marel while we were . . . while I was . . . away."

"She was our joy." Darea kissed Fasala's cheek before she turned to Xonal. "ClanUncle, may I have a moment alone with the healer? I have a message to relay to her that requires some privacy."

Salo frowned until he met his bondmate's gaze, while Xonal's expression turned shrewd. "Do not keep her away too long, Darea, or my ClanSon may well call for a search of the pavilion."

Four

I followed my friend out of the hall and down a corridor to Xonal's offices, which like all the others were empty. As soon as we were inside, Darea secured the door panel and turned on the external viewer.

"Are you expecting someone to barge in?" I asked.

"Not at all," she said, while making a discreet affirmative gesture at the same time. "So many wish to speak with you, I dare not keep you long." She removed a device from her tunic and set it on a table in the center of the room before she switched it on. "Your pardon, Cherijo, but this will disrupt any recording drones in the immediate vicinity. I do not think anyone would dare plant monitors in the ClanLeader's chambers, but we cannot be too careful."

I looked around. "Why would they bother?"

"Xonea has sent some oddly worded messages since leaving oKiaf space," she admitted as she began moving around the room and checking things. "Both before and after you were returned to us. He also despised Jarn, as I am sure you have guessed by now, and kept her under constant surveillance."

I needed to give my ClanBrother another hug the next time I saw him. "Good for him."

"You do not understand the implications, Cherijo." Her voice went tight. "Xonea never accepted what happened to you on Akkabarr. Over time his obsession with bringing you back to your mind and body grew unmanageable. It drove him to behave in an unseemly manner toward Jarn. Salo and I feared his anger would unbalance him, perhaps even drive him to do the unthinkable." She made a gesture of frustration. "Now that Jarn has gone and you are returned to us . . ."

"He'll settle down and be very happy?" I suggested.

"He honors you, Cherijo—you know this—but over these last years his feelings have become darker, more violent. Now they are unnaturally fixated." She began pacing around me. "Xonal and Salo and I have discussed this at length. We are agreed that the only action that will appease him in his current state is to Choose you again."

Now I was confused. "He can't. I broke his Choice years ago." I eyed her. "Can he?"

"We cannot say. There is no precedent." When she saw my frown, she added, "No Chosen has ever embraced the stars and then come back to us. You have done so twice now."

"I can't be compared to other Jorenians," I reminded her, "not with my immune system."

"You were not born to us, Cherijo, but still you are Torin by Choice and, as such, one of us." Darea thought for a moment. "It has been said to us by some of the crew members that the bond between you and Duncan has been severed. I would know if this is true."

I didn't want to talk about this, not with Darea. She'd had a front-row seat to most of my relationship with Reever, and she knew how much I loved him, and what I'd sacrificed to be with him. But for those reasons and the friendship we'd once shared, I forced the words out.

"Duncan doesn't want me anymore. He's still in love—he still honors Jarn," I amended. Jorenians didn't have the word *love* in their language. "Under the circumstances, I can't be with him anymore. So yes, I think our bond is history."

"Duncan is not Jorenian, nor has he been adopted by the House, so the endurance of your bond is not subject to our laws," Darea said. "If you should declare yourself free of him, and make this known to the House, I think Xonea will Choose you. And if you refuse his Choice—"

I finished that thought for her. "He'll go crazy, just like Ktarka did."

She nodded.

"I can't believe this." I sat down on one of the chairs by Xonal's desk and rested my face in my hands. "So my choices are stay with Duncan, who I want to kill, or drive Xonea insane again, until he kills himself. Not a tough decision, is it?"

"Should you choose not to free yourself of your bond, I believe our ClanCousin will at last accept that he cannot have you." She stopped roaming the room and came over to me. "For all the wrong he has done, Xonea has acted only out of honor and affection for you. Xonal is certain that with time and distance his improper feelings will fade. He may perhaps find another who will fill his heart and join his path."

But until then I was stuck in a loveless relationship.

"Tell Xonal and Salo that I understand, and I'll explain things to Reever." I stood up. "Is there anything else I should know?"

"The Hsktskt have come to Joren to speak with you."

"Xonea mentioned it. Any particular reason why?"

"They brought a young male of their kind who was alterformed with alien DNA," Darea said. "They seek the means with which to reverse the process so that the male may be restored to his natural appearance."

"I seriously doubt that's possible." I hadn't read about that in Xonea's secured files, and I knew very little about alterforming, a recently developed practice of body modification through genetic grafting. "What did they try to change him into?"

"A Jorenian." Darea's mouth went tight. "I have seen vids of the male. The alterformation was quite successful."

"That's really not good." The last thing anyone in the universe needed was a Hsktskt running around disguised as a Jorenian. "Where did they get the genetic material? From a dead captive?" Jorenians did not tolerate enslavement; at the first opportunity after capture, they committed suicide.

Darea made a negative gesture. "The cells were harvested from the body of one who was sent to embrace the stars."

I had a bad feeling about this. "Tell me the rest."

She put a comforting hand on my arm first. "The DNA was taken from the remains of your former Chosen. ClanSon Kao Torin."

*   *   *

In the past I'd often been tempted to violate my physician's oath and do a little harm. I might not have been completely human, but certainly I had all the ugly, petty emotions of one. After discovering from Darea that SrrokVar had used my first love's DNA to alterform a rogue minion, I felt like wiping out a few species. Starting with the Hsktskt.

At least Darea understood that I was in no shape to return to the festivities, and promised to make a convincing excuse for me. I left Xonal's offices and slipped down a side corridor to a communications room, where I notified HouseClan Adan of my presence on planet and requested a meeting be arranged with the Hsktskt delegation for the next day.

"Healer, we understood you were to stay at House-Clan Torin's pavilion for a welcoming celebration," the Adan communications officer said. "The Faction representatives are quite willing to wait to meet with you at a more convenient time."

"Well, it's convenient now." The sooner I got this over with, the better. "I'll be arriving in the morning. Would you please notify the ClanLeader and request a security detachment for me?"

"I will see to it at once, Healer." The young, handsome blue face on the viddisplay darkened, and his tone deepened. "Do you have knowledge of some threat made against you by these offworlders, Lady?"

According to Xonea's files I was still considered ClanJoren, which made me the honorary kin of every House on Joren. If I so much as hinted at a threat, the Adan would happily declare ClanKill on the Hsktskt and eviscerate the entire delegation on the spot. Even now I could see the dark blue tips of the young com officer's claws emerging.

Maybe I don't have to violate my oath personally.

The dark twinge of glee that accompanied my ugly thought made my stomach roll. When had I become so conniving and bloodthirsty? Had she done this to me?

"No," I said firmly. "I misspoke. No threat has been made against me." I had to come up with some excuse. "I've been away for a long time, ClanSon Adan. I still have to adjust to current political situations, which are very different now."

"We are eager to assist you in any manner during this difficult time, Lady. Should you have any need while you are among our House, know that my name is Apalo Adan."

"I thank you, Apalo. Until tomorrow, then." I ended the signal, sat back in the console chair, and pressed my palms against my eyes. Behind me the door panel chimed. "Go away."

The panels opened and closed. "Darea Torin told us that you were not feeling well."

I swiveled around to face Shon Valtas. He was wearing a modified ceremonial robe of dark green and brown, and had braided several interesting-looking gold ornaments into his mane. He also wore a belt made of black daggers sheathed in some kind of dark blue leather and carried a short spear, the shaft of which had been decorated with fringes and tiny wood carvings. "Don't you look ready to hunt down and kill something."

He grimaced down at his garments. "These are oKiaf ceremonial garments. The Senior Healer insisted I dress for the occasion. He also sent me to check your condition."

"Darea lied for me. I'm fine." I got to my feet. "Excuse me. I need to arrange transportation to the capital for tomorrow morning."

"I will accompany you."

I gave him a suspicious look. "Are you still in love with her?"

The fur around his neck shifted as he realized what I meant. "My feelings for Jarn were inappropriate. After she made her commitment to Reever known to me, I struggled for some time—"

I whipped up a hand. "As much as I'd love to hear how you survived rejection, a simple yes or no will do."

"No."

"Great." I eyed his weapons. "Disarm, get packed, and be ready to leave at dawn." Now I had to go and lie to the Torins, requisition a glidecar, and have a conversation I didn't want to have with the man who no longer loved me. I'd probably lie to him, too.

Xonea met me halfway in the corridor outside the great hall. "Darea said you were not feeling well."

All this hovering was really beginning to get on my nerves.

"Bad headache. It's starting to let up." I touched my temple and tried to look pitiful. "I'll have to skip most of the party, though. I have to take a trip to the capital in the morning to meet with the lizards. I'm on my way to tell Xonal now." I walked past him.

Xonea caught up with me. "I will accompany you."

"That's very sweet of you, Captain, but I know how busy you are, and I've already arranged an escort." I kept my tone bland. "Healer Valtas is going with me."

He didn't like that. "Why take you the oKiaf?"

"Well, Shon was alterformed before being infected by the protocrystal and reverting to his original form," I said, making a casual gesture. "Since the Hsktskt are interested in reverse-engineering the alterform process, it seems like a good idea to have him come along."

Xonea tugged me to a stop. "I do not like you meeting with the beasts."

"I'm told that we're all good friends now." Although his grip was a degree too tight for comfort, I tried to look puzzled instead of pained. "What's not to like?"

"You have been through an arduous ordeal." The lines around his mouth and nose deepened. "You should remain with kin so that we might care for you."

Meaning I should stay behind so he could keep an eye on what was happening between me and Reever, and jump at any chance to Choose me. I still couldn't believe the Torins had allowed this to go on for as long as they had. Why hadn't Xonal talked to his ClanSon about his unnatural fixation?

"Shon Valtas is a qualified physician, and he's well acquainted with my condition," I reminded him. "Should anything unexpected happen, I'm sure he can cope. You can stay here and do whatever it is you need to do while you're on planet."

I didn't sound very convincing, and Xonea wasn't stupid. "What has Darea said to you?"

"The usual. 'Hello. How are you? We missed you. We honor you. . . .'" I shrugged. "You're not going to make me try to copy all the hand gestures, are you?"

Reever came into the corridor, and didn't even glance at Xonea. "Cherijo, the Torin are waiting for you to address the assembly."

"Speech time. Wonderful." I rolled my eyes. "See you later, Xonea. Duncan." I dodged between the two men and hurried into the hall.

This time Reever caught up with me and took my arm as I made my way through the assembly toward the flowery platform at the head of the hall. "Darea has apprised you of Xonea's emotional condition."

"She did." I felt the brush of his thoughts against my mind and glanced down at his hand. "Just so you know, if you try to link with me, ever, I will kick you in the groin."

"Have you forgotten that I can control your body?" he asked, as politely as if he were asking about the weather.

"You have to sleep sometime, Duncan. I can wait and cripple you after I come out of it." I stomped up the steps of the platform and walked to the center. I couldn't stop Reever from accompanying me, and it was probably best that we show a united front, but I didn't have to stay up there all night.

The crowd immediately fell silent, which made my voice ring out through the hall. "I've never been very good at making speeches," I warned them, "so this will be brief." I sounded too loud, too harsh, and took a moment to clear my throat. "I've been away for a long time, and I'm still trying to catch up on what's happened since I last left Joren. I want you to know how much it means to me, to be able to come home, here, to the Torin. I never had a family of my own on Terra, and I never expected to find a new one. When I lost Kao"—I tried to smile—"I felt as if my one hope of happiness had died. Here, tonight. . . ."

I knew I had to say more than that, but my throat didn't want to cooperate.

"Gratitude and honor overcome my bondmate," Reever said. "HouseClan Torin rescued Cherijo, protected her, and brought her into their hearts. You have done more for me and my bondmate than simply providing a new homeworld for us and our ClanDaughter. You have taught us what it means to be part of something bigger and better than ourselves."

It wasn't only self-pity that made tears stream down my cheeks. In that moment I could have killed him. "Duncan is right," I said, the words rasping past the constriction in my throat. "You have done so much for us, for me. You saved me from loneliness and despair by accepting me as your kin, and for that, I will honor HouseClan Torin forever."

The applause nearly deafened me as Reever guided me down from the platform. I was passed around from one Torin to the next as my family embraced me and murmured words of encouragement. Somewhere between the fiftieth and sixtieth hug Reever took charge, gently extricating me and making excuses as he guided me out of the hall. In our wake I heard Xonal telling Xonea to let us go.

I managed to compose myself by the time we reached the guest quarters the Torin had allocated to us. "Is Marel here?"

"She is staying with Fasala in her family's rooms tonight," he said. "I thought we should have some time alone."

"What for? We've already adequately dissected

the situation. It's a dead issue." I reached for the door panel controls. "I need to rest. Go away."

He put an arm across the opening panels. "How will you convince Xonea that our bond remains strong if we occupy separate quarters?"

I didn't have an answer for that, so I ducked under his arm and went inside. The rooms were decorated in Torin colors but with Terran-sized furnishings, and the prep unit had been programmed with all my old favorites. I dialed up a server of chamomile, added a touch of spice, and carried it to the nearest single chair. Reever made his own cup of something vile-smelling and came to stand beside me.

"Don't look so smug," I advised him sourly. "We'll have to keep up appearances until Xonea stops obsessing over me, but as soon as he settles down, we'll be going our separate ways."

"I do not want a separation."

"What a shame, then, because you don't actually get a vote." I sipped my tea, but the usual relaxing effect it had on me wasn't happening. "You need to spend some time with Marel," I added when he opened his mouth to respond. "It's clear that she seriously bonded with your alien girlfriend while I was gone. Since I'm back in the same body, I really can't help her adjust to the fact that Jarn is dead. While you're at it, you might remind our kid that *I'm* her real mother."

"I overheard what she said to you at Main Transport." He touched my hair. "I regret that her affection for Jarn has hurt you."

I got up and faced him. "Don't pretend you feel anything for me, Reever. You're no good at it. Just shut up and play your part. And while you're doing that, keep your damn hands off me."

"You still love me." He sounded slightly amazed.

My rage finally boiled over, and I threw the lukewarm remains of my tea in his face. "I never stopped, you bastard."

I went into the sleeping chamber and secured the door before I stripped out of my tunic and trousers. Inside the tunic were odd loops I hadn't noticed before, and I realized it had been altered to accommodate and conceal a blade harness. I tore the tunic apart before I flung the ragged pieces across the room.

Then I collapsed on the sleeping platform, buried my face in a pillow, and wept myself into unconsciousness.

I slept like the dead thing I felt I was inside, and woke an hour before dawn to cleanse and dress. Fortunately none of Jarn's clothes had been brought over from the *Sunlace*, and what I found in the storage container looked newly made from an array of gorgeous Jorenian fabrics, cut down and tailored specifically for an adult female of small stature.

"Thank you, Xonal," I murmured as I sorted through them and selected an outfit made of dark amethyst and deep green.

After last night's ugly scene I dreaded another confrontation with Reever, but when I came out of the bedroom, he was gone. The only sign he'd stayed was a pillow and a neatly folded coverlet left on one of the lounges. *Good riddance,* I tried to tell myself, but it didn't do anything to loosen the knot in my chest. All I could do was hope that Xonea got over his stupid crush soon and I could bury what was left of my marriage before it started to rot.

Despite my complete lack of appetite, I made myself eat a light breakfast. The delicious morning bread, one of my favorite native foods, tasted like chalk, and the more I tried to eat, the more it choked me. If this kept up, I'd have to start infusing myself with calorie supplements.

Shon arrived just as I finished tidying up. He'd dressed in plain, light-colored garments that offset his dark pelt and made him seem a little less menacing. He didn't say much, although he noticed the bedding Reever had used and gave me a sharp look.

"Don't ask," I advised him.

I collected my medical case and accompanied him to the glidecar waiting at the front of the pavilion. He manned the controls, which was fine with me, and from there we drove across the province onto the throughway used by the HouseClans to travel from one territory to another.

I tried to take an interest in the scenery, but the silvery yiborra grass fields all looked dull and gray to my jaundiced eye. I caught myself counting t'lerue as we passed the Torin pasturelands, and closed my eyes. I needed to pull out of this depression before we reached the capital, or I'd never be able to face what was waiting there for me.

"They still speak of you on Kevarzangia Two," Shon said, his voice startling me. "You are greatly honored for what you did to save the colony."

The faces of all the people who had died during the Core plague flashed through my mind, merging into one much-beloved face: Kao Torin's. "I didn't save all of them."

"Jadaira—a female 'Zangian pilot who befriended me—nearly died of the effects of the plague on her dam. She was pregnant with her when the infection spread to the native inhabitants." He went on to describe the damage the Core had inadvertently done to Dair in utero, and the drastic measures taken to alterform and save her after her mother died. "You would like her, I think. She is as stubborn and independent as you."

"Must be the Terran parts they stuck in her. We're not known to be sweet and submissive." He'd gotten my interest, though. "How does an aquatic who can't be out of water for more than a few hours become a pilot?"

Shon began to explain the 'Zangians' evolutionary problems—they were making a slow and difficult transition from an aquatic to a land-dwelling species—and how the young 'Zangians had been alterformed by the League in order to defend 'Zangian space and fly patrol missions around their homeworld. I was happy to hear that the former military starjocs were currently using their expertise to help rescue civilian ships in trouble, although from some of Shon's stories it sounded at times as if it was as risky and dangerous as fighting the Hsktskt had been.

After a brief lull in conversation, Shon glanced at me. "Would you mind if I ask you a personal question?"

That instantly put me on my guard. "How personal?"

"It is related to your professional philosophies." When I rolled my hand, inviting him to go on, he added, "After all you have experienced and suffered since leaving Terra, why do you continue to help others?"

"Why wouldn't I?" I wished he would go back to being the strong and silent type. "I'm a doctor. It's my job."

"During your medical career, you have accomplished extraordinary things, and yet you have never personally profited from it." He decreased speed as we reached the exit from the throughway for the capital. "From what I have observed, few seem to appreciate what you have done."

"Obviously you're not counting the welcome-home party the Torins threw for me last night," I snapped. "Or the fact that they rescued me from being taken back to Terra and treated like a lab rat there. Hell, I was even made one of their rulers for a while."

"What if their true motive was not to express appreciation at all?" he asked. "What if the Jorenians wanted to control and possess you? What better way to accomplish that than to maneuver you into devoting yourself to their species through such a blanket cultural inclusion as formal adoption?"

No one had ever suggested such a thing, not even Reever, who wasn't especially fond of the Jorenians.

"I don't like the way you think," I told him. "You came to Joren not just to practice medicine but to hide out from the League. You used them for your own purposes, Shon, and now you've got the nerve to suggest that they're using me?"

"It is only a thought."

I *hmph*ed. "On Terra we call that living in a plas domicile and throwing rocks."

"You have a point," he conceded. "But consider this: The Jorenians have never before offered to adopt me. Yet as soon as we arrived back from the sojourn

to oKia, I received a formal offer from ClanLeader
Xonal to join his House."

My temper simmered a little higher. "Maybe he
was being nice."

"The crew almost certainly reported to him the
facts about my abilities and immortality, which were
revealed during the expedition," Shon said. "Having
two immortal kin instead of one to serve his people
would greatly elevate the Torins' status among the
other HouseClans."

"You know, almost everything in my life has happened because of someone else's selfish desires, private agendas, or dastardly plans," I told him. "The
only people who have ever treated me like a person
have been the Jorenians. Call me an idiot, but I'd like
to keep on believing they actually care what happens
to me."

"I cannot blame you for that," he said. "Only keep
an open mind, Healer. There is more at work here
than the kindness of strangers."

Mercifully he shut up after that, leaving me to
wonder if he was simply being paranoid, or I didn't
want to accept another painful truth.

All the HouseClans on Joren lived together with
their kin in huge, communal pavilions that were stra-
tegically located in the center of their territories.
These communities had evolved from a massive cultural shift in the past, when the first Jorenian tribes
had abandoned their nomadic existence as hunter-
gatherers and instead had settled down and laid claim
to the most fertile and favorable areas on the planet.

The Adan had a slightly different situation, in that
they were both a HouseClan and the hosts of Joren's

ruling government, which comprised members from every HouseClan. To provide for the various council members and representatives as well as the visiting merchants and officials from other regions, they had built around their pavilion various accommodations, business centers, and other communities. Over the years these satellite structures had expanded out from the original pavilion in a series of rings—hundreds of them.

I had seen a few vids and images of the capital, but until now I'd never realized the size of the developments surrounding the Adan pavilion. The gratis guest quarters and offices had grown into a small city.

"We're supposed to meet ClanLeader Adan and his men at the Center for Planetary Peace," I said to Shon. "How are we going to find it?"

"I signaled the HouseClan last night to obtain directions." He tapped the vehicle's console display, and a detailed glidemap appeared. "The meeting place is here, at the north curve of HaloFourteen."

Suddenly I wanted him to reverse the glidecar and take me back to my HouseClan. "I don't suppose you could take a wrong turn or something."

"If that is what you wish." He slowed the vehicle and pulled off the glidepath into a curving park planted with unfamiliar, brilliant orange and white flowers. He coasted to a stop beside a crescent-shaped reflecting pool and shut down the engine. "You do not have to meet with the Hsktskt, Healer. You do not have to do anything."

I didn't want to talk about it, so I got out of the glidecar and walked across the short blue green moss that served as decorative grass on Joren to stand at the edge of the pool. Thin flashes of light sparkled on the surface, and I crouched down to look at the small aquatics stocking the pool. I couldn't remember the Jorenian name for them, or if they were native to the Adan territory, or why I'd agreed to come here when the safest, sanest thing would have been to conduct this meeting over a console.

Shon sat down beside me. "Cela'dnor."

"What?"

"The name of the creatures in the water." He looked more comfortable on the ground than he had behind the controls of the vehicle. "It is Cela'dnor."

I felt suspicious. "Can you read my mind?"

"I have a sense of you, but it is not telepathic in nature." He leaned back on his elbows. "When you meet with the Hsktskt delegation, I will remain at your side. I will not leave you alone with them."

"I'm not afraid of the lizards." The past I thought was long dead and gone, however, was terrifying me. "Why are you being so nice to me? What do you want? Another shot at romance and true love? I'm not Jarn, and I'm not interested."

"My younger brother was murdered by the League," he said instead of answering my questions.

"So were a bunch of my friends." I sighed. "What happened?"

"They drowned him. Like many of my people, he feared water. The only time we go into it is when we are dead. They knew this." He stared at the pool. "They wanted him to die in terror. They wanted me to know that he did."

I got to my feet. "I'm sorry, I shouldn't have reminded you of . . . I'm sorry, Shon."

He looked up at me. "I do not think of you as I did Jarn, Cherijo. When I look at you, I think of my little brother. So know that for as long as I breathe, you will never again go into the water alone."

I didn't understand, and at the same time I did. "And what if I jump in and start to drown?"

He stood up. "Then I will breathe for both of us until I can bring you back to the shore."

I glanced at the water, and then walked slowly back to the glidecar with my oKiaf brother.

Five

I expected to see a lot of Jorenians inside the stately
building that served as the Center for Planetary Peace,
but when Shon and I entered the reception area, we
were greeted by only one young male wearing a fitted gray robe over a white tunic and black trousers.
His attire seemed so unusual for a Jorenian—all the
HouseClans had vivid, distinct colors that they used
in everything from decor to garments—that I couldn't
help staring a little.

"I am Apalo Adan, Healer Torin." He made a
modified version of the elaborate formal gesture of
greeting between members of different Houses. "On
behalf of the Adan, I welcome you to the capital."

"I'm happy to be here." I covered the lie with a
smile as I introduced Shon. "Is everyone here, or are
we early?"

"The Hsktskt delegation and our negotiators are
presently in conference on the summit level." He
gestured toward a lift. "Would you care to rest after
your journey? We have arranged rooms for you and
Healer Valtas at the pavilion."

I almost leapt at the chance to put off seeing the

Hsktskt dressed in my dead lover's DNA, which made me all the more determined to get it over with. "No, I think I've kept them waiting long enough."

Apalo's eyes gleamed with discreet approval. "Then if you please will accompany me?"

The lift took us to the top floor of the building—where else would they have put a summit level?—and opened to a gallery of Jorenian sculptures of various historic figures, all carved from gleaming sapphire-colored stone in life-sized proportions. Most were in benign poses, but here and there were famous warriors armed to the teeth, claws extended, and looking as if ready to disembowel someone.

"Impressive," Shon murmured, pausing to study a statue of Tarek Varena, sculpted in an attack stance over a fallen enemy.

"Sure," I muttered back. "If you like serial killers."

Shon eyed me. "Tarek Varena effectively put an end to the ancient territorial wars between the House-Clans."

"Which he did by one hundred straight days of single-handed combat in the quad, during which he slaughtered the best warriors from every House on Joren," I reminded him. "I think the final count was somewhere around six hundred, seven hundred men?"

"I approve only of his results, Healer," the oKiaf said. "Not his methods."

"Good," I replied. "Now stop admiring his statue so we can get on with this."

Beyond the gallery was a large, formal area with a single long, wide table interspersed with dimensional image projectors set into its surface. At that moment several holoimages of Jorenian anatomy were being projected. These were being studied and discussed by the twenty or so Jorenian physicians present and several Hsktskt in Faction uniforms. Everyone stopped talking as soon as we stepped into view, and the oldest of the physicians politely rose to her feet.

"Healer Torin, welcome." She came around the table to finish the greeting and clasp my hands in Terran fashion. "I am Healer Apalea. I trust my ClanSon has inquired after your needs?"

I smiled at Apalo. "He's been terrific." I didn't want to look at the Hsktskt, but one tall female had gotten up from the table and was heading toward us. In a lower voice, I asked, "How are things going with them?"

"The path has not been the smoothest," Apalea admitted. "The Faction representatives have not yet accustomed themselves to speaking to humanoids as equals."

For centuries the Hsktskt had regarded warm-blooded species as inferior and fit only for enslavement or execution. Even with all that Jarn had done to save their species, I had doubted they would completely abandon their prejudices.

Apalea turned to the Hsktskt female as she joined us. "Healer ChoVa, I believe you know Healer Torin."

"As her designate, very well." ChoVa bowed toward me while letting her head fall back, which was a public declaration of regard and respect.

It took me a moment to process what she'd said. "My God. You're little ChrreechoVa." I noticed the medical emblem on her tunic. "I'll be damned. You kept your promise to become a physician."

"I always keep my word, Namesake." She straightened and inspected my face. "We were told of your return, but I was not certain I believed it to be true until now." The forked end of her black tongue tasted my air. "You are as I remember you on Catopsa. Not at all like the other who wore your hide."

"I will take that as a compliment, thank you." I introduced Shon, who was polite but distant. "Where is this alterformed male you want to tinker with?"

"I am here."

He came to stand beside ChoVa, and when I looked into his face, I felt as if I'd been punched in the belly. Seven feet tall, matte black hair, smooth blue skin. Four parallel scars that scored one of his lean cheeks, and a purple streak blazed in his black hair, but other than that, he was the image of Kao Torin, right down to the gleam of humor in his white-within-white eyes.

"Well, hello." Emotion welled up inside me as I took him in. "You have a nice face."

"It is too blue. I feel exposed without my scales. But these work well enough." He smiled, and showed Kao's perfect white teeth, filed down to sharp points.

The unsightly alteration to his dentition instantly shattered the illusion, which allowed me to get hold of myself and offer my hand. "You're called PyrsVar, is that right?"

"Yes." He handled the Terran gesture of greeting without a hitch, and didn't crush my fingers in his. I noted that his skin was several degrees cooler than a Jorenian's should have been. "And you are Cherijo."

"It is not proper to use family names among the warm-bloods until you are invited to do so," ChoVa chided him. To me she said, "He is yet learning how to conduct himself around your kind."

"Oh, yes." PyrsVar rotated his eyes in a distinctly un-Jorenian fashion. "One must not utter insults, or make unguarded gestures. One must not offer an opinion on warm-blooded matters. Now one must not use the wrong name, however many there are." He grinned again. "One has not yet mastered the ridiculousness of diplomacy and protocol."

"One could have remained behind on the ship," ChoVa said sharply, "performing maintenance on the lavatory and atmospheric-control units."

"When one is the primary reason for the sojourn?" PyrsVar made a scoffing sound. "I think not."

Although they sounded like bickering adolescents, and behaved as if they disliked each other intensely, I had the feeling there was more to these two than what I was seeing. Even sniping at each other, they seemed comfortable, like old friends.

"From what the Torin told me, the Hsktskt are interested in reversing the bioengineering performed on PyrsVar." When ChoVa nodded, I glanced at the console. "Would you mind giving us a quick overview of what you've discussed so far?"

That sent everyone back to the console table, and Apalea seated Shon and me in the center before running through a series of holoimages that had been provided by the delegation. I had to force myself not to stare at the Hsktskt who had been so drastically alterformed. He might have changed his teeth and picked up some scars, but there was still far too much of my lost love in the set of his expressions, and the elegant, purposeful way he moved.

He's not Kao. He's a lizard wearing his stolen cloned body.

"Four years ago unknown methods were used to

transform PyrsVar's body from that of a healthy adult
Hsktskt male to a duplicate of Kao Torin," Apalea
told me. "After capturing the private facility where
these procedures were carried out, the Hanar's forces
were able to recover some information from the medical database, but much of it was destroyed during the
final battle." She brought up a holoimage of a young
Hsktskt adult male.

"That is as I was born," PyrsVar said, inclining his
head toward the projection. "Hsktskt. Pure of blood.
Clear of thought."

"Simple of mind," I heard ChoVa mutter.

"What sort of information did they recover?" I
asked Apalea.

"Not a great deal, Healer. Some charted entries
and assessment scans on the progression of the alterformation." She pulled up a second image of PyrsVar
in Hsktskt form, only now with new, blue skin that
was visibly shedding scales. A third showed the begin-
nings of soft-tissue and musculature changes to his
head, torso, and limbs. "There were no details regard-
ing the process used to transform PyrsVar. The healer
who experimented on him may have refrained from
keeping notes or destroyed them once the process
was completed in order to safeguard his methods."

"He wasn't a healer," I said, thinking of SrrokVar
and the monster he had been. I looked at ChoVa. "I
assume you've run some comprehensive scans to determine what percentage of his anatomy is currently
affected."

She nodded. "The outward appearance is that of
a Jorenian, but this is deceptive. His internal systems
were actually augmented rather than altered, so he
possesses both Jorenian and Hsktskt organs. He has

also retained certain congenital aspects of bone structure and musculature."

From what I knew of the two species, that was on the order of a miracle. "He shouldn't have been able to merge the two physiologies. Hsktskt and Jorenians can't produce children." I glanced at Apalea. "Can they?"

"There is no record of a Jorenian/Hsktskt hybrid," she said, shifting in her seat. "However, we know from the members of HouseClan Kalea that certain other reptilian species like the Tingalean and the Korpa are capable of siring children with our females."

"The Korpa are completely different from the Hsktskt, but the Tingaleans . . ." I paused to consider and compare the anatomical details. "There is a remote possibility, then."

"PyrsVar proves that it can be done, Healer." ChoVa gestured to the living, breathing paradox in the room. "Genetic scans indicate that SrrokVar did not recombine the DNA from each species, but forced them onto the body, which he used as both a scaffold and an incubator. Based on the internal scarring, I believe that he first grew the Jorenian organs inside PyrsVar's body, and once they were fully developed, he surgically integrated them."

If he'd done that, he would have had to also force the body itself to accept . . . "Oh, God." My eyes widened as the implications sank in. "ChoVa, please tell me that you continued administering the antirejection drugs."

"As soon as we realized that his body was beginning to attack itself, I began a new regime of immunosuppressant." She glanced at PyrsVar. "At present his systems are stable."

There was more to it than that, and I sensed none of it was good, but I guessed she didn't want to give me the bad news in front of him or the other delegates. Now I had to prod another sensitive area. "All right. What I need to know now is, why do the Hsktskt want to reverse-engineer the alterformation process? Or is it just this male?"

All the lizards looked at one another, as if waiting for someone else to spill the beans. ChoVa fiddled with the console. Apalea's expression became strained.

"It is only me they wish to change," PyrsVar said. "The Hanar does not wish me to breed as I am now. Nor do the warm-bloods. They will not say this to you for fear of offending each other and breaking the peace between our people."

"Is he right?" I asked ChoVa and Apalea. Both females exchanged a long glance before the Jorenian said, "It would be best for both species if a third, hybrid species does not come into being."

"You don't have to go to all this trouble," I said. "Sterilization will keep him from breeding."

"Yes." PyrsVar folded his arms. "But that is the thing that *I* will not allow them to do to me."

Procreation was as important to the Hsktskt as it was to the Jorenians, but so were their cultural boundaries, so his attitude made no sense. "You'd rather risk your life?"

"Your brain problem prevents you from remembering what happened between us on Vtaga. I wish very much to have young." He showed me again how he had ruined Kao's teeth. "Had you not escaped me on Vtaga, I would have taken you as my woman and bred you."

Shon went rigid beside me. Apalea covered her eyes with her hand. ChoVa looked ready to save me a lot of trouble by killing the patient with her bare hands.

I did the sensible thing and laughed. "Given my unique physiology, Hsktskt, I think you would have found that a little more difficult than you imagine."

He shrugged. "Then I would have found another female and kept you for my pleasure."

Every female in the room looked appalled, but I had to chuckle again. "Thank you. I think. Is it absolutely necessary for us to go to all this trouble simply so that you can be a daddy?"

"Every being has the right to breed and secure the future," he told me. "Now that my line has been restored to me by the Hanar, I wish to be as any other male, and have the life that SrrokVar stole from me." He looked at his blue hands and their twelve fingers. "I cannot do that in this hide and with these parts."

He sounded determined . . . and painfully young. "Have your people told you exactly how dangerous this kind of experiment is? It's unprecedented, so we'll have no set procedure to follow. It will definitely not be painless. We'll do the best we can, but it's almost certain that we will make some mistakes. In the end, this could cost you your life."

"I survived this." He made a fist and thumped it against the vault of his chest. "A life without a mate or young is pointless. I will have what was—I will be as I was—or die trying."

In that moment I should have flatly refused. Undoing the genetic stew of his body promised to be a nightmare, and the odds were against his survival.

An uncomfortable life was better than no life at all. He could find a tolerant mate; they could adopt young.

But I also knew how strong the desire to have a child was. After he had Chosen me, Kao and I had shared our dreams of someday having a family together. Later, after I discovered that my hypervigilant immune system would spontaneously abort any pregnancy, I'd taken extreme measures to save the fetus that Reever and I had conceived together.

"Be sure this is what you want," I told PyrsVar. "I can almost guarantee you that any separation we attempt will not be reversible."

"I will endure what I must. I am Hsktskt." He swept his arm in a dismissive gesture.

"You're a hybrid," I corrected, "and not a very well-built one at that." I turned my attention back to the holoimage of his internal organs, and noticed his Jorenian spleen was taking up more space than it should. "What caused the enlargement here?"

"An immune system response to the presence of his Jorenian augmentations," ChoVa said. "Reinstituting regular doses of antirejection drugs has stabilized it."

I punched up specific scans of the spleen and studied the data, which knotted my stomach. Not taking the meds, even for the short time that his regime had been interrupted, had resulted in a significant amount of damage. It couldn't be reversed and made him more vulnerable to infection. "What other organs and vessels were compromised?"

"Infection has scarred his lungs and cardiac organs." She magnified the affected areas to show me the damage. "He has also suffered several seizures, both from exposure to the plague of memory and from immune-response enzymatic spikes."

"I'll need to see all the medical records on him, complete or not, and a full list of the drugs you've administered before we decide what direction to take." I thought for a moment. "We should draw his blood and see if we can synthesize more. I want enough for at least three complete transfusions."

"Surgery is not practical," ChoVa said. "His body is too dependent on the augmentations."

"No, we can't cut them out of him," I agreed. "However, that's not the only option. Have you run a complete microcellular series?"

"Yes, but the results indicate the alterformation was not entirely induced by standard viral methods." She sounded frustrated now. "We cannot discern what SrrokVar did to accomplish the genomeld."

"We will." That monster wasn't getting the better of me again, not from the grave.

"I do not understand what any of this means," PyrsVar complained.

"It means you must be quiet and do as you are told," ChoVa snapped. "Or we will make errors in your treatment, and you will die."

"All things die." He folded his arms. "Are you so easily distracted?"

"I'll explain this to you later," I promised him before ChoVa could reply. "Right now you do need to let us work." I stood. "Healer Apalea, I'd like to admit PyrsVar to your HouseClan medical facility for a preliminary workup. We'll also need access to a genetics lab and some staff to assist. Would the Adan be willing to accommodate all that?"

She made a reassuring gesture. "The Ruling Council has indicated that you are to have whatever you deem necessary. I will personally supervise the resource management and act as official liaison."

"The Hanar will wish to be consulted about this," one of the delegates predicted.

"I'll deal with TssVar personally," I told him, enjoying the way his eyes bulged. I turned back to Apalea. "I'd like to work with a team of doctors and nurses who have experience in treating genetically compromised patients. ChoVa, I hope you're not planning to return to Vtaga anytime soon, because I need your knowledge and experience on this case."

She inclined her head. "I will be happy to stay and provide whatever assistance you require, Namesake."

"She would not go even if you asked her to," PyrsVar said. "She enjoys watching me suffer."

"Not as often as I wish," ChoVa muttered.

The Hsktskt rarely joked about anything, but I didn't think they were serious. In fact I was picking up something else from both of them, in the way they looked at each other and the distinct lack of viciousness behind their cold words. It wasn't friendship; I could see that they weren't good buddies. Then I understood. Somehow the daughter of the supreme ruler over the Hsktskt Faction and a renegade male trapped in the body of a warm-blooded offworlder had developed feelings for each other.

These two were in love.

I turned to Apalea. "Before we do anything, I need to contact the Hanar on Vtaga."

An hour later I sat down in front of an interplanetary-communications array. I didn't recognize half the console controls or the design of the unit. "This looks like something I could seriously damage."

"Establishing interplanetary relay channels requires rather more than a standard com unit provides," Apalo told me as he bent over to adjust something. When I reached for one of the keypads, he caught my hand. "I have preset all the controls, Healer. It is best that you not touch the console while you are signaling Vtaga—unless you wish to damage it."

"Sorry." I put my hand in my lap.

Apalo smiled a little as he indicated the display. "Speak clearly and directly to the monitor, like so." He ducked his head and pressed a key. "Centuron KssetaVa, Healer Torin is ready to commence her relay."

"Acknowledged," a Hsktskt voice growled over the audio. "Now transferring relay over to the secured channel."

"When you are ready to speak, press this switch." After showing me which one, Apalo straightened. "And should you need assistance, Healer, I will be waiting outside in the corridor."

I glanced at the switch as my stomach clenched. "Thanks for your help."

The communications officer withdrew, which left me alone with the beast. I pressed the switch and watched the face of my old enemy coalesce on the screen.

Seeing him made me idly wonder just how many strange and exotic patients I had treated in the years since I'd left Terra. TssVar—or, more precisely, his mate and their young—had been among my first.

My charge nurse's four eyes rolled wildly toward me, and I saw why she had choked out her report—the business end of a pulse rifle was pressed tightly against her larynx. Terror had mottled her smooth vermilion hide with dark splotches.

On the other end of the weapon was a monster. A big, ugly green monster.

It was a sextipedal, reptilian being with a number of minor contusions on its head and upper limbs. Close to ten feet tall and weighing over four hundred kilos, it towered over T'Nliqinara. An unfamiliar metallic uniform covered a brutal frame thick with broad ropes of muscle. Whatever it was, it meant business.

As TssVar did now, judging by the look in his glaring yellow eyes. The former OverLord spoke in his native language, a series of clicks, grunts, and hisses that the ship's translator muted as it translated it into Terran for me.

Reptilians generally didn't age in the same way humanoid species did, and the years had left little mark on the former OverLord's brutal features. The only way I knew he was five years older was the subtle darkening of his scale patterns.

"SsurreVa."

"TssVar." I didn't know how a measly warm-blood was supposed to address the supreme ruler of the Hsktskt Faction, so I didn't even try. "How have you been?"

"I have enjoyed better decades." He took a moment to study me. "So, it seems, have you."

He looked tired, I thought, feeling a little sorry for him. The former OverLord had never been especially fond of politics, and now he was permanently swamped in them.

"It's not been all bad," I lied. "I didn't have a plague

make me into a supreme ruler overnight. I just took a nap for five years."

"It was never my wish to rule," he informed me. "The surviving elected me to the throne."

"Being possessed by an alien persona wasn't on my to-do list, either." I had learned to read some Hsktskt body language when TssVar had enslaved me, and the set of his facial muscles was saying he was unhappy as well as tired. "Are you planning to stay with it, or give it up?"

One of his huge yellow eyes rolled upward while the other glared at me. "One does not 'give up' supreme rule, SsurreVa."

I considered that. "Who would yell at you if you did?"

TssVar's species couldn't smile, but he flashed me a couple rows of teeth in an approximation of the expression. "Now I remember why I have missed you."

"Same here." He seemed surprised by that, and I added, "It may shock you, especially after all we've been through, but I do consider you one of my oldest friends."

"Since I regard you as the same," he said, "it does not."

We sat together in a comfortable silence until some underlings appeared behind him, evidently to check on him. As I watched them grovel, I wondered how I was going to tell him that his daughter had fallen in love with a rogue hybrid. Maybe he already knew. Maybe he didn't, and PyrsVar would have his Jorenian organs removed in a less civilized fashion.

TssVar dismissed the talon kissers before he spoke to me again. "It would seem my courtiers grow impatient. You have examined the crossbreed?"

"I've looked at him in a meeting room," I corrected. "I'll do an examination once he's in the hospital. Fortunately HouseClan Adan has agreed to let me use theirs."

"The Jorenians have been very accommodating, but they like this situation no better than I." He propped his taloned hands against the edge of his console. "Do you believe that the rogue can be restored to what he was?"

There was some hope in his voice. *So he doesn't want him dead—at least, not yet.* "I think I'm going to have to run a lot of tests on him before I answer that question."

He blew some air through his nostrils. "One can never obtain a reasonable response from you healers."

"Having one in the family now, you should know." I felt as if I were walking through a field of invisible proximity-triggered explosives. "Since your daughter has been the lead physician on this case, I've asked her to stay and work with me. Is that going to create a problem?"

He eyed me. "She has a security detachment. I trained them myself."

"That's not what I mean."

"I know what you say and do not say." He seemed to be mulling it over. "I suppose I cannot persuade you to end this rogue's life during the course of his treatment."

"No more than the colonists on K-2 could talk me into killing you and your mate before I delivered your kids," I agreed. "Nor would I take kindly to you ordering one of your entourage to arrange a helpful accident or discreet assassination for my patient."

"You seem to forget, your patient wears the hide of your dead mate," he grated.

"Not by his choice," I reminded him, "or mine. Look, I know PyrsVar is not a sterling example of your species. Every time he opens his mouth, *I* want to thump him. But he's the victim here, TssVar. The way SrrokVar used him—the sick things he did to him—were beyond reprehensible."

The Hanar didn't say anything.

I decided to push a little more. "All he wants is what was taken from him: a normal life. He's willing to die for that. I think he deserves a second chance."

"I am not concerned with him." He swept his hand to one side. "It is ChoVa. If anything untoward happened to the crossbreed, she would never forgive me."

"Neither would I," I mentioned.

"Someday, when your child attains mating age," he growled, "I will have this conversation with you again."

After I promised to send him regular updates on our progress and accepted his not so fond farewell, I terminated the relay. I had promised after signaling TssVar to meet everyone at the medical facility, but I needed a break from all the unrequited Hsktskt hormones and some time to think.

Apalo escorted me to the guest quarters the Adan had arranged for me at the pavilion, and after signaling Apalea and letting her know I would be another hour or so, I went to change into some fresh garments. That was when I found a disc that had been tucked into the clothing I had packed.

It was unmarked, so I carried it over to the room terminal and placed it in the reader. Instead of the medical text I was expecting to see, the feed from a surveillance drone popped onto the screen.

The drone had been recording in darkness, so the scene on the monitor was displayed in the reds, oranges, and blues of thermal signatures. Even with the fine detailing, it took me a moment to recognize the field of yiborra grass, one that had been cultivated near the Torin pavilion.

A small figure stood alone in the center of the field, and as the drone drew closer and took a stationary position on the closed bloom of a d'narral flower, I took in the waist-high grass, the outline of the nose, and the long hair. The woman in the vid, who stood there looking up at the stars, was me.

I frowned. *When did I do this?* I heard grass thrashing, and saw a taller figure come up behind me on the screen.

"When Kao Torin died, a part of Cherijo died with him," I heard Reever say over the terminal speaker. He stopped next to my figure. "That did not happen to me when she died."

The female figure turned to look behind them. "Marel is alone," she said in my voice, but in a form of Terran that was so slurred and garbled I almost didn't understand her. "We should go back."

My jaw dropped into my lap. This wasn't me and Reever standing in a pasture. This was my body and Reever.

This was *Jarn* and Reever.

"Fasala was happy to come and stay with our daughter for a few hours." Reever put his arm around her. "You dislike it when I speak of Cherijo's first love."

"He is dead," Jarn said in her awful Terran. "We do not speak of the dead on Akkabarr."

"No," I told the terminal, "you just steal other women's bodies and husbands and children."

"Indulge me this once." Reever began petting her hair, the way he had so often done with mine. "Do you know why Cherijo's death did not affect me as Kao's passing did her?"

"Let me guess," I snapped over whatever Jarn replied. "Having sex with my possessed body kept you from weeping yourself to sleep every night."

He turned her around to face him. "I became Cherijo's lover, and eventually her husband, so that I might take Kao's place in her heart, as I promised him that I would. But I could not."

That jolted me a second time. He'd promised *Kao* that he'd marry me? When had that happened? Then I froze as I remembered that, just before his death, Kao had made Reever his Speaker.

"She was an idiot to refuse your love," Jarn said.

"I never refused anything!" I shouted at the terminal.

"It had nothing to do with her," Reever said calmly. "I told you that I loved her, but the truth is I did not. I could not."

I groped blindly until I found the console buttons and stopped the replay. Then I sat and stared at the frozen thermal images without seeing them.

It was easy to understand now why he'd fallen so hard for the slave girl. He'd been faking with me. All these years, everything he had told me had been a lie.

I restarted the disc, and sat and listened and

watched as Reever explained it all to Jarn. His voice never wavered as he told her how he had never felt a thing for me. He admitted that he had been curious, and the sex had been a nice bonus, but toward the end he'd decided that he was never meant to love me. I'd just been the means for him to reproduce and learn how to be a daddy.

Unlike me, Jarn seemed confused and upset. She asked him why he'd stayed with me when he hadn't loved me. And then Reever said something that struck me in the chest like a blade.

"It was you. All this time with her, I was waiting for you."

After that, I sat and watched them make love in that pasture. The thermal imagery made it quite clear that they both enjoyed themselves thoroughly; by the time they were finished, both of their bodies glowed with heat and satisfaction. As they cuddled and murmured to each other, I shut off the replay.

So now I knew.

It was funny how detached I felt. Later, I suspected, the humiliation would set in, and I would wish I were dead, but now I felt nothing. I got up, put on my footgear, and wandered out of my quarters.

The HouseClan was very fond of greenery, and had allocated the center portion of each outlying city halo to serve as public parks and gardens. I found one that wasn't crowded with flowers, Jorenians, or offworlders, and sat on a flat rock beside a small artificial waterfall.

Focusing on PyrsVar had kept me from thinking about Reever and Marel, but I could admit now, I had been nursing a tiny flicker of hope about the future. Before tonight, I'd been utterly convinced that

Reever had loved me. Maybe that erroneous assumption had nursed and kept alive a shred of hope. If I hadn't seen the vid, I'd have continued on in ignorant bliss. My pride would have healed; it always did. It wasn't impossible to think that with time I might have even grown willing to give him another chance.

All my hope was gone. The love I had believed in had never existed.

This wasn't my fault, and I knew that, but it still ripped at me. I'd always taken that love for granted, and now that I knew it had never been real, I felt as if my heart were curdling inside me.

All I wanted was to be loved. Why couldn't he love me?

Something tickled my ankle, and I looked down to see a thin ribbon of faintly glowing blue trying to crawl under the edge of my trouser leg. It reminded me of the dancers I had seen on the vid, and I felt like kicking it into another halo.

"I know. It wasn't your fault, either." I bent down and coaxed the wind dancer into my hand, where it curled around my fingers and brightened as it warmed itself with my body heat.

Wind dancers were nocturnal creatures, and generally spent the daylight hours draped over a nice warm stone basking in the sun. Another, dark green dancer appeared and fluttered slowly around me until I offered it my free hand.

"I think they like you."

"Yeah. I have great body heat. According to Jorenian folklore, if you're nice to them, they're supposed to grant your dearest wish." I glanced up at Shon. "But no. You're still here. So, want to tell me why you're following me?"

"I bring news."

I straightened my fingers and watched as the dancers, now glowing with borrowed warmth, began to unwind themselves. "Am I going to *like* this news?"

"That is for you to decide," he said. "Senior Healer Squilyp has arrived. He wishes to speak with you and Reever as soon as possible."

"He's out of luck, then," I said. "Reever is in Marine province."

"Not any longer." He turned to the side, and I saw two Terrans waiting at the entrance to the gardens.

My daughter didn't look happy. Neither did my husband.

"So much for wishes." I watched the wind dancers flutter up and away.

Six

I wasn't sure why I went with Reever to see Squilyp
at the Adan's medical facility. Idle curiosity, maybe.
Nor did I object when Shon volunteered to take
Marel for a walk around the grounds while we spoke
to the Omorr.

Reever didn't say a word to me as we went to the
conference room where Squilyp was waiting for us.
He seemed tense and unhappy, not that I cared.

"Did you bring me the data on the alterformation
cases treated on Joren?" I asked after greeting my
friend.

"I have it here, but there is something else we must
discuss. Sit down, both of you." Squilyp stood behind
the console until we did, and then punched up a ho-
loprojection of two human brains illuminated by tiny
blue veins and minuscule flashes of bright blue light.
"This"—he indicated the right image—"is a scan I
made yesterday of the synaptic activity from your
brain, Cherijo."

I folded my arms. "Why?"

"I wished to map your higher-level functions so

that I might identify any areas of the mind that are not being utilized."

"I don't see any," I said.

"Neither did I, on your scan or this one." He turned to the left image. "This, in fact, shows the exact same patterns of activity, which indicate brain function was not compromised by the head injury."

"If you have a point, Senior Healer," Reever said, "I would appreciate you making it."

"Observe." Squilyp tapped the console, and the two images merged, overlapping each other. "Do you see any variation in the pattern?"

"Why would we?" I countered. "They're synchronous. Which means they're identical."

He nodded. "The left image shows the same activity because it is your brain, Cherijo."

"That's terrific." I got to my feet. "If you'll excuse me, I really have to—"

"The second image of your brain was scanned a year ago." The Omorr paused. "From Jarn."

I sat back down as the implications sank in. "There are variations; you're just not seeing them."

"I ran both scans through the neuroanalyzer," Squilyp said gently. "There are none."

"Run it again," I suggested through my teeth. "Use a different medsysbank."

"I ran it through four."

I glared at him. "Is this some type of new therapy? You lying to me, too?"

Reever looked at me and then the Omorr. "I do not understand."

"Thought processes are like Terran fingerprints, or Hsktskt scale patterns, or oKiaf fur coloration. They are unique to the individual," Squilyp said. "Two different people cannot display the exact same synaptic activity. It is impossible."

Reever eyed the overlapping images. "Jarn and Cherijo shared the same body, the same brain."

"But not the same thoughts, the same language, or the same memories," I tagged on. "We had the same brain but different minds. There can be similarities, but not exact synchronicity." He still didn't get it. "What Squilyp is trying to tell us is that— synaptically speaking, anyway—Jarn and I are the same person."

"You are not."

"Exactly. Nice try, Squid Lips." I jumped up and headed for the door panel.

"In a recovery state, a patient who has experienced massive neural-tissue destruction will form a new persona in response to its environment," the Omorr called after me.

I whirled around. "Then how do you explain me?"

"I cannot," he admitted. "But I can confirm that you suffered severe memory repression. Think on the stressors involved. You witnessed the Jado Massacre. You were abducted and enslaved. You were nearly killed in the crash on Akkabarr. You believed Reever and Marel were dead, and when that native shot you, you must have wanted—"

"You shut up." I strode toward the console. "I'm not a coward. I've never run from anything in my life. I would never have done this to myself."

"You were alone, terribly injured, and left to survive in a hostile environment." His gildrells drooped. "Cherijo, you did not do this. Your body did."

I leaned in. "Do me a favor, Squid Lips. Go back to Omorr. See your mate and your sons. Enjoy your life, and forget about this." I straightened and looked at Reever. "We're done here."

Reever maintained his silence as we retrieved Marel and returned to the HouseClan pavilion. My daughter offered me a distant greeting, and a polite peck on the cheek. She also responded politely to my questions about their journey and her opinions of the capital, but resentment glittered in her eyes and had erased her usual cheerful attitude.

If she's still that way, I amended silently. I could see that someone Jorenian had taught her manners, and she remained well-spoken for her age, but other than that, I knew next to nothing about my own child.

Except that she didn't want to be here.

Shon remained with me as I took my family to my quarters, and then asked to have a private word with me before he left. I didn't consult Reever, but stepped out into the corridor with the oKiaf and let the panel close behind me.

"If you wish to change your accommodations," Shon said in a low tone, "I will give you my quarters and stay in one of the halo hostels."

"He'll just come after me again." I checked the time on my wristcom. "Reever and I have to settle some things. Get something to eat, come back in an hour, and then we'll head over to the medical facility."

He wanted to argue with me—I could see that—but I think he also realized I needed to do this. Finally he touched my shoulder and then left.

Back inside my quarters, I heard Reever speaking to Marel in the spare sleeping chamber. His voice sounded firm, while hers was definitely tearful. I caught only a couple snatches of the conversation, but it soon became apparent that she wanted to go back to the Torins. Reever reassured her, and once I was pretty sure I heard her sobbing into his tunic, but he didn't give in to her.

He emerged ten minutes later and joined me at the dining table, where I was transferring a few things from my garment bag into my medical case.

"She is sleeping," he told me.

"Good." I slipped the datapad Squilyp had given me with all the records he had gathered on alterform procedures into my case and closed it. "Are you hungry? I'll make you something to eat before I leave."

"Why did you abandon us?" he demanded.

"Abandon." I paused on my way to the prep unit and then kept walking. "You know, if you don't want to take another bath in my tea, you should try rephrasing that."

He didn't have the good sense to keep his distance, but came over and stood beside me at the menu panel. "Why did you run away from me and our daughter?"

"I didn't *run* anywhere." I dialed up a bowl of vegetarian chili and a thin, crusty Jorenian morning bread that I thought would go well with it. "Shon Valtas and I came by glidecar to the capital to meet with the Hsktskt. He operated the vehicle; I sat and watched the scenery through the viewer." I carried my food over to the table. "Did you feed Marel before you left Marine province?"

"Yes. Sit down." He waited until I did and then took a moment to compose himself before he continued. "When I returned and found you gone again, I was very angry. I wanted to find you." He looked back at the closed panel to Marel's room before he added in a lower voice, "I wanted to punish you."

I took a bite of my bread. "And you thought you'd bring our kid here to watch you do it? My, my. Is this really your idea of quality parenting, Reever?"

"When TssVar freed me from the slavers' arena, I swore never again to resort to violence against a helpless being." He leaned down. "You made me forget that. You made me want to beat you. As you do now."

"You should hear some of my newer fantasies," I confided casually. "With a lascalpel, full body restraints, and my anatomical knowledge?" I shook my head. "I could introduce you to realms of pain that you haven't even dreamt of, pal."

"I would never lift a hand in anger against you, Cherijo." He straightened. "Just as you would never harm me."

I shrugged. He was right, but I had no problem with letting him worry a little. "Meeting with Squilyp put me behind schedule, and I have to eat and get ready for work. Can you talk a little faster?"

He sat down beside me. "I do not completely understand human emotion, but I do know about its absence. If I had no feelings for you, Wife, I would not care where you went or what you did."

I tested my chili, but it was still a little too hot to eat. "Did I ever explain to you the Terran allegory of the dog in the manger? No? It's pretty simple: You don't want me, but you don't want anyone else to have me. So until you accept that I don't belong to you, you're going to continue to do stupid things like this out of anger and misplaced possessiveness. No doubt you will wreck my life—again—and make me and our daughter and yourself miserable in the process."

His eyes had shifted to such a dark color of gray

they looked black now. "You truly believe that I have ruined your life?"

"I guess I could be wrong. Let's review exactly what you *have* done to me for the last ten years," I said, using my fingers to tick off each point. "You took control of my body on K-2. You lied to me about who you were. You arranged for me to deliver a killer's quintuplets at gunpoint. You lied about your friendship with him. You forced sex on me in order to infect me with a killer plague. You pretended to join a ship's crew in order to stalk me. You arranged a Hsktskt invasion of Joren just to capture me. You enslaved me and forced me to practice medicine on other slaves. You left me to rot as an alien-possessed slave on an ice world. Oh, and then you cheated on me with the bitch who took over my body for five years." I had run out of fingers, so I looked up at him. "Did I miss anything?"

"You know the reasons behind my actions," he said through his teeth. "Everything I did, I did out of love for you."

"But, Reever, I have it on very good authority that you never loved me." I smiled brightly at him. "Evidently you were just killing time and having gratuitous sex with me while you were waiting for Jarn to show up."

Something glittered in his eyes. "Who told you this?"

"You did." I nodded toward the room terminal. "Replay the disc that's sitting in the scanner. You're going to love the ending."

Reever went over and switched on the replay. He stood watching until the vid showed him and Jarn beginning to make love, and then shut it off. "Who gave you this?"

"I don't know. I found it stuck in my garment case."
Here was my supreme moment, the wronged wife tri-
umphant, and yet I couldn't feel anything. I was numb
from the heart up. "The graphics are pretty wonderful, don't you think? Did she like to be on top all the
time, or just when you were doing it outside in the
dirt?"

He stared at me, furious and appalled, unable to
speak.

"It's okay, Reever. I don't really need to know." I
propped an elbow on the table and rested my cheek
against my hand as I watched him. "The good thing
is that now I completely understand why you were
so upset over losing Jarn. After all, she was the only
woman you've ever loved."

"You were never meant to hear what I said to her."
He strode over to me. "Cherijo, I am convinced that
Xonea did this to break our bond, so he can Choose
you for himself."

"There is no bond. Maybe if you had been honest with me from the beginning, I might have had a
chance to have a normal relationship with someone
else. Who knows? Maybe even with Xonea." I looked
into his eyes. "At least *he's* always loved me."

He turned his face away. "You will never forgive
me for what I said."

"I'm afraid that was pretty unforgivable," I agreed.
"But you can do something to make it up to me."

Now he looked at me. "What?"

"Take Marel and go back to Marine province."
When he tried to speak, I held up one hand. "Our kid
doesn't want to be here; she doesn't know me and
she's mourning Jarn. She misses her Jorenian family
and friends. You have no reason to stay married to

me; you never did. There is nothing to salvage here. So just take her and go."

"I cannot leave you like this, not after what Squilyp said."

"The Omorr is wrong. I'm fine. I have friends here, and plenty of work to do. I don't need you hovering over me, waiting for me to have a psychotic break." When I saw him reaching for me, I shook my head. "Don't."

His hand fell to his side. "I will do as you ask."

"Great." I stirred my spoon around the server. "Are you sure you don't want something from the unit?"

"I know you are not as calm as you pretend to be." He sounded tired. "You are hurt and confused. You are afraid. I will send Marel back to the Torins, but let me stay. Let me help you."

"Reever, if I were on fire, I wouldn't ask you to spit on me." I tried another spoonful, found the temperature had grown tolerable, and began to eat.

He sat and waited for me to finish, but when I got up and tidied the servers, he seemed to run out of patience. "When will we see you again?"

"I'll come over and visit in a couple of weeks." I went to change into some fresh garments, clean my teeth, and braid my hair. I didn't hurry, and by the time I came out, Shon was waiting for me.

"Don't let Marel sleep too long. She'll be grumpy on the trip back." I picked up my case. "Say hello to Salo and Darea for me."

"This is not finished," I heard him say as Shon and I walked out.

Oh yes, I thought, taking every bit of agony inside me and locking it away for good. It was.

*   *   *

HouseClan Adan's newest and largest medical facility had been recently built in the very center of the halo city, and occupied nearly three-quarters of the multilevel structures in the circular construct.

Shon guided me to the physicians' entrance, where a friendly receptionist scanned our wristcoms before directing us to an isolation ward on the top level.

"Why are they verifying identifications?" I asked the oKiaf in the lift. The last time I'd been on Joren, no one had asked me to prove who I was.

"Someone attempted to use a patient at a Torin medical facility as a bomb," he said.

"Who were they trying to blow up?" When he gave me an ironic look, I groaned. "You've got to be kidding."

"The device was deliberately sabotaged before it was implanted so that it could be discovered before it detonated," he told me. "The mercenary who arranged it wanted Jarn and Reever to leave Joren so they could be forced to crash-land on Trellus."

"Those little details weren't in Xonea's encrypted files." I wondered what else had been omitted.

"Another version of the facts was presented to the Torins to avoid a subsequent invasion of Trellus. The colonists were shielded, but it would be best for everyone concerned if you discuss this matter only with Reever." The lift came to a stop, but he put out a paw to stop me from exiting. "I have no wish to intrude on your personal life, but you cannot hide in your work to avoid settling matters with your mate."

I smiled a little. "Oh, everything is settled now, Shon."

On the isolation ward we found an entire staff of Jorenian healers and nurses busy arranging equipment and preparing different work areas. Apalea appeared to be supervising, but the delegation was absent, and ChoVa and PyrsVar were also nowhere to be seen.

"Where are my Hsktskt?" I asked the Senior Healer.

"The delegates are meeting with our ClanLeader to strike a formal agreement between our peoples." She nodded toward the back of the ward. "The healer and her patient await you in assessment room one." She handed a stack of surgical shrouds to a nurse before she added, "The Hsktskt healer seems somewhat agitated by the alterformed male."

Poor Apalea, she hadn't picked up on the underlying reason for that. "If we can restore him, they'll probably mate."

"Mother of all Houses." Her eyes widened. *"Here?"*

I felt a surge of sour amusement. "I think we can persuade them to first return to Vtaga for the proper rituals."

I asked Shon to inspect the surgical suite while I went to check on my patient and his healer. I found both sitting in silence; ChoVa read a chart while Pyrs-Var toyed with his vocollar. Neither of them would look at each other, and I saw why when I spotted a monitor array in pieces on the floor, and a tail-shaped dent in the wall.

"All right, children," I said as I stepped in. "Before the Jorenians and the oKiaf join us, let's get something straight." I addressed ChoVa. "When you are on this ward, you are a physician, and my assistant. If you have a problem with the patient, you bring it to me." As I heard PyrsVar make a snickering sound,

I turned to him. "And you will cooperate and do as you're told without giving me or Healer ChoVa any lip, or I will see to it that you're realterformed into a mud-dwelling, slime-eating Ichthorii."

"He will not follow my orders," ChoVa told me, her tongue lashing the air between us. "He would rather behave like a youngling and destroy valuable equipment."

"I did not care for the sounds it made," the rogue snapped. "SrrokVar strapped me to a thing that made the same noise and left me to burn in my hide for three rotations."

"The equipment can look and sound a little scary," I agreed, "but we are going to try not to hurt you. If something causes you pain, all you have to do is tell us, and we'll stop the procedure. Do you understand me?"

"He says he wants this, but he cannot control his temper," I heard ChoVa mutter.

"Is that right?" I gestured to the wall. "What calm, levelheaded person in the room did that?" I dropped my hand and sighed. "This is going to be difficult for all of us. And remember, we're the guests of a species with zero tolerance for bad tempers. If you threaten or cause harm to a member of the Jorenian staff, whether you mean it or not, they can declare ClanKill and use their claws to have you eviscerated alive—and I won't be able to stop them."

ChoVa grimaced, but PyrsVar looked down at his alterformed claws and then grinned at me. "I knew these had to be good for something."

I decided the youngsters needed some time apart, and after I gave ChoVa the data I had obtained from Squilyp, I told her to download it into the ward's database. PyrsVar I took across to the wardroom he would be occupying for the duration, and had him strip down to his skin while I prepared my scanners.

"I cannot wait to have my other limbs restored to me," he said as he dropped his garments on the floor and stretched. "Four are not enough. Will you grow back what SrrokVar cut off?"

I glanced at the faint marks on his torso left by the amputation of two of his Hsktskt midlimbs. "We'll see. Now lie down on that berth and relax."

After taking his vitals, which were abnormal for both species, I began scanning at the top of his head and worked my way down to his chest.

His brain presented predominantly natal reptilian features and functions, and the few humanoid characteristics that had been added were mainly involuntary: the ability to produce his own body heat, adrenaline, sweat, and hair. When I got to his chest, however, I found two sets of cardiorespiratory systems, eight kidneys, a freakish-looking liver that appeared to be cobbled together from Jorenian and Hsktskt organs. And then there was the mystery mass that my scanner failed to identify.

I set the device aside and palpated a spot just to the bottom left of his chest plate.

He immediately scowled. "That hurts me."

"I'm sorry." I picked up my scanner again and studied the display before inspecting his hide. "Were you wounded in that place?"

"No. It has always been so, since my earliest memory."

Whatever was inside him was congenital, and definitely of Hsktskt origin. It didn't show any aspects indicating that it was a tumor or other form of malignancy. But with its complicated structures and vascular supply, and what looked like a rib it had at some time absorbed, it didn't even vaguely resemble any of their organs on record.

I'd have to take a biopsy and determine exactly what it was before I decided if it needed to be safely removed along with the other, redundant Jorenian implants.

"Why do you make your face like that?" PyrsVar asked.

I saved the new data before I met his gaze. "You are the most complicated patient I have ever had."

He flashed his pointed teeth. "No, I am simple. ChoVa has told me so, many times. Did her father ask you to kill me?"

"Let's just say that he cares for his daughter more than he wants your throat cut." I sat down on the edge of the berth. "PyrsVar, there is a group of crossbreeds on Joren who have formed their own HouseClan, the Kalea. All of them are like you: half Jorenian, half some other species. From what I've heard, at least two of them are part reptilian. It might be wise to take a trip to their territory and meet them."

He looked puzzled. "You wish me to befriend these people?"

"Friendships can lead to other things," I agreed. "As you are right now, you can walk out of here, live a seminormal life, and maybe, with a little luck and very selective mating, reproduce."

"But not with a pure-blood Hsktskt female."

"No." I went ahead and gave him the second option. "I believe I can also perform some cosmetic procedures to alter your physical appearance to that of a Hsktskt, which would allow you to reside on Vtaga and blend in better with your natal species."

"You mean you would not take out the Jorenian parts. You would only change my outsides." He muttered something under his breath that sounded vicious.

I sighed. "There is no need to get agitated. As your doctor, it would be irresponsible of me to attempt a full restoration without first offering some safer alternatives."

"I do not want safe," he informed me. "I want ChoVa." He seized my hand. "You will help make me worthy of her, so that her father does not slit my gullet, and she does not take another mate."

"All right." If I couldn't have my love, then maybe making it possible for my namesake to have hers would fill a little of the ragged hole in my heart. "I'll try."

Once I had inspected the ward and filed a few requests for some additional equipment, I called the staff together in an adjoining conference room and met my new crew.

Apalea had outdone herself in finding experienced professionals with backgrounds in genetics, reconstructive surgery, and hybrid physiology. Along with four other medical physicians of various specialties, I had six residents, ten interns, and a small horde of intensive care nurses.

After all the introductions had been made and work assignments handed out, I presented my preliminary scan results to the staff. The room fell quiet as I detailed the brutal amount of augmentation and alterformation that had been forced on PyrsVar, as well as some of my immediate concerns.

"Keeping him stable is our first priority, so your primary responsibility is to ensure that our patient remains on schedule with his meds," I told the nurses. "If his regime is interrupted again, his immune system will revert to its natal functions again and begin attacking the Jorenian organs. Given the amount of damage the last episode caused, he probably won't survive a repeat."

One of the physicians, a healer who worked in pediatric genotherapy, made a polite gesture to catch my attention. When I nodded to her, she said, "Healer Cherijo, since the process used to alterform this male has been lost, how will we know how to proceed?"

"PyrsVar remembers what was done to him," I told her. "He has no medical training, but already today I've learned that his midlimbs and tail were amputated before his remaining limbs were alterformed, and he was left in a dermal regenerating unit for three days."

Several of the nurses looked shocked while the healers murmured among themselves.

"He wasn't well treated by the psychopath who did this to him. He'll never admit it, but he's afraid. So when you work with this patient, take into consideration the amount of abuse he's already suffered, and try to be gentle." I turned to another resident who had gestured for my attention. "Yes?"

"That mass in the left lower quadrant"—he pointed to the odd organ I had discovered in PyrsVar's chest— "does not have an apparent function. What is it?"

"I don't know." I glanced at ChoVa. "Were you able to identify it?"

"We did not recognize the mass, so we assumed it was Jorenian in pathology," she replied.

That wasn't good. "It scans as reptilian, not humanoid, on the cellular level. He claims to have had it since early childhood, perhaps birth."

"May I, Healer?" Our pediatrician took my scanner and peered at the display. "These rows of echoes bisecting the central compartment suggest a pedunculated vertebrate tumor."

"The fibrous membrane could be a chorioamnionic complex," another healer put in. "The other incorporated structures are unfamiliar to me, but they appear similar to what is presented by a malformed monozygotic diamniotic parasite."

"Fetus-in-fetu." I nodded, and then caught ChoVa's blank look. "Hsktskt births are always multiple. PyrsVar must have absorbed another fetus while in utero."

ChoVa's jaw dropped. "He is impregnated with a sibling?"

"It happens." To the curious interns, I said, "The fetus becomes embedded due to a repercussion of vitelline circulation anastomoses. The absorbed twin probably suffered a developmental delay which resulted in multiple reversed arterial perfusion syndrome."

The pediatrician nodded. "We see the same mechanism at work in the gestation of acardiac twins. The reversal of the arterial flow retards the growth and cardiac development of the impaired twin, which is then embedded in the larger, stronger fetus." She frowned. "Healer ChoVa, this condition should have been detected at birth and the mass excised from the patient's chest. This disorder also becomes readily apparent from the parasite's slow but continued growth and compression of the adjacent organs. He has likely been in pain his entire life. Why does this remain untreated?"

"The male is the offspring of a disgraced pariah. As such he had no recognized bloodline, and was not entitled to the rights and benefits afforded to our citizens." ChoVa's inner eyelids drooped. "Other than what was done to him during the alterformation process, this is the first time in his life he has received medical care."

"I see." The healer didn't verbally express her contempt, but it was written all over her face.

"Many of my colleagues and I do not hold with our species' custom of punishing the young for the crimes of their sires," ChoVa said. "You are doubtless familiar with the cultural implications of disrupted or disgraced lineal status. For years your people were largely unsuccessful in integrating offspring of slave rape into your society."

"We refer to them as 'the ClanChildren of Honor.'" The healer's disdain abruptly faded from her expression. "Your pardon, Healer ChoVa. Perhaps our people are more alike than either world cares to believe."

"No one is seeing the value of this aberration," I pointed out. When everyone looked at me, I added, "The fetus-in-fetu is a twin. It will contain the same DNA PyrsVar had when he was born. We can harvest the unadulterated genetic material we need directly from it."

"How would you use it?" ChoVa asked.

"Rather than try to remove the Jorenian organs

from the Hsktskt, we could infect them with a retroviral compound that would deliver the natal DNA and encode it into the Jorenian sequences."

"That would work very quickly." Apalea looked thoughtful. "But would the body be able to withstand such rapid transformation?"

"It's worth exploring." The room intercom chimed, and I went over to answer it. "Yes?"

"Healer Cherijo, we have received a summons from the Ruling Council," Apalo told me. "They have requested that you attend them in chambers at once."

Joren's governing body probably wanted to be briefed on our project, but I still needed to run more tests and put together a tentative treatment plan. "Can't this wait until tomorrow?"

"Stand by." The intercom fell silent for a minute, and then Apalo's voice returned. "The council members have received an interplanetary signal that requires your immediate attention, Healer."

There goes my staff meeting, I thought glumly. "Very well. Tell them I'll be there in a few minutes."

I dismissed the off-duty staff for the rest of the day, wrote up quick orders for PyrsVar's care, and left the ward in ChoVa's capable hands. She and the pediatrician promised to run secondary scans on the fetus-in-fetu lodged in PyrsVar's chest and determine if it could be removed without compromising the blood supply to the surrounding organs.

"Don't tell him that he has a sibling in his chest," I advised the Hsktskt healer. "He's carrying around enough guilt."

Shon joined me. "Are you leaving now?"

"Yes." I started toward the lift, and then stopped

to look back at him. "Where, exactly, is the Ruling Council?"

After a little bickering (I didn't need an escort, the oKiaf didn't want me going alone) Shon accompanied me to the council's chambers, which were in a beautiful but tightly secured sector of the innermost halo. Built of neutral golden stone studded with panels of polished minerals from every inhabited province on Joren, the place looked like a small palace.

My admiration for the structure seemed to amuse the oKiaf. "You were chosen as a ruler of this world, and yet you have never once been in their chambers?"

"I've signaled them a few times." I made an exasperated sound. "Back in those days I was busy being a doctor, and a fugitive, and a ship's healer. Don't even get me started on how time-consuming it is to be enslaved."

"There are eleven seated members on the council," he told me as he parked our glidecar in a designated area. "They are elected based on provincial governing experience; most are high-ranking members of their HouseClans. Three alternates also monitor every proceeding from their home provinces and participate when necessary. While you were away from Joren, one of the three would have voted in your stead."

I'd never asked to be made a planetary ruler, so I didn't feel bad about the lousy job I had done as a council member. Still, I felt a little uncomfortable with the way the security team grinned and greeted me as we stopped at three identification checkpoints on the way to the ruling chamber. At the final gate, six guards stood smiling but with weapons ready as Shon and I were scanned from head to footgear and our mouths swabbed.

I didn't mind being searched, but I was never happy about giving up a DNA sample. When the guard verified we were genetically who we said we were, I asked for both our swabs back and dropped them into a small disposal unit.

The interior of the council chamber proved to be as interesting as the outer structure. Oversized screens encircled the room, and had been installed at an angled pitch so they could be easily viewed from the center platform. A long spiral of ClanSigns, one from every House on the planet, marched across the screens, and illuminated pedestals holding complex flower arrangements glowed underneath them.

The real show was on the center platform, a dais surrounded by gently sloping tiers of stone steps that ended at the edge of a polished expanse of old, scarred wood. The humble material used for the platform seemed out of place compared with the grandeur of the rest of the chamber, until I realized what it was.

"That's the base of an old warrior quad, isn't it?" I murmured to Shon.

He nodded. "It is the quad where Tarek Varena defended his honor."

My stomach rolled—I wouldn't have preserved a place where hundreds of men had been slaughtered—but I could see the symbolic power of it. Tarek Varena had not only created Jorenian path philosophy, he'd been responsible for instituting the first set of planetary laws. Without the hundred days he'd spent killing everyone who challenged him, there would be no HouseClans.

Atop the old warrior quad stood the eleven members of the Ruling Council, dressed in simple white robes with narrow belts woven from yiborra grass.

The five women and six men had calm faces, and plenty of purple in their hair, one of the few signs of age among their species.

One of the women stepped forward. "Healer Torin, we thank you for attending us so quickly."

"My pleasure, council member." I glanced up as another Jorenian face appeared on the room's screen panels. I recognized the handsome face and shrewd eyes of an old ally.

"Welcome back, Doctor," Ambassador Teulon Jado said from the screens.

I knew from the records that the ClanLeader of the Jado had been sent to Akkabarr to be sold as a slave to the Toskald. There he had somehow escaped to the surface, and united the tribes of slaves left to die there into a rebel force. With their help, he had cobbled together a fleet out of the thousands of shipwrecks on the planet, and taught the tribesmen how to fly the ships. Then he had begun staging attacks against their former masters, the Toskald, until the surface rebellion had developed into a full-fledged war.

The rebellion had given Teulon direct access to secret bunkers on the surface, which contained weapons stores and the Toskald's greatest advantage, crystals etched with command codes that gave him control over thousands of armies. He'd used the crystals to bring the Hsktskt and the League as well as the Toskald to their knees. His rebellion had been an engine of vengeance, a vehicle of justice for the Jado Massacre, but in the end he had used his power to force a peaceful end to the war.

Even I didn't have to be told that he was the most admired man in the galaxy.

He looked as young and vigorous as any Jorenian

male, his blue-skinned face austerely handsome and his long black hair coiled into a deceptively simple-looking warrior's knot. But his eyes were another matter altogether; they spoke of his soul, one that had been battered and pushed to the brink of madness while witnessing unthinkable tragedies.

He and Jarn had been allies, but I wouldn't hold that against him. "It's good to see you again, Ambassador. How may I be of assistance?"

"My bondmate and I are presently on Vtaga, negotiating some trade agreements with the Hanar," Teulon said. "We have received several signals from a number of border patrols and cargo vessels which have encountered a newly formed anomaly in an unexplored region between N-jui and Varallan. The anomaly appears to be a rift in space."

Rifts, or dimensional disruptions, were so rare that only a handful had been discovered and mapped over the last thousand years. While their bizarre properties were interesting, most were unstable and presented only a minor hazard to the shipping routes. No one knew what caused them to appear or vanish.

"Does this rift pose a threat to any populated worlds?" I asked.

"Not to our immediate knowledge," Teulon replied. "It is what came out of the rift that concerns us now."

The fuzzy image of a star vessel appeared on the chamber screens. It appeared to be drifting in front of an uneven ellipse filled with millions of tiny stars. I couldn't tell how large the ship was, but the sweeping design and intricate filigree of its hull arrays were unlike anything I'd ever seen. So were the red, white, and orange alloys or materials used to build it.

I frowned. "What is that?"

"We have been unable to identify it," Teulon said. "The hull reflects most of our scans, although our patrols have used a drone probe to determine there is a crew on board."

A vidfeed from the drone appeared on the screens, and showed the little mechano using some exhaust shafts to gain access to the mysterious vessel. It passed through several conduits and into what appeared to be a fuel tank filled with some dark, gelatinous liquid before it emerged into an interior compartment. There it widened the view from its lens to take in a series of clear vertical columns suspended from the upper deck.

Inside each column a motionless humanoid body hung suspended in a silvery white fluid.

"Are those stasis chambers?" I heard Shon say.

I didn't see any breathing tubes or monitor lines attached to the bodies, but their heads were completely covered by some sort of helmet that might have been providing them with oxygen. Each column had also been equipped at the base with a series of control panels.

The technology we were seeing was so far advanced that it appeared unlike anything in existence.

I also saw something on the exposed skin of the bodies. "Ambassador, can you magnify the image and focus on one of the hands inside the tank?"

"Yes." The image zoomed larger as it was magnified, until it showed a close-up of the back of one hand, glittering as if it was gloved in clear crystal. As we watched, the mineral attached to the skin grew a few millimeters.

"Those tanks are filled with protocrystal," Shon said.

I glanced at him. "Are you sure?"

"I have seen it many times on my homeworld. The matrix is unmistakable." He kept staring at the image. "But why isn't it attacking or absorbing the bodies?"

I studied the images. "Maybe they're somehow immune to it." I raised my voice. "Ambassador, have you determined if the crew of this vessel is still alive?"

"Not as of yet." Teulon Jado's face reappeared on the screen. "We have sent out a salvage crew to secure the ship and tow it a safe distance away from anomaly, but for obvious reasons we do not wish to bring it to an inhabited world."

"You can't leave it to drift through space, either," I said.

The council member made an elegant gesture. "Ambassador Teulon, the Hsktskt Hanar and our council agree that the first to board should be a medical response team, in the event the crew is still alive and require treatment. Healer Torin, Healer Valtas, you have had much experience with this mineral. You understand the dangers involved."

"Seeing as the protocrystal almost ate Healer Valtas," I said politely, "I guess we do."

"Ambassador, this mineral is unpredictable, aggressive, and very dangerous," Shon said. "As this appears to be the same substance, I advise against having any contact with this ship."

"But if this crew belongs to a species unknown to us, one that has found the means with which to control the protocrystal," Teulon countered, "they may be willing to share their knowledge. It could save your homeworld, oKia, from being consumed by it."

I'd feel better if we first found out who the crew were. "Have you been able to determine if the ship came out of the rift?"

"Both appeared on a cargo vessel's long-range scanners simultaneously," he said.

Which meant that the ship could have been caught in the rift when it formed, or may have created it. "Have your patrol ships sent in any drones to see what's on the other side of the rift?"

He nodded. "There is an unusual energy field within the perimeter of the anomaly. It has destroyed every drone sent through it."

I didn't want to go any more than Shon did, but the ambassador was right: we had the most experience in dealing with the effects of protocrystal exposure. "I'll need time to assemble a team and arrange transport."

"HouseClan Torin has put the *Sunlace* and her crew on standby," the council member told me. "The Hanar's delegation has also been instructed to provide you with any assistance the Faction may provide."

Jarn had worked with ChoVa to cure the plague of memory, and with her experience in stasis medicine ChoVa would be invaluable. It meant putting PyrsVar's restoration on hold, but I had no doubt if the Hsktskt healer came on the sojourn, he would insist on accompanying her. I could also work on designing the retroviral compound.

"If the *Sunlace* is ready, we can leave tomorrow," I told Teulon. "I'll go, on one condition."

"Which is?" the ambassador asked.

"There is one person I don't want on this expedition," I told him. "He is to be kept on planet while I'm gone. Under guard, if necessary."

Teulon's brows rose. "Who is this male?"

"The ship's linguist," I said. "Duncan Reever."

Seven

At my request, Ambassador Teulon sent orders for the *Sunlace* to land at Adan Main Transport while I put together a medical team. As soon as Shon and I explained the situation to ChoVa, she immediately volunteered to go along, and as I'd expected, so did PyrsVar.

"There are some species that use different mineral compounds in their stasis suspensions," the Hsktskt healer told me. "It is possible that these people have mastered the use of the protocrystal as a life-support system."

"We've only just begun discovering its properties," I reminded her. "And since it doesn't occur outside our galaxy, that implies that this rift may have come through time as well as space."

"You think this ship jumped here from the future?" PyrsVar chuckled. "No one can do that."

"No one can now." I looked over the roster of residents and nurses. "The *Sunlace* has a competent medical staff on board, but I'd like a couple of extra hands. If this crew is still alive but in distress, and we can extract them, they're probably going to need intensive, round-the-clock care."

In the end we recruited another dozen Adan medical professionals to join the expedition, as well as a xenogeologist and several engineers who were very interested in getting a good look at the ship.

Xonea Torin was waiting for us at the docks when we reported the next morning. He greeted the Adan, ordered the medical equipment be brought on board, and then pulled me to one side.

"I know this is a time of great personal distress for you," he said, his voice gentle, "but know that whenever you need to talk, you have but to ask for me."

Ask for him. The man who had destroyed the last of my illusions just so he could have me for himself. Yeah, I was going to do that.

I kept my expression blank. "That's very nice of you, ClanBrother, but I'm not in any distress that I know of."

"You are not." He frowned. "But surely you have been subjected to some recent unpleasant revelations."

"Nope." Now that I knew he had been the one to slip me the disc, I wanted to punch him in the face. Pretending nothing had happened between me and Reever would hurt him more, though. "Duncan came up yesterday with Marel to see me before I left, which was wonderful. I am glad he's decided to stay behind with her. She's had enough upheaval in her life, don't you think?"

His eyes narrowed. "As you say."

"I'd better get to Medical and check on my staff." I picked up my case. "See you later."

Shon met me at the boarding ramp and glanced back at where Xonea stood watching me. "The captain does not appear pleased."

"The captain can go jump out an air lock," I said pleasantly as I walked up into the ship.

I made an appearance in Medical to greet the ship's staff, introduce the extra hands, and issue orders for shifts and work assignments. I designated Shon and ChoVa as alternate shift supervisors but left the running of the bay in the hands of the residents and nurses. Everyone seemed much more comfortable around ChoVa than PyrsVar, but the rogue decided to make himself useful by joining the crew in the cargo hold and helping them transport our equipment and supplies up to the bay.

When the ship's navigator gave the five-minute warning before transition, I had Shon accompany me into one of the treatment rooms.

"The last time we did this, I was someone else," I joked as I lay on the berth and let him strap me down.

"I will stay with you." He brushed back my hair before he attached the monitor leads to my temples. "I would also like to scan you during transitional phasing, if that is acceptable to you."

"Sure." I stifled a yawn. The panic attack I had been expecting hadn't arrived, and all I felt was a sinking feeling that had been boring into my belly since I'd listened to Reever tell Jarn he'd never loved me. "While we're waiting for reality to take a vacation, why don't you tell me something about Jarn?"

He adjusted the linens covering my legs. "What would you care to know?"

What did she have that I don't? seemed like a pathetic thing to ask. "What was it about her that you loved?"

He sat down on the stool beside my berth and thought about it. "She was direct, like you, but she could be kind, as well. The first time I saw her was when she was making rounds with the Omorr. She looked across the ward at me, and in that moment I knew her. As one hunter recognizes another."

He described his first meeting with Jarn, and how she had paid him what sounded like the ultimate compliment by deferring to him as a female to male.

"She put an end to that as soon as we were alone," he admitted. "But even as she exercised her authority, she remained courteous."

So she'd had great manners. Mine were okay, as long as my temper wasn't involved. "What else?"

"She had a tenacious respect for life," he said. "In every instance when she had to choose between her personal safety and someone hurt or in danger, she never gave herself a single thought."

I'd been reckless that way a few times myself. "Immortality is very reassuring."

"She jumped into an open pit of protocrystal to save my life," the oKiaf advised me. "Your body may be as inviolate as mine, Healer, but it is the one thing that can kill us."

"Is that why you jumped in the pit?" I asked softly.

He nodded. "I was very depressed and lonely. Jarn had soundly rejected my overtures, just as Jadaira had on K-2. I did not want to face eternity alone."

I closed my eyes. "No one does."

Distantly I heard the final warning before transition, and felt the soft warmth of Shon's paw cover my cold right hand. Even with my eyes closed, my head began to spin, and then I was pulled down into that whirlpool of blackness until it consumed me.

I floated above the deck of a Jorenian ship, where a group of people stood around Reever and a cloaked woman holding Marel in her arms. I spiraled down, pulled toward and then into the woman, until I saw the others through her eyes.

"Teulon," I said in a harsh voice. When he came to me, I handed Marel to him. "We are taking her with us. The Iisleg are my people; I don't know any of you. I am Jarn, not Cherijo, and you cannot stop me."

Squilyp took a hop toward me, but Xonea put a hand on his shoulder and held him back.

Then my husband got in my face. "I challenge your right to take her from me. I am her father. We are the only family she knows."

"You have each other. I have nothing." I slipped a dagger out from the sheath on my belt. "No, Reever. You will not take her from me."

"Squilyp." Reever waited until the Omorr came to us. "Is what she says true?"

"I will have to run some tests, but she has suffered at least two point-blank pulse fire shots to the head," the Omorr told him. "If there was enough brain damage, the cells would have regenerated, but the memories belonging to Cherijo would not. Cherijo, in essence, would no longer exist."

"We will leave now," I told the men.

"You would kill anyone who tried to take your daughter, would you not? Is this the way of the Iisleg women now?" my husband demanded. When I nodded, he said, "So would I. Anyone but you."

"But he took the kid away from you anyway," a deep female voice drawled.

The faces around me paled like ghosts of themselves, and then faded away, leaving me standing on an empty deck.

I turned around slowly, looking for her. The subliminal implants in my brain that allowed my dead surrogate mother to communicate with me seemed to work only whenever I was seriously disoriented, unconscious, or having a near-death experience. "You might as well show yourself. Transition won't last forever."

"You'd be surprised at how long I could keep you here." Maggie stepped out of the shadows.

She was dressed in an inappropriately fitted Jorenian flight suit, her red hair coiled up into a sleek knot atop her skull. She brought a cigarette to her lips, inhaled, and blew out a stream of smoke before she dropped it on the deck and crushed it out under her bootheel. "Nice of you to come back, though."

"I never chose to leave."

"That's not true." She waggled a finger at me. "You see, when your kidnapper crashed you on that frigging ice cube of a planet, you'd already decided to end it in the big way. You'd watched the Jado ship blow up; you knew Reever and Marel were dead. You didn't give a damn about the promises you made to me. No, Joey, it was all over long before your pals the skela showed up to skin you."

I wondered why I didn't feel any lingering emotion for her. On Terra she had been my best friend, the one person who had kept me from becoming a miniature of my creator. But the cutting tone of her voice, the silly, provocative way she dressed, and the stink of her illegal tobacco had become as tiresome as her demands. Whatever good she had done for me in the past, she'd also done a great deal of harm. I didn't owe her anything.

"Reever and Marel weren't dead, and I didn't die, and here we are." I folded my arms. "What do you want, Maggie? An apology? Sorry I haven't been around. Alien-possessed body and all that. Kiss kiss, bye-bye." I shut my eyes and concentrated on regaining consciousness.

"I've not really missed that mouth of yours," Maggie said as she circled around me. "But apology, such as it is, accepted. Now, we have some black crystal to talk about."

I opened my eyes. "I'm on my way to investigate a ship full of infant crystal. You'll have to get in line with your doomsday mineral and wait."

"Baby, I'd like nothing better, but your stupid little war with the Hsktskt accelerated the things," she snapped. "What we assumed wouldn't be happening for quite some time is now coming at us like a runaway glidetrain. It's time to do the job you were created for, Cherijo. Time to pay for all the gifts you were given."

"I never asked for any of this," I reminded her.

She made a contemptuous sound. "But you never gave it back, either."

"Why don't you spare us both the usual song and dance," I suggested, "and just tell me whatever it is that you want me to do."

Her snide smirk disappeared. "Don't go anywhere near that ship or that rift. Turn the *Sunlace* around, go back to Joren, and get your family. We're moving you to a safer neighborhood."

"So now I'm in *danger*?" I laughed. "If that's the best you can come up with, Maggie, I think you're out of luck this time."

"Mistakes have been made. Timelines miscalculated." She spread her hands. "We can correct the problems, but we need to get you out of here, and for that, you need Reever and the kid."

There was only one reasonable response to Maggie's demands. "Go to hell."

"Honey, that's right where you're headed." She patted my cheek so hard it was more like three slaps. "I haven't endured all this grief to let you blow it now. So be a good kid and do what I say, or I'm going to have to get nasty."

"Why would that be any different?" I countered. "Come on, Maggie. I'm not going to turn the ship around, I'm not going to get my family, and I'm not going anywhere with you."

"You spent the last five years drifting mindlessly through my backyard." She caught my chin and looked into my eyes. "And you don't remember. Shit. I keep forgetting how primitive your brain is."

"Let go of me," I said nicely.

"You ascended, Cherijo, but you couldn't assimilate. We were kind of shocked, actually, but without corporeal existence, you were your basic mindless bowl of vegetable soup." She released my chin. "I'm sorry, kiddo, but after we tried nudging you a few times, we had no choice. We had to send you back."

"So you killed Jarn, and shoved me back into my body?" I grabbed the front panels of her suit. "Is that what you're saying?"

"No. We can't do anything like that." She pushed me away with a flick of her fingers. "Jarn understood that a sacrifice had to be made. How she knew, I can't tell you, but she vacated the premises voluntarily. As much as you hate her, she's the one who brought you back. She traded her life for yours so that you could save Reever and the kid."

"I don't believe you."

She shrugged. "Free will, Joey. It's the bitch that keeps on wrecking."

Something welled up inside me, and a lower, harsher voice came out of my mouth. "No being undergoing a dimensional transformation preserves its sense of spatial relation."

"Jarn?" All the color drained out of Maggie's face as she stared at me. "You can't be—not after—"

I backhanded her, taking vicious pleasure in it, and knocked her to the deck. Then I stepped over her, straddling her as I bent down and grabbed her by the throat.

"I think you miscalculated more than the timeline, Jxin." I could have snapped her neck in that instant, but I knew it wouldn't kill her. Nothing would. She was as invulnerable as the black crystal. I released her, and stepped away as she coughed and gasped in air. "Now release me from this dream, or I will show you what more I can do."

Maggie staggered to her feet. "Fine. Be it on your head. If you board that ship, your timeline will end in a matter of weeks."

I didn't look at her. "Now, Maggie."

The deck around me began shrinking, and I floated up and back until I hovered horizontally above it. A berth appeared under me, and monitors sprang up all around me. Then Shon was there, scanning my head and baring his teeth in a grim snarl.

"Are you going to assess me," I said weakly, "or bite me?"

"Cherijo." He fumbled with the scanner, almost dropping it before he tossed it aside. "You've had hardly any brain activity at all. We were about to move you into intensive care."

That sounded ominous. "How long was I out?"

"Three days."

"I need to find another way to travel." I sat up, groaning as my stiff muscles protested. "Are we there yet?"

"We will arrive at the rendezvous point in a few hours." He helped me out of the berth. "I should run some tests."

"It's always like this," I assured him. "Just point me toward a cleansing unit, and let everyone know I'm back. Again."

He saw how wobbly I was, and put an arm around my waist. "Where did you go?"

I thought of Maggie, and how frightened she had looked. For the first time since she had begun hijacking my mind, I didn't feel afraid of her. "No place important."

I didn't dwell on the nasty end of my mental visit with my surrogate mother; everything that happened in those dreams usually defied explanation anyway. Instead, I took a long, hot cleansing, had a quick meal at the nurses' station, and began organizing what we'd need to examine the crew of the rift ship.

Shon didn't hover exactly, but he kept a close eye on me until the *Sunlace* reached the rendezvous point.

ChoVa was less diplomatic and insisted on scanning me herself before letting me out of the bay.

"You were unconscious for seventy-one hours," she said when I tried to complain. "You would not permit a patient that had been in such a state out of their berth."

"I'm a doctor, not a patient."

"Neither are mutually exclusive states, as you certainly know. Open your jaw." When I did, she used a penlight to inspect the interior of my mouth. "The monitors occasionally displayed some fluctuation in your brain activity during the three days you were unconscious."

"They were probably echoes from me shifting in and out of REM sleep." I endured another light-response check of my pupils. "Shon should have mentioned that when he told you about them."

"I observed the fluctuations personally." She seemed satisfied that my optic nerves were still functioning, and straightened. "I relieved Healer Valtas each night so he could rest, and remained at your side to observe."

"I know you're not entirely nocturnal, and one of the nurses could have monitored me just as well," I pointed out.

"I was concerned that you were experiencing another identity crisis." She sniffed as I laughed. "What else would you call it?"

"Nothing, that's perfect." With an effort I controlled my mirth and sighed. "I'm glad you came along on this jaunt. You're a good friend, ChoVa."

That seemed to mollify her. "The Hanar would not be pleased if we were to lose you again."

"I don't know about that." I plucked at the hem of my tunic. "Jarn cured your plague, not me."

"She was an excellent physician, and fortunate in her discoveries." The Hsktskt checked her scanner and made a notation. "But she did not understand the patterns of your hide. She was not born to it. She wore it because she had no choice."

"We call that being uncomfortable in your skin." And why hadn't Jarn liked mine? "You liked her, though, didn't you?"

"Well enough for a warm-blood." Briskly she completed the exam, and issued a stern warning for me to report to her the moment I felt any weaknesses or disorientation.

It was a little annoying, having the baby I'd once delivered treat *me* like a child, but since it was done mostly out of affection, I let it go.

Shon and I decided it was best to minimize the risk of exposure by limiting the size of the first response team. ChoVa stayed behind in Medical while he and I went with a senior engineer and two security guards to the shuttle bay.

Xonea stood waiting by the launch that had been prepped to transport us over to the rift ship. "Cherijo," he greeted me with a smile and a warm gesture.

"Captain." I nodded and kept going.

"I neglected to mention something," Shon said in a low voice as we carried our cases into the launch.

I stowed my case under a passenger seat. "What?"

"I didn't inform the captain of your reaction to transition." He hefted one of the packs onto an upper rack. "When he signaled for you, I told him that you were working on extraction simulations for the ambassador, or preparing reports for the council. And once I said you were cleansing. When he asked why you would not return his signals, I indicated that your memory impairment had made you somewhat absentminded."

"For an oKiaf, you're a pretty decent liar." I glanced at him. "Why go to all that trouble to keep Xonea away from me? I was unconscious."

"ClanLeader Torin signaled me before we left the planet. He felt it prudent to keep you and the captain separated as much as possible."

So now the Torin had Shon running interference. "Thanks, but I can handle Xonea on my own."

That's exactly what I did, too, when the captain indicated that he intended to accompany us to the rift ship.

"I appreciate the offer, ClanBrother, but we don't know what we're dealing with yet, and the risk of infection is too high. Besides, I have plenty of protection." I nodded to one of the security guards boarding the launch. "I'll signal and let you know what we find."

He glowered at me. "You will maintain an open channel at all times, or I will come and retrieve you myself."

I made my smile insultingly sweet. "I know Duncan would appreciate your concern for my safety and well-being."

Once our launch had left the *Sunlace*, I briefed the engineer and the guards and discussed how best to access the crew compartment.

"We don't know if the protocrystal is completely contained," I warned them, "so until we do, we stay in envirosuits and proceed with extreme caution. Alert me or Healer Valtas if you see anything that doesn't look right."

The engineer peered out through one of the viewports. "There is the rift."

I turned to have a look at the anomaly, which appeared much larger than it had in the drone feed Teulon had transmitted. About half the size of the *Sunlace*, it stretched out in an elongated oval, narrow at each end but very wide in the center, almost diamond-shaped. There were no discernible edges or perimeters I could see, only clusters of tiny, twinkling lights that became denser in the center of the rift. They didn't emit light the way stars did, however; they were more compact and seemed to have an even number of discernible axis points. They also flickered in and out of view at random intervals and speeds.

"Not stars at all," I murmured. "More like energy bursts."

The derelict ship appeared, still glowing with bright colors but obviously adrift. Two Hsktskt patrol vessels paralleled its meandering course, reminding me that if this didn't go well, we might end up being fired on by the Hanar's well-meaning militia.

"There is an air lock on the port side," the engineer said. "We should be able to dock with it."

As the pilot brought the launch up alongside the rift ship, the rest of us donned our envirosuits and took down our supply packs.

"Until we test the interior for atmosphere and run a biodecon, everyone stays on tank," I told the men as I fastened on my breather. "Keep your suitcoms enabled at all times. Healer Valtas and I will go in first."

The launch rocked as its docking clamps fastened to the derelict, and air hissed as the pilot sealed our compartment and opened the air lock. The rift ship's hull panels slid open silently, inviting us in.

"Ready?" I asked the oKiaf, who nodded. "Let's go."

The first thing I noticed when I stepped into the other ship's air lock was a panel of unfamiliar controls that sparkled with frozen condensate. There were no etchings or pictographs to indicate what purpose the controls served, only a series of colored light pads, only two of which were still illuminated.

"Some power systems are still online," I said to Shon. As soon as we had all crossed and our air lock closed, so did the derelict's. "And the proximity sensors are functioning." The lock flooded with atmosphere, which I scanned and found to be a harmless mixture of oxygen and nitrogen. "They're air breathers."

Shon initiated the portable biodecon unit, which detected no harmful microorganisms inside the ship. "The internal temperature is rising."

"I guess it knows we're here." I waited until the atmosphere wouldn't flash-freeze my face off, and then removed my helmet and breathed in. "Cold, but tolerable." I nodded to the others.

Our exhalations made a few white puffs as we moved forward into the ship. The first compartment was largely empty, containing only a few odd-shaped objects that seemed to be containers of cargo or supplies. The deck had been fashioned from some sort of orange alloy in a solid sheet that curved up into walls and continued over to form the upper deck. There were no visible seams, emitters, or other devices anywhere, but a soft amber light appeared and filled the compartment. Then one of the walls lit up and showed a series of complicated-looking symbols.

"We've been welcomed, I think," I said over my suitcom. "Captain, are you seeing this?"

"Yes, but our archivists cannot identify the language."

"Transmit it to Joren," I suggested. "Reever may be able to do something with it."

How simple it was for me to say that, now that I'd disconnected my feelings from my husband and our wretched relationship. I expected by the time I returned to Joren, I'd be able to look at Reever and feel nothing at all.

"The crew compartment is this way," Shon told me, pointing to an opening in the back.

I looked at the other men. "Stay here."

The oKiaf and I made our way through the opening and along a narrow passage into the adjoining compartment. The amber light preceded us like a guide showing the way.

"An interesting form of energy conservation," Shon observed as he studied the fluctuating light. "The environmental systems must be designed to respond to the presence of the crew."

"Hopefully the air isn't working off the same system." I stopped to scan some racks from which hung strange-looking garments too small to fit an adult. "Odd. I didn't see any infants in those tanks."

Shon took down one garment, which seemed to melt the moment he touched it. Then I realized it was stretching itself into a larger shape. After another moment he was holding a one-piece fitted garment that appeared to be sized for his body.

"Biomalleable clothing with self-fitting sensors," I guessed. "Clever way to save space and still stay fashionable."

"Indeed." He hung it back on the rack.

Around a wall that brightened to show us more of the incomprehensible symbols, we entered the area that the drone had encountered. I counted twenty-one tanks, all of which were occupied by bodies. My first scan confirmed that the crew were locked in stasis; their life signs barely registered. The semiliquid suspension scanned as pure, partially solid protocrystal, identical to the mineral found on Shon's homeworld except for the structure of the hardened portions.

"The crystalline formation is different," he told me. "It does not correspond with the samples taken from oKia or my body."

"It hasn't killed them yet, so maybe it *is* different." I crouched down to study the eight control panels encircling the base of one tank. "These are monitors, I think." After my scanner showed no conduits leading into the deck, I glanced up. "Where's the power feed?"

"I cannot locate it." He scanned the length of one tank. "They are not drawing power from the ship."

"Well, something has to be keeping them alive." I spotted an aperture at the base of the tank and peered over it. "This looks like a shunt." I noted the tiny glyphs all around the outside rim, and the design of the membrane stretched across the interior. "Give me one of your specimen containers, and stand back."

I took out a syrinpress, and touched the infuser to the center of the membrane. It formed a seal around it, and I slowly drew out a small sample of the protocrystal fluid. When I drew the instrument away, the membrane sealed itself. I immediately dropped the syrinpress into the specimen container and sealed it.

A moment later my instrument became covered with hardened crystals, and then dissolved into a clear puddle.

"It will eat through the container," Shon murmured.

"I don't think so." I watched it for a moment, and when it didn't react to the container, I handed it to him. "We need to take this back to the ship for analysis before we attempt an extraction."

When we rejoined the rest of the team, I saw the engineer busy performing some scans of his own on the interior hull, but whatever was showing up on his device had him shaking his head in disbelief. "Healer Torin, you should see this."

I went over and eyed his scanner display. "It can't identify the ship's structural materials. Well, that's not much of a surprise."

"This is." He scrolled down through the data until he came to a series of readings. "I scanned the carbon content inside the air lock as well as this compartment. The readings indicate that they are approximately six million years old."

I didn't understand what he was saying. "Does that mean it took them six million years to make the jump through time?"

"It is a comparative reading," he corrected. "The carbon on this ship predates our time by six million years."

"So this thing came from the past, not the future." I gazed around the compartment. "Is there anything else you can tell me about it?"

"The power generating the light is not coming from the ship's systems," he said. "They operate on energy drawn from an exterior source."

"I did not see any reservoirs or reserve tanks on the exterior hull," Shon put in.

"The power is not contained on the ship; it is only being funneled through it," the engineer said. "According to my scans, it is being drawn directly from the rift."

Eight

After inspecting the rest of the derelict ship, we signaled the launch and returned to the *Sunlace* with the sample from the stasis tanks. While the engineer and the guards met with Xonea to brief him, Shon and I took the specimen to Medical.

"When Reever was studying the black crystal, he made use of a secured lab on another level that was not occupied by the crew," the oKiaf said as I initiated quarantine seals on the room and buffered them with a sterile field. "He felt there would be less threat to the ship if all possible precautions were taken."

"This isn't black crystal, and I'm not Duncan Reever." I placed the container in a shielded tank we used to test irradiated and infectious specimens. "It won't do anything to us."

He put a paw out to stop me from accessing the medsysbank. "How can you know that? You saw what it did to my body."

"Jarn saw. I just read your chart." I knew my actions must have seemed reckless to him, but I also knew I was right. "This is not the protocrystal that exists in our time, Shon. It's at least six million years old."

"Age has not rendered it harmless," he said. "You saw what it did to the syrinpress."

"But it hasn't hurt the crew of that ship, and it didn't try to attack me when I took a sample." I pulled off one of my gloves. "If you need proof, I'll put my hand in the container."

His eyes narrowed. "You are behaving irrationally."

I couldn't agree with him. I'd never felt more sure of anything in my life. But I also knew he could cause a lot of trouble for me, maybe even have Xonea toss me in a detainment cell. "I'm concerned about the people trapped in this stuff. I'd like to get them out of there. But you're right, I'm probably moving too fast." I thought for a moment. "We have air lock access through the waste venting system. We'll set up a specimen-collection probe and keep it handy. If this sample so much as twitches the wrong way, I'll dump it in the probe and flush it out into space. Satisfied?"

He didn't look happy. "Very well."

We spent the next six hours studying the sample, which behaved itself while we subjected it to a full spectrum of scans. It didn't register on the atomic level as being any different from common quartz, found in abundance on thousands of worlds throughout our galaxy. There was only one primary difference in its composition, and that was the energy infusing it.

"It is not kinetic, thermal, gravitational, radiant, or electromagnetic," Shon said after assessing the readings. "The scanners cannot classify it or its system. All they can determine is that the power level is constant."

"When the interactions of any particles aren't dependent on time, the total energy of the system remains constant." I went around the tank to take another image scan. "But I don't think this is the kind of energy that subjects itself to too many physical laws."

"Do you know what it is?"

"Not well enough to call it by its first name." I straightened and pressed a hand to the small of my back, which was aching slightly. "Maybe it's simply alive."

"Then our scanners would identify it as bioelectric energy."

"Not that kind of life. A different order of life. Maybe higher, maybe lower. Obviously not on the same playing field as we are." I went over to the console and downloaded the images I'd scanned, and then pulled them up and enlarged them several thousand times.

What I saw on the monitor didn't correlate with what I knew, at least until I began making the connections. However advanced the technology was that created the rift ship, it still had to pass through an anomaly that emitted extreme levels of radiation along with bizarre, multidirectional gravitational fields. The crew's fragile bodies would never have survived the passage without significant protection.

The lab around me slowly faded away as memories began flashing through my mind. I didn't want to think of that makeshift hospital, and the thousands of dying colonists I had been so desperately trying to save. Too many of them had died before I had discovered what had made them sick.

But I had to remember. There was something important that had happened to me that day, something I'd forgotten. . . .

When I returned to Reever's cot, I found Ana kneeling beside him, her hands pressed to the sides of his face.

"Physical contact helps Duncan to communicate," she said. *I didn't tell her I already knew that from personal experience. She concentrated for a moment, then shook her head. "There's something wrong. I can't reach him."*

"It's no use." I touched her shoulder. "We'll have to revive him, Ana."

She looked down at her hands on Reever's face, then back up at me. Something vital flared into her gaze. "Wait, I have an idea. Give me your hand." She joined it to Reever's and placed hers on top of both. "He won't respond to me, but I think I can act as a conduit for you. Duncan discussed it with me once, a technique used to assist a nonverbal species. You may be able to reach him through me."

"He's sedated," I said as I shook my head. "It's not possible."

"If we do this while he's unconscious, will it prevent another seizure?" I nodded. "Duncan has . . . unusual abilities."

"Ana, he's on continuous sedation. Whatever abilities he has are fast asleep."

"We have to try."

"All right." It was a last-ditch effort, but at least it was one that wouldn't kill him. Another seizure would. "Tell me what to do."

Her hand tightened over mine and Reever's. "Call

to him in your mind, Joey. Call to him as you would a lover." I closed my eyes, thinking of Kao. "No," she said. "Call to Duncan.*"*

I tried. It was difficult to shut out the sounds of the dying around me. I thought of the few times Reever had touched me, linking with me, and tried to summon that same sensation.

Reever. Come to me, Reever, I'm waiting. We need you. I need you.

Something slowly seeped into me, coalesced, became a presence. A semblance of Duncan Reever masked it, but I knew it wasn't him.

"Something else," I said. Ana made an encouraging sound, and I tried to intensify the connection by concentrating. "Not Reever."

I was plunged into a liquid, moving darkness. All around me, I felt not one presence but a multitude. Hundreds, thousands, even millions.

I blinked, and I was back on the *Sunlace*, sitting in front of the lab terminal and staring at the image display. The protocrystal looked nothing like the Core that had caused the plague on Kevarzangia Two, but it reminded me of that terrible day at the isolation facility because it shared something with the Core.

Intelligence. Consciousness.

Purpose.

"What are you doing?" I heard Shon ask.

"We were wrong." I shook off the feeling of déjà vu and set aside my memories. "It's not a liquid. Look."

He joined me and studied the magnified view, which showed billions of tiny, three-sided crystalline structures suspended in equally infinitesimal energy fields. "They look like nanites."

"No." I increased the magnification to show the interior of one of the little crystals. "Do you see it now?"

He peered at the screen. "Increase to maximum resolution."

The console would only magnify to one million times, but that was enough for Shon to see the internal structure of the crystal. It was made up of billions of tinier, triangular-shaped crystals suspended in their own energy fields.

"If I were able to zoom in on one of those," I said, "I imagine we'd find that they're made up of the same crystal matrix, too."

"What is it?" he murmured.

"There are a couple of inadequate names for it." My own wonder and excitement subsided, and something cooler took its place as realization began to sink in. "Infinity. Eternity. Forever. Take your pick."

He backed away from the monitor. "This is not possible."

"Look at it this way: The next time someone asks you how the universe began, you can tell them there was no beginning. It just was, is, and will be." I switched off the image. "I think we should call it quits; how about you?"

"How can you be so collected about this, this . . ." He gave up and gestured toward the tank.

"Immortality rock?" I regarded the specimen. "I guess I'm becoming hard to wow in my old age."

"You believe this is a different mineral from the protocrystal that inhabits my homeworld."

"Well, the atomic structures are quite different, and the three-sided formation is new, but it's the same rock. This specimen happens to be more evolved." I switched off the sterile field and pulled off my gloves. "I'd say this is what your protocrystal will look like in a few million years, once it's had time to grow."

His expression became exasperated. "We know from the carbon dating of the ship that this specimen came from the past."

"You're still thinking in linear terms: a past and a future, a beginning and an end. Those rules don't apply to something that isn't governed by them. Like this crystal." I patted his shoulder. "Try not to think about it too much. You'll just end up with a really bad headache."

I knew it was petty of me not to explain everything in minute detail to Shon, but we both had the same enhanced brains and upgraded diagnostic capabilities. If he couldn't figure it out on his own, maybe he'd sleep better tonight. I already knew I wouldn't.

After I secured the lab, I left Medical and went directly to my quarters. In the old days I would have stopped in the galley for a meal and spent some time socializing, but as much as I liked the Jorenians, I was in no mood for chitchat. I needed to think.

I took a shower, picked at a meal I didn't want, and then went to my terminal to do a little work. At first I ran some simulations on the retroviral compound I had formulated for PyrsVar's treatment, but then I closed the file and began reviewing all the available data we had collected so far from the derelict.

Energy was what bonded the crystals into a pseudoliquid state; I was certain that merging the field was what solidified the matrix. If I could figure out how to temporarily disrupt the energy fields being generated by the individual crystals, I might be able to release the derelict's crew from stasis.

The question now was, did I want to?

A light blinked on my console, indicating a new signal was waiting for my attention. Once I'd verified that it hadn't come from Command—I had no interest in verbally sparring another round with the captain—I opened the relay.

My daughter's face appeared on the display. She wasn't looking at the screen, but over her shoulder. "Like this, Fasala?"

I heard Salo's daughter murmur something in the background.

Marel turned toward the screen. "Healer Cherijo, this is your daughter. I'm signaling you from Joren. You left without saying good-bye to me or Daddy. I don't know why you did that—Daddy won't tell me—but ever since he brought me back to the pavilion, he's been different. Sad, and mad, and hurt. He won't tell me why."

"And he never will," I told my daughter, even though she couldn't hear me.

"I know you are my first mama, the mama who made me," Marel continued. "I wasn't very nice to you when you came back because I don't know you. I don't remember you. Jarn was my mama. I loved her."

My throat tightened. "I know, baby, I know."

"Daddy said you love me and him as much as Jarn did." She frowned. "That's why I don't understand this. You came back and then went away again so fast. Daddy says you may not come back to Joren for a long time. Now you don't have us and we don't have anyone."

I wanted to reassure her, but what was I going to say? *Your father doesn't want me? I can't stand to be in the same room with him? You're going to have to pick a parent, kid, because they can't live together anymore?*

I'd have to signal Reever and have him deal with this, I decided. He had her affection; I didn't. He was also there with her; what could I do on a ship that was light-years away?

"I was naughty when Daddy took me to the capital," my daughter confessed. "I didn't want to go and be with you. I fussed at him and I cried. I wanted to stay with Fasala and my friends here. They're my kin. But I didn't mean to make you go away again, Healer Cherijo." She made a beautiful gesture with her hands. "We should be with our family on the journey, so they can help us. That is the way."

"They turned you into a little Jorenian while I was gone, didn't they?" I didn't mind. There were far worse things to be in the universe than the beloved adopted child of a species who would rip to pieces anyone who tried to harm you—as I knew from personal experience.

"I didn't ask Daddy if I could signal you tonight, so I'm still being naughty," my daughter confessed. "But he's so sad and lonely now, Healer Cherijo. He doesn't eat or sleep, and when he looks at me, I don't think he sees me anymore. I didn't stop Jarn when she left Joren, even though I knew I wouldn't see her again. It's my fault she died. I don't want to lose my daddy, too."

I took in a ragged breath, and checked the time stamp on the signal. Marel had sent it five hours ago, and according to the time difference, it was currently the middle of the night on Joren. I couldn't even signal back and speak to her; she wouldn't get the relay for hours—assuming Reever would even let her view it. But I couldn't let her go on blaming herself for Jarn's death.

"I think you must be angry with us, and maybe you should be, but I am sorry. I don't want you to be alone out there." She put her hand to the screen, as if she wanted to reach through the monitor and touch me. "You've been lost and alone for so long, being away from us again now must hurt you, too. I didn't think about that. I never meant to make you feel that way."

Tears spilled down my cheeks. I put my hand on the display, pressing it to the image of hers.

"I ask your pardon for all my wrongs, Mama," Marel said in Jorenian, taking away her hand to make the formal accompanying gesture. "If you would come back to Joren, I will be a good ClanDaughter and behave myself. I will go wherever you and Daddy want me to. And I won't be mean to you anymore. Just please come back soon. Daddy and I need you here."

I watched Fasala Torin come up behind Marel, put an arm around her, and reach toward the console. The signal terminated and my screen went blank.

I got up and went to the viewport to stare out at space. I didn't know how long I stood there, my eyes filled with stars and tears; I couldn't think straight. Marel's pleading words echoed in my mind, over and over in a torturous loop.

. . . *You left without saying good-bye. . . . Now you don't have us and we don't have anyone. . . . Daddy and I need you here. . . .*

I slid down the hull wall until I sat on the deck and huddled with my arms around my legs and my forehead pressed to my knees. Whatever Reever and I had done to each other, Marel didn't deserve to pay for it. At the same time, I knew she would have to.

Although I loved my child, and would do anything to prevent her from suffering, I couldn't do as she had begged me to. I couldn't go back to Joren and pretend, not even for her sake, that everything was fine between me and her father. Reever might be the best liar in the universe, but I wasn't. Every moment I spent with him, I'd be replaying in my head that surveillance vid of him with Jarn. I'd hear all those lovely, terrible things he'd said to her. I'd see the flare of passion between them as they made love. And until the end of my days, I'd see the look on his face when I'd woken up in my body and he'd realized who I wasn't.

Marel had lost a mother she had dearly loved, and Duncan had lost his lover, but I'd lost both of them.

There would be no going back for any of us.

Two days of making trips to the derelict ship and studying the protocrystal that held the crew in stasis should have produced some definitive information about the rift, the ship, and why both had showed up in our time. But on the third day, at a briefing Xonea insisted we broadcast over interplanetary to both Joren and Vtaga, I had very few answers to offer.

"At present, we know that the ship came from the very distant past," I said as I displayed on the room monitors the readings that had been collected from the derelict. "Minimal life signs indicate that the crew is still alive, although we have been unable to determine a safe method of extracting them from the crystal matrix that holds them in stasis."

"Is it entirely necessary to rouse the crew?" TssVar asked.

"If you want some real answers, it is." I turned toward the monitor where his image was displayed. "These people traveled six million years to get here, Hanar. We have to assume they had an important mission, or at least an extremely good reason to attempt such an epic jump."

"Can we send the ship back into the rift?" Xonea asked.

My brows rose. "We could, theoretically. Why would we want to?"

"Perhaps they never meant to come here," the captain pointed out. "They may have become trapped in the rift during a routine jaunt and were transported here against their wishes."

"That would be a viable scenario," I agreed, "if every member of the crew had not placed themselves in stasis before entering the rift."

"What makes you believe they did so?" one of the council members asked.

"We've analyzed the stasis tanks thoroughly." I brought up a holoimage of one of them. "I can't tell you how they are able to function, but there are a few things we know about them. The control panels at the base of the capsules appear to be dedicated monitors that measure the occupant's vital signs; the readings that are displayed match those of our instruments. There also seems to be some sort of connection between the panels and some of the consoles located in a section of the ship our engineers had dubbed the helm."

"The ship controls the stasis chambers?"

"I believe that the controls for the tanks are located inside them, here." I pointed to the wide belt around the floating figure. "From the design, it appears that the crew first climbed into the tanks, and then initiated stasis."

"That cannot be the case. There must be an automated control system outside the tanks," TssVar argued. "Once in stasis, they could not release themselves."

"We should bring this ship to Joren," one of the council members suggested. "HouseClan Zamlon has some of the finest engineers in the quadrant. The vessel can be kept safely in their shipyards while it is examined."

"The ship is funneling power into all of its systems directly from the rift," Shon said. "If we attempt to relocate the ship, it will lose its power source."

"As the stasis chambers are dependent on that power," I added, "I can almost guarantee disconnecting it will kill the crew."

The chief engineer gestured, and after Xonea nodded to him, he stood. "My department has been working with several pilots during our analysis of the ship. As yet we have been unable to gain access to its database or computer systems, assuming it possesses such technology, but several of the pilots involved have recognized certain features of the star charts that appear at regular intervals on the interior walls." He indicated the imager console. "If I may?"

The captain inclined his head, and the chief brought up a holoimage of two star charts. "The image on the right is from the *Sunlace*'s chart archives. It displays the position of all inhabited star systems throughout our galaxy. The image on the left was scanned from one of the display walls inside the derelict. It is also an image of our galaxy, as you can see." He merged the two charts together, superimposing the stars.

"You are in error, Chief," someone murmured. "Most of the stars have moved, and many are gone."

"This was also our first conclusion, until we identified the star systems that had disappeared. Each possesses a star coming to the end of its life span." He removed the chart showing our galaxy and left up the one scanned from the ship. "According to database projections, this chart shows what our galaxy will look like in ten million years."

Xonea gave him a sharp look. "Think you they intended to journey sixteen million years into the future?"

"I cannot say for certain." He made an uneasy gesture. "But why would they project the decay of stars in such a fashion if it were not their destination?"

"Then what are they doing here?" one of the Hsktskt delegates asked.

"Something must have gone wrong," I said. "Something pulled them off course in the middle of their jump, and they landed here instead, in the wrong time."

"The rift may have formed in their jump path and caused the disruption," another engineer put in.

Shon shook his head. "The ship draws its power directly from the rift. It came with the ship through time. It may even be their method of propulsion."

There was a great deal of debate after that, and as I sat beside Shon and listened, the oKiaf leaned toward me.

"You did not share your findings on the nature of the stasis matrix," he murmured.

"I didn't tell them you were a touch-healer who can cure any injury or illness, either," I whispered back. "Should I volunteer that little fact?"

He made an amused sound. "We will have to destroy the sample."

"I don't think it can be destroyed," I replied. "I was thinking more along the lines of injecting it back into the tank." I caught Xonea frowning at us. "Let's talk about this later, shall we?"

After another hour of discussion, the captain finally gestured for silence. "We must decide now how to proceed. The ship's technology may take months or even years for us to understand; we may never be able to gain control of it. The rift is unstable and could collapse at any time. Healer Torin had theorized that moving the derelict away from it may threaten the lives of the crew, who are at our mercy. Council members, Hanar, based on what little information we have, I advise we send the ship back into the rift, in hopes that it will return them to their point of departure."

"Without ever knowing who they are, and what their mission is?" TssVar bristled with disapproval. "If their intentions were not benign, we would be sacrificing a valuable opportunity to protect our territories. No, I say we should take this vessel. We should tow it into the gravitational field of the nearest star."

I looked around the table, expecting to see plenty of horrified expressions. Most of the department chiefs instead looked thoughtful, as if his proposal had actual merit. "You can't be serious."

Xonea pretended he hadn't heard me. "We cannot predict what the ship's response would be, Hanar. It may possess systems to funnel energy from sources other than the rift. They may sense our actions and interpret them as a threat. Such an intervention could also trigger an awakening of the crew, who would doubtless respond. We have not yet identified any weapons systems, but it is unlikely they would undertake such a journey in a defenseless ship."

"This ship could just as well be a scout, and the crew put in stasis as a lure," TssVar countered. "Their technology may have already assessed ours and found it inferior. Sending it back could betray our weaknesses to an enemy. Who is to say that a fleet of warships is not on the other side of that rift, waiting to invade our time and conquer our worlds?"

"I can't decide which is more breathtaking," I said in the loudest voice I could manage. "The arrogance in this room, or the stupidity."

One of the Hsktskt commanders rose out of his seat as he drew a blade. "No warm-blood will speak so to the supreme ruler in my presence."

All the Jorenians present got to their feet, their dark blue claws ready as they looked toward Xonea, who had drawn the ceremonial seven-bladed sword he wore.

"I Shield the Hsktskt delegation," I said quickly. Then, before anyone could react, I added, "I name the occupants of the derelict vessel as my blood kin."

"They cannot be your kin," Xonea snarled. "They come from a world six million years in the past."

"They're very distant kin." I folded my arms. "Feel free to challenge my declaration if you like, Captain. All you really need is a DNA sample from one of them—and their permission to take it."

"What does this mean?" the Hanar demanded.

"Healer Cherijo has claimed kinship with the crew of the derelict," one of the council members said. "As such, they are to be protected by HouseClan Torin. Should harm be threatened or attempted against them, she may choose to declare ClanKill against the transgressor."

"It means," Xonea said through his teeth, "that we cannot destroy the ship or allow the crew to be harmed in any fashion."

"I have never regretted outlawing the practice of slavery," TssVar said as he stared down at me. "Until now."

"You had your chance." I turned to Xonea. "Assuming anything about this ship or this crew without more information is ridiculous, and you know it. Healer Valtas and I will put all of our efforts into reviving the crew, and then we will talk to them. Instead of imagining why they came here, tossing them back through an unstable rift, or shooting them into a star, we will behave like the civilized beings that we're supposed to be and *ask* them to tell us why they're here."

A guard came into the room and went to have a hushed conversation with Xonea, who abruptly announced that the briefing was over. He then gestured to me and Shon.

"Think he's going to throw us in the brig?" I said as we walked over.

The oKiaf chuffed out some air. "If he does, he will never get that DNA sample."

Xonea finished issuing orders to the guard in rapid Jorenian before he turned to us. "There has been a problem in Medical Bay. One of the crew passing in the corridor noticed that it appeared empty. Upon entering, she found the air supply had been tampered

with, and the entire staff had been rendered unconscious." He caught my arm as I turned to run. "They
are unharmed, Cherijo."

"But why? Why knock out my staff?"

"To keep them from interfering," Xonea said. "The
entry to your lab was found standing open, and the
sample of protocrystal you took from the derelict is
gone."

While Xonea and his men began searching through
the ship for the thief, Shon and I returned to Medical
to check on the staff. A few of the nurses had sustained
bumps and bruises from the spills they took—the gas
introduced into the air supply had been a powerful
anesthetic, and had caused them to literally drop in
their tracks—but no one had suffered any serious
injuries.

"There was no warning," the resident we'd left in
charge during the briefing said as I scanned the bump
on the back of his head. "We were reviewing mede-
vac procedures when one of the nurses standing nearest to the air duct fell to the deck. We tried to leave
before we were overcome, but the panels would not
open."

"Shon, tell Xonea to check the access log file for
the entry panel to Medical. Whoever locked down
the bay had to do it from the corridor." After ensur-
ing the resident didn't have a concussion, I infused
him with a mild analgesic and transferred him to a
berth for observation, and then moved on to the next
staffer waiting to be examined.

I didn't worry about the lab until I had checked
each and every one of the medical staff. I could have

delegated the task to someone else, but I was taking this very personally. Whoever had attacked my people might not have done any permanent damage, but that was just sheer luck. If one of the residents had been running a surgical training simulation with the interns, someone could have fallen onto the imager— or, worse, an activated lascalpel.

After I finished the exams, I went to join Shon in the lab, where he was scanning the remains of the tank where we had been storing the stasis specimen. One side of the tank was gone; the others appeared partially melted.

"I found a suture laser discarded on the deck. He must have used it to cut out this panel," the oKiaf told me, pointing to the missing section. "The beam setting was too high, which caused the damage to the other panels."

"So it wasn't anyone in Medical." No one on my staff would use a suture laser so clumsily. "But why do all this just to steal the specimen? Whoever did it can't take it off the ship. Even if he could somehow smuggle it off, it has no value to anyone but us."

"Perhaps the thief intended only to take it from us." He glanced over at the console. "Did you encrypt the last set of scans we performed?"

"Oh, I encrypt everything," I said, and went over to pull up our files. Which were no longer there. "It's all gone. The database has been wiped clean." I reached under and felt around until I retrieved a packet of discs. "He didn't think to check for backups, though. This guy is definitely an amateur."

"It could be one of the delegates. Even the Hanar's daughter." He caught the look on my face. "I know you are fond of her, Cherijo, but her first loyalty is to her people."

"I am a physician, Healer Valtas," ChoVa said as she walked in. "My first loyalty is to my oath." She studied the ruined tank. "How was this done?"

"We think he used a suture laser, not that he really knew how to use it."

"It appears that he misjudged the strength of the containment unit, as well." The Hsktskt made a contemptuous sound. "Were I your thief, oKiaf, I would simply use my fist and smash in the side of the tank."

"Healer?" one of the nurses called. "There is a signal at the station for you."

I went to answer it, and listened as Xonea described what he had found down in Engineering: more unconscious crew members, and an empty specimen container sitting on the deck next to a power conduit.

That meant the protocrystal could be anywhere. "You have to clear the crew out of there, and quarantine the entire level," I told him. "Right now."

Before he could respond, my console went dark, and the ship lurched under our feet. The light emitters overhead began flickering until they shut down, too, and the emergency lights snapped on.

"What the hell is going on?" I used my wristcom to signal the captain. "Xonea? What is your status?"

His voice was accompanied by the sound of men shouting in the background. "Someone has seized control of the helm. They have locked out all access to the navigation and propulsion systems. Evacuate your level to the emergency launches at once."

"Why are we abandoning ship?" I demanded, but he had terminated the signal.

I gave the order to the staff and cleared out the bay, sending Shon ahead to make sure everyone went to their assigned launch. Then I went to retrieve some triage packs. Through one of the viewports I saw the rift, no longer small and distant, but right in my face, impossibly huge, blocking out the rest of space. I thought at first it had somehow grown larger, until I felt the entire ship shudder violently, as if caught in some powerful force. Then I understood what was happening to us, and ran.

ChoVa was waiting in the corridor for me and took several packs. "Why did the captain order an evacuation?"

"Someone's taken control of the *Sunlace*," I told her, "and they're flying us into the rift."

Nine

We made it into the emergency launches, but that was all we had time to do. I heard the pilot engage the engines as I pulled my harness straps over my shoulders, and then the air in front of my face began to sparkle.

"It's here," I heard Shon say.

I felt his paw grope for my hand as the dazzling light expanded and streamed over me. A cascade of blinding golden stars pierced my eyes and poured into my mind, larger and brighter until I felt a scream well up in my throat and Shon's claws digging into my palm.

The feel of the soft fur and the bright pain jerked me back into the shadows of my memory.

"They ordered us not to kill you," the strange alien voice said, "but said we could use you as often as we wished."

I came to, but only just. My limbs felt heavy and dull, and my mind clouded, as if I had been drugged. Distantly I felt the restraints on my limbs; I'd been manacled and chained.

The cabin we were in slowly revolved around us,

items tumbling out of containers, equipment smashing against the interior walls.

"My brother has no taste for your kind." The claws that had been choking me only a few moments before caressed my cheek. "But I wondered. I wondered how you might be."

I wanted to look through the viewport and see how close we were to the surface. "Oforon, there is still time to send a distress signal."

"I've tried. No one will respond. The Toskald are blocking all transmissions." *Black eyes squeezed shut as he held on to my chains, the only thing keeping him and me from tumbling about the cabin.* "The League would not come even if they received it. We were always expendable, my brother and I."

The wind buffeting the transport began to howl outside the hull, a petulant child frustrated with a toy it could not break. "My husband and daughter care about me."

"You think they still search for you?" *Oforon uttered a sound of sour amusement.* "You're a fool. They believed Shropana's ruse, just as everyone else did. They think you long dead."

I had felt dead, until this moment. I wasn't Jorenian, but at last I understood why they left behind messages for their kin. I couldn't go into the embrace of the stars without speaking one last time to the ones I loved.

"Please." *I had no problem with begging, not when it came to Reever and Marel.* "Release me, let me send one signal. Only one, I promise. I must say good-bye to my family."

"No." *His grip on the chains tightened as the ship spun faster.* "If the signal is intercepted by others, they will relay it to Shropana in hopes of collecting the reward for you. He will use it as an excuse to invalidate our contract. My family will get nothing."

He punched me in the face, and I fell into the dark. I don't know how long I was there, but when I woke, I felt sweat slicking my skin, and my heart hammering with frantic fists under my breast.

I couldn't die. Not like this.

"You won't die, Terran," Oforon snarled, as if he could hear my thoughts. Hot flecks of his saliva pelted my face. "Not from the sickness, not from beatings. What will it take to kill you?"

I tried to answer him, but the silencer strapped to my face plugged my mouth.

"We're going to crash." He said this bitterly, angrily, as if it were my fault. His claws jerked the collar up, completely cutting off my air. "Maybe that will finish you. Do you wish for death?" He released the collar and reached up to wrench the silencer out of my mouth. "Tell me now."

"Don't be afraid, Oforon," I said. "It will be quick."

He curled his claws into a ball, and drew them back as if to hit me in the face. Then his eyes closed, and he fell to his knees, his head back, a terrible howl tearing from his throat.

I wanted to wrap my arms around him, to comfort him in these last moments. All I could do was rest my cheek against the top of his mane.

The void that followed that vision seemed almost merciful. In it, I had no thought, no awareness, no sense of self or surroundings at all. I wasn't unconscious or conscious. My abductor no longer existed; no one did. I hung between the two states, caught in a moment of time and trapped there, unable to go back or forward, helpless to do anything but be in that place.

I could leave it; on some level I knew that, because I had done it before. My body might have been bio-engineered to last forever, but it was a thing apart from me. I could shed it like a garment and move beyond this torment. I understood the path and where it would take me. I knew what was waiting beyond it. More of the same suffering and outrage and agony. An eternity of it.

So many things had been done to me during my brief life. So much had been violated, stripped away, and stolen, all without my consent. I had been drowning in the ugliness of that existence. But this, this decision, could not be touched or swayed or removed from me. I could leave behind all the pain and horror and wretchedness I had known. I could finally be free.

This time, I would stay. This time, I would be alone forever.

The between grew colder, and smaller, sinking inside me until I became the prison and the prisoner. Intolerable. Inescapable. If I didn't choose, I'd spend eternity shrinking down until I was the size of a crystal of a crystal of a crystal of a crystal. . . .

I opened my eyes, only vaguely surprised to find myself hunched over, half in and half out of my seat harness. The warm weight of Shon's head rested against my shoulder. The light had disappeared. The rest of the crew in the launch appeared to be unconscious.

I felt brittle and numb as I eased Shon off me and back in his seat before I staggered to my feet. Slowly I moved around the compartment, checking him and the crew. Their body temperatures were low, but their vital signs were strong. Everyone had survived the passage through the rift.

Shon was the first to regain consciousness, and he looked at me through unfocused eyes. "We're alive."

"Looks that way." I chafed his paws between my hands and tried to smile. "When your legs feel steady, I could use some help."

Another hour passed before the crew began to wake up. We used it to make rounds of the launches and the corridors, and found the Hsktskt to be in the worst shape. We wrapped them in emergency thermal packs where they lay; they were too large and heavy to move easily.

Some of my nurses stumbled out of the launches and came to assist us with reviving the rest of the crew, but it was slow going. I found Xonea behind the launch bay's main console, his hands still on the board. He had been trying to open the outer doors when we'd entered the rift, which would have killed him the moment the bay depressurized.

In spite of my ire with him I felt a reluctant admiration for my ClanBrother. He might be an interfering jackass, but he was the captain of his ship, and he would have sacrificed himself in order to save his crew.

White eyes opened as I took his pulse. "Cherijo. Did we embrace the stars together?"

"The rift embraced us, I think," I said as I scanned two ugly gashes on the side of his neck. "What did this?" I glanced down and saw blood on his hands, and lifted one to inspect it. "Xonea?"

"I could not open the hull doors," he said. "When the light came over me, I thought I would make it quick." He drew his hand away. "What of the others?"

"The Hsktskt aren't in great shape," I admitted, "and the crew is cold and disoriented and a little banged up, but I think everyone will be all right."

Some color returned to his face. "We must have passed through the rift."

"I don't know anything else that could have done this. We'd better keep everyone in the launches until we know if the environmental system is still functioning," I suggested as I applied a pressure dressing to the wounds on his neck. "This will hold you for now, but you're going to need some sutures."

"After I assess our situation." He tried to use the console, but the unit was powerless and off-line. "What need you now for the crew?"

"We have triage packs on the launches, and my people are all right," I assured him. "Once we know it's safe to stay on the ship, I'll need some glide gurneys and a couple of strong hands to transport the Hsktskt over to Medical."

"Healer." An intern waved at us from a launch I hadn't yet checked.

"I'd better get back to work." I hurried off.

Shon was already inside the launch and working on a pilot who had flash burns on his face and hands, and what appeared to be a pulse pistol embedded in his chest. On the other side of the deck, a second pilot sat holding a burned arm with a compound fracture near the elbow.

"Report," I said as I knelt down beside them and opened my case.

"The pilot attempted to use his weapon after entering the rift." Shon gingerly tried to extract the power cell from the base of the pistol, without success. "The copilot attempted to stop him."

I gloved and scanned the chest wound. "Punctured lung, internal burns, hemorrhaging—what the hell was he thinking?"

"He shouted that he was being crushed," the co-pilot said, his voice tight with pain. "I felt the same sensation, but when I heard the weapon being activated . . ." He looked at his arm. "I could not permit him to shoot me. I meant him no harm, lady."

"You were both hallucinating," I told the copilot as I measured the depth of the penetrating wound. "We can't remove the pistol; the end of the barrel is plugging the hole in his heart."

Shon gave me a direct look. "The weapon's power cell prevents anything I could do for him here."

Which meant he couldn't touch-heal the pilot, and I couldn't operate on him, not on the deck of a launch with no instruments. I shouted for a gurney.

The nurse touched my arm. "Healer, we cannot know yet if it is safe to return to Medical."

"That's why Healer Valtas and I are going." I glanced at the copilot. "Wrap that fracture, immobilize the limb, and try to keep him comfortable until you're permitted to transport him to the bay."

Xonea insisted on sending two guards with us, something I didn't think was necessary until we encountered all the debris in the corridors. Every storage unit seemed to have dumped its contents in our path, and the two warriors cleared and climbed and kicked their way ahead of us to clear a path to a still-operable lift.

"Remind me to talk to the captain about getting you guys some serious additional compensation," I told them, earning a grin from both.

Medical was likewise a mess, but we quickly confirmed that we still had power to some of the equipment and two of the surgical suites. I sent the guards back to launch bay to report on what we'd encountered, while Shon and I prepped the pilot.

He heard the faint whine before I did. "Cherijo, listen. Do you hear that?"

"No." I stopped scrubbing and cocked my head. "Yes. Sounds like power arcing." I glanced around, looking for sparks or smoke, and then saw a faint yellowish glow coming from under the drape over our patient's chest. "For God's sake, not now."

Shon pulled back the drape and scanned the pulse pistol. "The focusing unit and safeties must have been damaged during the transition through the rift."

I stopped scrubbing and grabbed the end of the gurney. "How long do we have?"

He shook his head. "Minutes, perhaps."

It would have to be long enough. I shoved the gurney into the surgical suite and maneuvered it over to the procedure table. Shon helped me slide the pilot's body off the gurney and into position under the laser rig.

"Go and get the probe from the lab," I told him as I grabbed a rolling instrument tray and dragged it over to the table.

"You cannot use the lascalpel," he reminded me before he ran out.

The whine came from the pulse pistol's power cell, which was still engaged and trying to feed pulse energy into the focusing unit of the weapon. If the pistol had been functional, that would have merely burned a hole through the pilot's spine and killed him. But the weapon was damaged, and the focusing unit disabled, which sent the pulses of power directly back into the cell. This was causing a critical-mass buildup that we had no way of stopping. The explosion would vaporize the patient, me, Shon, and at least half the deck.

Worse, I couldn't use a laser-powered instrument anywhere near the power cell, as its beam could also trigger a detonation.

I hunted through the manual instruments on the tray and found a dermal probe with a sharp enough edge to cut through flesh. After administering a neuroparalyzer, I made my first incision to the right of the embedded pistol, in a section of the rib cage that I knew would be wide enough for what I had to do.

This wasn't surgery; this was barbarism, and it went against every iota of my training. But with the weapon about to detonate, I didn't have time to do otherwise.

I shoved my hand into the incision, working my arm as I pushed my fingers past the tough outer membranes and muscles. The feel of his rib bones scraping against the back of my knuckles and the heel of my palm gave me the creeps. So did feeling the sponginess of his collapsed lung as I groped by touch for the compromised aortic junction.

My sensitive fingertips found the place where the tip of the weapon had penetrated. With my free hand, I gripped the heated stock of the pistol and used a steady pressure to work it free. As soon as the tip slid back, I put two fingertips into the hole it left behind, plugging the junction as best as I could. Then I pulled the pistol out of his chest with a fast jerk.

It had already grown so hot that it scalded my hand, but I didn't let go. "Shon."

"I have it." He took the pistol from me and, as the

smell of burning fur filled the suite, carefully placed it inside the specimen container within the probe. He sealed it and carried it over to the biohazardous disposal unit.

"Disengage the sterilizer first," I snapped as I felt the pilot's heart rate beginning to speed up. "And hurry. He's going into cardiogenic shock."

I held my breath as Shon placed the probe inside the unit, tapped the console to override the disposal's first-stage operation, and enabled the venting system. A moment later I bent over the patient as something exploded just beyond the hull wall, sending a wrenching shock wave through the entire level.

"That was too close." The oKiaf closed his eyes as he braced his hands on the unit and murmured something under his breath.

"You can pray later," I told him as I reached for a clamp. "For now, come over here and help me get my hand out of this man's chest."

The pilot's collapsed lung, along with injury to the aortic junction, which directly affected the left ventricular muscle mass, reduced his cardiac output to the point of imminent heart failure. Hypoperfusion had already begun, and if he didn't suffer a massive MI, then his organs would begin failing and there would be nothing we could do to bring him back.

Shon transferred the patient over to the heart-lung machine before cutting through the remains of the sternum and spreading open the interior chest.

"On three." I handed him the artery clamp. "One . . . two . . . three." I pulled my fingertips out of the artery, and he immediately clamped shut the perforation. After I applied suction to clear leaking blood, I in-

spected the wound. "The tissue is burned, damn it."
That meant the damaged section of the artery would
have to be replaced by a graft, something his poor
condition didn't allow us time to do.

"If you will permit me to try to heal him?" he
asked, and at my nod placed his paw directly over the
gaping chest cavity.

I watched, fascinated, as the pads of the oKiaf's
paw began to glow, infusing the area with a soft white
light. Gradually the wound in the artery began to pull
together, sealing its own edges. Instead of forming
scar tissue, Shon's power erased the wound, restoring
the vessel to its original condition.

He took away his hand, his breathing heavy now,
and swayed a little as he stepped back.

"Hey, don't quit just yet," I said as I reinflated the
collapsed lung. "You're the best natural lascalpel I've
ever met."

"Something is wrong." He swallowed. "I almost
could not finish. I do not think I can do any more for
him."

"No problem." I pulled down the laser rig. "I can
manage the rest the old-fashioned way. Why don't
you take a walk, get some air."

"I will stay and assist." He sounded shaken, but he
seemed steadier as he inserted a chest tube and repositioned the instrument tray between us.

"If you feel like passing out, please don't do it on
the patient," I warned before I went back to work inside the pilot's chest.

Several hours passed before I had repaired enough
of the internal damage to risk taking the pilot off life
support. If we couldn't restart his heart, it would have
all been for nothing, but our luck held. After direct

electrostim the organ contracted and began pumping vigorously.

"We do nice work together, Shon," I said as I checked for bleeders and then began to close. "It's just a shame you couldn't do the rest of his chest. Does that happen to you very often?"

"Never," he told me. "Even when I drew on every ounce of my power to heal Jadaira on K-2, I did not feel this weak afterward. Something is wrong."

"Something in here?" I glanced around the suite.

"No. This place is wrong—where the ship is now. I feel . . ." He hesitated, as if he didn't like admitting it. "Diminished. As if my ability to heal is somehow being drained away."

"You were just pushed through a rift in space," I advised him. "I think you're entitled to be a little off your game."

He eyed me. "But it does not seem to have affected you."

"I'm not a touch-healer." But even as I said that, I knew what he meant. I had been the first to regain consciousness, and I wasn't suffering any ill effects from the painful passage. Truth be told, I felt better than I had since waking back up in my body.

Then it occurred to me why he was giving me such an odd look.

"Shon, I had nothing to do with this. I was at the briefing with you when the specimen was stolen, and also when the ship was pirated. Nothing, not even that protocrystal, is worth endangering the lives of the crew. These people aren't just my friends and colleagues. They're the only family I have left."

Most of the suspicion faded from his expression. "I should not have assumed you were responsible. It is only strange that the ship would be taken so soon after you prevented the Jorenians and the Hsktskt from harming the crew of the derelict. Then to find that you alone were unaffected by the passage. You have had such violent reactions to transitions in the past that I expected . . . but perhaps the nature of the rift somehow protected you."

I considered telling him what I had experienced during the passage through the rift, and then discarded the idea. "I understand. Why don't you see if we can get the staff back here and start assessing the injured? I'm going to move our patient into recovery and clear some working room. And Shon." He turned back toward me. "I don't know if we really are brother and sister, or just two random victims of an unkind universe. It doesn't matter to me anymore. You're part of my family now."

He inclined his head and left the suite.

Shon returned to Medical with most of the staff, a dozen guards, and all of the Hsktskt on gurneys. Most of the lizards were semiconscious but still very sluggish from cold exposure. PyrsVar volunteered to tend to them in order to free up the staff, and I accepted immediately. We had five times as many injured crew members to assess and treat, and more would probably be arriving as search teams cleared corridors and checked other areas of the ship.

I asked Shon to supervise the treatment of the co-pilot with the burned, broken arm. Even if he couldn't use his ability, he was an extremely capable physician and was particularly gifted in dealing with orthopedic cases. While he worked on him, I ended up back in surgery with a female maintenance technician who had been loading temporary-shelter materials onto a launch, and reported with a plasteel rod protruding from one side of her torso. She'd limped to Medical on her own while using another rod as a makeshift crutch.

"Others needed the gurneys more than I," she said, glancing down at the rod in her side. "I would have removed it myself, Healer, but for what you taught us during our first aid training."

"You probably would have lost a lot more blood if you had." I couldn't remember her or the training she had mentioned. "When did you take that first-aid course?"

"Last year. I asked about the proper treatment of botanical poisons, and you said . . ." She stopped and made a quick gesture. "Forgive me, Healer, but it was your other self who trained us. Jarn thought all of the crew should be ready to minister to themselves and each other in times of emergency. She said that was the way of her people."

Jarn was dead and gone, but she was still managing to piss me off. "Her people were unwanted slaves left to die on a very nasty world. We're a little more civilized and sophisticated than they were."

She moved her shoulders. "Perhaps here we will be the same."

By the end of the day we had admitted twelve patients and had ordered twenty more back to their quarters to rest and recover from stress fractures, contusions, and lacerations. In addition to the impact injuries, every patient I saw had suffered a mild to moderate case of hypothermia.

I scheduled two more shifts in addition to our standard rotation so that no one worked in Medical for longer than a few hours at a time. None of my weary staff protested. Then I left the bay in Shon's hands as I went to find Xonea.

I found my ClanBrother coordinating repairs from the secondary command center in the heart of Engineering. The technicians and mechanical support crew were working feverishly to restore power and function to the rest of the ship while the engineers assessed the damage to the engines. Xonea listened without comment to my report on the condition of the pilot and the number of wounded we had treated.

"So other than waiting for the Hsktskt to warm up and keeping the seriously injured on close monitor, we should be all right," I finished, and then added, "I need to take care of those wounds on your throat."

He made a negligent gesture. "I will attend to them later."

"It *is* later, and I am the Senior Healer," I said. "That means you let me stitch you up, or I have to relieve you from duty until such time as you decide to allow me to administer the required medical treatment."

His face darkened. "You would not dare."

I smiled. "Who do you think the department chiefs are going to side with? The helpful healer who only wants to provide proper care, or the captain with the open neck wounds and bad attitude?"

He rubbed his eyes. "Can you do it here?"

"Why do you think I brought my case?" I looked around and nodded toward the chief engineer's briefing room. "Let's go in there."

Once inside the office, I secured the door panels and pointed to the top of the conference table. "Sit down on that and open the front of your tunic." I began removing the supplies I would need and laid out a sanitary mat on the table beside him.

"I am surprised you did not send the oKiaf or one of the other healers to attend to me," Xonea said as I gloved and then removed the temporary dressings.

"I needed to stretch my legs. Lift your chin, please." After scanning both wounds, I prepared some gauze with antiseptic solution. "This is going to sting, a lot."

Stoic as ever, my ClanBrother didn't even flinch as I began cleaning out the gashes. "Were there others who attempted to embrace the stars?"

"A few of the injuries I saw were a little suspicious in nature, but no one asked for their Speaker or tried to finish the job, so I let it go." I cleaned the dried blood from the flesh around the gashes before I dialed up a local anesthetic on my syrinpress and infused both areas. "You're not planning to have another go at your arteries, are you?"

"We do not fear death, Cherijo," he reminded me. "What we cannot tolerate is being taken from our kin and all we know."

I calibrated the suture laser before I eyed him. "We have plenty of kin on the ship, Captain."

He tilted his head back as I began closing the wounds. "There can be no Clan without the House. We may never again see Joren."

"We haven't lost the House or Joren. We're just separated for a little while." I finished one gash and went to work on the other.

He looked down his nose at me. "Is that how you think of this division between you and Reever? A temporary separation?"

I waited until I took the instrument away from his neck before I answered. "You seem very interested in me and Reever lately. Maybe you should mind your own business."

"I know you saw the vid of him with the Akkabarran," he informed me. "You heard what he said to her. He does not honor you, Cherijo. He never has."

"Also, none of your business." I looked down as he caught my wrist. "You don't want to do this with me right now, ClanBrother. Not when I'm holding a focused-beam laser close to your head."

"You resent me now, but it will not always be so," he promised. "I but showed you the truth that he denied you."

"He is my husband, my lover, and my bondmate." Technically speaking, anyway. "However we feel about each other, that is between us." I looked into his eyes. "I don't want you meddling in my relationship with Reever again."

"I had prior claim to you," he snapped.

"You seem to forget that I killed myself to break your Choice of me," I sneered. "And if you think I won't do it again, then maybe you should remember how you felt as the ship went into the rift."

His face turned a chalky pale blue. "Cherijo, you know not what you say."

"Don't I?" I uttered a cold chuckle. "I wouldn't even hesitate this time." I didn't want to blow up at him, and then I was. "I'm sure you told yourself that you were doing the right thing by sneaking that disc into my case, but all you really did was hurt me and Reever and Marel. What's worse is, you didn't even do it for my sake. I doubt you gave my feelings a second thought. You showed me that vid so you could destroy my marriage and have me for yourself. Frankly, Captain, I'd rather die than be with a man that selfish.

End of discussion." I looked at his neck. "Keep the wounds clean and dry, and let me know if you experience any inflammation, drainage, or bleeding."

He followed me out of the briefing room. "Cherijo, wait."

I turned and waited.

"You have every right to condemn me in front of the crew and, when we return to Joren, before the House." He ducked his head. "I would humbly ask your pardon, lady, for the wrongs that I have done to you and those whom you honor."

I didn't want his apology, but at least he was trying to make one. "I'll think about it." I looked around at the busy engineers. "Do we at least know where we are, and has anyone found the idiot who brought us here?"

"The saboteur has not made himself known to us, nor have we found evidence of how this was done," he said slowly. "The stardrives and the navigational array are still off-line, and we are depending on our launch engines to maintain orbit."

"We're orbiting something?" I glanced at the viewport. I'd been so busy with patients, I hadn't even bothered to look outside.

"We have not yet identified the planet, the star system, or the galaxy," he admitted. "Nothing correlates to our star charts. We may have been thrown into another region of the universe altogether."

Jorenian technology allowed our ships to jump through dimensions in order to relocate within the confines of our galaxy, but there was no ship in existence that could universe-hop. "Have we been able to communicate with anyone?"

He took a datapad from a waiting technician and

inspected the display. "We have been unable to pick up any relays, and our distress signals remain unanswered." To the other man he said, "Secure the launches before the crew attempts to cut through the bay doors. Assure that all safety protocols are followed."

"No relays." I was still trying to digest that. "But there have to be open transmissions that we can pick up or monitor. Merchant ships, ore haulers, colonial beacons. Something."

"The transceiver is fully functional," he said quietly. "It was among the first of the arrays I ordered repaired, so that we might signal our House for assistance."

I didn't like the despair I heard in his voice. "Joren is still there, Xonea. It has to be a problem with the equipment."

"Six million years ago, our world was awash in volcanic activity," he told me. "The atmosphere was still too toxic to sustain life."

I couldn't accept that. "You can't assume flying into the rift caused us to be thrown back in time six million years. We would never have survived a journey of that duration. Forget about us, the ship itself would be dust."

"That was at least how far the derelict vessel traveled," he reminded me.

"Sure they did, with a ship and technology that by comparison makes our own look like flint knives and digging sticks." He didn't like me insulting his ship, I could see that. "The *Sunlace* is a marvelous star vessel. There is nothing better in the Jorenian fleet. But it is not designed to travel through time, and neither are we."

"You should see this." He pulled up a close-up image of an icy hull panel on his console. "We discovered it as soon as we sent a team out on tethers to inspect the exterior of the ship. What do you see?"

"Frost-covered alloy with a couple of bad cracks." I frowned as one of the repair crew passed a light emitter over the panel and it began to glow. "And what looks like some kind of residual radiation."

"The metal is not covered with ice." He magnified the image. "Scans indicated that is coated with the same three-sided crystals you found on the derelict in the stasis chambers."

I tried to make the connection. "Okay. The saboteur must have ejected the specimen, and it stuck to the ship."

He made an encompassing gesture. "I cannot say what our enemy did, but the inspection revealed that the entire ship is encased in these crystals."

"That can't be from the specimen," I protested. "We barely had an eighth of a liter of the stasis matrix in that container."

"Nevertheless, it is the same," he told me. "Perhaps the passage through the rift accelerated the growth rate, or contained an additional quantity of it. In either event, the ship is completely enveloped; the crystal has sealed all of the stress fractures in the hull as well as the seams and apertures of every accessway into the ship."

I felt a surge of nausea until something occurred to me. "If we're sealed inside, how did the crew get out to inspect the hull?"

"The crystal retreated from the seams of the air lock as soon as the crew entered it," he said. "It seems it *allowed* them to leave the ship."

I didn't like this. At all. "Where are we?"

Xonea pulled up an exterior view of the space surrounding the *Sunlace* and the planet below us.

We were in orbit above a world that appeared to be a smaller, moonless version of Kevarzangia Two. Dense forested areas and smaller expanses of cleared land made pretty, multicolored splotches on the surface, framed into continents by dark blue green oceans.

It wasn't exactly the way I remembered it, but as I stared at the display, I found one of the more unmistakable features: an enormous valley of waterfalls on the northeastern continent.

"We will first launch a surface probe," I heard Xonea saying behind me to one of his men, "and determine if it is safe to send down a shuttle."

"There's no need," I said, my voice hollow. "The atmosphere is oxygen-nitrogen, and none of the indigenous life is toxic to us." Too bad I couldn't say the same about the nonindigenous occupants.

Xonea looked shocked. "You know this planet."

"Unfortunately I do. It's been a while since Reever and I made an emergency landing on it, back when we were trying to negotiate peace between Taercal and Oenrall." I turned away from the viewer and saw he still didn't recognize it. "It's Jxinok. Maggie's homeworld."

Ten

Days passed as the crew worked to bring the *Sun-lace*'s systems back online and repair the damages to the interior of the ship. All our patients in Medical, including the Hsktskt, recovered from the trauma they'd suffered during the passage through the rift. The pilot's chest wound was healing without complications, and I had begun regenerative therapy to restore the areas of his derma that had been burned.

PyrsVar never left ChoVa's side until she was ambulatory, and even then trailed around after her like a personal bodyguard. The other Hsktskt were at first outraged by the news that we had been pulled through the rift, but after a briefing with the captain grimly accepted the situation.

There were still problems that we couldn't resolve. The protocrystal encasing the ship did allow repair crews to exit and enter the air locks while they worked on the exterior of the ship, but it would not release the seal it had formed over the launch bay's outer doors. When the technicians tried to cut through the seam, the crystal didn't budge, but only absorbed the energy from their pulse torches and glowed a little brighter. None of our technology could pry it away from the hull.

We weren't completely trapped, but after several abortive attempts to free the bay doors, it became apparent that we weren't going to be permitted to send our launches to the planet's surface.

Although the ship's transceiver was thoroughly tested, none of the signals we transmitted were answered, nor could we monitor any other transceiver activity. Long-range scans of the space surrounding us revealed only two populated worlds in the vicinity: Jxinok and another, smaller civilization on a planet in a neighboring system. Neither planet responded to our distress calls or otherwise acknowledged our presence.

We had enough supplies to keep the crew alive for two years, longer if we instituted rationing, so we weren't in immediate danger. At the same time, we couldn't hang in orbit above Jxinok forever.

Everyone showed some signs of stress from our predicament, but Shon especially seemed to grow more distant with every passing day. I tried more than once to talk to him about it, but he would simply claim he was tired or preoccupied. We didn't have a psychologist among the medical staff, but when ChoVa and I were alone discussing charts as we prepared to change shifts, I asked her what she thought of the oKiaf's withdrawn, remote behavior.

"You are kin with these Jorenians, and I have PyrsVar and our delegates," she said. "The oKiaf has no one."

"He and I are friends," I said.

"Healer Valtas is also protective of you," she pointed out. "Perhaps he does not wish to worry you with his fears."

"I don't think so. He's never been shy about confiding in me in the past." I finished my notations before passing back one of the delegates' charts to her. "I know he's the strong, silent type. Maybe I'm reading into it too much."

"No, the change has been noticeable," she disagreed. "Many times I have approached him to discuss treatment, and before we came here, he was always forthright with his opinions. Now he merely listens and agrees unilaterally with my suggestions."

"You are our resident expert on Hsktskt physiology," I said, "and he's never treated a member of your species before this trip. Maybe he's simply deferring to you."

"I would agree, but I have been monitoring some of the Jorenian patients, as well, and he has far more experience with their species than I." She gave me a long look. "Do you believe he is experiencing some sort of emotional disturbance, and is attempting to hide it from us?"

"I haven't observed anything to make me think that." I turned around and accessed the medsysbank, pulling up the data we had on the oKiaf species, and searched for emotional disorders. "His people do experience some mental illness, most in the realm of phobias and reactive depressions. It could be a form of post-traumatic stress disorder."

"We should examine him and run a full neurological series." When I frowned at her, she added, "The oKiaf is supervising the fourth shift. If he may soon present a danger to himself, the staff, or the patients, we must know now and remove him from duty."

I checked the time on my wristcom. "He's been off since yesterday, and won't be reporting for duty until tonight. Maybe I'll go by his quarters for a friendly visit. See if I can coax it out of him."

"Take a scanner with you," was ChoVa's advice.

Shon's quarters were located on the same level as my own, so before I went to check on him, I stopped to cleanse and change out of my uniform tunic. Wearing my civilian garments might allay some tension and make it easier to convince him to be more forthcoming with me.

He opened the door panel before I had a chance to touch the panel. He looked a little better than he had yesterday, although his dark eyes remained wary. "Cherijo."

"Good morning, Shon." I smiled. "I thought I'd stop by and get your opinion on something. Got a minute to talk?"

He stepped aside in silent invitation.

I had never bothered to visit Shon's quarters, so at first I was startled to see how empty the rooms were. He'd removed all the conventional Jorenian furnishings and wall hangings and had disabled more than half the light emitters. The effect was a little like walking into a cave.

Instead of bare deck or a woven floor covering, Shon had spread out a patchy layer of dried leaves, stems, and flower petals, which crunched a little under my footgear. Four wide, flat stones formed a loose rectangle around a portable thermal generator that had been modified to cast off flickering light as well as heat. A few furs lay in neat bundles near the walls, and a primitive-looking tapestry had been hung to conceal the prep unit.

"Very Spartan," I said, breathing in the chilly air, which I guessed to be about twenty degrees colder than the rest of the ship's atmosphere. I caught a trace of what smelled like burned bone and greenery, which alarmed me until I saw a discreetly placed olfactory unit. Shon must have programmed it to produce the smells that reminded him of home. "Is this what it's like on oKia?"

"No. It is only pretense." His voice sounded flat and uninterested. "Why have you come here?"

"As I said, I thought we'd talk." I sat down gingerly on one of the flat stones and patted another beside me. "Sit down, Shon."

He came over, his movements a little uncertain, and crouched in front of me. He studied me as if I were a slide under a scope. "You are not like the others."

"Neither are you, even if you can't use this right now." I tapped the place on his tunic that hid the parallel marks in his fur. "I know not having access to your ability is upsetting you, but I'm sure it's temporary. The way we were jerked through that rift, we're lucky our minds didn't get a little scrambled, too."

"Minds are strange. Cut off from the others. Alone." He rose and moved away, going to stand with his back against the wall. "This is not as it should be."

"ChoVa and I compared notes," I said carefully. "We both think it would be a good idea to run some tests on you, see if there was any fallout from the transition. You haven't been yourself since we came here."

"I am not myself," he agreed. "You are afraid. Of this, of me."

The way he was acting was seriously starting to spook me. "Our patients depend on you to look after them. I don't think you can do that anymore, not until we find out what's bothering you. You need some help, Shon."

He watched my face. "That is why you came here. To help. To stop this. But it is too late. You came too late."

The disjointed, unfamiliar patterns in his speech had me deeply concerned. He almost stumbled through each sentence, terse as they were. I couldn't hear an ounce of emotion in his voice or see a glimmer of response in his eyes. It was like having a conversation with a drone instead of my friend.

Suddenly I knew I wasn't talking to Shon anymore. "Who are you?"

He pushed off the wall and walked toward me. "You have said the words to this one."

I got to my feet and backed away. "What words?"

"Infinity? Eternity?" Something shimmered in his eyes, icy and frightening. "These are not names. There are no names."

I turned and ran for the door panel, but got only a few steps before he seized me from behind. He turned me around and held me up to his face. There I could see what had caused the glitter in his gaze—tiny three-sided crystals, dancing inside his pupils.

"You know."

"I know you aren't Shon Valtas," I said tightly. "Please stop doing this and release him. We won't hurt you."

"You cannot hurt. You can see." He put an arm across my throat and dragged me to the door panel. "You must see."

Fighting him wasn't working; his grip was too strong. Hoping cooperation would win me a measure of trust, I stopped struggling and went along with him. "What do I have to see?"

"Them."

The corridor was empty. I could shout for help and someone would come running. They'd also attack Shon and probably try to kill him, if the protocrystal hadn't already.

"How did you take over Healer Valtas's body like this?" I asked.

"Caught inside." He touched the center of his chest. "This one save."

"The pilot. You were trapped inside the pilot's body." When he inclined his head, I thought quickly. "Did you come through the rift with us?"

He gestured toward his face. "This is rift." He made a gesture toward a viewport. "Rift is this."

"Then you were in the rift." He didn't say anything as he guided me around a corner. "I don't understand. Are you saying that you are part of the rift? You made it?"

"No. *You* made rift."

My blood ran cold. "How could I have done that?"

"You made it," he insisted, and then he said one more word that made my blood run cold. "Soon."

He didn't touch the controls to the lift; he only glanced at them, and the entry slid open. He kept hold of me as he took me down several levels and then walked me to the launch bay.

Dozens of crew members filled the bay; some were working on the damages to the launches, while others were inspecting the inside of the hull doors that remained inoperable.

"You tell them to go," Shon said, and nodded toward the main air lock. "I open."

After witnessing him operating a lift simply by

looking at it, I had no doubt he could do the same with any other mechanical system on the ship. "Why?"

"We go." He nodded toward one of the launches.

It was clear that he intended to take me off the ship, which meant opening the outer hull doors, too. The moment he disengaged the air lock, the entire bay would vent into space. "You'll kill everyone here if you do that."

"You tell them to go," he repeated.

He wasn't going to back down. "You must let me talk to them first, or they won't leave."

He released me. "Talk quickly."

I gestured to the chief of the bay, who looked puzzled as he came over to us. "How may I assist you, Healer Cherijo?"

"I'm ordering an immediate evacuation of the bay, Chief," I said, keeping my expression blank. "Tell your people to stop working and leave at once."

His eyes widened. "Why say you this? What is the matter?"

"There is a dangerous organism present that poses a threat to the crew." I just didn't say it was standing right next to me. "Healer Valtas and I will deal with it. Please, order your people out of here."

"As you say, Healer." The chief went to his console and gave the order, and a few minutes later the bay was empty.

"We don't have to leave the ship," I said as Shon marched me over to one of the launches. "We could stay here and discuss what you want me to know."

"Words are insufficient." He tugged me up the ramp and into the launch, guiding me to the copilot's seat before clipping me into the harness. "You must see."

"See what? Who?" I demanded as he took the pilot's position and I heard the engines engage. "Where are you taking me?"

"To them," was all he said.

He glanced out at the hull doors, and a visible gap appeared between them, causing an instant, explosive decompression. The bay's atmosphere along with everything that wasn't nailed down or held by a docking clamp flew out as the maneuvering thrusters came online and slowly guided the launch out into space.

The pilot's console lit up as it received multiple signals from the *Sunlace*. Shon ignored them, and when I reached for my console, he eyed me. "No."

"My friends will be worried about us," I said. "Let me tell them that I'm all right, or they will try to follow us."

"They cannot follow." He watched the front view panel as the launch dropped down out of the orbital path of the *Sunlace* and began a diagonal approach to the planet's upper atmosphere.

I checked the display and saw that he had closed the hull doors, which made me feel a little better, at least until I saw what happened next.

The seams of the launch bay's air lock sparkled as they were engulfed and sealed by the protocrystal enveloping the ship.

The protocrystal occupying Shon's mind and body seemed to have no difficulty piloting the launch, although he never once touched the controls. The ship flew as smoothly as if it were on autopilot toward the planet's surface.

"What do I have to see on the planet?" I asked,

and quickly added, "I know you said *them* before, but who are they? More like you?"

"Not like this," he said. "This one calls them the tribe."

"So they are not like you."

"Not like this," he agreed.

He seemed to have trouble identifying himself with personal pronouns. Of course, with all the billions of crystals making up the stasis matrix, he might not think of himself as an individual at all. "How many are you?"

"Not many," he corrected. "All."

"Do all of you share the same consciousness?"

"Not consciousness. All consciousness."

I was becoming frustrated with the limitations of speech. "I want to understand what you are. I can't help you if I don't know what you need from me."

"Need." He glanced at me. "This *you* need."

I jumped on that. "All right, then, why do I need to go to the planet? To see the tribe? To see the Jxin? Can they help us?"

He shook his head. "They do not help."

"Can I do something to help them?"

"You are them." He moved his shoulders. "You are not them."

I felt like screaming. "Do you know how frustrating it is, trying to communicate with you?"

"Yes." He gave me a direct look as he repeated my exact words back to me. "Do you know how frustrating it is, trying to communicate with you?"

I got the message. "I'm sorry. I know you're trying. I'm afraid because I don't understand you, I won't do what you want, and then you'll hurt my friend Shon because of it."

"No hurt." He turned back to watch through the viewer.

The launch landed in a small clearing bordered on three sides by dense, lush green forests. At the northern edge a wide path had been cleared and paved with immense disks cut from pale wood of tree trunks, and fitted together with diamond-shaped insets of golden brown stone. Over the path more botanicals floated, tethered to the ground by fine-linked wooden chains and providing shade from the bright yellow sun's light.

I looked for the shining towers I had seen in a vision during one of my many Maggie-induced hallucinations, but they were nowhere in sight. Neither were the ruins we had discovered when we'd actually found and landed on Jxinok during my investigation into the terrible age plagues inflicted by the black crystal on the Oenrallians and the Taercal.

"Where are they?" I asked Shon as he powered down the engines.

He nodded toward the north. "Coming."

Since the Jxin hadn't bothered to acknowledge or respond to our signals, I wasn't expecting a welcoming party to meet our launch. Shon gestured for me to disembark, and followed me down the ramp as it lowered to the soil. I watched the path leading out of the clearing, expecting the Jxin equivalent of a security patrol to appear at any moment.

I heard their laughter first: high, soft, and pretty. Then I saw four figures moving toward us, all dressed in sleeveless ground-length light blue robes.

They moved effortlessly, their limbs fluid and their gait unhurried. Their long, narrow skulls had slits rather than ears, and their eyes were tilted in an angular slant, but their blunted noses and small mouths weren't all that different from my own. From the subtle contrasts in their bone structures and the arrangement of their long hair, I guessed them to be two males and two females.

They halted a short distance from me and Shon and regarded us in silence. Now and then they glanced at one another as if they were having a conversation we couldn't hear, and since over the years Maggie had demonstrated vast telepathic abilities, I guessed they didn't need to use their mouths to communicate.

"Am I supposed to talk to them," I asked Shon, "or just look at them?"

"You may speak to us, primitive," one of the males said in flawless Terran.

"I'm Dr. Cherijo Torin. This is Dr. Shon Valtas." I thought trying to explain that Shon was possessed and had abducted me might not be a good idea right off the bat. "Have you received the signals sent to you from the ship in orbit?"

"We have heard them," one of the females said, sounding bored. To the others, she said, "We should return. The circle will be forming soon."

"Excuse me," I said in a louder voice when the four started to turn back. "Why didn't you answer our signals?"

Three kept going, but the second male remained long enough to say, "We had no wish to" before he followed the others.

I turned to Shon. "All right, I've seen them, and I've talked to them, and they're not interested in us. Can we go back to the ship?"

"See more." Shon pointed at the departing Jxin. "Talk more."

"I already don't like them," I mentioned as we started after them. "I don't think my opinion is going to improve on closer acquaintance."

Either the four Jxin weren't aware that we were tailing them, or they didn't care. From their complete lack of reaction to discovering that we'd landed without permission on their world, I was voting for the second. By now Xonea and the rest of the crew must have been frantic about me and Shon leaving on a launch; I wanted to get back to the ship before the Jorenians found a way to send down some launches, invade Jxinok, and begin disemboweling these people.

The walk from the clearing to the Jxin settlement took only a few minutes, and as soon as I saw the first of their dwellings, I realized why I hadn't spotted them as we landed. The shining crystal towers Maggie had shown me were nowhere to be seen; these Jxin had built their much more modest homes out of opaque white-gold and ivory stone that reflected the colors around them, allowing the dwellings to blend in perfectly with the surrounding forest.

The structures were also arranged in tall clusters of cylindrical white stone tubes that led up to oval chambers of the darker white-gold stone. What alloys they had used were pure gold in color and seemed to serve only as some sort of exterior decoration.

As beautiful as the Jxin colony was, I didn't see any drones, equipment, or other variety of technology. There were plenty of people in various colored robes, and the dwellings, but nothing else. To my eye the place appeared almost barren.

Some of the Jxin glanced at us as we walked into their settlement, but the majority walked by us as if we weren't even there. I didn't attempt to speak

to any of them as Shon and I stopped in the center
of the colony, where we stood and watched a large
group forming a standing circle in between the largest dwelling clusters.

I didn't like this. I hadn't yet seen one child or elderly person; everyone in the colony appeared to be
a young, healthy adult. "What are they going to do?
Sacrifice their young, or eat their old people?"

A female in a yellow robe walking past me heard
what I said and turned around. She came over and
touched my cheek, and then said, "We do not make
sacrifices. We have no young or old among us. We do
not eat."

My jaw dropped as I recognized her face. "Maggie?"

"We have no names." She tilted her head. "You do
not belong here."

"Are you forgetting who you're talking to? It's
me, Cherijo. The surrogate daughter you've been tor-
menting for the last ten years." When she didn't react,
I went to her and grabbed her by the arms to give her
a shake. "No more games. Why did you do this? Why
bring the ship here? Did you send the protocrystal to
infect Shon so you could get me down here?"

"I do not know you, Cherijo." She said my name
slowly, as if she was uncertain of the pronunciation.
"We do not have children, so you cannot be my
daughter. I have no control over you, this male, or
your ship. I have no reason to bring you here."

"You're lying." I was so angry I could have beaten
her into the ground. "Don't deny it. How else would
you speak my language so perfectly? You came to
Terra. You helped my father create me. You pretended to be my mother. Did you think I wouldn't
recognize you?"

"I absorbed your language when I touched you. I have never left our world." She seemed amused now. "I am too new. It will be a very long time before I am sent out to give life."

I glanced around us. "You've never left this world."

She laughed. "To depart, one must gather and perfect and purify for many eons. I have lived only a thousand years. I cannot leave."

"She speaks truth," Shon said to me. "Jxin child."

My hands dropped away as I tried to sort it out. "She's only a kid in this time?" He inclined his head. "So what now? Am I supposed to stop her from leaving? Kill her? Make sure I'm never born, something like that?"

"You cannot stop this," he said, pointing toward the circle of Jxin.

The people in the circle had joined their hands, and held their faces up toward the sun. The light streaming over them intensified and reflected into the center of the circle, where it formed into a glowing ball that grew brighter and whiter by the moment. When it was almost too bright to look at, some of the people in the circle let go of the others and began walking toward it. When they reached the light, they disappeared into it briefly, and then reemerged a few seconds later, their bodies glowing with the same energy.

"What the hell are they doing?" I murmured. "Sunbathing?"

"It is purification of the essence," Maggie said, smiling at the circle. "Soon our elders will attain the perfection required to shed their bodies forever. Then the Great Ascension will truly begin."

"You're dumping your bodies to become a big ball of light?" I shook my head. "Truly stupid, more like."

"It is so much more than you could possibly understand." She gave me a pitying look. "How tiresome it must be, to have such a primitive mind."

I showed her my teeth. "At least I'm not trying to turn into an ambulatory spot emitter."

The last of the Jxin in the circle went in and came out of the light, which faded as they joined hands and appeared to reabsorb it into their already glowing bodies. After that, they wandered away in different directions, their illuminated bodies making the watching Jxin smile and nod and laugh.

I suppose the whole deal would have sent a xenobiologist into raptures, but I found it about as interesting as watching a bunch of drones switch on.

"What happens to the people who can't purify their essence, or whatever?" I asked Maggie.

"There are no such people here."

I folded my arms. "Every species has failures."

"Not the Jxin." She made a negligent gesture. "Once, long ago, before we attained all that we are, there were such disappointments. They were known as undesirables. Our ancestors culled them from our bloodlines and sent them away."

I remembered the other civilization our long-range scanners had detected. "Were they sent to another planet in the next solar system?"

She nodded. "They were given a new world of their own, where they could indulge in their imperfections and harm and maim and destroy one another without our interference. Perhaps you should visit their planet."

I ignored her snotty suggestion as I mulled it over. How convenient for Jxin, to simply purge their gene pool until it was sparkling clear, like their crystal art. I could guess who those nasty rejects had grown up to be, but it wouldn't hurt to get a confirmation. "What do they call themselves, these undesirables?"

"We do not have contact with them," she told me. "We do not care. I am finished speaking with you now." She started to wander off.

"Oh, no." I caught her arm. "I have it on good authority that we need to talk more."

"We have spoken at length. I find you too limited to be of any interest to me." She looked down at my hand. "The Jxin do not feel pain, and we cannot be injured. Tightening your grip will do nothing but hurt your hand."

"I came here from the future," I said. "I have some information you may find of interest."

"You are not advanced enough to travel so." But even as she said that, she looked closer at me and Shon, as if seeing us clearly for the first time. "But you are not us, and you are not them, and there are no others."

"See? You worked it out, all on your own." I didn't want to discuss this out in the open, not when I wasn't sure how Maggie or the Jxin would react, so I gestured toward the cluster dwellings. "Which mushroom is yours?"

She pointed to one of the top levels of a smaller cluster. "I commune there with other new ones."

"That'll work." I led her in that direction, glancing back to see Shon walking to where the circle had been. He turned his head and gave me a nod.

"Do you have any star vessels on this planet I can borrow?" I asked Maggie as we entered the bottom level of her dwelling.

"We do not use star vessels. Why do you require one? You have one here and one in orbit."

That squashed my idea of escaping back to the *Sunlace* in a Jxin launch. "It's a long story."

They might have looked simple and beautiful on the outside, but on the inside the Jxin's homes were breathtaking. As they had evolved past the need for such commonplace things as water, food, and heat, the Jxin had evidently eliminated all the customary trappings that went along with them. Their homes were instead filled with art, music, and plants. The general theme connecting everything was native crystal: sculptures carved from it, music made by it, and plants growing from stunning arrangements of it.

The material used to construct the dwellings allowed the sunlight through, which made everything around us sparkle. It was a bit like walking into a home decorated almost entirely in diamonds. The only spaces I saw that weren't being used as display areas were several regularly spaced, arch-shaped recesses in the walls.

Maggie took me up to an observation deck that looked out over the forest and at the same time magnified the view so that I could see nearly half the continent beyond the settlement. As I gawked a little—all right, my jaw landed on the floor and stayed there for a good ten minutes—she grew impatient.

"You keep me from my interests," she told me. "Tell me what information you possess."

"The undesirables your ancestors evicted from Jxinok call themselves the Odnallak," I said, peering out the other side of the deck. "They're in the process of trying to ascend. In the process they will create a malignant substance that is harmful to all intelligent life. Is that really the valley of the waterfalls over there? I thought that was like a couple thousand kilometers away from here."

"It is the valley. You are mistaken about the undesirables. As they were, are, and will be, they will never ascend." She didn't even sound a little worried. "Can you find your way back to your little ship, or will you need directions?"

"Why do you think the Odnallak will fail to evolve like you?" I countered. "Up until you kicked them off the planet, they *were* you."

"The undesirables are impure beings, and as such have no hope of perfection. They first refused correction of the flaws ingrained in their cells and then the impurities could no longer be removed; it was why they were sent away. If they do anything, they will destroy themselves."

"Oh, they're going to do that, too," I assured her. "Their creation of the black crystal almost wipes out their species. The few survivors become shapeshifting criminals and killers who forget about all the nasty things their ancestors did."

She sighed. "And this is all the information you have?"

"This is what is happening in my time," I corrected. "What you told me was my reason for being. In the future, you created me to be immortal so that I would live long enough to find a cure for the black crystal. But there is no cure, Maggie. It can't be destroyed, or reasoned with, or sent someplace where it can't do any harm. It's infected nearly every inhabited world in my time. It's caused billions of species to suffer and become diseased or insane and die terrible deaths, and that's just while it's been napping. Someday it's going to wake up and start eating worlds, and no matter how long I live, I won't be able to stop it."

"You are immortal?" She inspected me from my head to my footgear and back again. "How did I make you so?"

"I don't care," I snapped. "Didn't you hear a word of what I just said? Billions of beings are going to die unless you stop the Odnallak from trying to follow in your footsteps. You have to keep them from creating the black crystal."

"But you are here," she said. "I created you, you said, to cure this black crystal. Thus, the black crystal cannot be destroyed or averted by me as I am now."

"You can still do something now," I insisted. "You can change the future."

"Obviously I cannot," she said. "If I had tried and were successful, you would never have come here, Cherijo. You would not exist."

Eleven

As much as I hated to admit it, Maggie was right. If there were some way for her to prevent the black crystal from being created, I would never have come to Jxinok. I'd have winked out of existence the moment the events that led to my timeline were altered. No black crystal, no reason for her to create me in the future.

I wandered back into the interior chamber, absently admiring the crystal version of the valley of the waterfalls. They really were beautiful, especially the tiny, interlocking specimens she'd used to form the flowing water; the play of light over them made them look just like real liquid. Then I frowned and bent closer.

The water crystals were three-sided.

So were the green crystals she'd used to form the flora around the falls, and the golden brown crystal she'd shaped into the rocky ledges.

I didn't let myself get excited until I inspected a dozen more sculptures and confirmed my suspicions.

Maggie joined me in front of a wall installation where one of the cluster dwellings had been reproduced in opaque white and gold crystal. "What are you doing?"

"All of these crystals you've used for your artwork have three sides." I turned to her. "Do all the crystals on this planet grow in the same formation?" She nodded. "Do any of them generate power?"

"All of them are alive," she said, "until we harvest them. The process strips the organics from them. Do you wish me to escort you back to your ship?"

"How do you harvest them?" I pressed. "By hand?"

She frowned. "Why would we do that? What does it matter?"

"Tell me how you do it and I'll leave," I promised.

"We use the collectors." Bored now, she walked over to one of the empty recesses I'd noticed before. "We think of the colors and sizes we need, and the collector gathers the crystals and deposits them here."

"Show me."

"You said you would leave if I told you. I have." When I didn't budge, she exhaled heavily and turned to the alcove, bracing both hands on either side. She closed her eyes, and a moment later a small heap of dark purple crystals appeared in the bottom of the alcove.

I stared at the crystals. "What if they're not suitable? Can you send them back?"

"Of course." She repeated the process, and the dark purple pile disappeared.

"Does the collector work only for you, or can others use it?"

"It is keyed to read the thoughts of any who activate it," she said.

"Thanks." I ran to the nearest exit cylinder.

Shon stood waiting just outside the dwelling. As I emerged from the lowest level, I cleared my thoughts.

I didn't know if he could read my mind, or even if what I had planned would work, but I had to try.

I waved at him. "Healer Valtas, I need you in here."

He slowly walked toward me. "What is it?"

"Something wonderful," I said. "A cure."

He stopped and shook his head. "No cure."

"They've just discovered it," I said. "It will change everything for us. Please, hurry."

He fell for it, and followed me into the dwelling. I stopped in front of one of the collectors and turned to him, smiling.

"You see?" I gestured to the interior of the alcove. "It's all right there."

He peered inside. "I see nothing."

"I know. I'm lying." I shoved him inside. "Sorry."

I braced my hands in the same places Maggie had, closed my eyes, and focused. I didn't know how to tell the collector to do as I wanted, so I just imagined it: the protocrystal being pulled out of his body and sent back where it belonged, back in space. Then I imagined Shon alive and well again.

I heard Shon make a strange sound as something bright shone against my eyelids. Then the entire dwelling began to shake, and just as abruptly stopped.

"Cherijo?"

I opened my eyes to see Shon standing inside the recess. He looked bewildered.

"Where are we?" He glanced around him. "Why am I in here?"

"It worked." Exhausted but satisfied, I dropped my hands. "Too bad I can't fit the *Sunlace* in one of these things."

Maggie joined us and looked from the oKiaf to me and back again. "What have you done?"

"I removed the crystal infecting my friend's body,"
I told her, "and now we're leaving. It's not really been
fun. Bye."

"Wait," Maggie called after us as I led Shon out of
the dwelling.

"All she's wanted me to do is get out of here," I
said to Shon, "but the minute I go, she wants me to
stay. It's really sad, how these higher-evolved life-
forms can never make up their mind. How are you
feeling?"

"Tired." He flexed his paws. "You said I was infected with another crystal."

"Yeah, whatever is all over the *Sunlace* got inside
you. I think it was an accident, but it decided to spring
me from the ship and bring us down here." I glanced
to the side as Maggie caught up with us. "What do you
want now?"

"You are more interesting than I thought," she
said. "I wish to speak to you now."

"You had your chance." Treating her like *she* was
the stupid primitive was probably unwise, given how
much power she and her people had, but I wanted a
little payback. And then something clicked. "There is
nothing for us here. We're going back to our ship."

"Wait." When we didn't, she added, "Please."

I stopped and turned around. "Say *pretty please
with sugar on top*."

"Why would I . . . ?" She saw my expression and
quickly added, "Pretty please with sugar on top."

I was starting to enjoy myself. "Now apologize to
my friend."

Maggie eyed Shon. "I have done nothing to him."

"He was in trouble, and you did nothing to help
him." I folded my arms. "Well?"

"I apologize to you for my inaction," Maggie said to Shon.

The oKiaf glanced at me. "This is unnecessary."

"No, pal, this is what we call fun." I regarded Maggie. "You know, you may be an omnipotent life-form on the brink of attaining evolutionary perfection, but you're also rude, inconsiderate, and selfish. We're not interested in you anymore. Have a nice ascension."

Maggie followed us all the way back to the launch. Shon looked over his shoulder a few times, but I acted as if she weren't there. I had the feeling that Maggie had never been ignored or dismissed in her life, especially by two primitives who should have been worshipping at her feet. I was gambling that the novelty might work in our favor.

"You cannot leave now," I heard her say as Shon and I started up the ramp. "I wish to know more about you. Why did you decide to put the male in the collector? How were you able to operate it? Your mind is too—"

"Primitive?" I gave her a snide smile. "Maybe it is and maybe it isn't. Guess you'll just have to wonder about that forever." To Shon, I said, "Come on, we're done here."

"I will go with you," Maggie said. When she saw my expression, she added, "If I may. Pretty please? With the sugar on top?"

"I don't know," I said, tapping my footgear on the ramp. "You're useless and nasty, and those are your *redeeming* qualities. We have a lot of work to do to repair our ship and return to our own time. You'll probably only get in the way."

"I will help you with this work," she offered.

Bingo.

On the jaunt back to the *Sunlace*, Shon took my lead and treated Maggie almost as brusquely as I did. By the time we were on final approach to the launch bay, Maggie had asked us a dozen questions that we hadn't answered, a situation that dumbfounded her as much as when I told her to shut up while Shon attempted to signal the ship.

"There is too much interference," he said, and changed the external viewer to display the transceiver array. Like the rest of the ship, it was encased in protocrystal. "That may be why our relays are jammed."

"Jxin crystal absorbs all forms of differentiated energy," Maggie put in. "You must align your devices to transmit at the same frequency for it to pass. As you did on the larger ship when you came here."

"We didn't change the frequency of our signals when we came out of the rift." I scanned the protocrystal and used the readings to calibrate our transmitter.

"Someone did," Shon murmured back to me.

"*Sunlace* Command, this is Healer Cherijo Torin," I signaled, using the new frequency. "Respond and confirm."

"Lieutenant Fasonea Torin confirming your signal," I heard one of the helm officers reply over the clear relay. He sounded relieved. "It is good to hear your voice, Healer. Are you in distress?"

"No, Lieutenant." We might be if what I planned didn't work. "Stand by, please." To Shon and Maggie, I said, "We have to get into envirosuits. Right now."

Shon didn't question my order, but Maggie began to argue at once. "My body is inviolate. I do not need this outerwear. Why are you doing this? You have breathable air in this vessel. These suits are badly designed."

I ended up shoving her into the envirosuit like an impatient mother dressing a fussy child. When she tried to struggle, I grabbed her chin. "Enough. You're wearing the suit, or I'm going to save myself a lifetime of grief and toss you out of the air lock."

"That will not harm me," she said.

"No, but it will give me a great deal of pleasure to see you encased in ice and floating around out there." I jammed the helmet over her head and sealed it to the collar of the suit.

Once we were all in protective gear, I went back to the console and signaled Fasonea again. "Lieutenant, please notify launch bay that we're on approach."

"Launch bay remains inoperable, Healer," Fasonea said quickly. "Do not attempt to dock. You will collide with the ship."

"It's all right, Lieutenant," I replied. "We've taken some safety precautions."

"Healer, do not approach, I repeat—"

I shut down the relay and turned to Shon. "Fly straight at the access doors," I said over my suitcom. "Slow and steady."

He brought the launch around into docking position. "What if they do not open?"

I watched the ship as we drew closer. "Then we're going to make a great big dent in the hull."

The launch's com panel lit up as we drew closer. I kept my eye on the doors, and the glittering crystal filling the seams.

"Come on," I muttered. "You took us off, you can let us back on."

Collision was imminent, and while I knew it wouldn't

completely destroy the launch, slamming into the *Sun-lace* wasn't going to do great things for it, either.

Slowly the crystal oozed out of the seams, and a gap appeared in the center of the doors. Someone on the other side had wisely engaged the air lock, so this time nothing was blown out into space. Then we were flying into the ship, hovering for a moment in the massive air lock as the doors closed behind us, then moving forward and landing on the docking pad.

"How did you know it would allow us access?" Shon asked me.

"I didn't," I admitted. "But if we had hit the ship, its orbit would have towed our wreck alongside it for a couple of hours, which would have given the crew enough time to come out on tethers and rescue us."

"Assuming we survived the collision," he amended.

"It was a risk." I saw half the engineering crew running toward the launch, led by the captain. "But you and I can survive pretty much anything, and as loudmouth back there has so often reminded us, she's inviolate."

"I want to take this suit off now," Maggie complained from the passenger compartment.

We removed our envirosuits while the launch went through biodecon, and then lowered the ramp. Xonea was the first one on board.

"Are you injured?" he demanded, eyeing Shon with a less-than-friendly glower.

"We're okay. Before you declare anything, I Shield Healer Valtas. Shon was not responsible for what happened." I gestured vaguely at Maggie. "She was."

"You blame me?" She looked astonished. "I did nothing to bring you primitives here, Cherijo."

"No," I agreed, "but someday you will."

*   *   *

While Maggie wandered around the launch bay to examine its equipment, Shon and I quickly briefed Xonea on what had happened on the planet and the complete lack of interest the Jxin had taken in us.

"I'm positive they didn't have anything to do with bringing us here," I added. "We're nothing more than a nuisance to them."

"If they are not concerned about our presence, then why has she come to the ship?" he asked.

"I lured her here. She's young, and for a Jxin, she's fairly stupid. But the protocrystal wanted me to see her people as well as talk to them. It seems to be the real reason we were brought here." I watched her inspect one of the security guards as if he were nothing more than an exotic bug. "I have to find out more about the Jxin of this time."

"It would be better to send her back to the surface," Xonea said. "If her people are as powerful as you say, then she could do a great deal of harm to the ship or the crew."

"That would require her to actually give a damn about us," I told him. "Which she doesn't. Generally speaking, we barely register on her radar."

"We might convince her to help us return to our time," Shon said. "If we can hold her interest for that long."

I gave him a grim smile. "Let me handle that."

After assuring Xonea that I wouldn't let Maggie out of my sight, I went over to her and informed her that Shon and I were leaving. "I have to examine Healer Valtas and determine if there is any damage to his body."

She flicked a glance in his direction. "There is not."

She pointed at the guard. "Why do these males carry such crude destructive devices?"

"They use them to shoot things they don't like," I advised her. "So be nice. How can you tell Healer Valtas has no damage to his body?"

"I can see his insides. They have already healed." She tried to touch the guard's pulse rifle, making him step back. To him she said, "I wish to examine that device. Give it to me."

"Uh-uh." I took her arm and guided her away from him. "We don't let kids play with guns."

"I am a thousand years older than any being on this vessel," she said, sounding sulky now. "And I do not play."

I stopped and turned to her. "If you're not going to behave yourself, I'll tell the captain to dump your ass on a drone launch and send you back to the planet."

She frowned. "But I cannot go back. You have not yet answered my questions." Her expression turned suspicious. "Are you going to tell me how you were able to use the collector?"

"I don't know. Maybe when I feel better about you." I nodded to Shon, who followed us out of the bay and down the corridor.

"Where are you taking me?" Maggie asked in between staring at everyone who passed.

"Medical." I marched her into the lift. "I want to see if your assessment of Healer Valtas is correct."

"I am not wrong," she said, her tone growing lofty again. "I am never wrong. We Jxin do not make errors."

I thought of what Future Maggie had said to me to try to keep me away from the derelict. "Someday you might revise that statement, honey."

She spent the rest of the time it took us to reach Medical explaining to me how she could not be compared to the food product of a hive insect, complaining about the inefficient design of the ship, and making general observations about how bored she was. As we had on the launch, Shon and I ignored her, which seemed to be the only way to keep her attention focused.

ChoVa was making rounds when we entered the bay, and handed off a chart to a nurse before coming over. "Cherijo, we were deeply concerned about your abduction. The captain just signaled and apprised us of your"—she glanced at Maggie—"situation."

"You are not like the others," Maggie said, inspecting ChoVa. "You cannot regulate your body temperature as Cherijo and Shon do. And you are green and scaly and have many teeth." She glanced past the Hsktskt healer and became riveted. "*What is that?*"

"I am called PyrsVar." The rogue came up to Maggie and sniffed her. "She smells strange. Did you find her on the planet?"

"It speaks." Maggie's expression filled with revulsion as she walked around him, staring at his body. "You made this, Cherijo?"

"I am not a *this*," PyrsVar told her. "I am a person, like you."

"You are not like me. Or like them." She squinted as she came around to the front of him. "You are two people. But you are one. Your insides are all wrong." She turned to me. "This thing was made, not born."

"Lots of us were made," I reminded her. "And PyrsVar is not a thing. He is a person, and you will treat him as such."

"But he is . . ." Lost for words, she shook her head. "How could you allow him to take apart another being and put the pieces inside himself so?"

"This was forced on me by an evil one who deceived me," the rogue answered for me. "Healer Torin is trying to restore me to be as I was born."

"You have to separate him," Maggie told me. "He must be made into the two again."

"I'm working toward a less drastic solution, but we don't have time for that now," I said, and turned my back on her to speak to ChoVa. "We need to do a full workup on Shon." Using my hands close to my chest, I made the Jorenian gesture for "no." "Nurse, can I have a blank chart?" When it was handed to me, I made some quick notes, explaining my plan to ChoVa, and handed it to the Hsktskt. "Set up assessment room five for the examination, and monitor him from the main console."

"There is nothing wrong with him," Maggie said as she followed us into the room. "I told you that."

"We primitive beings have to follow certain procedures," I told her. "None of which include relying on the word of Jxin as a diagnostic tool."

"You could be employing your time to do other things." When I didn't react to that, she said, "How long will this take?"

Through the view panel I saw ChoVa working at the main console. "Oh, no time at all."

While I performed a thorough exam of the oKiaf, ChoVa used the scanners embedded in the walls—the room had been designed for healers to remotely assess dangerous or quarantined patients—to scan Maggie, me, and Shon. I wanted to be sure the oKiaf and I were not contaminated with any more protocrystal, but more important, I wanted to find out exactly what Maggie was.

Shon's vitals and scans read normal for his species, with a slight elevation in synaptic activity. "Any headache or aftereffects?"

"I feel as I did before we came into the rift," he said carefully, and touched his chest. "I think my difficulties after the passage were caused by the protocrystal infection."

"It did not infect you," Maggie said. "It merged with you. Do I have to stay here? I want to look at that PyrsVar person again, and this is taking forever."

I glanced at ChoVa, who nodded to indicate the scans were completed. "You can talk to him, but don't be offensive. He can't help what he is."

"None of you can." She left the exam room.

As soon as we were alone, I rubbed the back of my neck. "She's like my daughter was when she was a toddler."

"She is quite childlike." Shon looked thoughtful. "She has no parents, I assume."

"I didn't see any kids down there. Maybe after they attained immortality, they lost the need to reproduce." I saw his gaze turn shrewd. "What are you thinking?"

"She maintains that she is superior to us, and yet since we came from the planet, she has been recurrently boasting about herself to you," he said. "It is as if she wishes to impress you."

I thought about it. "You mean if she genuinely believed that she was superior, she wouldn't bother bragging to me. The same way I don't go around telling my cats how wonderful I am."

"I think it more accurate to say that she wishes

to obtain your approval. In the same manner a child wishes a parent to admire their accomplishments," he said.

I covered my eyes and groaned. "She has to grow up and be my mother someday. I can't be hers."

"Perhaps you were *her* maternal influencer." Shon fastened the front of his tunic. "You remarked on how different her speech is from the Maggie you knew in our time. And yet just now she used Terran slang: 'This is taking forever.'"

"She absorbed the language from me when we were on the planet, she said. The language she taught me from birth." My head whirled. "When I was a kid, I always wondered why she talked the way she did. And I'm the one who taught her. God."

Shon touched my shoulder. "I do not mean to upset you. But everything you do in this time, especially in Maggie's presence, could have a direct effect on you in the future. Be careful, Cherijo."

Maggie seemed to be getting along with PyrsVar, who was showing her how to operate the prep unit, so I called ChoVa into my office, where she related to me and Shon what the room scanners had revealed.

"She appears to be somewhat humanoid," the Hsktskt healer said as she pulled up a holoimage of Maggie's form. "Her internal organs are similar in size and arrangement to that of certain biped species from our time, but they no longer appear to have active function. There are some other, startling differences, such as this." She stripped the derma, musculature, and organs from the holoimage, reducing it to a skeleton.

"Her bones are transparent." I magnified the image. "No cells. No marrow."

"She does not possess any blood cells, either. Her

body fluids are as clear as her skeletal system. Here is the most interesting aspect of the scan." ChoVa switched the display to thermal, and we saw Maggie's bone structure begin to twinkle with millions of tiny white lights.

"What is that?"

"Our medsysbank could not identify it," she advised me. "It does not register as matter or heat, only light."

"They absorb sunlight," I said. "Maybe they're converting it into this light. Some kind of advanced photosynthesis. It would explain why they no longer need to eat or rest."

"Are their bones made of crystal?" Shon asked.

"They don't scan as mineral, bone, or any other matter." ChoVa turned to me. "I never believed I would encounter a living organism whose physiology is beyond our comprehension, but it would appear that this female's species has evolved beyond the limits of our knowledge and understanding."

"Maggie told me on the planet that they are purifying themselves for this Great Ascension. From what I observed, they're preparing to discard their corporeal bodies and transition to a higher-level existence." I thought for a moment. "Once they abandon their bodies, they won't be able to exist here anymore. The process has to be irreversible."

"What has that to do with us?" Shon asked.

"From the time I left Terra, Maggie has been communicating telepathically with me, manipulating me and using me to carry out her orders." I turned to him. "The Jxin didn't make us immortal healers just so that we would live long enough to combat the black crystal. They couldn't do it by themselves, or they would have. After they ascend, they're going to realize they screwed up. They're going to create us to clean up the mess they left behind." I uttered a single bitter laugh. "We're not doctors, Shon. We're janitors."

He didn't like it any more than I did. "We must stop them from ascending."

"How? They aren't going to listen to us. On the planet, they barely acknowledged our existence." I pulled up the scanner readings again. "Why didn't their synaptic activity register?"

"It did, briefly," ChoVa corrected. "The scanner's display stopped registering when the comparative exceeded the maximum scale of nine hundred and ninety-nine trillion."

A nurse called in on the com panel. "Healer Cherijo?"

"Hold on." I looked at the Hsktskt. "Their synaptic activity is a quadrillion times more than ours?"

"At the very least," she agreed.

At last I understood why Maggie's people had been so quick to dismiss us. "A Jxin having a conversation with us would be about the same as me trying to having a heart-to-heart talk with bacteria."

"Healer Cherijo," the nurse called again over the panel.

Feeling impatient over the interruption, I punched the button. "What is it?"

"It is the female visitor," the nurse said. "She and the crossbreed went into one of the surgical suites."

The last thing I needed right now was Maggie fooling around with the equipment. "Please tell them to come out of there."

"I attempted to, Healer. The female secured the entry from the inside before she initiated a sterile field." The nurse sounded frightened. "According to the power console, she has enabled the lascalpel."

ChoVa shot to her feet the same moment I did. "PyrsVar."

The three of us ran to the suite, which was in procedure lockdown. The panel refused to accept my emergency override codes.

I tried the intercom. "Maggie? Open this door."

"There is no need for you to come in," she said calmly. "I am helping you with your work."

"Open it this instant," I insisted.

"I will when I am finished." She shut off the com.

ChoVa used her fist to punch a hole into the entry panel, from which a shower of sparks exploded. Then she dug her claws into the panels' center seam and wrenched them apart.

"Deactivate sterile field," I called out as she rushed in, and then Shon and I followed her. We stopped beside her as we saw Maggie and PyrsVar, or what was left of him.

"You should not have done that," Maggie said as she passed her hand over the rogue's gaping chest cavity, causing it to glow with light as one of his hearts floated out of it. "The air on board this vessel is not pure."

She deposited the heart into a second body that lay on another gurney, a body that also had an open chest wound—one that was filled with PyrsVar's bloodied Jorenian organs.

Twelve

"What have you done?" ChoVa said as she rushed over to PyrsVar's side. "You have killed him."

"I removed the organs that do not belong in him," Maggie said. "He is not dead."

Nor was he anesthetized, I saw, but mercifully he was unconscious. "Was he awake when you started cutting into him?"

"I made him go to sleep," Maggie said. "The other one was already asleep."

"What other one?" I demanded. "Who is that? One of the interns? Where did you get him?"

"I did not get him. I made him." She nodded toward the Jorenian body on the second gurney. "I used the stunted, sleeping one trapped in the Hsktskt's chest to make the form. I needed something to serve as the receptacle, and he was not using the other."

As soon as she had transferred the organ into the Jorenian body, I shoved her aside and inspected the rogue's chest cavity. She may have been using some form of light energy to perform the horrific surgery, but she was no surgeon. She'd butchered him.

"Shon, get into your gear." I pulled on a shroud, a mask, and gloves. "ChoVa, see to the Jorenian."

"I will help you," Maggie offered.

"You will stand aside," I told her, "while I try to repair what you've done to this man."

She looked mystified. "I have done the work. I have separated him."

"You've hacked him to pieces." I put PyrsVar over onto the heart-lung machine and pulled down the lascalpel. Maggie had cauterized the severed vessels as she removed the organs, which would buy me a little time. "I need four scrubs nurses in here," I shouted.

ChoVa had pulled on her gear and was now focused on the Jorenian, although she kept looking over at PyrsVar.

"It's all right," I told her. "I've got him."

"We could put him in stasis now," she said desperately. "You could use the retroviral compound to rebuild his body."

"I designed it to work in an immersion tank, and he'd never survive that." I turned my head and saw the monitors weren't hooked up. "Shon, scan him and give me his vitals."

"BP is dropping, heart rate decreasing," he told me as he performed the scan and then started anesthetic. "He needs blood, but what type?"

"Auto-infuse him for now." I looked over at the nurses coming in. "Do we have any crossbreed blood synthesized?"

"He is not a crossbreed any longer," Maggie announced. "I have purified him."

"Shut up," I snapped, and turned to Shon. "Type his blood."

"I already have." He met my gaze. "It's Hsktskt, type J."

Thirty minutes ago PyrsVar had been a crossbreed. "It can't be. Do it again."

"I have, three times. All the readings are identical." Shon sent one of the nurses to retrieve all the units of Hsktskt J blood we had stored. "Maybe we should permit the Jxin to complete the separation."

"It is done," Maggie told him. "You said you wanted them separated, Cherijo. That is what I did."

"Can you repair all this damage?" I asked Shon.

He gave the chest cavity a long look. "The organs will have to be in their proper position for me to heal them."

"That I can do." I pulled down the lascalpel and started on the heart. "ChoVa?"

"The Jorenian's heart has begun to beat on its own," she told me, her voice harsh. "I am completing the liver transplant. Can you save him?"

I exchanged a look with Shon. "We'll bring him back."

As I worked on putting PyrsVar's remaining organs back in their proper places, I cursed myself for leaving Maggie alone. Her literal interpretation of our casual remarks might cost the rogue his life, and ChoVa the love of hers. As soon as I could, I was putting her on a launch—or pushing her out of the nearest convenient air lock.

"You are angry with me," I heard Maggie say in an astonished voice. "That is why you behave this way. But why?"

"I'm not angry," I assured her. "I'm furious. I could kill you with my bare hands."

She looked sulky again. "No, you cannot."

"What makes you think you can rip open a man's chest and start pulling organs out of it?"

"He was dying."

"He was fine." But even as I said that, I moved down and saw the condition of his only remaining kidney. It was atrophied, but with a little luck Shon could heal it. "What did you do with his other kidney?"

"It was dead tissue, and it was poisoning him," she replied blithely. "I removed it and destroyed it."

ChoVa made a strange sound. "That explains the strangeness in his color. He was very pale today; he must have been in renal failure. But he never said anything to me."

PyrsVar probably thought admitting something was wrong was unmanly. Since his Jorenian kidneys had not been functioning, without treatment he probably would have died in a few hours.

"Why didn't you come and tell me this?" I asked Maggie.

"I wished to, but the male said I should not," she told me. "He believed that you would not permit me to separate him. He said it was his decision, not yours." She came over to the table. "The derma will take several weeks to regenerate. I promised that I would also help regrow the two missing limbs and his rear appendage."

"You're not to touch a single scale on his body," I said through my teeth. "Or anyone else on the ship. Ever again. Is that clear?"

"Your language is quite simple," she assured me. "I understand you perfectly."

I finished reconnecting the organs in PyrsVar's lower abdomen and checked over the major vessels in the rest of his limbs. "All right," I said to Shon. "Your turn."

He stripped off his gloves and came around the table, inspecting the open chest. "I will begin with the heart, and work out from there. It will not take long. As soon as his pulse and respiration restart, you must remove him from the machine."

I took Shon's place by the equipment. "I'm ready when you are."

The oKiaf placed both paws over the open chest cavity and closed his eyes as his pads started to glow.

"He uses the light as we do, for purification," Maggie said, astounded. "Why did you not have him separate them?"

"Be quiet," I snapped at her, staring at PyrsVar's organs as Shon healed them one by one. As soon as the heart pulsed and the lungs inflated, I took the rogue off life support. "His heart is beating, ChoVa," I said over my shoulder. "He's breathing on his own now."

She murmured something under her breath, maybe a prayer. "I will need your assistance when you are finished there," she said. "This Jorenian could awake before I am able to close."

When Shon nodded to me, I left him with Pyrs-Var and went over to the second gurney. Despite her distress ChoVa had done an excellent job transplanting the remains of the Jorenian liver, although there appeared to be another half still intact in the chest.

I started anesthetic to keep him unconscious before I inspected the rest of her work. "The heart looks good. What about the bowel?"

"It was not as lengthy as it should be, and then ..."

She looked at me over the edge of her mask. "It began to grow inside him."

"I accelerated the growth of some of the organs that required enlargement to attain the correct size," Maggie put in. "That is the only way they would work."

"I'll take it from here," I told the Hsktskt. "Go and see if Shon is ready to close."

Once I had scanned the Jorenian's chest and ensured all the organs were functioning, I closed the cross-shaped incision Maggie had used to open his chest. The last of my sutures ended just below the collarbone, and I noticed a small black spot on the side of the throat. It was the male's ClanSign, the uplifted wing that was the mark of HouseClan Torin.

I hadn't thought about what Maggie would build out of PyrsVar's Jorenian organs—or whom.

The male's black hair had already grown several inches out of his scalp and had fallen to cover half his face. I knew that mouth, but I still tugged off my glove and brushed the hair back so I could see the nose and eyes and brows. The four parallel scars that had been on PyrsVar's face were gone.

I looked down at the face that I had never expected to see again in this lifetime or any other. "Kao."

Maggie pushed me away from the gurney, tearing my shroud at the same time. "Cherijo, you must go out into the large room now."

I wanted to deck her, but as she'd pointed out on the planet, I'd just hurt my hand. "I'm not done here."

"You are needed." She wrapped her hand around my wrist, used her other hand to blow a hole through one of the wall panels, and dragged me through. She gestured at the gaping medical staff. "Make them move."

"Move where?" I tried to pull free, but she had a grip like a snow tiger's. "Stop it."

Maggie turned to the staff. "Move back. Hurry." When several of them extended their claws, she jerked on my arm. "Make them move. If I do it, they will be hurt."

I didn't want her to kill my people. "I Shield the Jxin," I said to keep them from attacking her. "Evacuate immediately to the corridor."

The staff quickly filed out, although several still looked back at us with murderous expressions.

I turned to Maggie. "Now, what is the big—"

A wide, powerful surge of energy shot from the lower deck and punched a hole through the upper, scorching the alloy and then melting through it. The blast fanned out from there into a dozen and then a hundred crackling streams. The displaced air slammed into me, and only Maggie's hand kept me from being knocked flat on my back.

In the center of the energy streams a dark vortex formed, pulling in the power all around it and billowing outward. Every piece of equipment in the bay went dark, while datapads, charts, and instruments flew into the air and began whirling around the twisting mass like debris until the last of the energy was swallowed up. The vortex brightened and began to shrink as if it was collapsing in on itself.

"Can you move it off the ship?" I shouted to Maggie over the noise.

"Wait," she said, peering into the mass. "They are almost through now."

DREAM CALLED TIME   241

"They?" I echoed, squinting as the light grew blinding. "Someone is in that thing? Who is it?"

"I do not know." She looked almost afraid now. "Now they come."

Without warning the vortex disappeared into itself, and the small cloud of debris that had encircled it fell to the deck. A few crackles of residual energy still buzzed in the air as two figures appeared: a tall adult and a small child.

I didn't believe my eyes, even when they solidified. "Reever?" I had to walk over and reach out my trembling hand so that I could touch my daughter. "Marel."

Her face looked dead white, and when she spoke, her voice came out in a whisper. "I found her, Daddy."

Reever caught her as she fainted, and lifted her against his chest. Over her golden curls he stared at me, becoming my mirror, both of us gaping at each other as if we were seeing ghosts. "Cherijo?"

I took Marel from my husband and carried her over to the nearest berth. She lay limp and unresponsive in my arms, and as soon as I checked her vitals, I knew she was in shock. I shouted for a nurse as I checked her pupils, which barely contracted, and quickly her small form for external injuries.

"What happened?" I demanded.

"I don't know. We were on Joren, at the Torin pavilion." Reever's voice sounded hollow. "Marel and I were sitting in the courtyard."

"Where you were sucked into an energy vortex that transported you six million years into the past, where you just happened to land on this ship in my medical bay?" I glared at him. "You might want to run that by me again, Duncan. Starting with, how?"

"We were in the courtyard," he insisted. "She has been trying to signal the *Sunlace* without success, and asking me each day when you would be returning. I felt it was time to tell her the truth. I explained to her that your ship had vanished into a rift in space."

I scanned her for internal hemorrhaging, but found nothing. "Then what?"

"She claimed she could find you. I told her that the rift had disappeared, that it was impossible even to know where you were." He flexed his fingers as if they were stiff. "She put her hand in mine and smiled up at me. The next thing I knew, we were here."

"You're telling me that our daughter can teleport through time?" I snarled. "Have you lost your mind?"

"He speaks the truth." Maggie appeared beside me and looked down at Marel. "She can sense the places where space is thin and conduits can be made. She is not particularly skilled at making them stable, however. I felt it begin to collapse before they emerged."

My daughter was in shock, I was surrounded by crazy people, and we were all stranded millions of years from the nearest medical facility. I shouted for the only person who could help me save my daughter's life. "Shon."

"Here." He didn't spare Reever a second glance as he looked at my kid. "She is very weak. I can hardly feel her."

I could barely take in enough air to speak. "Can you bring her back? Please?"

"This is not damage to the body, Cherijo," he said.

He turned to Maggie. "You know what has to be done, do you not?"

She lifted her chin. "She said I was not to touch another being on this vessel."

I grabbed the front of her robe and yanked her close. "Don't you dare start acting snotty again. If you can heal her, do it. Now."

"The conduit was unstable. As she tried to keep it from collapsing on her and the man, she left some of herself between. She cannot live without it." Maggie looked down at my fist. "You are angry with me again."

"I apologize." Knowing my daughter's life hung in the balance, I could afford to lie through my teeth. "Please, if there is anything you can do to repair the damage, help her."

"I do not have what she needs," Maggie told me. "What she left behind is lost. It can be replaced, but it must come from the source. It must come from you."

"I don't understand."

"She is not exactly like you," the Jxin said, "but she has some of you, and some of him." She nodded at Reever. "She needs what you gave her before, when you made her."

"What? What exactly does she need?"

Maggie tapped my wrist. "It is in your blood."

"My blood is poisonous," I snapped. "I can't give her a transfusion. It'll kill her."

Maggie nodded. "You must take away what is lethal before you give her what she is missing. I can do this."

My daughter's pulse had grown so faint I could barely detect it on my scanner. "What do you need?"

A few moments later we had rigged a transfuser

from my arm to Marel's. I clamped off the tubing halfway and fitted a dialysis reservoir between us.

"All right, now what?" I asked Maggie.

"I will purify it." She crouched down, releasing the clamp and slowly filling the reservoir with a pint of my blood. As soon as it was full, she cupped it between her hands, bombarding it with the strange light energy she used.

I watched my blood turn clear. "You're removing the platelets. If all she needed was some plasma, why didn't you say so?"

"It is more than plasma," Maggie murmured as she concentrated. "It does not have a name because you have not yet discovered it. Now shut up."

I bit my lip and looked over at my husband. He was kneeling beside the berth and holding our daughter's hand, but he was staring at me.

"How long has she been able to do this?" I asked him.

"She teleported herself and TssVar's son on Vtaga," he said. "That was the last time that I know she attempted it."

I was still angry with him. "Why didn't you just lie to her when the ship disappeared?"

"After you went missing from Oenrall, I lied to her for years," he said, the lines of weariness around his mouth and nose deepening. "I told her you were still alive and just waiting for us to find you. That we had to keep looking."

"That wasn't a lie."

"I knew you were dead. I wouldn't admit it to myself—I couldn't—but somewhere inside me, I could feel it." His eyes turned to a glassy blue. "Lying to myself and our child was all that kept me sane during those years. Finding Jarn was . . ." He trailed off and shook his head. "It was wrong to take Jarn from her friends and her people. But we needed you, and she was all that was left."

"You can stop there." I didn't want to hear the story of his big romance again. I looked at Maggie, who had taken her hands away from the reservoir. "Is it ready?"

"Yes." She released the clamp on the transfuse tube and allowed the clear fluid to slowly seep into my daughter's veins.

"If this poisons her," I said in a low voice, "I will spend the rest of my existence finding a way to kill you, Jxin."

She looked more puzzled than worried. "Even if you could, then you would die."

"Why would I want to live without her?" I felt dizzy and closed my eyes.

It took what felt like an eternity before I saw the first signs of color returning to my daughter's small face. Then her blood pressure rose and her heart rate steadied. As I removed the needle from my arm, her breathing became more regular.

I didn't relax; what we had done was beyond foolhardy. But after another hour of constant monitoring, and no signs of any toxic reaction to the transfusion, some of the tension eased out of my shoulders.

"She will be well now," Maggie said. "You have saved her life."

"So did you." I studied her lovely, indifferent face, and wondered how she could rip apart a man and then save a little girl, all within the space of a few hours. "Thank you."

She imitated my smile. "Now will you tell me how you were able to use the collector?"

ChoVa and Shon took over monitoring PyrsVar and Kao in recovery so that I could stay with my daughter. Maggie seemed content to watch the maintenance crew repair the damage from the vortex, and when that palled, she created exotic concoctions at the prep unit and tried to coax the nursing staff into sampling them. To be safe, I summoned a couple of security guards to keep an eye on her. That left me alone with Reever in the isolation room where I'd moved Marel so she could rest undisturbed.

I expected that my husband would want to know what had happened to us since the *Sunlace* had been swallowed up by the rift. When he held his hand out to me, I realized giving him access to my mind was the simplest and quietest way to update him. So I let him initiate a link, but I didn't try to project any thoughts to him. Instead I let him search through my memories and see whatever he wanted.

You have not discovered how to return to our time, he thought to me. *Can Maggie re-create the rift that brought the ship here?*

I don't know, I admitted. *Maybe. She has tremendous power, but she's also unpredictable. I'd rather find our own means of getting back home.*

I could attempt to communicate with the protocrystal and persuade it to help us. He winced as the memories of the Core plague and the possession of the oKiaf welled up into my thoughts. *Then again, perhaps not.*

After seeing what it did to Shon, I vote no. I could feel the edge of something dark in his mind, an emotion he was trying to suppress. All of it centered around Marel. *I have been through this before, Duncan. If my blood had hurt her, I would have found the beginning stages of toxicity by now. She's going to recover.*

I believe you. He seemed a little uncomfortable that I had picked up on his negative emotion. *I can't lose her now, Cherijo. Not after losing both you and Jarn. I would not survive it.*

You found me again. Resentment still filled a few corners in my heart, but the prospect of never seeing my family again had made his betrayal seem less monstrous than before. If I was going to be completely honest, he hadn't betrayed me; he'd simply tried to cope. It wasn't his fault he'd fallen in love with Jarn, or because of it he'd realized that he'd never been in love with me. None of this had happened by my choice or his.

Maybe, I thought, if I let go of the last of my pride and tried to take Jarn's place in his life, eventually he might learn how to feel some affection for me again.

What are you thinking?

You're occupying my mind, Duncan. If you can't tell, we're both in a lot of trouble.

He laced his fingers through mine. *You are not as simple to read as you once were. Part of your mind is closed to me now. It has been since you returned.*

I was thinking I'd rather be a poor substitute for Jarn than go on living alone. I squeezed his hand. *When all this is over and we're back on Joren, we should do like you said, and talk about it. Try to work things out.*

You would do that? He touched my cheek.

My motives are completely selfish, trust me. I glanced up and broke the link between us as I saw ChoVa gesturing at me from the view panel. "I'll be back as soon as I can," I murmured before I slipped out of the room.

"I regret disturbing you, but the Jorenian male has regained consciousness," she told me. "Shon thought you should be the one to first speak with him."

"Signal the captain and ask him to come down here," I said. "Assign one of the nurses to keep an eye on Marel and Reever for me, too."

It wasn't easy to walk into recovery and see Kao Torin sitting up in his berth and looking around him with his gentle, curious eyes. When he saw me, he made a simple gesture of greeting and smiled when I returned it.

"How are you feeling, ClanSon?" I asked as I scanned his chest.

"I fear I am a little confused." He politely waited until I had completed my first scan before he asked, "Where am I?"

"You're on the *Sunlace*." Giving him too much information might cause him to panic, so I kept the details to a minimum as I briefed him. "What's the last thing you remember?"

"I cannot say for certain. I had left Joren to serve as a pilot at a new colony. I remember being on patrol." He peered up at me. "May I know your name, Healer?"

"I'm Cherijo Torin," I said, watching his face. He gave no reaction to my name. "Your HouseClan adopted me some time ago. I'm the Senior Healer on this vessel."

"Tonetka Torin retired at last, did she?" He chuckled. "Captain Pnor often despaired that she never would. May I speak with the captain?"

"Pnor embraced the stars some time ago, Clan-

Son." His readings were in good ranges; he was simply weak from blood loss and, I imagined, the shock of being built out of an alterform's spare parts. "We have a new captain now."

"Kao?"

Xonea strode into recovery and stood over his ClanBrother, his eyes wide as he looked all over him and then at me. "How has this happened?"

"You would have the Senior Healer explain the matter of our kinship, ClanBrother?" Kao joked. "Surely you have not forgotten the hundred times ClanFather has told that tale at the gatherings."

"Mother of all Houses. He is Kao." Xonea turned chalk white. "Returned to us as you were."

"There's a bit more to it than that." I touched Xonea's arm. "Your ClanBrother's last memory was his last assignment as a pilot."

He pinned me with a sharp glance. "He does not recall you?"

"Have we met before, Healer?" Kao asked mildly. "Your pardon, but I do not remember you."

"No pardon is required, ClanSon. Would you excuse us for a moment?" When he nodded, I led Xonea out of recovery and closed the door panel. "Maggie removed all the Jorenian organs and DNA from Pyrs-Var, and re-created Kao from them. He has retained some memory of his past life, but evidently nothing beyond his transfer to K-2."

"These organs taken from the Hsktskt were cloned from my brother's cells. This male never lived as Kao Torin. And yet . . . he is my ClanBrother. His voice, his hands . . ." He looked through the viewer. "I know that bodies can be duplicated, but how could anyone re-create a life lost?"

"His life was not lost, Jorenian." Maggie came to stand by the viewer and looked in on our patient.

"That man died in my arms ten years ago," I told her, my hands curling into fists. "Don't you tell me he was still alive when we put him in that capsule."

"The body died," she assured me. "Before that, you gave him your blood. It changed his cells. It preserved what he was."

"No." I swallowed. "My blood is what killed him."

"This is because you are impure. Like the other, but more complicated." She regarded me. "Do you wish me to separate you?"

I thought of Jarn, and how happy Reever would be to have her back. "Sorry, but I don't have another body sitting inside my chest."

She shrugged, and started to say something else, when she frowned and turned toward the starboard side of the ship. "There is another vessel approaching."

"You claimed that you did not have any ships," Xonea said.

"It does not belong to the Jxin." Her expression cleared. "It is only the undesirables."

Something hit the side of the *Sunlace*, rocking the deck under our feet.

"They are shooting at you," Maggie said helpfully.

Thirteen

Xonea left Medical while the staff and I secured our patients and prepared for incoming wounded. I went to the isolation room to check on Marel, who was still sleeping, and brief Reever on the situation.

"Unless Xonea needs you to negotiate with these people," I told him, "I want you to stay here with her."

"I am not leaving her." He glanced out at the nurses hurrying to prep our staging area. "What provoked this attack?"

"We've been signaling for help since we got here." I bent down to kiss my little girl on the brow. "This is probably why they didn't respond."

Maggie didn't protest when I put her to work preparing triage gurneys and instrument trays, although she seemed a little bewildered by our response to the attack.

"They have a faster vessel, and more powerful weapons," she told me. "You should not shoot back."

I'd already heard the sonic cannons booming as Xonea returned fire. "Maybe we'll get lucky. Why are they attacking us, Maggie? What did we do?"

"It is not what you did; it is what they do." She shrugged, and then said something even more ominous. "That is why there are no others. They attacked and killed all of them."

The first wave of wounded arrived from a lower level that had suffered heavy damage and some sort of explosion. The crew's injuries were a combination of impact fractures and serious burns. Whatever weapons the Odnallak were using employed a lethal phosphorous compound I'd never seen before: one that flash-burned on contact and then continued to burn through the derma down through the muscle and bone tissue, charring everything in its path. Three crew members died before I found the right counteragent to neutralize it.

Shon joined me as I finished assessing a navigator with spinal trauma. Jorenian blood spattered the front of the oKiaf's tunic, and he looked ready to maul someone. "I will do what I can here."

"Don't overextend your ability," I warned him. "I'm going to need you in surgery."

Grimly I reported our status to Command, issued orders for the neutralizer to be administered to every burn victim who came in for treatment, and then took my first patient, a female with severe head trauma, into surgery.

The battle raged on, and as the ship shuddered and jerked around us, I wondered how long the stardrive core would hold up. If the Odnallak were able to successfully locate and target it, this fight and the ship wouldn't last much longer.

I worked as fast as I dared to remove tiny fragments of bone from my patient's brain before I closed and called for the next patient.

Time and faces began to blur as I operated to save patients with crushed rib cages, fractured spines, and battered organs. At some point I realized the fight had ended, but then we began having disruptions in our power supply, and I had to give the order to switch the bay over to the emergency generators in order to maintain life support systems for the critically wounded.

When I had a minute between cases, I looked in on Shon and ChoVa, who were working in the other surgical suites, and the residents, who were handling the now-overflowing triage. I issued orders to our logistics technicians for them to set up every available chamber on our level as temporary patient wards. Our caseload surpassed twenty, then fifty, then reached a hundred before security stopped carrying in wounded.

Six hours after the battle, almost one-third of the crew had reported or had been brought to Medical for treatment.

Xonea signaled me sometime that night. "We have negotiated a cease-fire."

"Thank God." I stripped off one bloody glove before I rubbed my tired eyes. "What are the terms?"

"We are to follow them to their homeworld and surrender some of our people to them for questioning."

I didn't like that. "Who do they want?"

"Maggie, you, Duncan, the Hsktskt, and the oKiaf." Before I could ask, he added, "They would not explain how they knew your names, or why they wish to question you."

I glanced at the isolation room. "Can we jump away from here?"

"Only if we wish to finish what the Odnallak started.

The stardrive is inoperable and on the verge of implosion." He sounded old and very tired. "Cherijo, we cannot escape or continue to fight. Presently the only thing holding the ship together is the protocrystal. If I am to make repairs and save the crew . . ."

"I'll speak to the others, and we'll get ready," I promised. I already knew what their answer would be. "All I want in return is for you to protect Marel, and get everyone home. Do whatever it takes, even if it means leaving us here."

"I will, ClanSister."

We arrived at Odnalla two days later and assumed orbit above the planet. I caught a few hours of sleep now and then on a cot in Marel's room in between caring for our patients. Reever never left her side and ate only when I brought food to him, and slept in the chair beside her berth only when I threatened to sedate him. Our exhausted daughter slept a great deal, but the few times she woke, she was alert and coherent, if a little confused. She had no memory of teleporting to the *Sunlace*, and in particular watched me with wary eyes.

"Healer Cherijo," she said on the second day, when I paid her a visit during my morning rounds, "you are my mama, aren't you?"

"Yes." The lapses in her memory did concern me, but considering the trauma she had suffered, they weren't unexpected. "Do you remember being with me on Joren?" Her curls bounced as she shook her head. "I came to see you after Jarn left."

She looked at me, and then her father. "Daddy? Who is Jarn?"

Reever exchanged a look with me before he said,

"She was a friend of ours who stayed with us while your mother was away."

"Oh." She yawned and her eyelids began to droop. "Was she nice?"

"She was very nice." I sat down on the edge of the berth and held her hand. "Marel, try to stay awake a little longer. I need to ask you some questions to see how well you can think now. Do you know how old you are?"

"Four." She frowned. "No. Nine. I'm nine years old."

I didn't have time to run a full neurological series on her; I'd have to hope I'd have the chance when we returned from the planet. If we returned. "Can you tell me where you were before you and Daddy came to the ship to see me?"

"In the courtyard at the pavilion. I was finishing my schoolwork. I was sad." She sighed. "I'm very tired, Mama. Can't I rest now?"

"All right, baby. Go back to sleep." I held her hand until she drifted off, and then gestured for Reever to come with me.

Outside her room, we both watched her through the view panel.

"Has she suffered brain damage?" my husband asked, his voice tight.

"I don't think so." I rested a hand on his shoulder. "This amnesia was trauma-induced, and it's not completely retrograde. She remembers only select events and facts. I think her mind has chosen to forget what has hurt her most."

"Losing Jarn."

I nodded. "She feels responsible for what happened to Jarn." I related what Marel had confessed to me during the surreptitious signal she had sent from Joren, and added, "I tried to reassure her that it wasn't her fault, Duncan. I wasn't happy about her transferring her affections to Jarn, but I would never allow her to think she was to blame for her death."

"She tried to warn Jarn and me of what was going to happen," he said slowly. "Somehow she knew when we left Joren for oKia that she would never see Jarn again."

Xonea signaled to let us know that the launch was ready to take us down to the planet, and that during preflight checks the bay chief had discovered the protocrystal had already retreated from the hull doors.

"It wants us to go down there," I said as I peered through the viewport at the Odnallak's dark and dismal-looking homeworld. "But why?"

"Perhaps we were meant to meet them as well as the Jxin," Reever suggested.

None of it made sense to me. Both species had advanced well beyond our capabilities; even if the Odnallak were less evolved than the Jxin, the massive ship they had sent to attack us had more than enough firepower to vaporize the *Sunlace*. One of the technicians I'd given a follow-up exam to had mentioned scanning a number of worlds we had passed on the sojourn to Odnalla. All of them were dead worlds that appeared to have been attacked from orbit, so viciously that every trace of life had been wiped out.

"PyrsVar was displeased when I told him we were sojourning down to the planet," ChoVa told me as we left Medical. "I was obliged to sedate him so that he would not try to follow us."

"Smart idea. His body is still adjusting to all the changes." I glanced at Maggie and lowered my voice.

"She doesn't seem to be worried about meeting the enemy."

"I can hear you," Maggie said. "I do not worry. The undesirables can do nothing to me."

ChoVa flicked out her tongue. "She has no fear."

"Or common sense," Shon put in.

Maggie sighed. "I can still hear you."

None of us were carrying weapons, but Reever went to weapons storage and helped himself to several daggers. After a thoughtful glance, Shon joined him, and the two returned looking slightly more at ease.

"You know they're probably going to disarm you the minute we step off the launch," I advised my husband and the oKiaf.

"They may try," Reever said.

"What is it with males and the unknown that makes them resort to weapons?" ChoVa asked me as we boarded.

I hefted my case onto an upper rack. "It's probably the reason our response is to pack extra medical supplies."

With the exception of Maggie, we were all on edge. We were surrendering ourselves to an enemy that had likely destroyed almost all the other civilizations in this region. Not knowing their intentions or what we would be facing down on the planet didn't help matters.

During the flight Reever briefed us on the surface conditions. "The climate is harsh, and the atmosphere thin. Gravity will be half of what we are accustomed to, so curtail your movements. The Odnallak appear to have resurfaced most of the landmasses to serve their population. Natural resources have been exhausted; they rely heavily on their technology and offworld sources to support life."

"Are they raiders?" ChoVa asked.

"Scans indicate more than a thousand types of nonindigenous life-forms," he told her. "We must assume they imported these creatures from surrounding solar systems."

My husband's information was chilling, but even so it didn't prepare us for what we saw as we approached the landing coordinates the Odnallak had transmitted.

Towering structures, industrial facilities, and transportation systems covered every inch of land as far as the eye could see. Which wasn't very far at all, considering how much the Odnallak had polluted their atmosphere. A thick, dirty-looking fog hovered over the metropolis, darkening from a maroon color at the outer limits where their sun still penetrated to an ugly gray at surface level. The only water I saw was a sickly-looking green color, and was funneling through wide alloy canals between the structures.

"Open sewers." ChoVa drew back from the viewport. "What manner of people are these Odnallak, that they would dwell in their own filth?"

We got the answer to that as soon as we landed, and our pilot was instructed to lower to the docking ramp. My first inhalation of the planet's air made me choke—it was so tainted—and I grabbed breathers and quickly passed them around to the others.

"Keep them on until we get inside a sealed structure," I ordered, and then took Reever's hand and walked down the ramp.

The group waiting for us on the dock all wore helmets and protective garments, and carried their own air supply on their backs. They also held glowing spheres that they extended like weapons. One of them pointed at us and swept his arm around toward a nearby elevated transport system while the others flanked us.

We walked to the rail transport, climbed inside one of the compartments, and stood waiting as some of the Odnallak came in behind us. The compartment's doors closed, and I nearly fell over as the transport took off at high speed.

"This is like a visitors' tram," I murmured, watching the Odnallak city flash by as the transport sped along. "Only who wants to tour this place?"

One of the Odnallak's helmets turned toward me, and through it he issued a stern command.

How were we supposed to answer their questions if they weren't going to make the slightest effort to communicate with us? "I guess that means be quiet."

The transport stopped at one of the largest structures at the very edge of the city, where we were escorted off the compartment, then led through a tunnel and into the gigantic building. We passed through three different chambers that scanned us and blasted us with different gases before we reached the interior.

Once inside, our captors removed their helmets and began speaking to one another in hard, clipped voices. I didn't recognize their language, but their features held me riveted.

They were all male, each with the same black hair and dark blue eyes. Their faces were scarred, bitter masks, some showing open sores, broken capillaries, and other signs of ill health, but other than those aberrations their features were nearly identical—and their features were Terran. I couldn't believe what I was seeing until one of them moved and a light emitter illuminated the gray sheen of his dark hair.

The Odnallak all looked as if they could be my brothers.

I shook my head, wrenching my hand from Reever's and backing away. "This is a mistake. A trick. They're shape-shifters—they're doing this deliberately." I turned and ran toward the decon chambers.

Our pilot caught me and smiled down at me. "You cannot leave. You have just arrived."

I knew I was behaving irrationally, but I couldn't overcome the terror I felt. "Get me out of here."

"This is your home, Cherijo." The pilot's face began to pale and seemed to dwindle as his body shrank inside his uniform. His black hair pulled back into his skull and took on a gray cast, while his white-within-white eyes formed new, dark blue irises. He smiled, baring Terran teeth, and when he spoke, it was in the same language as that of the other Odnallak. Then he looked into my eyes and tried to touch my face.

I staggered back. "Stay away from me."

"Cherijo." He stood there beaming like a benevolent demon. "Is that any way to speak to your father?"

Reever caught me from behind and clamped an arm around my waist as he initiated a link. *That is not Joseph Grey Veil,* he told me firmly. *We watched him die on Terra. He is a shape-shifter trying to frighten you. All of these men are shape-shifters.*

"Your theory, while admirable, is flawed by your ignorance," the Odnallak said to my husband. "The Joseph Grey Veil you witnessed being murdered on

Terra was simply a clone. I have employed many over time."

"He read your thoughts." I watched him stroll over to the other Odnallak, who engaged him in what sounded like a loud, furious argument. "How could he do that?"

"He is telepathic," Maggie advised me. "And not like the others. He is very old. They are not shape-shifters, Cherijo."

"What else do you know about them, Maggie?" Reever asked.

"They have changed since we put them here. They bred with some of the others before they killed them to have new ones." She frowned at the group of arguing men. "The undesirables wish to hurt us and kill us, but the old one does not."

"He's not Joseph." I didn't sound convincing, even to my own ears. "Joseph is dead."

Reever didn't look at him, but focused his attention on me. "It doesn't matter who he is, or who these people are. They mean nothing to us. Do you understand me?"

I nodded tightly, and wrapped my arms around my waist.

The Odnallak wearing my creator's face returned to us. "If you wish to avoid pointless torture and painful death, you will come with me now."

"I'm not going anywhere with you."

"Very well." He gestured toward the men. "They are very curious about the Hsktskt and the oKiaf, as they have never seen their species. I imagine they will be the first to be dissected."

"We agreed to come here to be questioned," Reever said.

"My ancestors have lied to you, dear boy. When they have carved you up and harvested what they want from your bodies, they'll signal the ship and tell them to send another group, and threaten to execute you if they do not. It will take a few weeks, but eventually they'll collect the entire crew that way."

Shon stepped between us. "We will go with you."

"Excellent." Joseph beamed at us and gestured toward another chamber. "This way, please."

We followed him into a complex industrial center where hundreds of Odnallak were working. The group that had argued with him followed behind us, still bickering among themselves, so there was no chance for us to escape. We walked across alloy bridges suspended above massive pits where enormous machines operated.

"Those are this city's air and water purifiers," Joseph mentioned as he noticed my interest. "As you observed outside, my ancestors have thoroughly poisoned the atmosphere and razed the planet in their efforts to make it hospitable."

"It did not look like this when you were brought here," Maggie remarked. "It was cold and there was much ice, but there was also much life."

His smile faded. "My people were accustomed to being warm, well fed, and comfortable. What they did here was merely in an effort to reclaim what you stole from them."

"We stole nothing. We made you leave our world." Maggie gestured toward the equipment. "Had we permitted you to stay, you would have done this to it."

"We'll never know, will we?" He pointed to a passage leading from the industrial center. "In there, if you would."

We walked into a storage facility where the Odnallak had filled launch-sized bins with towering piles of ore and minerals. In the center of the facility were a complex array of equipment and wide tanks filled with molten liquid.

"This is where they have been rendering the native ores to power their city and provide fuel for their vessels." Joseph led us into the equipment complex and pointed to a series of archways spanning circular platforms. "Stand on the alloy circles, please. Everyone but you, my dear." He nodded at Maggie.

I didn't move. "What are you going to do to her?"

"The Jxin and I have much to discuss." He gave me a push toward the archways. "If you do not wish to be fired upon by my impatient brethren, you will stand on the circles now."

Reever took my arm. "Do as he says."

My husband led me over to one of the circles and positioned me on it before stepping onto one beside me. ChoVa and Shon did the same. Joseph waved one of his hands over a console, and dark liquid streamed down over us.

"I would suggest you hold very still," he advised as ChoVa thrashed her tail and I ducked my head to keep the liquid out of my face. "The matrix hardens on contact."

The liquid turned ice-cold, solidifying over our bodies while at the same time sending out thin tendrils that connected to the inside of the archway. A moment later we were all trapped in dark gray webs of oily-looking crystal.

"It is a crude form of life native to this world, and quite unbreakable," Joseph advised as ChoVa cursed and writhed. "It is also reactive to movement. The more you struggle, the tighter it will contract."

He retrieved a device and brought it over to me. "From you, dear daughter, I need some blood."

"I'm not your daughter." I hissed in a breath as he stabbed the device into my arm and used it to draw out several vials of blood. "What are you going to do with it?"

"It's a gift for our friends." He handed it over to one of the waiting Odnallak, and then strode over to Maggie, who was watching everything with visible boredom. "Now, I think some scans are in order."

The Odnallak who had taken the vials of my blood quickly left, but the others took up positions around us. I soon discovered that Joseph's claims were true, and had to force myself to be still to keep the crystal matrix from tightening around my throat and cutting off my air.

After Joseph had performed several scans of Maggie, he handed his scanner to one of the Odnallak, who studied it and uttered several sharp words.

"It seems that my ancestors want very much to boil you alive in one of their mineral vats," he told Maggie.

She didn't look alarmed at all. "That will not harm me."

"They know. It is more a symbolic act, to show their contempt for you and the rest of the Jxin." He walked around her. "Why did you accompany the primitives here?"

"Unlike you, they interest me." She walked over to me. "This one is unlike any of the others. Her mind is simple, but she is unique. She was able to operate one of our collectors."

"Ah, yes. That is because you tampered with her many millions of years from now. I was very displeased when I discovered your meddling in my experiments. But I am not one to hold a grudge." Joseph smiled at me. "Over time she has proven to be most entertaining."

"Go to hell," I told him.

"There is no hell," Maggie advised me before turning to Joseph. "How long will you keep them like this?"

"Indefinitely, unless you answer my questions."

"I do not want to stay here. I want to return to the ship." Maggie moved down to ChoVa, who was having difficulty breathing. "Loosen this one's bonds, or she will expire."

Joseph passed his hand over ChoVa's web, and the tendril wrapped around her neck eased away. Immediately she began to curse him, until he caused another to wrap around her muzzle.

"There, all better. Now, your people have been devoting themselves to ascending to the next level," he said to Maggie. "How close are you to attainment?"

She thought for a moment. "Within the solar year the eldest will acquire perfection and ascend."

He inclined his head. "My people are also very close to attainment."

"You cannot ascend." She made a negligent gesture. "You are impure."

"My people have already discovered the equations, and acquired enough power necessary to make the transition," Joseph informed her. "In fact, their entire civilization has been quite devoted to that end. Their intentions are to ascend before the Jxin."

"They cannot. They are still flawed." Maggie frowned at the other Odnallak. "They have already sickened themselves with the things they have put in their bodies. They would never survive exposing their flesh."

"On the contrary, they can and will, as soon as they collect the last element they require." He grinned at her. "Where is the infinity crystal?"

"Maggie, don't tell him," I shouted.

"It is inside the Jxin," she told him. To me she said, "You need not shout. He must know that he and the other undesirables cannot take it from us."

"We are not interested in what you have used for your own selfish purposes," Joseph said. "What we wish to know is, where is the source?"

Maggie moved her shoulders. "It came to Jxinok long ago. Some of it left. We do not care where it went."

"But you do know where it is now."

She pointed up. "It protects the vessel you attacked."

Joseph turned to the other Odnallak and spoke quickly to them. They lowered their weapons and immediately left the facility.

"What are they doing?" I demanded.

"They will be launching drones to collect the crystal from the *Sunlace*. Hopefully your captain has finished his repairs to it." He took Maggie's arm. "We're through here now, my dear. Come with me."

"Where are we going?" I heard her ask as Joseph led her away, but I couldn't hear his response.

He was probably going to drop her into one of those molten-ore vats. "Reever, we have to get out of here and warn the ship."

"I can't free myself."

"I can," Shon said, and out of the corner of my eye I saw an intense white glow. "Close your eyes."

Minutes passed as the light enveloped us, and the gray crystal began to tighten. I couldn't breathe, couldn't blink, and a scream rose in my throat as the matrix contracted and began grinding into my bones. Just when the pain grew unbearable, the tendrils encasing me began to crack and then break apart. Shards of the ruined web pelted the alloy circle and the floor all around me as I struggled to free myself of the remnants.

By the time I'd worked my way out of the web, Reever and Shon were free. ChoVa was the last to stumble out of the archway, and shook herself, flinging the shattered crystal all around her.

"If we try to leave the way we came, the Odnallak working in that industrial center will see us," I said, looking around until I spotted a small vehicle of some kind. "Shon, can you pilot that?"

He went over and looked inside the cockpit. "Yes."

The vehicle turned out to be a multipurpose transport, which could be operated on the ground as well as in the air. As Shon activated the controls, I checked the interior and tossed out some equipment to make room for the four of us.

"We have to find Maggie, get off this planet and transition the *Sunlace* out of here before they can get the protocrystal they need from the hull," I told him. "They're not going to be happy about it."

"I was a combat pilot," he said. "I know what to expect. Duncan, take the copilot's seat. ChoVa, you and Cherijo get into those harnesses."

By the time we were strapped in, Shon had engaged the engines and tested the craft's controls. "It's fast, which we'll need. Hold on."

With a maneuver that upended the craft and rolled it in a complete three sixty, Shon flew the craft across the storage facility and into the industrial complex.

Below us everything was in chaos, with smoke belching from the equipment and several small fires burning. On one of the walkways I saw Maggie standing and looking down at Joseph, who was sprawled in the bottom of one of the pits.

"There she is." I reached up and pointed. "Can you land there?"

"No, but I can hover close enough for someone to grab her." Shon changed direction and headed for the walkway.

As he descended, Maggie beamed and waved at us, squinting as the engine's backwash blasted over her.

I opened the back compartment door and turned to ChoVa. "Hold my legs."

The Hsktskt wrapped four limbs around me as I pushed the upper part of my body out of the compartment and reached down to Maggie. "Grab on to me."

She jumped up, seized my hands, and hung dangling from my grip. "You freed yourselves. I was just coming to do that."

I turned my head and yelled to ChoVa, "I have her."

The Hsktskt jerked me inside, but I lost my grip on one of Maggie's hands. She clasped my arm with her free hand and began climbing up me with ease, until she was inside. At the same time, some of the Odnallak beneath us opened fire.

I hauled Maggie over my lap and slammed the compartment door shut. "She's in," I told Shon. "Go."

"Cherijo, that was very unexpected." Maggie

struggled into an upright position. "How did you free yourselves? Were you able to operate the undesirables' machines? You are not angry with me again, are you?" She glanced at ChoVa. "You wish me to shut up now."

"That would be nice," I said.

We didn't escape the industrial complex unscathed; the Odnallak hit us with a barrage of ground fire, damaging the hull and taking out one of the engines. Still Shon somehow managed to evade the worst of it and emerge on the other side, where we had been brought in from the tram.

I saw why he had put the craft into a stationary hover. "It's too big to fit through those chambers."

Reever put his hands on two spheres set in the console, turning them until they glowed. When he pressed in on the top of the spheres, twin energy blasts shot out of the front of the craft and blew an enormous hole through the air locks.

"Now it's not," he said.

Shon flew through the ragged gap and up to the rail transport station, where I saw innumerable trams coming to a stop and a horde of armed Odnallak pouring out of them. But rather than fly over the rails, Shon darted the craft under them.

There wasn't more than a few feet of space on either side of us as he flew beneath the elevated rails, turning the craft sideways here and there to squeeze through even narrower spaces between the support struts.

I looked back and saw several other craft in pursuit. "We've got company, coming up fast." I winced as one pilot misjudged his distance, clipped a strut, and slammed into the ground, exploding on impact. Then

I glanced ahead and saw we were headed straight for some kind of blockade of other craft. "Shon."

"Brace yourselves, this is going to be ugly." He brought the craft to a sudden stop amid a hail of weapons fire from the blockade, wrenched the nose up, and shot in between the rails.

The craft bounced into something that careened away, and through the side view panel I saw it was one of the transports, which fell directly on top of the blockade. Things began exploding as we cleared the rails and Shon righted the craft.

"They will have the launch surrounded," Reever said, "and the docking area guarded. Our power cells are almost drained."

"They believe we're primitive, so this should work." Shon banked the craft, circling around the docking area and drawing fire away from our launch. He began to descend on the far side, half a mile from the launch, and stopped just short of landing.

"They're coming right at us," I said, watching the Odnallak running and firing as they swarmed across the docks.

"They are."

"I will not die if they implode this vessel-propulsion system," Maggie said. "You and Shon and Reever will be badly hurt. ChoVa will expire."

"Maybe you should land, Shon," I suggested, "and we should run?"

"Wait for it." He turned his head and showed me his fangs. "This will be better."

As soon as the Odnallak began hitting the craft with powerful blasts, Shon rammed the nose up, fired the engines, and shot away. By the time the Odnallak realized what had happened, he had landed the craft on top of our launch.

Maggie frowned as she looked out. "Why did you not set down beside it? This will not work."

"There are emergency access hatches on the roof of the launch. Follow me." I thrust open the compartment door and jumped out, hurrying to the nearest one, stopping only when I heard ChoVa cry out. I turned to see her clutching a bloodied shoulder and Reever and Shon moving quickly to grab her from either side and haul her to the hatches.

There was no time to perform a preflight or even check the fuel levels; as soon as we were inside, Shon and Reever ran to the helm and fired the engines. Maggie and I had just managed to get ChoVa strapped into a seat when the launch shot from the docking area up into the fog.

"Grab my case," I told Maggie, and then gently eased the Hsktskt's hand away from her shoulder. The wound was deep, wide, and bleeding profusely.

"It is not so bad," she said, her teeth grinding. "My arm is still attached."

While I put a pressure dressing on ChoVa's wound, Reever launched several probes, scattering them around us as Shon continued the steep climb. I understood the ruse as ground fire erupted all around us, hitting and destroying several probes but missing the launch. The dirty sky darkened to black and stars appeared as we escaped the planet's atmosphere and entered space.

"*Sunlace*, this is Shon Valtas," the oKiaf signaled. "We are en route to the ship now, ETA five minutes. Prepare for emergency departure as soon as we land."

"Confirmed, Healer Valtas," Xonea's voice said over the speaker. "Should we expect to be pursued?"

Reever checked the console. "They have not yet launched any of their star ships."

"Unknown, Captain," Shon said. "But we did not part on good terms."

"Understood. Report to Command as soon as you are on board."

I made sure ChoVa was secure in her harness before I joined the men at the helm. "May I?" When Shon nodded, I signaled the captain. "Xonea, ChoVa is injured and losing a lot of blood. I'll need a mede-vac team standing by in launch bay." When he confirmed my request, I added, "Did the Odnallak send up any probes while we were on the surface?"

"They did. They surrounded the ship for several hours, and then returned to the surface."

I looked through the viewer until I spotted the *Sunlace*, and then magnified the view.

The protocrystal that had covered the hull had vanished.

"They got what they really wanted," I said, glancing at my husband. "Do you think they'll try to use it?"

"Of course they will," Maggie said as she wandered up from the passenger compartment. "They will feed it to their machines now. Then they will release it according to their equations into their water and air, and it will kill them all."

I stared at her. "How do you know that will happen?"

"The old one had it in his head. He brought you here so that you would make it happen." She bent over the console and peered at the scanner. "They are very impatient. They have already begun."

"How were they able to remove it from the ship, Maggie?" Reever asked.

She nodded at me. "They put some of her fluids into the probes. Although if they had waited, it would have come down to the surface to find her."

I touched the spot on my arm where Joseph had tapped me. "Why would my blood lure the protocrystal into the probes?"

"You are its child, Cherijo," she chided. "Its child and mine. The old one said that in the future I used it to make you." She beamed. "That is why you were able to operate the collector."

Fourteen

Shon landed the launch on the *Sunlace* without incident, and while the men went to Command to brief Xonea, I called for a gurney and took ChoVa to Medical. Halfway there a Hsktskt male I didn't recognize came barreling down the corridor, blocking our path and leaning over the gurney.

"ChoVa?" When she didn't respond, he dropped his head back and roared in agony.

She opened one eye. "Stop making that noise. I am not dead. I am wounded. Move out of the way so that the healer may convey me to Medical."

The Hsktskt male's enormous yellow eyes glared at me. "Who shot her?"

"Who are you?" I countered.

He displayed several rows of jagged teeth. "If she lives, her betrothed. If she dies, the one who will gut you alive."

"Oh, it's you, PyrsVar." I turned to Maggie. "Are you responsible for this?"

She nodded. "I accelerated the growth of his scales before we left on the launch. He did not look well without them. Now he and ChoVa can mate."

ChoVa opened both eyes, inspected PyrsVar, and then dropped her head back. "I am not mating with a male who would let me bleed to death on a gurney."

"The romance will have to wait a little while," I agreed, and grabbed the handles of the gurney. To PyrsVar, I said, "You look very handsome. She's going to be fine. Now move or I'll have Maggie turn you into a Barterman."

PyrsVar flattened himself against a wall panel to allow us to pass, only to trot behind me and breathe down my neck as we continued on to Medical. "She is bleeding too much."

"I know."

He bumped into my back as he tried to look over my shoulder. "Her breathing sounds wrong. It is too rapid."

"She's panting because she's in pain," I told him as I wheeled her into the lift.

As soon as we were inside, he got in my face. "You must give her drugs at once."

I lifted my brows. "And which drugs would you like me to administer, Dr. Romeo?"

"I do not know," he said, scowling. "You are the healer."

"Exactly. And you"—I prodded his chest with my finger—"are not. Since I wouldn't presume to tell you how to attack a settlement, please return the favor."

"What does that mean?"

Maggie tapped his arm to get his attention. "It means shut up and let her do her job."

We made it to Medical, where with the help of several nurses we transferred ChoVa to a berth, where I personally prepped her for surgery. Since PyrsVar made it clear he wasn't going to leave her side, I sent him to cleanse and dress in scrubs.

Once we were alone, I started an IV and then prepared the anesthetic.

"How bad is it?" ChoVa asked as she watched me.

"It's not going to be easy," I admitted. "I'll need to repair the vessels and see what I can do about the severed tendons." I scanned the wound and showed her the displayed results. "As you can see, you're missing a good chunk of muscle. I'm also concerned about the length of the extensors."

"Harvest what grafts you need from my legs," she suggested. "I would rather limp than lose the use of an upper appendage."

That was what I needed to know. "I'll do my best."

"That is more than I could hope for," she assured me, her voice slurring as the anesthetic took effect and her eyelids drooped.

I signaled Command, and informed Xonea that I was going into surgery. That was when he gave me the news that a small Odnallak shuttle had managed to intercept the ship and, despite being badly damaged, had entered and landed in our launch bay. Smoke from the battered shuttle had filled the level, and by the time the emergency crews had put out the fires, the Odnallak pilot had escaped.

"We are searching for him now, and I am ordering guards stationed at Medical and every other vital area of the ship," Xonea said, "but you should advise your people to stay alert."

"Do we know who he is?" I asked.

"He was not seen by the crew," Xonea admitted. "If he is the shape-shifter, he will try to disguise himself as one of the crew."

"The only way to identify him is with a DNA sample," I told my ClanBrother. "Send one of your search team to me, and I'll give them handheld sample readers."

After I briefed the staff and told the nurses to round up as many DNA readers as they could for the search teams, I joined PyrsVar at the cleansing unit. I didn't want to think about Joseph, so as I scrubbed, I explained ChoVa's condition and how I planned to operate in words he could understand.

"Her shoulder is mangled," he said. "I have seen such wounds before on Vtaga, during the raids. Her limb will no longer function. You must have the oKiaf heal her."

"It's not that simple," I told him. "Shon can heal some wounds, but he can't regenerate missing tissue and tendons. I have to replace what was destroyed by the blast she took."

"I do not care if her limb functions," he said suddenly. "I would take her as my mate if she had no limbs." He chuffed some air through his nostrils. "But with the affection she has for her work, such a thing would cause her to suffer." He gave me a direct look. "Can you repair this damage and make her as she was?"

"I'll do whatever is possible, PyrsVar." I nodded toward the surgical suite. "We'll be working on her in there. I'll allow you to come in and observe, but you can't disrupt the procedure or distract me during surgery, or it could cost ChoVa the use of her limb. Is that clear?"

He nodded.

Once I had drafted two nurses and a resident to scrub in, I had PyrsVar move ChoVa by gurney into the suite. The gentle way he handled her touched me almost as much as what he had said. He did love her, more than I'd realized, which made me all the more determined to make the procedure as successful as possible.

After PyrsVar had placed ChoVa on the table, I initiated a sterile field and draped her body so that only her wound and her lower right leg lay exposed. I then examined the wound, cleaning out some charred tissue before I inspected the damage under the scope and confirmed my readings.

"I'm going to take some tendon and muscle from her leg now," I said to PyrsVar as I prepared to make the incision down the center of the femoral muscle sheath. To my nurse I said, "Prepare a catch basin."

I mentally reviewed what I knew about Hsktskt limbs and techniques used to repair them, and abruptly recalled the last time I had used them.

I ran in front of his gurney to the infirmary, shouted for a scrub team to move faster than the speed of light, and checked the still-twitching limb in the cryo-unit.

"I need the full text on Hsktskt limb replantation," I said as I scrubbed. "If they're not in our database, signal Command and tell them to relay them now."

A nurse brought it in on a datapad as I geared up, and I studied the data carefully. Had GothVar torn off TssVar's tail, it wouldn't have been a problem—Hsktskt regenerated those naturally. But the limb was going to require some very special, fancy cutting, especially in areas where the ruptured vessels were not as easily accessible, in and around the major shoulder joint. . . .

I pushed the laser rig up out of the way. "PyrsVar, help me turn ChoVa onto her uninjured side."

He carefully repositioned her. "Like this?"

I nodded. "That's fine. Now hold her in that position for me."

"Will it distract you if I ask why?"

"Not at all. I'm going to amputate her tail." I was already scanning it. "She doesn't need it, and it contains all the different tissues for the grafts I need."

"But if you cut it off, it will . . . grow back in a matter of weeks." His mask stretched. "And she will not limp or lose her limb."

"That's the plan." I cleansed the derma around the base of ChoVa's tail and pulled down the rig. "Nurse, we're going to need a bigger catch basin."

As I removed ChoVa's tail and dressed the stump, I told PyrsVar about that other surgery I had performed on my patient's father.

"Of course, immediately after I reattached his limb, SrrokVar had me dragged out of the infirmary and tossed back in the solitary-confinement pit," I said as I transferred a section of tendon from the dissected tail over to ChoVa's shoulder. "But if he hadn't, I would never have met the Pel, and I'd probably still be patching up slaves on Catopsa."

"That is why the Hanar looks upon you as a comrade and friend," PyrsVar said. "You saved his limb even when you knew you would likely not profit from it."

"Oh, I definitely paid for that surgery." I didn't want to think about what SrrokVar had done to me after I'd operated on TssVar, or how close I'd come to losing my mind in the crying chambers. "Nurse, a little suction, please."

Reconstructing ChoVa's shoulder took several hours, approximately a third of the tissue harvested from her tail, and many, many grafts and resections.

The most delicate part of the procedure was repairing and reattaching the extensors, which were a complicated mass of muscle and tendon that gave the Hsktskt motor control over her arm and claws. I did most of that while looking through a scope.

Finally I grafted a new outer layer of octagonal keratin scales from the tail by color to match her scale pattern—something the Hsktskt used to identify one another—and closed the last gap in the underlying layer of flesh. I wouldn't know until she healed and began physical therapy if the grafts had worked, but I felt a lot better about her chances than I had before.

"Let's take her out to recovery. Hey." I squeaked the last word as PyrsVar snatched me off my feet. "She's going to be all right. I promise." I groaned as he squeezed me. "Don't snap my spine."

He set me down on the deck and cupped my face between his claws. "I owe you a life-debt, Healer," he said formally. "For me, and for my ChoVa. Anything you may require, you have only to ask, and I will make it yours."

"You're welcome, big guy." I endured another reptilian hug before I stripped off my gloves and rolled my head to stretch the tight muscles in my neck. "She'll be out for a couple of hours, so maybe you should—"

I never got to complete my suggestion, as something hit the ship and the deck rocked under my feet.

"Not again." I rushed out of the suite and ordered the nurses to put the patients in restraints as a second blast hit the *Sunlace*. I'd just made it to Marel's room when the air turned icy and the first dazzling lights appeared.

My daughter opened her eyes. "Mama?"

I made it to her berth and climbed onto it, pulling her into my arms. "I'm here, baby. Hold on to me."

"Don't be scared, Mama," she murmured as light filled the room. "We're going home now."

I opened my eyes to see red frost forming on the buckled plasteel in front of me. The compartment where Oforon had stowed me had somehow survived the crash, although it looked as if it had been crushed in the grip of some giant hand.

The impact had also snapped my restraints, what good that did me. I tried to move and my breath rushed out as shattered bones ground together. My wrist was broken, and I couldn't feel the left side of my face. Numbing cold seeped in through the metal, spreading over me.

If I didn't get out of here, I was going to freeze.

I managed to push one shoulder against the access panel, but it wouldn't budge. The frigid temperature stole first my feet, then my legs. I wasn't walking away from this. I'd be lucky if I could crawl.

Time passed as I did, in and out of consciousness. Voices roused me, and then metal screeched and I fell out into dazzling white and blue light.

The fall stunned me as much as the icy ground, but as soon as I saw the furry, humanoid forms of my rescuers, I reached up. My hand flopped on the end of my shattered wrist, and cool blood streamed down my face.

A smaller form appeared. "Skjæra, it lives!"

The taller one jerked back. "Not for long."

They spoke Terran, although it sounded wrong. The head injury I'd sustained must have affected my hearing. The small one dropped down beside me and shouted for someone named "Skrie." Then it looked up at the taller one. "Skjæra, can you heal it?"

Another one came, and they began arguing in their muddled Terran while I tried to stay conscious. The little one touched me with its funny hand coverings, and pulled its face covering down, and I saw it was a little girl. It babbled something and then ran off. The other two followed it.

I blinked the blood out of my eyes and rolled onto my side. I could see the others now, some standing together by sleds on the ground, and others in some type of airborne vehicles. I couldn't hear what they said, but one of the taller forms dragged the child away from the hovering craft.

The one who had found me, the healer, followed, arguing again, but nothing stopped the one dragging the child. It threw the little one down on the ice, and drove two stakes through her mitts. It handed a blade to the healer and barked out an order.

I understood what they were doing then. They wanted the healer to kill her. To kill a kid.

"No." My voice hardly made a puff in the cold air. I tried again. "Stop."

The healer straddled the child, and held the blade over her chest, but didn't move. Shots were fired from the hovering craft, and one of the people by the sleds fell.

The one who had dragged the kid away took hold of the blade and the healer's hand, and forced both down. I heard the snap of a wrist, a gurgled word.

The child was dead, and the healer was coming toward me.

The blood had frozen on my face, and I couldn't

feel my body anymore. I don't know how I reached up again, but I saw my limp hand rise between us.

The healer pulled off one mitt with her teeth, revealing a human hand, and curled long, skillful fingers around mine.

The touch made tears spill from my eyes.

"Her name was Enafa. She was born twelve seasons past, and her mother often favored her above her sisters." The healer gently placed my hand against my chest. "I could not favor her above mine." One long finger touched my cheek.

The healer wept, blind tears of sorrow and regret and rage. I didn't understand what had happened, but I knew it had destroyed her. Just as it had destroyed me.

I couldn't do this anymore. No matter where I went or what I did, life would never change. Every species in the galaxy would go on breeding and butchering. That was all they wanted. Sex and death.

I could put an end to it. Something inside me told me I could. I could stop the killing, and the breeding. I could be merciful and put life itself out of its misery.

The healer rose, and lifted a pistol.

Yes. I kept my eyes open, waiting for the shot that wouldn't kill me. *Let her decide how it will be.*

Instead of shooting me, she pressed the weapon to her own head, and pulled the trigger.

"Mama." A small, cool hand patted my cheek. "You have to wake up now."

I came to with a jerk, bolting upright as I reflexively clutched Marel to my chest. Everything rushed over me as I shed the remnants of the horrible dream and climbed off the berth.

"Are you hurt?" I sat her down and checked her over quickly.

"Mama, I'm fine," she insisted, and pushed my hands away. "We're home now."

We'd gone through another rift, judging from what little I remembered. "Look at me." I checked her pupils. "How do you know we're home?"

"I can feel it." She looked past me and smiled. "Daddy."

Reever came over and wrapped us both in his arms. "I was in the corridor on my way here when the wave hit," he murmured. "I'm sorry I didn't reach you in time."

"We're okay," I assured him.

Once I was satisfied that Marel and Reever hadn't suffered any ill effects from the transition through time, I left them to check on the other patients and my staff. Everyone was shaken, and the abrupt jump had frightened some of the patients, but there were no new injuries. I quickly checked in with Command, and Xonea confirmed that we were indeed back in our own time.

"All levels report no new casualties," he added. "We were quite fortunate. The blast from Odnalla was so powerful it could have easily vaporized the ship."

I didn't remember a blast. "Did they attack us again?"

"No, something happened on the planet, a chain reaction of some sort," he said. "According to our last readings, it detonated the gases in their atmosphere. The entire world would have been engulfed in a firestorm."

No matter how clever the Odnallak had been, nothing could have survived that. "I should say how sorry I am that an entire civilization was wiped out, but good riddance."

"Agreed." He sounded very satisfied. "I am taking the ship back to Joren for repairs now. Our stardrive is still inoperable, but the blast threw us just outside Varallan. We should reach the homeworld in a few hours."

I saw Maggie wander out of one of the treatment rooms. "Thank you, Captain." I left the console and went over to her. "Are you all right?"

"Of course I am." She turned around in a full circle, her brow furrowed. "We have traveled a great distance. This is your time."

"So it seems." And we had accidentally removed Maggie from hers, which made me wonder why I still existed. "Can you go back to Jxin? To your own time?"

"No," she admitted. "But your timeline appears to be intact, so I will return eventually." She rubbed at her ear slits. "What is that unpleasant resonation?"

"We're flying back to Joren, but the engines are damaged. It could be from them." I couldn't hear anything, but I felt a vague discomfort settling over me. "Maggie, what sent us back through the rift?"

"The undesirables. They destroyed themselves with their machines and their equations, just as I told you they would." She studied my face. "Since I made you, Cherijo, you should call me Mother."

There was no way I was doing that. "You haven't made me yet. How did the Odnallak setting their world on fire create a new rift?"

"It did not create it. They did not collect all of the infinity crystal from your vessel." She turned away from me. "Some of it stayed hidden from them. It must have created the rift and brought the ship through it to protect you."

"Is it still on the *Sunlace*?"

She shook her head. "It is inside you now."

"It's *in* me?" I glanced down at myself. "Where?"

"In your fluids and parts and things." She glanced back at me with an odd expression. "You should be happy. Nothing can harm you now."

I felt a cold trickle of fear inch along my spine. "Maggie, does the crystal being inside me make me like the Jxin?"

"No. Are you hungry?" She seemed eager to change the subject. "I can make a meal for you."

"Thanks, but I'm fine." I thought of how the oKiaf protocrystal had nearly devoured Shon. "What will the crystal do to me?"

"It will care for you," she said, sounding impatient now. "The crystal will not allow anything to harm you. It is a good thing. You should be happy."

I wasn't. "Will I infect others?"

"It will stay in you." Another vague gesture. "None of the others could . . . it does not want others."

Trying to get her to explain something was like slamming my head into a plasbrick wall. "Why, Maggie? Why did it come into my body?"

"You are necessary." Bored again, she let her gaze wander. "I will make food in the wall machine for the nurses. They like the things I make with the sweet-tasting flowers."

I let her go and play with the prep unit. As soon as we reached Joren, I decided, I'd have Squilyp run a microcellular series on me. After that, we'd figure out some way to remove the crystal from my body.

I performed rounds, and changed ChoVa's dressing

while I updated PyrsVar on our situation. "Xonea will signal the Hanar and let him know we've returned. I imagine he'll send a ship for you and ChoVa and the delegates." But before we let anyone off the ship, we would have to find the Odnallak; we couldn't risk letting him escape again.

"That is good. I wish to present myself to him." He lifted a scaly hand. "Now that the Jorenian has been separated from me, he will have no objections to our betrothal."

"Let me give some friendly advice," I said. "Where TssVar's concerned, don't assume anything. He can still veto this love match."

"My father will not oppose it," ChoVa said, her voice rasping out the words. "I told him that if he did, I would leave the homeworld and live with PyrsVar elsewhere."

"You never said this to me," the rogue complained.

"Your skull is large enough already." She looked up at me. "I cannot feel my tail."

I grimaced a little. "That's because I amputated it and used it for the grafts you needed."

Instead of becoming angry, she nodded. "A clever alternative. I should have thought of that myself. The shoulder?"

"I was able to completely rebuild it." I went over what I had accomplished with the surgery, and then ordered her to rest.

"You should do the same, Namesake," she said before she closed her eyes. "You have not slept in days."

As I left recovery, I tried to remember the last time I had slept, and couldn't. I should have been dead on my feet, but I didn't feel tired in the slightest. I hadn't lied to Maggie; I didn't feel hungry, either. Then it struck me, what else I didn't feel. I put one trembling hand up to my throat, and felt for my carotid. Then I checked my other pulse points.

My heart beat only once every two minutes.

I didn't panic right away. I calmly went into my office and carefully scanned myself several times. Only after every reading displayed the same results did I come to a grim diagnosis.

The function of all my organs had slowed dramatically; my heart was barely pumping any blood at all. My core temperature had also dropped twenty-one degrees. My platelet counts had been reduced to an eighth of what they should have been, thanks to my bone marrow, which was disappearing. My skeleton still scanned somewhat normal, but sections of my largest bones had begun to turn transparent, as if they were made of crystal.

I ran a dozen simulations, and all of them indicated that reversing the process was impossible. I then calculated the rate at which my body was being transformed, and discovered that the process was a little less than half-complete.

Maggie was wrong. In roughly forty-eight hours, I would be exactly like the Jxin.

Fifteen

I signaled Shon, asking that he come to take over for me in Medical, and then left. I walked through the corridors without speaking to anyone or thinking; it was all I could do to keep moving.

Somehow I ended up in my quarters, standing by the viewport, watching the stars slide by. Soon we'd reach Joren and safety, and the HouseClan would throw another welcoming celebration, and everyone would be happy.

While I walked among them with my dying heart and my crystallizing bones, and pretended to be the same.

"Cherijo."

It was Reever; he'd followed me here. He was always doing that. Ever present, ever vigilant, forever waiting on me to finish an operation or cure a plague or save a planet. If I didn't respond, he'd wait until I did. No one was as patient as my husband.

This time he didn't wait; he turned me around to face him. "Tell me."

I took from my pocket the scanner with the last set of readings I'd taken in my office, and handed it to him. While he read them, I went back to my sleeping platform. The bed adjusted to the slight weight of my body, and the upper deck remained thankfully as blank as ever.

Not that it mattered. In two days I would outlive the bed and the deck. In two days I would outlive everything.

"Did Maggie do this to you?" I heard Reever ask.

"I don't know. I don't think so. What would be the point?" I frowned as I spotted something. "There's a crack in the ceiling up there. I'll have to report it to maintenance."

He stretched out beside me, his body touching mine. That, I thought, was because this platform was smaller than the one we'd always shared in our old quarters.

"Did Jarn like our bed?" I asked him.

"No." His hand stroked my arm. "She preferred to sleep on the deck."

"That must have been hard on your back."

"At first it was. But I have slept in worse places. Cherijo—"

"Shhh." I pressed my fingers against his lips. "It's done. There's nothing to say. Nothing you can do to fix it. Nothing I can do."

"There must be something. Some cure."

"I'm not sick, Duncan. It's not an infection like Shon had, or a disease, like the ones the black crystal causes. I'm evolving." I rolled over and buried my face in my pillow, and then sat up. "I can't even have a good cry anymore." I glanced down at myself. "I guess no body functions, no tears."

"Your body still functions. You're alive, *Waenara*,"

he said quietly, rising onto his knees and holding me by the arms. "Don't let this destroy you."

My dry eyes closed. "That's precisely what it's doing, Duncan. In a couple of days this crystal will take away everything that makes me human—not that there was much left to begin with—and complete the transformation." I pressed my forehead to his shoulder. "I don't know what I'll become."

He kissed me, a gentle brush of his warm mouth over mine. I could still feel that, and smell his scent, and while my heart would never again beat faster, his touch enveloped me like a soft cloak. I felt the vast emptiness inside me evaporate as I opened my mouth to him.

I couldn't remember why I had been so angry with him, not when he touched me like this. We unfastened our garments and pulled them away so our skins could touch and glide against each other, and to my surprise, nothing had changed. Making love with him was as thrilling and powerful as it had ever been. As it always had been between us.

For now, we were still us. Still lovers. Still human.

I stopped thinking, and immersed myself in the moment. I ran my hands over his body, stroking each sensitive spot, murmuring to him in wordless pleasure as he did the same. When he glided into me, I felt complete again, and gave myself over as he began to dance inside me.

He sank into me over and over, his eyes locked with mine. They changed colors, from gray to green to blue, and darkened as we came to the edge. It was so easy to lose myself in him, in this simple act, and then we both came together, merging and pulsing with heat and sensation.

Our bodies cooled. Duncan held me tightly against him as he rolled to his side, his hand tangled in my hair, his mouth tracing the curves of my lips. "My wife."

I smiled beneath those slow, lingering kisses. "My husband."

He fell asleep in my arms, and since I couldn't do the same, I held him and watched his peaceful face. It was funny, but in the past I'd always resented the need to sleep, and considered it a waste of time. Now that I would be wide-awake until the end of time, I felt a pang of regret. I would miss drifting off into that sweet, mindless oblivion.

I heard the console chime, and slipped off the platform. Careful not to disturb Reever, I pulled on a robe before I went out into the other room.

I answered the signal from Command. "What is it?"

"The captain requests you and Linguist Reever attend him in the main briefing room, Healer," the com officer said.

I sighed. "What now?"

"The captain needs to consult with you about the disposition of refugees."

"What refugees?" Before he could answer, I said, "Never mind. We'll be right there."

I woke Reever, and once we dressed, we took the lift up to the briefing room. Xonea and every officer on the ship were there, and on the room monitors was an image of Joren. There were so many ships flying in orbit around the planet it looked like an invasion, and I could see more approaching.

When Xonea saw us enter, he called for order, and then began the briefing. "We received several distress calls from ships en route to Varallan, which I relayed to the Ruling Council. At that time they informed me of their current situation, and that Joren will provide temporary asylum to all refugees who can reach our homeworld."

"What situation?" I asked.

Xonea pulled up several star charts of nearby solar systems. "Over the last three hours, the entire populations of fifteen planets in the quadrant have been destroyed." He illuminated the worlds, but each appeared to be in shadow. "Another fifty have been invaded, and if their inhabitants are not able to escape, they are not projected to survive."

I blinked. What Xonea had said made no sense; if it was true, then billions of lives had been extinguished.

"Who is waging this war?" Reever demanded.

"They are not being attacked by anyone." Xonea brought up a vid transmission. "They are being enveloped."

The poor quality of the vid made it hard to see many details; static occluded most of it. There was enough, however, to follow what had happened.

A humanoid with orange skin spoke urgently into the screen, and then turned his recorder away to show the view of a colony. The inhabitants were pouring out of their dwellings and businesses and trampling over one another as they ran. In the background a dense shadow rose up over the colony and came crashing down like an enormous wave of dark water. Everything it touched vanished beneath it as it crushed the colony. When it reached the humanoid recording the disaster, a wall of strangely glittering black filled the display. The transmission abruptly terminated.

"What is that?" I heard one of the engineers say. "A flood? Some sort of solar bombardment?"

"No." Unfortunately I had immediately recognized the way the blackness had refracted and then swallowed up the light. "It's the black crystal. It's awakened."

Due to the influx of refugee ships, Xonea could not land at HouseClan Torin's Main Transport; there simply wasn't room for anything larger than a launch. Instead he joined the fleet of Jorenian vessels to help police the refugee ships and keep their evacuation to the surface orderly.

Some of the species fleeing the black crystal refused to land on the planet, fearing it would be invaded, and demanded supplies be delivered to them so they could continue on their journey out of the quadrant. The squabbling over resources soon stopped as reports of black crystal invasions came pouring in from other quadrants, as well as warnings of several well-armed fleets raiding planets not yet affected by the destruction.

The Ruling Council ordered the Jorenian fleet to assume defensive positions around the homeworld and throughout the system. I returned to Medical and prepared our patients to be shuttled down to the planet with all other nonessential personnel. ChoVa wanted to stay, and argued with me until I threatened to signal her father.

"The black crystal hasn't reached Vtaga yet," I told her. "The Hanar is evacuating the planet and coming here. He'll want you to be safe on Joren."

She snorted. "How can any of us be safe?"

We hadn't told anyone that, thanks to some unique

planetary features, the only two worlds the black crystal couldn't invade were Joren and oKia. If we had, they would be quickly overrun by refugees and the raider fleets, and wars for possession would break out. "You'll just have to take my word for it."

Happily, Reever didn't argue with me when I sent him to take Marel down to the surface. "As soon as I have her settled, I will return."

"I'd feel better knowing you were there with her," I told him. "Especially if the situation escalates."

"Very well." He took me in his arms. "But if it does, I want you to come home."

There wouldn't be any reason for me to remain on the *Sunlace*. "I'll be on the first launch I can catch," I said, and kissed him good-bye.

Maggie seemed amused when I suggested she shuttle down to the planet with the others. "Why would I go there? It is a null world."

"*Null* meaning . . ." I rolled my hand.

"Nullify," she prompted.

I could already feel the headache she was going to give me. "What does Joren nullify, besides your interest?"

She pondered that. "You do not have a word for it. There was one that was close. . . ." She trailed off and began thinking again.

After a few minutes I asked, "Can you describe it?"

"It does not have a description. It was, is, and will be. Wait." Her face brightened. "Forever."

I blinked. "Forever what?"

"That is the word I wished to remember," she chided. "It is like that—forever—only more."

"Are you saying that it's the infinity crystal?"

"It can be anything. Except on null worlds."

This could be the cure we had been searching for. "What happens to it on a null world?"

"It becomes null." At my expression, she spread her hands out in a wide circle. "It loses cohesion and purpose. It sinks into the ground. It waits. We do not know why."

I thought of the deposits of liquid protocrystal on oKia. "What does give it form?"

"Anything made by the Jxin. We plan to start life-forms like you on many worlds. You are the legacy we will leave behind before we ascend. You, and the other primitives." She gestured at me and some of the nurses. "People."

"How nice of you." My version of Maggie had claimed to be the fabled founding race. This version confirmed it. "Too bad your legacy is quickly coming to an end."

"There will always be life," she said, her tone patronizing now. "You do not understand how it will be, but we will see to it."

"You'll *see* to it?" She had no idea of what was happening. I dragged her over to a console, and I showed her the vid of the colony being destroyed. "Is this how the Jxin saw to it?"

She drew back. "We did not make that."

"That's right, the Odnallak did," I snapped. "Do you know what it is? I didn't until now, but I finally understand. It's a malignant form of the infinity crystal."

"There is no such form."

"In your time there wasn't any—yet," I corrected. "Not until you gave the Odnallak the last element they needed for the experiment. You told them where they could find the infinity crystal. After they used it to blow themselves to kingdom come, this is what it became."

"I did not know." She stared at me. "But it cannot be the same. The infinity crystal creates all life, while this—"

"Destroys it," I finished for her. "We know."

She wobbled, putting out a hand to brace herself against the console. "How far has it spread?"

I told her. I showed her the lifeless, crystallized planets it had consumed, the worlds where it was just awakening, and the refugee ships that had fled the destruction.

"They cannot escape it," she said as she looked down at the display, and the waves of ships speeding toward Joren. "The people on those vessels are carrying it with them. If it was on their planets, it is in their bodies."

"Even when it was in its dormant state, the black crystal still caused suffering and disease on many worlds," I said. "What will it do now that it's awake to the people who are infected with it?"

"It will use them as the infinity crystal does," she said softly. "It will take over their minds and send them where it wishes to go—especially to the two worlds it has never been able to infiltrate and infect by itself. But it will not go to create life. When they land, then it will consume them and all other life it finds on that world."

"How do we stop it?" I demanded.

"It cannot be destroyed." She met my gaze. "Cherijo, the old one knew this would happen. He brought you to Odnalla so that you would think you were one of them. He wants you to help him save the undesirables."

"He was wrong." I had assumed all Joseph had been interested in was Maggie. "I'm not Odnallak."

She looked at the deck.

In that moment, I could have personally fed her to the black crystal. "Maggie, this is when you tell me that I'm not Odnallak."

"I do not know what you are," she burst out quickly. "You are different. Not like us, not like the undesirables, not even like the primitives. You exist outside the timeline, the old one said to me. You were made to. He knew something, but he was destroyed with the other undesirables."

"We think he's still on the ship. One of them boarded just before we were thrown back through time, and he's the only one who would have known to leave the planet." I switched off the console. "We have to find him. Will you help me?"

She gripped my hand. "I will do anything to make this right."

Maggie didn't need a DNA sample to determine if someone was who they appeared to be, or an Odnallak in shift form. All she had to do, she assured me, was scan their minds. Unfortunately she could do that only in their presence, so we formed our own search team and began working our way through the levels.

"Angry, worried, saddened, frightened," she chanted as she passed different crew members. "Longing, angry, hungry, angry."

"What are you doing?" I asked as we entered Command.

"That is what they are feeling," she said. "You should know this so you do not mistake them for the old one."

"That's fine, but you don't have to say it out loud."

Her brows rose. "But you cannot read my thoughts."

She had a point. "If I suspect someone is the shifter, or you find him, do this." I winked. "That will be our signal."

"But that is an eye movement, not a data transmission." She grinned at my expression. "I am having fun with you."

God help me, she was joking. "Just wink if you identify him. What will he be feeling, by the way?"

Her amusement vanished. "Not what you do."

"They have no emotions?" I'd seen plenty of anger on the Odnallak's homeworld.

"The undesirables knew only greed and hatred." She frowned. "The old one has lost those feelings, but he replaced them with something uglier. He is filled with endless rage."

I stopped to inform Xonea of what we were doing, but refused his offer to send a detachment of guards with us.

"You need your men on the launches. Maggie can handle whatever Joseph throws at us." I glanced at his busy console. "How are things on the surface?"

"The council is doing what they can to provide sanctuary for the offworlders and defuse tensions," he said, "but there have been several attempts by refugees to take control of our territories."

He didn't have to tell me they'd failed. "How many dead?"

"Forty thus far, and they will not be the last." He gestured toward the image of Joren on the viewer. "Soon there will be more refugees than we can accommodate, and our ships will move into position around the homeworld."

I knew things had grown desperate, but surely it wasn't this bad yet. "You can't fire on refugees, Xonea."

"We will not attack them," he said. "We will try to turn them away. If they still attempt to land, then we will disable their engines."

Leaving the refugees adrift in space.

"There's something you should know." I related what Maggie had told me about the refugees being infected with the black crystal brought from their homeworlds. "You have to tell the council so they can prepare."

"I will," he promised. "Cherijo, there is another decision that has been made by the HouseClans. Joren has never fallen to an invader, and we do not intend to begin now. When it is clear that the black crystal has come to our world, the HouseClans will send out one final signal to our kin. We will board our vessels, leave the homeworld, and fly into our sun."

He was talking about committing mass suicide, I realized. "Isn't there some other way?"

"There are many paths," he reminded me, "but under these circumstances only one destination. We will not run in terror. We will walk within beauty together."

"If it comes to that, just do one thing for me, please." The tears I thought I'd lost stung my eyes. "Save some room on the *Sunlace* for Reever and Marel and me."

He kissed my brow. "I could not go without you, little ClanSister."

My wristcom chirped, and I answered the signal from Medical. "Yes?"

"Healer Torin," one of the interns said, "you are needed here. A nurse on her way to report for her shift was attacked in the corridor. She was struck from behind and suffered a skull fracture and internal hemorrhaging. We have treated the injuries, but we cannot stop the bleeding."

"I'll be there in five minutes. Prep her and take her into surgery." I excused myself and went over to where Maggie was making rounds of the helm officers. "One of my people was attacked. We have to return to Medical."

As she followed me out to the lift, Maggie said, "These people do not hurt each other. The old one must have attacked your nurse, to stop us from finding him."

I nodded. "That or he attacked her to serve as bait to lure us back to Medical. I want you to scan everyone in the bay as soon as we get there."

"He should not have hurt the nurse," she said suddenly. "They are kind and helpless. He is an evil bastard."

At the rate she was picking up all my bad verbal habits, she'd be talking like the Maggie I'd known in no time. *Not that we have much time left.* A thought occurred to me. "Maggie, if the black crystal attacks us and destroys Joren, what will happen to you?"

"Nothing." She glanced around the lift. "I will be left alone here until I can return to my time."

If I didn't fly into the sun with the Torin, I might face the same fate. "Doesn't that scare you a little?"

"Once I spent two hundred solar years in solitude, so that I could rid myself of uncertainty." She grimaced. "I would rather be with my people, or you."

I felt a surge of unwilling pleasure. "I thought we primitives bored you."

"You did at first," she assured me. "But now I think

you are the most interesting prim—female that I have ever encountered. I am very glad that someday I will create you."

"When you do this next time," I said as the lift came to a stop, "could make me a little taller?"

We entered Medical, where Maggie scanned the minds of the staff, and then looked at me and shook her head. I went to scrub and put on my gear while the charge nurse identified my patient for me.

"Intern Qrysala found Manal unconscious in the corridor," she said. "He attempted to slow the bleeding, but his scans indicated the pressure on her brain was increasing."

"How diligent of Qrysala." And highly suspicious, as well. I turned to Maggie and deliberately dropped one eyelid. "Why don't you come in and observe the procedure?"

She winked back. "I would very much like to do that."

Before we went into the suite, I had Maggie put on scrubs and a mask. If the Odnallak assumed at first glance that the Jxin was a nurse, we might be able to catch him off guard.

We found the wounded nurse on the table and Qrysala busy hooking up her monitor leads. He saw us and gave me a very convincing, relieved smile.

"Healer Torin, thank the Mother you have come." He walked around the table with a tray of instruments. "Manal's condition is rapidly deteriorating. I would like to remain and assist you, if I may."

I glanced at Maggie, who gave me another wink. "Oh, I think you've done enough, shifter."

As Maggie came up behind him, the intern's smile faded. "Why do you call me that?"

"I guess because every time I even think of the name Joseph, I want to puke." Why was Maggie moving past him? "You do remind me of him, though. Attacking a woman from behind is the same kind of cowardly thing he would do."

Manal suddenly sat up, the terrible wound on her head disappearing as she slid from the table. "You jump to conclusions so easily, daughter."

I lunged at her, but she pushed me back with a simple sweep of her hand. Qrysala caught me before I fell, and held on to me with one arm as he extended his claws with the other.

"You've failed, shifter," I told him. "Miserably. Your people are dead, and you didn't stop the black crystal from being created. But I'll give you another chance to try again."

"Will you?" Manal seemed amused as Maggie took hold of her.

"You're going to help us create another rift," I told him. "Then we'll all go back together to an earlier time, when the Odnallak were more reasonable, and you'll tell them to stop the experiment."

"We were never a very reasonable people, Cherijo," was all she said.

"Or clever." Maggie watched as Manal's form shifted into the Odnallak. "This ruse was especially foolish. You have no avenue of escape now."

"Why would I want to leave, now that I have you both exactly where I need you?" He tossed a sphere at her, and when it struck her chest, it exploded into the liquid he'd used to restrain us on Odnalla.

This time, however, it was black.

Maggie looked down as the liquid wrapped her in its tendrils. "You know this will not kill me." She froze as the tendrils inched up and pierced her ear slits. "Cherijo, you must . . ." She fell silent, her jaw still hanging open.

"Maggie?"

"No matter how one feels about the Jxin, one has to admire the stunning breadth and depth of their conceit and arrogance." Joseph pulled a gurney up beside the operating table. "Doubtless she has told you ad nauseam how inviolate her body is. But while the young Jxin may be invulnerable, their minds are still not disciplined enough to resist true power."

I didn't know what he planned to do with Maggie, but he had black crystal, and I had to protect the Jorenians.

"Qrysala," I said, never taking my eyes off the shifter. "Get out of here. Evacuate the bay. Tell the captain to initiate emergency breach protocol." Sealing the entire level wouldn't save the ship, but it might give the crew enough time to abandon it.

I stood between Joseph and the intern, prepared to do whatever I had to in order to give the Jorenian the chance to get away, but Joseph didn't attempt to stop him from leaving. I reached out and groped for a panel, then punched in the code that engaged a quarantine seal.

"You have wasted entirely too much time and effort on these beings," he said as he and Maggie moved around the table, coming at me from each side. "Now it is time for us to stop playing hide-and-seek. We will finish the work and return to our homeworld."

"Terra doesn't want us," I said as I backed up against the door panel.

"A part of you has always known you were not Terran, Cherijo." He stopped in front of me and reached out to catch some strands of my hair between his fingers. "Just as you know that I am your father."

I struck his hand away. "You didn't make me. Maggie did."

"Interfering in my work does not constitute maternal privilege. But this time I am rather grateful that she meddled with you." He glanced down and back up again. "Your new radiance is lovely, but it is not entirely natural, is it?"

"Maybe I've been exercising and watching my weight," I countered.

"Maggie has deceived you," Joseph confided. "How do you think the last pure source of the infinity crystal ended up in your body?"

"I'm just lucky that way."

"Maggie put it there." He brushed his knuckles against my cheek before I could move my head. "She has never cared for you. You're a primitive. The unnatural offspring of an undesirable. You might have a formidable immune system, but to the Jxin you were nothing more than a suitable storage container."

I kept my expression blank. "Maybe I volunteered."

"Give up your precious humanity to serve the Jxin? I think not. But you needn't worry about it." He patted my shoulder. "Maggie and I will be separating you from the infinity crystal, and everything else that has tainted you. Then you will assist me in saving our homeworld."

"Odnalla is a great big dead scorched rock," I reminded him. "So are your people."

"Now they are." He gestured at Maggie. "When the Jxin opens a new rift for me, we will do exactly as you wished. We will return to an earlier time in my people's past, and use the crystal to help them finally attain what is rightfully theirs."

I shook my head. "You'll just blow up the planet and create the black crystal sooner than you did the last time."

"Not if we go back to the time before the Jxin marooned us on that wasteland of a world." He smiled. "When those self-righteous idiots were still mortal enough to be killed."

The Jxin hadn't simply created me. They had been the mythological founding race, the first species of intelligent life in the universe. Before they had vanished from history, they had planted the seeds of life on countless worlds. If the shifter murdered them, he would wipe out all life in my time.

"Maggie," I said carefully. "I know you can hear what we're saying. You have to fight this. You have to help me."

Her gaze shifted to my face, and for a moment I saw a glimmer of understanding. Then the whites of her eyes disappeared, swallowed up by liquid black.

I turned to Joseph. "I'm not the only immortal in this time. One of the others will stop you."

"Who? Reever? He is on the planet with your brat. The oKiaf and all the others will soon be infected." He grabbed me by the throat. "Now it's time for surgery, daughter."

I fought him, of course. I punched and kicked and clawed as he dragged me over to the table and strapped me down. Maggie followed him like a drone, moving equipment out of the way and helping to hold me down as he put me in restraints. She didn't respond to anything I said to her, and when I looked into her eyes, I could see the black crystal glittering inside her, ugly and cold.

Joseph grew tired of me fighting, I suppose, because he slammed a mask over my nose and mouth and held it there until whatever he pumped into my lungs made my vision blur and my body go limp. It seemed I was still human enough for him to knock out, because I went from there into blackness.

I woke up stretched out on my back, staring up at Terran sky. I was in a shockball stadium, dressed in a uniform, holding the object of the game, the beautiful cold silver sphere. The shockball that had been programmed to murder my husband.

Someone helped me to my feet, and led me out onto the field. It was a drone official, moving me away from the crowd. Everyone had fallen silent.

"We cannot disable the game computer," the official was saying. "If you do not release the sphere, you will die."

Even now, if I released the sphere, it would automatically seek out Duncan. I wasn't going to let that happen. Going out on the field was to protect everyone else, I realized. I stumbled along, ears ringing, vision blurring.

Jericho was dead. Joseph was dead. I clutched the hot sphere tighter between my palms. They were dead, but Reever would live.

The official checked the players' board. "The last penalty shall be administered in five, four, three . . ."

The hysterical crowd chanted down the clock, then suddenly hushes. Behind me, a woman screamed. Everyone was standing on their feet, looking up at a lone figure, standing on the edge of the highest tier of seats.

Another crazy fan, determined to have the best view. What a game.

The final, lethal jolt hit me. It knocked me flat on my back. The alloy between my hands began to glow a dull red. I clenched my chattering teeth and endured the charge, holding the sphere up, high above my head, so everyone could see.

Look at me. Watch me burn.

I forgot about the pain when I saw the lone figure leap out into space. Thousands of voices shrieked their shock and horror as the figure hurtled down toward me and certain death.

As I twisted and writhed, so did the figure. Was it some kind of poltergeist, suffering with me, burning with me? No, it was tearing off its outer clothes. Another dark-haired twin who arched up and at the last moment spread out his two enormous, gleaming black wings.

Released.

I shed that memory along with the confines of my agonized body, and flew up not into the sky but through the ship. I had never felt such utter lightness, such freedom, to glide through the corridors, and zip around the crew as they moved past me. They didn't see me, and to my view their movement seemed slow, their voices a dull, droning jabber.

I left the ship to hover outside and look upon Joren. The only world that had ever welcomed me was trapped by rings of ships packed with frightened, angry strangers. They were burning inside, where no one could see. They wanted to die, as I had, that bright and beautiful day on Terra, but not to save the ones they loved, and not even to end their unseen torment.

They wanted to die because they were afraid to live.

I looked back at the ship. I didn't have to return there, to the body that I'd left in Medical, or the two immortals who were tearing it apart. I could go on to where I had traveled before, where no one would ever touch me or need me or hurt me again. Where I would never again feel tired, or cold, or lonely.

I would feel nothing, forever.

A flare of light caught my eye, and I turned to see debris streaming around me, the remnants of a refugee ship that had just exploded. Parts of the ship flew past me to pelt the hull of the *Sunlace*. Instead of bouncing off it, they clung, spreading black tendrils as they ate into the alloy.

Without even thinking, I lifted one hand, and a lovely golden light shimmered out of me. As soon as it touched the black crystal, the malignant mineral stopped burrowing and crystallized.

I knew it was only a temporary measure. Even with the power I possessed now, I couldn't destroy it. Nothing could.

I felt an invisible tidal wave of terror pass through me as another world was taken by the black crystal. The terrible emotion was not mine; it belonged to every being consumed on that world. There would be more soon, and still more, and then the last flickers of life would be extinguished, and what had been would never be again.

And then I knew.

As much as I wanted to go, I couldn't leave them to die like this.

I slipped back into the ship, and moved through its corridors, my soul growing heavier the closer I came to my flesh. I stopped only outside the room, afraid now to see what he had done to me. Still, I knew that the end of his work was the beginning of mine.

I passed through the door.

People shouted all around me, and when I opened my eyes, Shon was standing over me and calling for help. It felt wrong, to be on that table, to be where I was. Everything remained the same . . . except me.

I pushed myself up with heavy hands, and saw Shon bare his teeth. "What happened? Where is Maggie and the shifter?" What was wrong with my voice? I sounded terrible. I touched my throat, expecting to feel bruises.

The oKiaf grabbed me by the shoulders and looked into my eyes. "Who are you?"

"I'm Cherijo." I frowned. "Who did you think I was? Jarn?"

"What was the name of the 'Zangian who taught me to swim?" he demanded.

"Jadaira. Why are you testing my knowledge of you?" When he didn't answer, I swung my legs off the table and lurched to my feet. All my muscles felt thick and strange. "We have to track down the shifter before he—" I halted as I saw the pale reflection of my face on the inside of the view panel. "What?"

As I said that final word, I saw the jaw move, and the image reach up to cup it and hold it. I watched as blunt fingers moved across the thin lips, up over the prominent nose, and across the wide brows.

I looked down, and saw my breasts were gone. I reached down and felt the ridges in my abdomen.

I didn't touch the unfamiliar, suspended weight between my legs. I didn't have to; I already knew what *that* was.

No.

I reached for an instrument tray, dumping its contents before I held the shiny surface up to my face. In it, I saw a young, hard face. The face of a brilliant physician as it had been twenty years ago.

Maggie and I will be separating you from the infinity crystal, and everything else that has tainted you. . . .

Joseph had kept his promise. I had been changed to what I had been before he and Maggie had altered me. The clone of Joseph Grey Veil's cells. A perfect copy of all that he had been.

I had been changed back into a male.

Sixteen

"How far has the black crystal progressed?" I said in a younger version of my father's voice.

"Hanar TssVar has sent part of his fleet to form a blockade of Varallan," the oKiaf said. "It seems to have slowed the invasion in this part of the quadrant."

"What about the shifter, and Maggie?"

"He took her to his launch," Shon said. "They escaped from the ship an hour ago. We saw you go with them."

I sat down on the edge of the table before I fell down. "He must have assumed my appearance in order to get past the guards."

"No. The shifter used another form." He checked the results of the DNA sampler and gave me a bleak look. "Your DNA is very close to the profile in Cherijo's medical records. If you are her, the most significant change has been made to your chromosomes, in order to change your gender."

"If I am? You still don't believe me?" I felt a surge of unfamiliar aggression. "How would you like me to prove my identity, Shon? Retinal scan? Fingerprints? They've all been altered. Since the Odnallak are telepathic, any memory I offer would be suspect. I'd perform an operation, but we don't have any patients who need surgery."

"I can confirm who you are," a deep voice said.

I couldn't believe Reever had returned to the ship. "What are you doing here?" I demanded as he came and tried to take my hands in his. I jerked them away. "Tell me you didn't bring Marel back with you."

"I left our daughter on the planet, *Waenara*." He glanced at Shon. "This is Cherijo."

Now I knew why he'd grabbed my hands. "You brought him up here just to confirm my identity, when we could already be going after the shifter and Maggie?"

"We signaled Reever as soon as we reviewed the security vids. I thought he would want to join us." Shon started to say something else, and then turned to my husband. "Perhaps you should be the one to tell him."

"Her," I corrected. "I don't care what they did to my body; I'm still female. What about the vids?"

Reever put a hand on my shoulder. "I will replay them for you."

"While we do that, I want you to prepare a suspension tank," I told Shon. "Prep the solution for tissue and organ reconstruction."

"Why?"

I went out to my office, ignoring the hateful looks my staff were giving me, and took the blood samples I'd drawn from my specimen storage unit. "This blood contains the DNA I had before he did this. You're going to use it to alterform me."

"I cannot," Shon said. "The process takes months."

"Not if we use the retrovirus I designed for Pyrs-Var." I sat down at my console. "Show me the vids, Reever."

He pulled up the images recorded by the monitors in launch bay. They showed Maggie and Xonea flanking a small, hunched-over figure. The three walked toward the Odnallak craft, when suddenly the figure in the middle wrenched free and grabbed a cutter from a toolbox. She brandished it like a club, and managed to hit Xonea several times in the head and chest before he knocked it away, hoisted her up under his arm, and carried her kicking and screaming up the ramp.

I reached out to enable the audio, and listened to the struggling female's shrieks. She used a garbled form of Terran that I barely understood, and hearing that voice was like being punched in the chest. As Xonea struggled to carry her inside the craft, she turned her face toward the recording drone and called again for help. I knew the face, of course, but this was the first time I'd met the mind behind it.

"This is why you came back to the ship," I said to Reever.

"It is why they signaled me," he said.

Of course he'd come back to the ship. It all made perfect sense now. "How do you think he did it?"

He sat in the chair opposite mine. "We cannot know what happened in the surgical suite, but the nurse he impersonated has not been found on the ship."

"He probably used her body as a scaffold for the DNA sequences he removed from mine. Maggie had the power to do the rest." I paused the replay so I could look at her a little longer. I felt a strange sense of the inevitable, as if this moment had been coming since the League transport had crashed on Akkabarr. "Nice to finally meet you, Jarn."

I replayed the vid another time. The Akkabarran fought like a combat veteran, with quick, economical movements that conserved energy and at the same time delivered the maximum amount of force. She also wore my body like she had been born to it. In a sense, she had; twice now.

Suddenly I couldn't look at her for another second, and switched off the display. "Just before he put me under, the shifter said he was going to create another rift and go back to an earlier time to save the Odnallak and kill Jxin. Maggie said something about space being thin in certain places. To create a new rift, he might have to go back to where the first one appeared. TssVar will probably be happy to lend you one of his attack raiders; they can jump there in no time."

Reever blocked my path. "I will relate that to the captain, so that he can alert the Faction. But I am not leaving you."

"I'm going to be naked and floating in a tank for the immediate future," I advised him. "If the retroviral delivery system works, I should be a little more interesting to look at in approximately three hours. If it doesn't, I definitely won't."

"You don't have to do this for me."

Oh, that hurt. "I'm glad Jarn is back. I hope you two are very happy together. But you'll have to forgive my vanity. I really don't feel like standing up to urinate for the rest of my life." I went around him.

He followed me into the submersion treatment room. "You mistake my meaning. You do not have to risk your life in order to be female. I will love you no matter what you are."

"If you haven't noticed, Reever," I said, my big hands becoming very large fists, "I've turned into my father."

"No," he said. "You could never do that."

"Right. Well, as tolerant as you might feel toward the prospect of a same-gender relationship, I really can't see you having sex with Joseph Grey Veil." I folded my fists under my upper arms. "Not when you could have Jarn in my body."

"I don't want Jarn."

"Hello. You were in love with Jarn. And she's back, and I'm a guy, and . . ." I threw up my hands. "Why are we even arguing about this?"

"*You* are arguing." He pulled me into his arms and kissed me.

Although my mouth was different, kissing my husband felt the same. Unfortunately other things began to happen, and I pulled back as all sorts of muscles and things I'd never had as a woman began to tighten and throb.

"Well, it seems the new equipment works." I glanced down and winced. "Are erections always this uncomfortable? No, don't tell me."

Shon made a polite, coughing sound before he joined us. "The tank is ready, and I've placed your DNA sample into the solution. As soon as you're submerged, I'll infuse the tank with the retrovirus."

I began stripping out of my clothes, trying not to look at my body and, of course, failing. "I can't believe all this body hair. You men must do nothing but sweat." I glanced at Shon. "Sorry."

He shrugged. "I could never imagine how it feels to walk around in all that bare skin."

Once I was naked, I went over to the tank and

climbed up the short ladder on the side. "This had better not be freezing. I hate cold baths."

"I warmed it to the same temperature as your body." Shon brought a large syringe over to one of the infuser ports on the side of the tank, and handed me a tube with a mouthpiece on one end. "Oxygen feed," he said. "You will have to be completely immersed. I would sedate you, but you will have to remain conscious in order to keep from aspirating the fluid."

Which meant I was going to feel everything. Oh, joy.

"Don't remove me from the tank until it's finished. Whatever happens, I'll survive it." I looked at my husband. "See you when I'm a girl again." I inserted the mouthpiece, lifted my feet, and sank into the fluid.

I saw Reever through the side of the tank, his hand pressed against it. I matched my palm to his before I turned my head and nodded to Shon, who injected the compound.

Minutes ticked by as I breathed through the tube and let the fluid soak into me. The first sensation I felt was a faint prickling sensation all over my body as the compound entered my pores.

The harsh in-and-out of my breathing echoed in my head as warmth spread over me, and my skin tightened. I closed my eyes, trying to relax as the warmth became heat. Nerve endings flared as my muscles knotted and contracted, making me feel as if a million insects were crawling over my skin. I clenched my teeth against the mouthpiece as those insects stopped crawling and began biting.

I was burning up, the tank's fluid cold against my fiery skin. Spasms racked my limbs steadily, and I fought back the panic and sense of smothering. I could still breathe, I could endure this. Just as I had before. . . .

I looked around, and saw I was back at the Free-Clinic, suspended in a lukewarm solution filling one of the fluid tanks used to treat aquatics. I was also stark naked.

"Don't move," Reever said.

"I'm not exactly in the mood for a swim," I said. "Would one of you mind telling me what's happened?"

"The contagion has stopped spreading since your contact with the Core. No new cases." Ana sighed. "The epidemic is over."

The Core. I recalled everything now. "Not for long. I've got to get out of here." I felt disoriented, my limbs rubbery. "Give me a hand, Duncan."

"Try not to disturb the fluid," he said as he leaned over. I saw how he averted his eyes as he reached for me. It was a little late for him to be worried about my modesty.

"Try not to drop me."

Reever carefully lifted me out. Once I was standing, Ana helped me dry off while Reever sealed the tank.

Puzzled, I asked, "What are you doing that for?"

"To preserve the Core that are still alive. The tank will have to be transported and drained in the groves."

Just as I thought I couldn't take any more of the pain and suffocating spasms, my muscles slowly went lax. The heat took longer to dissipate, but in time that passed, too. I was so grateful for the relief that when the bones in my pelvis began shifting around, I hardly noticed.

My immune system had prevented me from giving birth to my daughter in the traditional fashion; after

I miscarried Squilyp had transferred her tiny fetus to an embryonic chamber we had constructed. Now that I was in essence giving birth to myself, I wondered how any woman survived such pain.

The fluid began to seep away from me, and my body came to rest on the bottom of the tank as it emptied. I lay there on my side, my eyes closed, my heart thudding under a soft weight. I pressed my hand over it and felt the slope of my small breast.

"Cherijo." As he had so long ago on K-2, Duncan lifted me out of the tank, and wrapped me in a soft, warm towel. He carried me to a table and gently placed me there. When he straightened, I held on to his arm.

I hadn't opened my eyes yet. I was afraid to.

Don't be, Duncan said in my thoughts. *The compound worked. You are yourself again.*

As Shon began to examine me, I opened one eye and took a quick peek. The female body had never looked quite so beautiful to me.

"Couldn't you have made me taller?" I asked the oKiaf.

"For that I would have to use Jorenian DNA, and I do not think blue skin would suit you." He helped me sit up and scanned my back. "You have significant muscle strain and a few tears, but they are already healing." He infused me with an analgesic. "How do you feel?"

"Sleepy." I climbed off the table and swayed on my feet, which felt crinkled around the instep. "Wrinkly."

"I would keep you here, but I think you would be more comfortable in your quarters with Duncan."

Shon turned to my husband. "Signal me at once if her condition changes."

"I can't go to bed now," I protested. "We have to find the shifter and Maggie and Jarn. Stop them"—a huge yawn split my face—"from going back."

As we passed the immersion tank, I noticed Reever walking oddly, as if he was trying to block my view of it.

I stopped and looked up at him. "What are you doing?"

He forced a smile. "I am taking you to our quarters."

"No, you're not." I tried to look around him, and he countered my move. "I'm not moving until you let me look at it."

Slowly he stepped back, and I saw that Shon had sealed the open top of the tank, and covered the entire unit with a clear plas biohazard shroud.

The inside of the tank was covered in a thin, shimmering layer of black crystal.

I did go with Reever to our quarters, but only to cleanse and change into a fresh uniform. After seeing what Shon had removed from my body, I doubted I'd ever close my eyes again.

"Why didn't I feel it?" I muttered as I yanked a brush through my damp, tangled hair. Reever came up behind me, pried the brush from my tight fingers, and began doing a much better job. "There had to be, what, ten kilos of that waste inside me?"

"Twelve point three."

"Twelve. Jesus, that's the same as having triplets." I handed him a clip. "Why dump all that black crystal

in me? He had to know it would have killed me—
should have killed me—almost immediately." And I
still wasn't sure why I was breathing.

"You said that Maggie used you as a vessel for the
last of the infinity crystal," my husband said. "Perhaps
Joseph hoped to preserve some of the black crystal in
the same manner."

"Go back in time to keep it from being created,
but put some in your clone first for safekeeping. Sure,
that makes sense."

As soon as he clipped the braid he had woven in
my hair to the back of my head, I stood and went to
the viewport. Joren was gone, and we were moving
toward another solar system.

"Xonea is pursuing the Odnallak craft," Reever
said, answering my next question before I could ask
it.

I turned around. "He thinks they have me."

"He saw the security vids; we were not sure we
could convince him otherwise," Reever said. "Cherijo,
while you were in the tank, we received a signal from
TssVar. Some of his commanders have taken their
ships and left Varallan."

"What?" I had been so sure we could count on
the Hsktskt to help protect Joren and oKia, the last
two uninfected worlds, at least long enough to give us
time to find a solution. "Why?"

"The commanders of the League fleet are not responding to any signals or League base command.
They have left Sol Quadrant, and their trajectory in-
dicates that they are en route to Varallan."

"The Hsktskt wouldn't run from that."

"Long-range scans indicate that ships from
other worlds have joined them." He hesitated, and

then added, "The fleet now has over ten thousand ships."

While the Hsktskt barely had two thousand. No wonder the commanders had deserted. "Do you think the black crystal is controlling the League fleet?"

"That, or the League commanders have decided to invade Joren and oKia in order to escape it." He stopped me from heading to the door panel. "You have been through an extraordinary ordeal, Cherijo. You have to rest sometime."

"I can sleep when I'm dead." I frowned as I remembered how I'd felt when I'd faced the prospect of being awake for all eternity. "Did Shon detect any crystal in my bloodstream?"

"He scanned you several times while you were in the tank. You shed all of the black crystal in your system, and he did not detect anything else." He studied my expression. "What is it?"

"I took those blood samples when I was infected with the infinity crystal. They should have contained traces of it." And now that the retroviral compound had altered my DNA, it should have also deposited the infinity crystal in my bloodstream, but when I performed a quick scan of myself, I found no trace of it. "Well, at least my bones won't crystallize before the League comes and starts a new war."

Reever and I went to Command, where my presence seemed to stun the flight officers. The captain overcame his shock soon enough; he called for security and ordered Reever away from me.

"I'm not a shifter, Xonea," I snapped. "If you don't believe it's me, signal Medical. Shon has all the scans to prove it."

Xonea did just that, but even after the oKiaf assured him of my identity, he seemed unconvinced. "I saw you abducted by the Odnallak."

"No, you saw a nurse who was alterformed to look like me." Given my ClanBrother's dislike of Jarn, I decided not to elaborate further. "Have you been able to locate the Odnallak craft?"

"We will intercept them within the hour." He lowered the pulse rifle he had trained on me. "Why did you not signal me before this?"

"In the shape I was, you wouldn't have wanted to talk to me," I assured him.

One of the com officers handed Xonea a datapad, which he read and passed back. "The Ruling Council has ordered me to return to Joren."

"We can't go back yet," I said. "We have to stop the Odnallak from creating another rift."

"The council has received an ultimatum from the commander of the League fleet. Our people and the refugees we are harboring must leave Joren, or they will attack."

"It's the black crystal. It knows it can't invade the planet by itself or by using infected refugees," I explained. "So now it's trying to get the people to leave so it can attack them in space. I bet the League made the same threat to oKia."

"They signaled them after contacting the council," Xonea confirmed. "What will it do if we do not leave our homeworld?"

"It has ten thousand ships under its control," I reminded him. "With that kind of firepower, they could bombard the planet from orbit. Joren wouldn't stand a chance."

The captain's expression grew thoughtful. "Do

you believe this Odnallak can put an end to the black crystal invasion?"

"I don't know. But if anyone can, it would be him or Maggie." I sighed. "If he is successful in returning to the past, he intends to destroy the Jxin. If he does that, then the black crystal won't be created. Neither will any other species in our time."

Xonea summoned his com officer. "Signal the homeworld. Inform the Ruling Council that at this time I respectfully decline to follow their orders."

Seventeen

Reever and I went back to Medical and joined Shon, who had been scanning the minerals my body had shed in the tank.

"It is black crystal," he confirmed, "but it is inert."

"It's just taking a nap," I said. "I suggest we blow it out an air lock before it wakes up and attacks the crew."

"I do not believe it will." He handed me the scanner he'd been using on the tank. "See for yourself."

I checked the display, and saw the usual readings for the mineral's atomic structure, element content, and energy levels. "Unknown, unknown, and what the hell is this?" I glanced up. "It's turned into rock?"

"As I indicated—the crystal does not contain any energy, and it is no longer generating it."

"It's dead."

He shrugged. "For want of a better word."

"It's a trick." I saw Reever by the tank. "Duncan, don't you even think about it."

He placed a hand on the side of the tank. "I feel nothing." Before Shon and I could stop him, he thrust his hand through the infuser port. Hunks of black crystal fell to the bottom of the tank as he pulled one of the formations free and drew it out.

"Do you have a death wish? Shon, seal the room." I looked around frantically for a specimen container.

"It is harmless now." Reever brought it over and offered it to me.

Without thinking, I swiped it from him. "It eats planets, Reever, so I hardly . . . think . . ." I looked down at the eight-sided crystal shaft, which sat in my hand like a pretty, harmless bauble. "Shon."

"It is as he says." The oKiaf took the crystal from me and held it up to the light. "It refracts the light as any prism would. I can feel nothing from it." He gave me a direct look. "You neutralized it."

"Wait a minute, I didn't do anything," I argued.

"The shifter placed the black crystal in your body because he must have known you would survive being infected with it," Reever said. "Just as you survived carrying the infinity crystal."

"My immune system is great, but it's not *that* great." I turned to Shon. "The blood samples you used to alterform me had to contain infinity crystal; I took them when I was infected with it. That's what must have happened."

He shook his head. "I found traces of three-sided crystal embedded among the black formations. Also in an inert, harmless state."

I refused to believe I had anything to do with this. "Maybe they neutralized each other."

"Or your body did. There is something else I discovered from the readings I took during the alterformation process," Shon said. "Something the shifter brought out of dormancy when he separated you into two beings. I confirmed it when I compared your sequences to Maggie's."

"I know I have Odnallak DNA," I told him. "Don't remind me."

"You were created with Odnallak DNA, and bioengineered with Terran DNA to appear human," he agreed. "But you also have chromosomes that are identical to the Jxin's. Approximately twenty-three."

"What does that mean?" Reever asked.

"It means that Joseph cloned me from his cells," I said slowly. "But Maggie added some of her DNA." I met his gaze. "It means Maggie *is* my mother."

A warning signal came over the com, and I went over to answer it. "Medical Bay."

"Cherijo, we have intercepted the Odnallak craft," Xonea said. "The shifter is not responding to our signals. Readings indicate that the craft is on a direct course for an unidentified, newly formed anomaly."

"He has also created a new rift," Shon said.

"Cherijo, we can pursue the Odnallak, but not before he reaches the anomaly," Xonea told me.

I knew what he was saying. The crew of the *Sunlace* had barely survived the first passage we had made through the derelict's rift, and our ship was still in desperate need of repairs. But if the shifter escaped into the past and destroyed the Jxin, we would wink out of existence, and none of this would matter.

I exchanged a long look with my friend and my husband. "Under the circumstances, ClanBrother, the only thing I can advise is that we follow them in."

"Agreed," he said. "Prepare for time transition."

We barely had enough time to alert the medical staff before the *Sunlace* reached the rift. As Xonea issued orders for the crew to brace for impact, Reever and Shon and I left the immersion room and joined my staff. I didn't mind Reever pulling me into his arms as the first of the rift's lights appeared around us.

If we didn't make it this time, there was no place I would rather have been.

The passage was just as cold and frightening as it had been the first time, but it didn't seem to last as long. When we emerged from the blinding light, we were on the deck but uninjured. This time everyone regained consciousness almost immediately.

"Something's already changed," I said, spreading my hand over an odd lightness in my abdomen. "Do you feel that?"

Shon touched his chest. "Yes." He opened the front of his tunic, and revealed the touch-healer marks in his fur. Now there were three: one golden, one black, and a new silver mark between them. "What does it mean, Cherijo?"

"I don't know." I looked at Reever, who was studying his hands. "What is it?"

"My scars." He showed me the smooth backs of his hands. "They have disappeared."

"Our coming here may have already altered our timeline." I didn't feel changed in any way, however, and my memories were still intact. So were Reever's and Shon's, or they wouldn't have noticed the subtle changes. I went to the nearest console and signaled Command. "Xonea, where are we?"

"We are in orbit above Jxinok," he said. "The Odnallak has just entered the upper atmosphere and is preparing to land."

I looked at the men. "Notify launch bay. We're going after them."

The jaunt from the ship to the surface gave me time to think, although I still didn't know what we could do to stop the shifter. Nor did I know what power he would have with the infinity crystal in his possession. The only hope I had was what my body had done to the crystal in the immersion tank. Maggie had told me over and over that both crystals couldn't be destroyed. I knew from my encounters with the black crystal that it was impervious to everything. How had I managed to neutralize them?

The Jxin use the infinity crystal to create life. The Odnallak created the black crystal, which destroys it. What am I missing?

We landed a few minutes after the Odnallak touched down, near a small Jxin settlement. We found the shifter's craft, but it was empty.

"They have gone to the village," Shon said, pointing to two sets of footprints in the dirt, and a third set of elongated marks between them.

Reever knelt and touched the soil. "She must be unconscious. They dragged her."

I hadn't thought of how this must be for him. "We'll get her back, Duncan." And then I'd be gracious and let him go to her. Somehow.

The settlement appeared to be much more primitive, with dwellings built close to the ground out of crafted wood and quarried stone. The people we saw as we walked into the settlement were also different—dressed in handmade garments, and using hand-tooled implements. I saw the faces of children, young adults, and elderly people among the settlers, and caught a glimpse of a cleared field beyond the tree line, and planted crops.

"Just how far back did we come?" I murmured to Reever as the Jxin settlers noticed us and began walking toward us.

"It appears we are in the time before their first industrial age." Reever stepped forward and held out his hands in a peaceful gesture. After some hesitancy, one of the older men came and took his hands.

My husband closed his eyes as he absorbed the Jxin's language. Then he spoke to him and the settler replied at length.

"They saw them pass through the settlement," Duncan told us. "They were headed for the quarry." He exchanged a few more words with the settler, who nodded. To us he said, "This male will guide us there."

Another man called out something in a loud, unpleasant voice. Most of the other settlers gave him some placid looks but didn't respond. After a few moments he stalked off in disgust, followed by three other scowling settlers.

"Let me guess," I said, watching them go. "Those are the undesirables."

The friendly settler gestured for us to follow him, and led us along a winding trail with deep ruts into the forest. We emerged from the trees onto a rocky plain, the center of which had been dug out in tiers that descended out of view. I noticed the sunlight glittering on some of the stones, and bent to pick up a small pebble near the edge of the pit. It was studded with tiny golden crystals.

Shon scanned it. "Dormant infinity crystal." He moved his scanner around in a slow sweep. "The soil here is saturated with it."

"Something is happening down in the pit," Reever said, and then the ground shook, throwing us all off-balance.

A transparent bubble rose out of the pit, enlarging as it grew and attaching itself to the sides of the quarry. Wherever it touched stone, it crystallized into clear, three-sided formations.

The settler paled and babbled something at Reever before he ran off.

"What did he say?" Shon asked.

"The translation is difficult," my husband said. "It was something like, 'The stars have awakened.'"

"Not the stars." I watched the upper vault of the bubble solidify into a shining dome. "The crystal has." Something jabbed into my back, and I whirled around to face the unfriendly settler and a small group of his pals. He held a curved blade fastened to the end of a shaft made from a root that curled around his hand and forearm.

Reever offered his hands again, palms up, and spoke to him gently. The settler snapped back at him and gestured toward the pit.

"Tell him we didn't do this," I suggested.

"He knows we did not," Reever said. "He is ordering us to go into the dome."

I saw the hair around Shon's neck rising. "I think that would probably be a good idea."

As the settlers marched us down into the pit, I noticed some of the scars on their hands: slashes that looked exactly like the ones that had disappeared from Reever's skin. "Duncan."

"I know. I see them." He said something to one of the men, who responded with a snarl. "Jxin children of this time are taught to control their emotions and desires from an early age. These men could not learn those disciplines."

"That is why they're forced to live on the fringes of society," Joseph said as he met us outside the dome. "They are used for the manual labor that the other settlers do not wish to perform themselves, and they are not permitted to breed outside their caste. But they are not called undesirables in this time. That won't happen for another thousand years." He smiled at me. "I had expected to see my son, not my daughter."

"I'm your clone, not your kid. Where are the women?"

"Inside, waiting for you." He gestured toward the dome, and an archway formed. "Come. Let me show you what you have made possible."

We followed Joseph inside the dome, which was still forming on the inside. I saw enormous shafts of infinity crystal shooting up from the rocky ground to serve as supports for the upper dome, and others growing into complex shapes that weren't as easily identified.

"What is all this?" I demanded.

"You must have a name for everything. It is as annoying a habit now as it was when you were a child." He gazed around, almost beaming with pride. "This is a place of transformation, where the future will shortly be decided. Call it whatever you like."

Maggie appeared, dragging a struggling Jarn behind her. Her black eyes told me she was still being controlled by the shifter. At the same time, the settlers seized Reever and Shon from behind and held their sharp blades to their throats.

"Duncan." Jarn looked at him and then me. "Cherijo?"

I forced a smile. "I'm sorry we had to meet under such unpleasant circumstances, Jarn." I turned to Joseph. "Why bring her here?"

"Balance, which now must be restored." He gestured toward Maggie, who dragged Jarn over to one of the crystal archways. As soon as she thrust her inside, dazzling lights enveloped her, and she vanished.

I felt sick. "What did you do to her?"

"She has been sent back to your time. Now that I have you, I have no more use for her."

None of it made sense to me, but the shifter was insane, so it probably never would. "Now you're going to do what? Destroy the Jxin, and the future, and take over the universe?"

"As much as I wish to, I cannot." He grabbed my arm. "That is for you to do."

"You're out of luck, then." I didn't fight him; there was no need to. "I'm not doing a damn thing for you."

"You wish to stop the black crystal, and save your timeline. It's time you faced the truth about who created it." He pushed me into the center formation, which was formed from a series of clear crystal panels. "Observe the Jxin, several thousand years after you met young Maggie. They have left their homeworld and have spread out among the stars." He sneered. "To pass along their precious legacy."

I watched the images. They displayed the Jxin being taken from slaver ships and left on hundreds of different worlds. "They weren't passing anything. They were enslaved."

"No, as I'm certain Maggie has told you, they merely needed transportation," he chided. "Now watch."

The enslaved Jxin seemed remarkably unconcerned about their pathetic situations. As they were abused and worked, they began to falter and then fell in their tracks. Their bodies were tossed into pits and off the sides of ships and into enormous fires. Each time a body was destroyed, a faint glow rose from it and twinkled out of sight.

"They ascended," Joseph explained, "but the bodies they left behind were riddled with pathogens. They rotted into the ground and infected the plant life, and dissolved into the waters, polluting the aquatics. They tainted the scavengers who devoured their corpses. Even the wind that blew the ashes of their burned remains spread their disease over the face of those worlds."

The crystal panels displayed new life emerging on the slaver planets, humanoid life. It crawled down from the trees and out of the swamps and emerged from the woods. The humanoids joined together in tribes and occupied caves, and then began making and using tools to kill game and build crude shelters.

"I know the Jxin were the founding race," I told him. "But I don't believe they used a disease to create life."

"Then you tell me, Doctor: how else could the Jxin have done it?" He produced a small container filled with black liquid. "The Odnallak knew. They had developed a cure for the plague the Jxin intended to release. When my ancestors were destroyed, it created the black crystal. Their final vengeance against the Jxin."

He opened the container, spilling the black crystal onto the rocky ground. I staggered backward.

"It will not harm you. You are as much its child as you are mine," he said.

"It's not a person, Joseph," I told him. "It's a rock. A deadly, contagious, malicious rock that, according to you, was created to wipe out all life in the universe, but still, a rock."

"You're wrong. It knows you. It helped me bring you to life." He smiled. "I showed it to you when you came to me on Terra. Don't you remember?"

Central Analysis was a research scientist's fantasy-land, fully stocked with all the latest in medical examination tech. Some of the scanners were so new I didn't recognize the models. Several worktables stood ready for human subjects, but there was a sterile, unused feel to the room.

I wiped up a little dust from a console with my fingertip and examined it. "Been suffering mad-scientist block lately?"

"I generally work in Development and Engineering." He pointed to another panel. "Through there."

I walked through the door and entered an equally sterile, cold environment. However, here there were signs of ongoing experiments, centrifuges spinning, culture dishes cooking, and an entire wall of containers stuffed with organs and other, less recognizable objects preserved in duralyde solution.

I nodded toward the wall. "Spare parts in case you mess up?"

"Some are continuing experiments in cloned organ scaffolding. Others are failures. As were these."

He pressed a button on a console, and an entire section of the opposite wall slid away. Behind it were endless rows of glittering plas bubbles, filled with black liquid, and hooked to dozens of data cables. Each had a drone clamped to its base, and from the flickering lights many were still active.

That didn't get my attention as much as the contents of the bubbles. Inside the murky fluid were small, pale objects enmeshed in a web of monitor leads. They were human. Human fetuses in various stages of development.

Hundreds of them.

I could feel the color draining from my face. "Embryonic chambers, I presume?"

"That is correct. This one"—*he went over and placed a hand on the only empty chamber*—*"was where I developed you."*

I walked toward it, morbidly fascinated. Memories stirred with every step.

The sea of warm, black fluid . . . the intricate web held my body suspended . . . warm and safe. . . .

I shoved out of my head the memories of the artificial wombs I had seen in Joseph's hidden laboratory on Terra. I wanted to vomit. "You put black crystal in the embryonic chambers."

"Of course. The crystal may not be benign, but it is immortal," he said. "I knew if I eradicated the Jxin sequences from the Terran DNA I used to create you, and replaced them with my own, it would not harm you. I was correct. As soon as I introduced your embryo to the fluid matrix, the crystal recognized you. It nurtured you. It gave you the gift of eternal life."

"That rock," I said through my teeth, "is *not* my mother."

He shrugged. "Not in the traditional sense, but it served quite admirably as a surrogate, and it still regards you as its offspring." He watched my face. "Once we destroy the Jxin, the black crystal will be ours to command. Think of all that we can do with such an ally. Any world we want will be made ours. Our children will live forever."

"I'd rather eat black crystal."

Dark tendrils wrapped around my feet and inched up my legs, leeching the warmth and the life out of me. I wanted to move, but I couldn't.

"I regret that I have to force your hand," I heard Joseph say. "But once this is done, you will see that it was the only possible cure."

Eighteen

I felt the frigid weight crawling up my body, tightening around my throat before I could scream. Then it inched into my ears, and streamed inside my head, closing off my thoughts to everything but the beautiful darkness inside me.

As the black crystal filled me, my body accepted it, and my mind expanded. I still saw the crystal panels displaying Joseph's images, but they were unnecessary to me now. The darkness was not evil or good; it simply was. I felt foolish for ever having feared it.

What I had always thought of as Jxin DNA was a contagion, a carefully engineered, encoded gene that the Jxin had inserted into their own DNA. They had created it exactly for the reasons Joseph had told me, to infect primitive life-forms on other worlds, and duplicate their evolution. They had believed that by forcing intelligent humanoid life to evolve on other worlds, they were contributing to the future of that level of existence. They saw the infection they spread as a means of reproducing one last time, so that the universe would remain under the control of their offspring.

It was horrendous. A disease without a cure that they had released without a second thought. By doing so, they had interfered in the natural evolution of millions of worlds. And they had done it out of conceit and pride. They believed their species was superior to all others.

I understood now what Joseph meant to do. Once I separated the Jxin from my ancestors and destroyed them in this time, I could use the infinity crystal to safely evolve the Odnallak. They would take their rightful place in existence, and one day attain perfection. It would be the Odnallak who traveled to other worlds, and left behind their legacy to existence before they ascended. Life would evolve, not from the plague of the Jxin, but from the same species that had created me.

"That won't happen, baby, and you know it," a voice drawled.

A light penetrated the cool darkness, glaring into my mind like the unwanted intruder it was.

I didn't want her here, but she wouldn't go. Not until I acknowledged her presence, and listened to more of her nonsense, and then drove her away. "Mother."

"After several million years of waiting for the kid to grow up and catch up," Maggie said, "you'd think she'd call me Mom. But no. It's Mother."

We faced each other in a featureless void, no bodies, no meaningless settings to provide her with her usual amusements. I didn't have to see her to know why she had come.

"Joseph told me I would know who created the black crystal. It was you."

"Technically it was both of us, but I'll take the

blame. I was very young, Joey. I hadn't yet learned the value of a good, bald-faced lie." She drew closer, bathing me in her light. "Don't feel so superior. You're still trying to be Daddy's girl."

She was vicious and selfish and had never cared about me. How could I have ever loved her? "Joseph told me the truth."

"Joseph told you what you wanted to hear," she corrected. "I liked that part about how the Odnallak are going to save the future as soon as you kill off all of us. These future saviors would be the same Odnallak who never stop for a nanosecond to think about anyone but themselves and what they want."

"Because of you," I reminded her, "and the way you treated them."

"Guilty as charged. When we see trash, we call it trash, and we treat it like trash. Because, oh, what do you know, it *is* trash, and it always will be." She appeared in front of me, beautiful and cold in her Jxin form, her hair floating around her as if we were both underwater.

"If the Odnallak were trash, it was because you made them feel that way."

"Oh, please, spare me the eternal sob story of the poor beleaguered, deprived, abused Odnallak." She swatted the air. "They were defectives who refused to improve themselves. They preferred to steal what they wanted instead of earning it. They always took the easy way out." She gave me an unpleasant smile. "And what do you know? Now you're following in their footsteps."

"If I don't destroy the Jxin now, they will exile the Odnallak, and create the same situation that led to their destruction." I didn't want to feel this anger. It was tearing at me, making it harder to think. "It's the only logical solution."

"No matter how many mistakes my people and I have made, Cherijo," she said, "we spent millions of years working toward the wisdom and the compassion we needed to ascend. The Odnallak haven't. We always tried to be better than we were. The Odnallak didn't. We will ensure the future of all existence. The Odnallak won't."

Joseph stepped between us. "You've done enough damage, Margaret. You've hurt our daughter for the last time."

"There's something he hasn't told you," Maggie said. "I can end his existence now. I could have done it at any time. We made you and the others so that you existed outside the timeline. No matter how he altered events or shifted time, at any time I could have sent you or one of the others back to destroy the Odnallak and finish this. But my people and I believed you deserved to make the choice freely. He doesn't."

"Shut up," my father shouted.

"It's all right, Joe. She's all yours now. Cherijo, while he's telling you all the reasons you have to destroy the Jxin, remember one thing. We never once asked you to destroy the Odnallak." Maggie spread out her arms. "No matter what you decide, I will always love you, baby."

Joseph swept his arm toward her, and black crystal smashed over her, erasing her and her light.

I felt her go. She disappeared from existence as if she had never been.

My father turned to me. "That is what must be done, Cherijo. To all of them. Kill them. Remove them from existence now, before they destroy all life."

I stared at the blackness where Maggie had been. "She never asked me to kill you."

"This is what they do," he said quickly. "They twist everything so that their lies sound like the truth. You know it isn't. She's still trying to pollute your mind. *Cherijo*."

I looked at him. "No more of this." I brought up my hands, and let the power building inside me flow through them. "No more."

My father did not go quietly, as Maggie had. Before he winked out of existence, he screamed his rage. Then he was gone, and I was alone.

I emerged from the darkness as I forced the black crystal out of my body, just as I had in the immersion tank on the *Sunlace*. Something had changed inside me, something that the crystal could not control.

I looked at the crystal panels around me, and reached out to touch the surface of one. It showed me the settlements where the ancestors of the Jxin and the Odnallak lived. I could feel their simple minds, the manner in which they had already divided themselves, and the first link in the chain of events that would end with the destruction of all life.

I felt power still growing inside me, and by instinct sent it out into the crystal panel. All around me the shafts and structures began to glow with silvery light. In turn I felt the enormous complexity of the dome, and how it eagerly responded to me, awakening more of the sleeping crystal in the soil, sending out golden tendrils toward the settlement, capturing and imprisoning the Jxin where they stood, holding them suspended in time and space. They would never move again unless I willed it.

I felt the timeline I existed in, but I also became

aware of others, waiting to form. I called up images from them on the crystal panels, and studied the time constructs.

I discovered that if I destroyed the Jxin, the Odnallak would not save my timeline. Without the Jxin to keep them in check, they would become conquerors and spread throughout the universe, first creating life, then enslaving it. They crushed every rebellion, and destroyed the children in their endless quest for ascension. Nothing I could do would alter their timeline, or its grim conclusion: In their desperation, the Odnallak would once more destroy themselves, creating and unleashing the black crystal.

If I destroyed the Odnallak, I discovered, the Jxin would never ascend. Without the existence of the Odnallak to drive them toward perfecting themselves, their civilization would continue peacefully for several thousand years and then it would simply die out of existence. Maggie's species had never fully appreciated the one thing the existence of the Odnallak among them had bestowed: the Jxin's desire to better themselves. Now because they had not evolved, they would never begin life on other worlds. But the universe had a way of correcting things, and the DNA left behind by the extinct Jxin would be blasted into space by an asteroid collision, where it would crystallize, spread to other worlds. Several million years after the Jxin died out, another species would rise to take their place, evolve, weed out their undesirables, and seek perfection. And the cycle of the black crystal would be repeated again.

If I did nothing, the black crystal would remain in existence, and the same timeline would play out. I called it up to see if any life escaped the scourge of the Odnallak's final weapon of vengeance. Joren and oKia did not escape, and once the black crystal wiped out all life, it began attacking stars, devouring them until it eradicated all light and all possibility of life in the universe.

Maggie had said I would have to make a choice, but there was no choice, except . . .

I called up one last potential timeline.

Once I had found the solution, I collected the last of the black crystal Joseph had brought back from my future, placing it in the specimen container he had discarded and sealing it.

"Cherijo."

Nineteen

I had forgotten about Reever and Shon, and stepped out of the time matrix to see the settlers imprisoned in crystal, and Shon lying unconscious on the ground.

My husband stared at my hair. "What has happened to you?"

I glanced at my reflection in one of the crystal shafts. My hair had turned completely silver, as had my eyes. "I've been changed again. This will be the last time."

He followed me back into the matrix. "Did Joseph do this to you?"

"Joseph, and Maggie. They're both gone now." I set the container aside and focused on reviewing the time constructs I'd called up. "I've found a cure for the black crystal."

"You told me that there is no cure."

"Not now, there isn't." I scanned the images, looking for the precise time sequence I needed, the moment when the Jxin and the Odnallak had separated as a species. I found it further along in the timeline than I'd imagined. "I'm going to make one. Step back from that archway, Duncan; I need that."

"You can control the crystal now."

"That's one way to put it." He had a gift for understatement, but his mind couldn't grasp what mine had attained in the last hour. I felt a little sorry for him. "It's all right. This will only take another minute or two."

I sent power into the archway, manipulating the time and space within its boundaries until it formed a small conduit. I could have made it much larger—big enough to swallow a fleet of ships—but for my purposes it didn't need to be big.

My final adjustment was to activate the energy well within the archway, and I stepped back as the portal began to open.

"What are you doing?"

"My last surgery." I sealed off the portal from the rest of the matrix—leaving it open would have sucked me and Reever into the portal—and returned to the crystal panels. "Bring me that container over there, will you?"

Reever picked up the black crystal I had collected. "Why do you need this?"

"Don't worry." I had to walk over and take the container from him. "I'm destroying it and the rest of the black crystal."

"As you said, the crystal cannot be destroyed."

"Not in the conventional sense, no." I lifted it up and looked at the angry, glittering contents. Now that I was immune to the effects, I could see the dark, ugly beauty of it. "But when I'm done, it will be destroyed, and there won't be a single trace of it anywhere in the universe."

Reever eyed the portal. "You cannot send it to an alternative dimension."

"Seeing how it can jump dimensions, that would be an exercise in supreme futility. What I'm going to do is give the black crystal exactly what it was designed to kill. The Jxin."

"Cherijo."

"And the Odnallak, too." I almost had enough power channeled to stabilize my tiny time rift. "I'm sending it to the moment in time when the Jxin still had bodies, and undesirables, and all the other little grubby problems that spoiled things for the ascension. The black crystal will infect them. They won't evolve. They won't discard the undesirables. And they damn well won't ascend."

"It will wipe out their species."

"Both species, to be exact. By the time it's finished, there won't be a single trace of their DNA left. At which point, the black crystal will cease to exist." I set down the container. "Say bye-bye to the Jxin, the Odnallak, and everything they've done to wreck our timeline."

"You cannot do this," he said at once.

I eyed him. "It's already done. I just have to send the crystal through."

"If you infect the Jxin and destroy their DNA, they will never become the founding race. Millions of species will be lost."

"Life will evolve again; it always does." I shrugged. "Only this time it won't be polluted by the Jxin or the Odnallak. It will be something different. Something new. Something that will not continue the cycle."

"You will kill everyone we know. Everyone we have tried to protect." He grabbed my wrist. "Cherijo, stop this."

"If I don't send it back, the crystal will destroy all

life anyway," I reminded him mildly. "And it will prevent any new life from evolving. This construct is the only way that sentient life has a chance."

He wouldn't let go. "There has to be another option."

I felt the frantic energy that had kept me going slowly draining out of me. "I've run thousands of time simulations through the matrix. Every other construct ends with the advent of the black crystal. Nothing survives it but me. It has to be destroyed, Duncan."

He frowned. "Why do you survive?"

"I don't know," I told him. "According to the time constructs I've run, no matter what happens, I am the only thing in the universe that never dies."

"So you would do this and condemn yourself to an eternity of solitude?"

That was the part I didn't want to think about. "It's the price tag, Duncan. Someone has to pay. I'd rather it be me." I tried to smile. "When it's done, I'm going to give myself to the protocrystal. It won't kill me, but it should keep me company while we wait for new life to evolve. Should only take a couple of billion years."

He let go of me and backed away. "I understand now." He looked blindly at the images flashing around us. "I was wrong."

"It won't hurt," I promised. "Not you or anyone else. You'll just stop existing."

"I was wrong about Jarn," he said.

"I don't want to talk about her." I turned away. "Would you leave now? I really don't want to watch you disappear."

"Why will you not be affected by the shift in the timeline, Cherijo?"

"I don't know." And I didn't care. "The matrix can't confide in me. It can only show me what will happen. Maybe Joseph did a better job cloning himself than he thought he did."

"It wasn't only Joseph," he said softly. "Maggie also gave you her DNA."

"She meant well, I suppose." I didn't want to think about my surrogate mother anymore. "Reever, I have all the time in the world here, but the rest of the existence doesn't. Let me do this. Let me end this."

"But you will not end. You will never die." He came to the console and took my hand. "Because you are not Odnallak or Jxin. You are both. You are neither."

"Whatever."

"Listen to me, Wife." He pressed my hand between his. "You are Jxin, but you chose not to ascend. You are Odnallak, but you chose not to harm. No crystal can kill you. The Jxin cannot control you, and neither can the Odnallak. You became Jarn, and Jarn became you. You are the paradox, Cherijo. The one true paradox in all of this. Why is that, do you think?"

"Shut up." I pulled away from him and accessed the control grid. I channeled the power grid into the matrix, and opened the portal.

"Squilyp told you there was no Jarn. I am telling you there is no Jarn. The woman who Joseph brought here was you. There is only you. It is the same with them. In you, there is no Jxin, no Odnallak. You are neither and both. You are their child, beloved. Their only child. The beginning and the end. The path changes, Cherijo. So, too, must the traveler."

"I have to stop them," I shouted.

"No." He swept me up into his arms. "You have

to do what you were created to do. You have to save them."

Reever carried me to the portal, and jumped through.

Light streamed around us, and then I stood in the center of a field, surrounded by Jxin. Reever lay at my feet, unconscious. I didn't see any familiar faces this time, but their expressions ranged from stunned to frightened.

Jxin with normal emotions, dressed in ordinary garments, gathered closer. Beyond them I could see a city, one that was much more advanced than the primitive settlement of the past, but not yet the metropolis of the crystal towers and mind-boggling technology.

"Are you injured?" I heard one of the men ask.

"I don't think so." I crouched down to check my husband. His pulse and respiration were normal, and after a few moments he opened his eyes. "That was unbelievably stupid."

He smiled up at me. "I know."

I looked up at the now-worried faces of my ancient ancestors. "My name is Cherijo Grey Veil, and this is my husband, Duncan Reever. We came here from the future."

It took them a minute or two to digest this. Finally one of the women asked, "Why?"

"To talk to you." Reever wasn't the only one who could make a crazy leap. "To save you."

It took a lot of talking. Several weeks of it, in fact, that I spent answering questions and mapping out timelines and submitting to medical examinations. The Jxin were nothing if not skeptical.

Fortunately they were also advanced enough in this era to grasp what Reever and I told them, and civilized enough to be horrified by their imminent future.

"It has always been the dream of our people to explore space, and colonize other worlds," one of their leaders, an older male known as an Elder, admitted. "But we have no wish to abandon our world or our bodies in order to evolve. And yet you say our descendants will do this."

"If you go on as you are, they will. The means by which they do it are the problem." I sighed and rubbed my forehead. "The Jxin must evolve into the founding race of the future. But it has to be all of the Jxin, not just the genetically perfect."

"How can we stop our descendants from causing this division?"

"Celebrate your diversity," Reever suggested. "Seek balance instead of perfection."

"We could outlaw bioengineering," one of the council members said.

"That might stop your people from tampering with your genetic future for a few generations, but eventually they'll forget why it had to be outlawed."

"Not if they preserve the records of our visit to this time," Reever said. "Etched in crystal, they will last forever. Then you only have to pass them and the warning we have given you to each new generation."

"If we do this," their leader said, "the future will be changed. Your timeline will be altered." He looked at me. "If there is no division among our descendants, you . . ."

I knew what he didn't want to say. "Reever may

never be born, and I'll probably never be created. We know."

He looked shaken. "You would give your lives for an unknown future?"

I leaned forward. "Billions of generations are depending on it. The future of the universe. So tell me, Elder, wouldn't you?"

The portal remained stable throughout the length of our sojourn, and once we had convinced the Jxin to alter their future, Reever and I had one last decision to make.

"We can remain here for as long as our timeline remains cohesive," he said to me as we walked out to the portal. "It will be several generations before the changes affect it."

"As much as I like them, I'd rather go back to our own time." I looked into the shimmering depths of the rift. "Marel could still be waiting for us on the other side. Or maybe we'll go to wherever she is."

"I love you, *Waenara*."

"I know, *Osepeke*."

We said our good-byes, and then held hands and walked into the light.

Twenty

I could end my story here. All things considered, I probably should. But while no one may ever believe what I've written in these journals, I think the truth is worth the risk.

Time lost all meaning as we traveled through the portal, but I wasn't scared. I had no idea what would happen to us, but Reever was with me. On some level I knew we weren't going back to our future; I could sense the enormous shifts in the time and reality taking place just beyond the portal. Whatever lay on the other side, I wouldn't face it alone.

We emerged not into my crystal matrix on Jxin, and not in the blackness of oblivion, but in a field of yiborra grass. As the portal vanished behind us, I looked into the docile, mildly curious eyes of a t'lerue.

"Hello, bovine," I said, holding out my hand for it to sniff before I gave it a gentle pat. Some of my tousled hair fell over my cheek and I began to push it back, and then stared at it. It was no longer silver, but had changed back to black with a silver sheen.

"Your eyes are dark blue again," Reever said.

"Good. I never liked silver that much." I used them to glance at my husband. "As happy as I am to see the place, why are we on Joren?"

"I cannot say." He scanned the horizon. "This is Marine province, but I do not see the HouseClan pavilion."

Neither did I. "Maybe they moved it." I turned around, and nearly fell on my face.

"What do you here, Terrans?"

The Jorenian male standing behind us was as big, strong, and handsome as the rest of his people, and he had the requisite black hair and white-within-white eyes. His skin, however, was not blue but tan, and as he made a gesture of greeting, I saw he had five fingers.

He'd also spoken to us in StanTerran.

"We're just visiting, ClanSon," I said carefully. "I'm Cherijo. This is my husband, Duncan."

He didn't react to our names. "I am Kol Kalea." He glanced around us. "Do you seek the settlement?"

"Yes," Reever said before I could ask what that was.

The crossbreed smiled. "I am meeting my bond-mate there. Come, I will take you along the path."

Kol led us across the pasture and up a hill. "Are you and your husband cattle buyers?"

"No," I said. "We're . . . travelers."

"I did not see you when I left the settlement earlier," he said. "You have no vehicle. How did you come to be in that field?"

"It's a long story," I advised him as we reached the top of the hill, and I stopped for a moment so I could absorb what I was seeing.

HouseClan Torin *had* moved their pavilion, which

was now atop some cliffs overlooking the sea. It was also surrounded by thousands of smaller structures that appeared to be housing, businesses, and gathering points. All of them were definitely not of Jorenian design.

"Okay, this is new," I murmured to Reever.

He took my hand in his. "ClanSon Kalea, could you tell us something about the settlement? Who lives here?"

"This is Torin territory, of course, but anyone may live here. This was the first open settlement on Joren, but it has proven to be such a success that all of the other HouseClans are opening their territories and developing their own merchant colonies."

"Really." My adopted people had always been friendly, but at the same time extremely territorial. "What made the Torin decide to build this open settlement?"

"It was part of the Expansion Treaty." Now he looked puzzled. "Where have you been traveling?"

"Oh, here and there." I exchanged a look with Reever. "We've been out of touch for a long time."

"I see." It was pretty obvious that he didn't. "The terms of the treaty required at least one multispecies colony to be established on every world, so that each species might develop tolerance through free trade. It has not been without its difficulties, but the Terrans have done a great deal to help smooth the path for others."

I wanted to laugh. "The *Terrans* have been helpful."

He inclined his head. "Their customs of embracing diversity and expanding knowledge through exploration have been adopted by thousands of worlds. Your people are highly regarded as ambassadors of peace and understanding wherever they go. But I do not understand. How could you not know this?"

"Our journey took us away from the explored quadrants for many years," Reever said.

"Before the treaty was struck," I added without thinking.

"That, lady, was more than two hundred years past." The Jorenian folded his arms. "I know Terrans do not live so long."

I couldn't tell him that we were immortal—assuming we still were—so I'd have to come up with a convincing lie. Fortunately my husband was much more skilled in that department.

"There was a problem with the stasis equipment on board our ship," he told Kol. "It did not rouse us when it was programmed to."

His dark brows rose. "Stasis travel was not developed until the year of my birth, Terran, and I have not yet celebrated thirty name days."

"It was an experimental prototype," I assured him. "That's probably why it malfunctioned."

"As you say." He didn't seem entirely convinced, but the lines around his nose and mouth eased a fraction. "I will ask one more question: Do either of you mean to do harm here?"

"I'm a physician and my husband is a linguist." I smiled at Reever. "We've taken vows to do no harm."

He nodded. "Then you are welcome."

That night, in the quarters the Torin had given us, Reever and I sat together at a terminal scanning history files. Many of the events from our past were still recorded, but many of the details and outcomes had changed.

After humans discovered they were not alone in the universe, Terra had struggled with an ugly period of rampant xenophobia. This time, however, some wiser souls had instigated a social revolution to address the problem. Tentative contact with offworlders was made, first to prove they were not a threat to humans, and then to find out exactly what they were. As the benefits of becoming part of a much larger intergalactic community became apparent, the governments of my homeworld actively encouraged interspecies events and enterprises.

The humanoid and reptilian species had still clashed on occasion, especially over the practices of enslavement and free colonization, but many of the massacres and wars had been prevented—by, of all species, the Hsktskt and the Terrans, who had somehow become partners in diplomacy.

"I can't believe they're running around the quadrants settling territorial disputes and disbanding slaver depots," I muttered. "The Hsktskt hate humanoids. Dear God, the Hsktskt used to *eat* humanoids."

"TssVar remains Hanar," Duncan said as he scrolled through another file. "He rose through the ranks by his work creating slaver-reformation programs and establishing reptilian-humanoid trade cooperatives. The arenas never came into being."

I thought of all the suffering Reever had experienced as an arena slave. "Good riddance. Are Squilyp or ChoVa still around?"

"The Omorr practices as a surgeon on his homeworld, and lives with his mate and their twin sons," Reever said. "TssVar's eldest daughter is now named

UtessVa, and recently was mated to a Hsktskt who looks remarkably like PyrsVar after he was changed." He read a little more. "TssVar began his career in the militia as a slave liberator," he added. "He saw to it that freed slaves were given sanctuary on Vtaga until they could be returned to their homeworlds."

"The universe always corrects itself. He took your place." I grinned. "Maybe that's why you two always liked one another." I saw a strange expression come over his face, and touched his arm. "What is it, sweetheart?"

"Kao Torin lives." He turned the monitor toward me. "So does his bondmate, a former Akkabarran physician named Jarn."

I looked at the image of the happy couple, taken during their bonding ceremony. Kao smiled down at his Choice, a lovely female with pale skin, light brown hair, and dark eyes. She was very attractive, but she didn't look a thing like me.

At first I wasn't sure what to say, and then I did. "I'm glad they found each other. How about you?"

He pulled me onto his lap. "I have my woman."

My first search had been through Terran census records, but I hadn't found any listing for Joseph Grey Veil, his daughter Cherijo, or her husband, Duncan Reever.

I leaned back against Reever's shoulder. "I wish I knew what happened to us."

"You were never born," a familiar voice said.

I stood up and turned around to see Shon Valtas standing just inside the door panel. "I secured that panel."

"You're still using the same codes you did before the time shift," he chided. "We weren't sure if you would be coming back, but when I heard a rumor about two Terrans suddenly appearing out of nowhere, I thought it might be you."

"You know where we've been," I said cautiously.

"Yes. All of us do." He turned and opened the door panel, and several beings entered: a crossbreed 'Zangian, a Jorenian whose skin was covered in a layer of crystal, and others I'd never seen.

Shon introduced the others by name before he said, "Like you, we were unaffected by the time shift. Our memories of the past are unaltered."

"So you remember the war between the League and the Hsktskt?"

"That, and the Core plague on K-2, the destruction of Skart, the rebellion on Akkabarr, and the attack on Trellus," Jadaira Rask said. "Although we soon found out that none of them occurred in this new universe."

"Maggie once told me that we were created to exist outside the timeline." I rubbed a hand over my face. "Does anyone know about us and what we are?"

"Happily, no," Renor, the crystalline crossbreed, said. "Nor have we revealed ourselves to anyone."

"After witnessing the changes in reality, we thought it best to remain silent and observe," the Tingalean added in its soft, hissing voice. "You and your bondmate were successful, Healer Grey Veil. The Jxin did not separate their species or attempt to ascend."

I looked at Shon. "So the black crystal was never created."

"No. The Jxin are gone now, but before their species died out, they became space explorers, and colonized over seven hundred worlds. They caused life on those worlds to evolve, and spread to others, and eventually founded every sentient species known to us."

Renor came forward and held out an etched crystal disc. "This was discovered in the ruins on Jxinok centuries ago, and since has been preserved in a museum of curiosities on my sire's homeworld. When I saw the mark on it, I knew it was for you, and so I . . . borrowed it."

The mark on the crystal was simple: three parallel lines, one golden, one black, and one silver. I carefully inserted the disc into the computer and opened it.

The image of a Jxin male who looked a little like my creator appeared on the screen. He began speaking in an ancient dialect.

"We send this prayer of gratitude to the healer of all things," Reever translated out loud. "The one who brought great wisdom to our people thousands of years ago. We are the last generation of the Jxin, and we would have you know that we have kept the promise made to you. We hope that you have made safe passage, and that you will always watch over our children among the stars."

The man who might have been Joseph bowed, smiled, and then disappeared from the screen.

I didn't know quite what to make of it. It had taken hundreds of thousands of years for the Jxin to reach the end of their species' existence. To think that they had passed along our warning for so many generations . . . "I didn't think they'd give up ascension to save the future."

"You gave up your future to save the Jxin," Jadaira said. "Sounds like a fair trade to me."

Maybe it would be, in a couple thousand years, when I got over the loss of my child. Because Reever and I had not been born in this timeline, neither had Marel. We couldn't risk trying to have another child, either, not with the genetic curses we carried.

But there were plenty of orphans in the universe who needed parents, for when we were ready to start a family again. I looked at Shon. "We should talk about where we go from here."

There wasn't a lot of debate during the discussion that followed. Because time no longer affected us, and eternal life would still attract mortals who wanted it for themselves, we would have to be careful not to draw too much attention to ourselves. That meant living simply and blending in with surrounding populations. We could all simulate aging, but we couldn't settle in one place for longer than a few decades.

"We should establish our own colony," Renor Kalea suggested. "A place where we can gather or take sanctuary when necessary. Perhaps on a world that would be inhospitable or unattractive to mortals."

"I suggest oKia," Shon said.

"Last time I checked, oKia had a native population of a couple million," I reminded him.

"You have been gone for several million years," he countered. "Protocrystal drove my people from our world at the turn of the last century. They convinced the Skartesh to relocate with them to one of Kevarzangia Two's moons. To date, oKia, Skart, and the entire solar system remain uninhabited."

"The protocrystal cannot harm us," Reever said thoughtfully, "and since her last transformation, Cherijo has the ability to communicate with and control it."

I never wanted to see another form of crystal for as long as I lived, much less reside among evolving, intelligent pools of it. Then something occurred to me. "Was the protocrystal affected by the time shift? Or is it still eating oKia?"

"It was somewhat altered. Now it merely tries to absorb other intelligent life into its matrix," Shon said. "Since the Great Exodus, that part of space has been quarantined by the Allied Faction. All trade routes have been abandoned, and even the worst of slavers and mercenaries avoid it."

The Allied Faction. I was never going to get used to hearing that. "Then if it's still willing to listen to me, I think I can work out some living arrangements."

"We will still need a mission," Jadaira said. "Immortality without purpose would be torture, I think. I would rather fly my strafer into the nearest star than spend eternity adrift among the living."

"We won't be drifting," I assured her. "The Jxin are not the only species who will ever discover or take a shot at ascension. Not now that their DNA is a part of every intelligent race in existence."

Shon seemed surprised. "So you believe our mission should be to suppress such evolution?"

"We could stop them, but I think we can accomplish more by guiding them," I replied. "We watch, we check, and when someone goes astray, we help them find their way back to sanity. We've got the rest of eternity. It'll probably take that long."

The Tingalean's eyes gleamed. "And if they choose to ignore our guidance?"

Reever answered him. "Then we stop them by any means necessary."

We all agreed to meet in a few days to solidify our plans and make arrangements to discreetly sojourn together to oKia. Then everyone left except Shon, who stayed behind to discuss the current status of several troublesome races, including the Toskald, who had abandoned their homeworld but had chosen ship life over settlement, and were now existing as pirates on the fringe of colonized space.

After figuring out how to work the prep unit, which was stocked with a bewildering variety of Jorenian and offworlder dishes, I prepared a meal for the men and then excused myself.

"Where are you going?" Reever wanted to know.

"I thought I'd take a walk and check out the settlement." I bent down and kissed his cheek. "Don't worry, I'll be back in an hour or so."

Beyond the settlement, Joren's moons arced above the horizon, a floating giant's neck ornament of light and dark pearls. The moonslight glided along the streets with me, illuminating the faces of the settlers and merchants I passed. Most were happy, some appeared preoccupied, and a few scowled at everyone and everything in their path.

I saw so many odd pairings and groups it was difficult not to gape. A pair of Hsktskt and Jorenian males stood by a screen display of the latest agri equipment and gestured while they discussed seasonal planting. Warriors turned farmers.

A trio of young Terran girls giggled as they glanced back at three boys trailing after them: one lean, tough Omorr, one healthy-looking Taercal, and a sound-shielded P'Kotman. All the adolescents alternated between whispering to their friends and casting flirtatious looks at the other group. Young courtship, it seemed, would never change.

Time had crossed more than a few barriers, I thought as I saw aquatics socializing with desert dwellers, and avatars mixing with miners. I stopped counting the Jorenian and offworlder crossbreeds I spotted; they were everywhere. Although Shon had told us there were still disputes and skirmishes between some species, it seemed intelligent life had decided to be more intelligent.

Balance, it was a beautiful thing.

I didn't know where I was going, but something guided me through the settlement. It had begun tugging at me as soon as we came down the hill, and now it wrapped around me and through me like a suture, closing up a wound I couldn't see or feel. If Maggie had still existed, I would have blamed her for it. But this was something far more primal, and it was coming from inside me and beyond me at the same time.

I found myself standing in front of a multilevel gallery designed completely out of plas. The lighting had been dimmed for the night, but inside I could still see a series of sculptures. They were all hewn from green, blue, and violet stone, and depicted figures from Jorenian history. Tarek Varena I recognized from the features, not the pose; he was sculpted alongside a lovely and very pregnant female. While I was glad to see that Tarek's sad fate had somehow been averted, the loss of my own friends and loved ones cut into me like a cold blade.

"Your pardon, lady."

I turned to discover Darea Torin standing just behind me. Just before I spoke, I remembered that in this timeline she had no memory of our friendship or kinship. "Can I help you?"

"My bondmate and I saw you from the café across the street." She glanced back over her shoulder at a dining establishment. "Would your name be Cherijo?"

"It is." I saw no reason to deny it. "How did you know?"

"Actually, I did not." She made a confused gesture. "I know it is impolite to delay you, but would you come with me for a moment? There is someone who wishes very much to speak with you. Her name is Salea."

I couldn't see whom she was talking about, but guessed it was another immortal healer who had recognized me. "Of course."

I followed her across the street and into the café, which was crowded and noisy. We wove our way through to a section where it appeared a celebration was being held. Then I saw the small, smiling face of the child dashing toward me, and the astonishment drove me to my knees.

I looked at the door panel for the hundredth time. If my ClanBrother and that damn Omorr didn't show up soon, I was going to go hunt them down myself.

"One of the pilots told me we're going to the Liacos Quadrant."

Hawk was talking to me again. "That's right."

"My father's homeworld lies along our route there. Would it be possible, I mean—"

"Can we make a stop? Of course." Reever came over, and I automatically blocked my thoughts. I patted Hawk's arm. "You're among my friends now. I hope you'll give them a chance to be your friends, too." I smiled at Alunthri. "They've enriched my life quite a bit."

"Cherijo, may I have a moment?"

I excused myself, then went with Reever to another unoccupied corner. As I looked back, Hawk began hav-

ing a conversation with Alunthri, and two fascinated Jorenians who had approached them in my wake.

"I think we have another potential member for HouseClan Torin." I looked back at Reever. "What's up?"

"Why are you so agitated?"

"I'm just, uh, excited to be back where I belong."

"If that's so, why are you blocking your thoughts from me?"

"Because I'm thinking about killing two crew members with my bare hands."

Duncan turned to the viewport and made a frustrated sound. "I could understand why you were blocking your thoughts on Terra. But we are among friends now, Cherijo. It isn't necessary."

Maybe it was time I went to find Xonea and Squilyp. "Stay here and I'll—"

The crowd between us and the corridor door panel suddenly parted, forming a wide gap between them. I saw why, and froze.

Xonea was standing at the other end of the gap. In his huge arms he was holding a yawning, blond-haired toddler.

There she was.

"I know you think my telepathic abilities are an intrusion, but if you would only consider how they deepen our intimacy—"

She was a tiny thing. Of course, the Jorenians made everyone look dinky. Her hair was so blond it was almost white, dead straight, and nearly touched her shoulders. Her features were rosy and yet not baby-pretty. No, she looked like a miniature adult.

"Uh, Duncan?" I blindly swatted at him, unable to take my own eyes away. "Turn around."

Xonea started walking toward us. The sleepy child rested her cheek against the wide vault of his chest, making her look even smaller. Given her rapid gestation, the six months I'd spent in sleep suspension on the League ship, plus the time on Terra, she would be about a year old now.

Reever took me by the arm. "I love you, Cherijo. I don't want there to be any more walls between us. Let me in."

"I will, in a minute. Would you please turn around?"

"Even now you are distracted. Has someone—"

I grabbed his arms and shoved him around. He went very still. "Xonea."

The child Darea had called Salea stopped short, and her expression turned grave. "It is you, isn't it? I still remember."

I could manage only a slow nod, fast tears, and open arms. Then I was holding her, and laughing, and crying, and saying her name.

"Everything changed when you and Daddy went away," she whispered. "Everything except me. I had to pretend it was okay until I could find you again. Did Daddy come back, too?"

"Yes, honey. He's at the pavilion now, with Healer Valtas." I couldn't quite catch my breath. "Are you all right?"

Her curls bobbed as she nodded. "It didn't hurt me, but no one remembered who I was after the last big ripple. When they asked about you and Daddy, I told them I was lost from you and I hit my head, so I couldn't remember our names." She wrinkled her nose. "They gave me a new one."

"Salea?" Darea sounded worried. "Do you know this lady?"

"Yes, ClanAunt." My daughter looked up with shining eyes. "This is my mother. Her name is Cherijo."

The Torins swarmed around us, but I knew I had to take her back to the pavilion, back to Duncan so he would know. But as I stood, I looked across the broad shoulders and past the concerned blue faces, and saw my husband walking toward us.

"Cherijo." He glanced down and then froze as he saw Marel.

"It's me, Daddy." Our daughter reached up, and he lifted her into his arms. "I'm still here. I'm still me."

He kissed her brow and tucked her head under his chin, closing his eyes for a moment. When he opened them, his lashes were wet, but his expression was filled with astonishment and joy. And then I knew no matter what happened now or in the future, or even when time came to an end, I would be safe. In that moment I had been given all I could ever want, all I would ever need. Eternal life might be a gift or a curse, but it would never touch the truth of what I knew now.

Love is the only thing that lives forever.

The Stardoc Novels

by

S. L. Viehl

"Continously surprising and deviously written."
—Anne McCaffrey

STARDOC
BEYOND VARALLAN
ENDURANCE
SHOCKBALL
ETERNITY ROW
REBEL ICE
PLAGUE OF MEMORY
OMEGA GAMES
CRYSTAL HEALER

Available wherever books are sold or at
penguin.com

Get to know
the Darkyn side of
S. L. Viehl
(writing as Lynn Viehl)

The Novels of the Darkyn

Stay the Night

Twilight Fall

Evermore

Night Lost

Dark Need

Private Demon

If Angels Burn

"Erotic, darker than sin, and better than good chocolate." —Holly Lisle

Available wherever books are sold or at
penguin.com

THE ULTIMATE IN
SCIENCE FICTION AND FANTASY!

From magical tales of distant worlds to stories of
technological advances beyond the grasp of man, Penguin has
everything you need to stretch your imagination to its limits.

penguin.com

ACE

Get the latest information on favorites like
William Gibson, T.A. Barron, Brian Jacques,
Ursula K. Le Guin, Sharon Shinn, Charlaine Harris,
Patricia Briggs, and Marjorie M. Liu,
as well as updates on the best new authors.

ROC

Escape with Jim Butcher, Harry Turtledove, Anne Bishop,
S.M. Stirling, Simon R. Green, E.E. Knight, Kat Richardson,
Rachel Caine, and many others—plus news on the
latest and hottest in science fiction and fantasy.

DAW

Patrick Rothfuss, Mercedes Lackey, Kristen Britain,
Tanya Huff, Tad Williams, C.J. Cherryh, and many more—
DAW has something to satisfy the cravings of any
science fiction and fantasy lover.
Also visit dawbooks.com.

*Get the best of science fiction and fantasy
at your fingertips!*